"Come with me," she whispered. She led him away to a corner of the verandah, away from the animated knot of their friends. The fragrance of night-flowering jasmine was strong in the air. Behind, there was laughter and joy, sparkling like the pink champagne in the frosted bottles.

"Charles?" she had to ask, so different did he look, but she had to know it was him as he had to know it was her.

There had been the words, the explanations, the bones of the "betrayal" laid bare, the sources of the actions that had flowed from it . . . but it had been unnecessary. He had moved toward her, as he did now, sleek and scented, and he had held her for an age as the words fluttered like leaves on the dry breeze of the desert, hardly heard, hardly mattering. She had drunk water from his bottle, and he had wiped her mouth with his fingers and the tears of love and sorrow from her eyes, and she had simply whispered, "Marry me."

"Yes," he had whispered back.

ALSO BY PAT BOOTH

MARRY ME

Pat Booth

Kensington Books
Kensington Publishing Corp.
http://www.kensingtonbooks.com

KENSINGTON BOOKS are published by

Kensington Publishing Corp.
850 Third Avenue
New York, NY 10022

Kensington and the K logo Reg. U.S. Pat. & TM Off.

First Kensington Paperback Printing: August, 1997

Printed in the United States of America
10 9 8 7 6 5 4 3 2 1

To my son, ORLANDO,
with all my love.

To the women in my life who have had the courage to make dreams come true. This book is about us.

Fredrica Friedman, Anne Sibbald, Bobbi Berkman, Martine Verbrugghen, Jane Buffett, Inger Anderson, Marilyn Grabowski, Kimberley Hefner, Sharon Stone, Martha Stewart, Anouska Hempel, Di Cummin, Diana McAndrew, Barbara Boote, Philippa Harrison, Nell Campbell, Norma Moriceau, Andrea Baines, Patty Boyd, Adie Hunter, Jose Fonseca, Susan Magrino, Joanne Benjamin, Eve Pollard, Joan Price, Tara Solomon, Nicole Miller, Davina Belling, Winifred White, and Claudia Peltz.

One

Rachel stared at the red roses. Once again, she read the plain card with its simple message . . . "Marry me." She sighed as she looked around the suite at the Hacienda Inn. This Santa Fe resort for those who valued pampering and privacy resembled paradise, but it didn't feel heavenly. It was full of her uncertainty, despite its understated luxury, the Navajo rugs, and the antique four-poster bed.

Had it been a good idea to come here the day after Christmas for a spa retreat? It was another thing Rachel couldn't decide. She looked at her watch. It was almost time for dinner, the last meal with fat, cholesterol, and alcohol that she could eat for five days. She'd better enjoy it, if she could rediscover a world in which genuine enjoyment was possible.

She walked to the glass doors that led to the terrace. Pulling them back, she felt a wall of cold air hit her. The desert could fool you. The sunset had looked as warm and inviting as the late afternoon. Now, as she wandered outside, she shivered in the thick terry-cloth robe. The sky was blood red from the slaughtered sun, and as she watched, other colors crowded in from the edges, marmalade orange, magenta, and a purple too fake for postcards, almost too real for life.

She sat on the edge of a chaise, far from Manhattan, and tried to face herself. Here it was, the crossroads: she was forty. Decisions had to be made, and for the first time in her life Rachel

Richardson didn't know what the hell she wanted. In a sense, she had it all.

She remembered the President in the green room after the show, charmed by the rough and smooth of her interview technique. "Well, Rachel, I'll tell you this. I never thought of myself as a masochist, but I actually enjoyed that." He had laughed the famous laugh and put his arm around her, and Rachel remembered the little squeeze that meant he would come back.

Over his shoulder she had seen admiration in the eyes of the research assistants and television journalists who knew that she had achieved a more or less impossible task. She had asked the tough questions, but still had not alienated her guest.

In her mind's eye, she could see the telegram from Charlie Rose, pinned to the board above her desk. "Congratulations. You passed me in the ratings once, now watch your tail." Then there was Steve, her impossible producer, leaning in the doorway, laconic and laid back, forcing the compliment past reluctant lips. "I always knew you were a celebrity, Rachel, and a professional, but when I watched you tonight I saw a Pulitzer journalist. Of course, one swallow doesn't make a summer . . ."

Again, she sighed. On the surface, everything seemed to be working for her, but reality was destroying the fantasy. Although from a distance it looked glamorous, up close she was getting lost in the minutiae: the long hours of preparation; the ongoing battles with Steve; the ratings game that called endlessly for the compromising of principles. Once she had prayed for that, but she had forgotten the danger of answered prayers.

All her spare time was spent networking. She was fodder for the gossip columns as she partied with interesting people, flirting easily between the uptown/downtown worlds of politics, art, and media. She was no longer sure what was business and what, if anything, was pleasure.

A graduate of Smith, and a participant in the women's movement, she had done what she had been supposed to do . . . she had become a success. But why the hell didn't it feel good *inside?* Where was the joy of arrival? Where on earth had the magic gone?

The sound of a distant carol broke into her thoughts, reminding her that it was the Christmas season. It *was* a silent night, still and holy, as it had been all those years ago in Chicago. Christmas was for children, but Rachel had never really been a child. That was baggage she carried with her, and it could still bring tears to her eyes. It did now, on the terrace of the Hacienda Inn, as she watched the desert sunset.

There had usually been a present. On Christmas morning as her parents slept, oblivious of her excitement, Rachel would climb on a chair and find her present on top of the old dresser where it was always "hidden." Her father would stagger from bed midmorning, his hungover mood foul, and Rachel and her mother would try to keep out of his way.

At eleven there was the good news and the bad news of his departure to O'Shaugnessy's saloon. It was the time Christmas would briefly be Christmas. Rachel would help her mother cook the large chicken and the trimmings they had been able to afford, and her mother would laugh and joke. Lunch was ready at one, but neither of them would dare to touch it until her father's return. An hour or two late, he would be back, but he would not come home alone.

He would bring with him drunks and drifters, and they would devour the lovely Christmas chicken. At that time Rachel had found it hurtful, but not odd; she had loved both her parents. But now with distance came judgment. She felt robbed of the childhood that so many others had enjoyed, full of cuddly toys stacked in warm, tidy rooms. Life owed her one, but Rachel was enough of a realist to know that life didn't pay up unless you forced it to.

Her childhood was gone forever. But she could make up for it. She would give her own child all the wonder and security she had never had. Rachel lay down flat on the chaise and looked up at the stars. She ran a hand over her flat abdomen. She wanted life to live in there. She needed someone to love and someone to love her. And before the child there would be a man—a strong, dependable, wonderful man who would blow into her life and carry her away to a brilliant and different future.

Now Rachel laughed out loud through the remains of her tears because the truth was this . . . Rachel Richardson, the tough career woman, the Manhattan socialite, the TV personality, longed for the miracle of romance. Above all things, Rachel hated clichés, but there was a part of her that yearned to be rescued from the castle tower of lonely fame.

"Grow *up,* Rachel," she whispered. But even as she scolded herself, the fantasy lingered. Could she change direction now? And if so, what would become of her former love, success? Could she give it up?

Christmas lanterns danced on the terrace as Rachel wrestled with her dilemma.

Across the nation, people envied her. Recently, she had been in the top ten of a *Vogue* survey in which readers had been asked, "Which woman in America do you most admire?" In suburban malls and country villages, women bored by the drudgery of family life fantasized about escape into Rachel's exotic world. What was a woman for? That was the question she was struggling to answer. Were men and women fundamentally different, with distinct and separate roles? Should women abandon their femininity and compete on male terms for power in a male world?

Matt was everywhere in the questions. His roses filled her suite. His proposal of marriage still rang in her ears. She had answered it with a definite "maybe." What did she feel about him? Was it love? She was attracted to him, to his power, his charm, and his intelligence. And then there was loyalty, something she had never been able to ignore.

Matt had been there for her from the beginning. He had given her her first job in television and he had been her mentor ever since. If she owed anybody anything, she owed Matt. But was that enough? Was this *it,* whatever *it* was? All her life she had been frightened by feelings. They had been dangerous things to indulge in the twilight world of alcoholic poverty. So she wasn't very good at emotions, relying instead on the safer, more ordered world of the intellect. Perhaps this *was* the genuine thing called love; maybe it was just that her standards for love were impossibly high.

Rachel stood up. She forced herself to stop thinking. She was here to relax and enjoy herself. This was her Christmas present to herself, and at a thousand dollars a night she should damn well have a good time even if she had never been much good at fun. Tomorrow she would lose herself in the spa life, but tonight she would eat up a storm and treat herself to a killer bottle of Chardonnay. That was an advantage of the Hacienda Inn. The main building, a converted hacienda of great charm and antiquity, was a hotel whose restaurant had an international reputation. The modern spa, close by but quite separate, was where Rachel would spend her days, returning to the old inn each night.

She began to dress for dinner. She didn't mind that she would be alone. Loneliness was a welcome rarity in her crowded life. Nor was she intimidated by the thought of handling the waiters and the stares of the other diners. Audiences, and getting people to do things for her, were not her problem. Her problem was knowing what to do with *herself*.

"Oh, Matt," she murmured as she sat down at the dressing table and peered at herself in the mirror. "Can you give me the life I need?"

Two

Carol McCabe sat at the easel in her room at the Hacienda Inn in the short black dress she would wear for dinner. She leaned forward to tidy a pencil line with an eraser. She looked at her watch. Damn! It was almost time to eat, and at last the painting was going well. She picked up a brush and leaned toward the canvas. As she did, her arm caught against the lamp she had rigged as a spotlight and a gob of yellow paint fell into her lap.

For a second she didn't move. It was a metaphor for her life. A perfect dress ruined in a second—the clean made dirty, the neat untidy. She had been blissfully distracted by the painting. Now, she remembered. She mopped absentmindedly at the stain, increasing the damage. She didn't care, and the old Carol would have cared desperately. Messes were like that. They bred bigger messes, and before you knew it your whole life was submerged in chaos. She smiled wanly as she realized how much she had been changed by what had happened. One single sentence had started it. Carol could remember everything about the moment. She had been driving Whitney to the garage to pick up his car. Her son had tossed his new haircut out of his eyes and turned to her with a strange expression on his face. He had reached forward, turned down the volume of Aerosmith on the CD player, and said simply:

"Mom, is Dad having an affair with Page Lee?"

Carol had wanted to laugh out loud. "Whitney! You're crazed! Whatever gave you that idea? What an amazing thing to say!"

Whitney had paused, fazed a little by his mother's total disbelief. Then he had plowed on. "I think he is." He had turned to her, uncertain, and she had noticed the flush high on his cheeks.

"What makes you think so?" She had been quiet then, calm. A misunderstanding of giant proportions needed to be cleared up. She had always thought of Whitney as being a bit detached, but that was surely a teenage thing to go with the music, the locked door to his room, and the moody monosyllables.

"I don't know whether I should be saying this."

That had made it worse. She had been cold in the warm car, and yet she could feel the blood rushing to her face. Whitney had lost a button in the middle of his shirt. The bright sun was filtering through the branches of the sycamore trees.

"Go on, Whitney."

It had been the end of the beginning and the beginning of the end. Page Lee and Daddy. Page Lee was the new associate at Jack's law firm. Young and pretty, she had been a protégée of Jack, who was one of the senior partners. Page Lee came to their house for parties and barbecues. In many ways she had been the image of Jack and the opposite of Carol. Fiercely intellectual, she was cold and sharp, dressed always in immaculate business suits, with young-Republican values as accessories. Page Lee's face had wrinkled in surprised horror, as had Jack's, when she beheld the pink, tail-finned, blow-up Cadillac float that Carol had bought for the pool. She had made the right noises, but had totally failed to see the point of the life-size jungle animal cutouts that Carol had painted for the garden. Carol was amused by Page Lee, actually tried to like her, because according to Jack, she was an enormous help to him at work. The fact that her yuppie ways were a stark contrast to Carol's cheerful bohemianism was beside the point, as was the fact that at twenty-five she was fifteen years younger than Carol. But on the day that Whitney told his mother about seeing

Page Lee and his father in a passionate embrace on the porch of their home, it had been beside the point no more.

Now, Carol stood up, her face grim with the memory. She reached around and undid the zipper of the black dress that had been one of Jack's favorites. She stepped out of it, letting it drop to the floor, and kicked it away from her. "You bastard," she whispered.

For a moment she stood there, catching a glimpse of herself in the mirror. At forty, she had far from given up. She was still pretty, with a fawnlike Goldie Hawn face, saucer blue eyes, and a firm, womanly body. Page Lee, in contrast, resembled a newly sharpened hard pencil. How the hell had Jack been prepared to sacrifice their marriage for that prickly anorectic?

Carol had always been in love with him. She had stood behind him in the canteen at college as he had spooned a mound of meat loaf onto his plate. He had turned and grinned as he watched her watch him, and he had said, "I love meat loaf." And she had said, smiling, "I can see that." In that instant she had known she would marry him. It had been the magic that not many people experienced.

For her, it had not faded in eighteen years, although now, with the twenty/twenty vision of hindsight, she could see how their roles had changed. In the beginning they had been equals, although opposites. Jack had been ambitious, popular, a fraternity man who excelled at sports. Carol had been a promising artist, an individual who spoke her mind, a bohemian dressed mostly in black who didn't care what people thought. But the chemistry between them had effortlessly overcome the superficial differences. Then Carol had metamorphosed, so gradually that nobody really noticed the change, from the spunky artist that Jack had fallen in love with all those years ago into "Mom," an enormously efficient suburban housewife, a good mother to her two children, and an important adjunct to Jack's career. Carol was content, but somehow, somewhere, in the endless service of the people she loved she had lost herself. The person she had once been had disappeared. She was aware of this. She had even colluded in the process. Carol the artist, she had come to feel, was the enemy of Carol the mother and wife.

As time moved on, Jack had learned to take her for granted. His formerly tactful requests had graduated to gracious commands, and then to not so very polite orders. The children were no longer sweetly dependent. They became teenagers, inconsiderate, self-centered, and often surly. They, too, took Carol for granted. She was no longer a person with her own needs, opinions, and dreams. She was "Mom," who loved them, whose role was to serve them. After all, they had never seen her act otherwise.

Carol's small dreams grew. In secret, she fantasized about becoming a real artist. She found a heroine, Georgia O'Keeffe, and became an expert on the painter's life. She thought endlessly of the wild desert and of painting all day. But whenever Carol dreamed of coloring her life, of escaping to a distant place, her fantasies foundered. Because, of course, Jack and the children had to be fitted into the jigsaw puzzle of a reborn Carol, and the short answer was that they did not fit. So that was the end of it. Or that had *been* the end of it.

Carol felt the anger build inside. She walked quickly to the bathroom and put on a terry-cloth robe. She tried to stay calm. Carol McCabe had a reputation for being good in a crisis. But what crisis? Whitney's appendicitis? The day she crashed the Volvo? The time they thought Devon was pregnant? Those crises she had handled with dignity. But Jack, her own Jack, and the snake at the office—that was different. It had turned her whole apple-pie life into a disaster. She had sacrificed herself on the altar of marriage and children, but Jack had made no sacrifices. Instead, he had helped himself to a parallel universe full of romance, excitement, and sex. Page Lee was not "Mom," rushing lemminglike from one trivial pursuit to the next. Page Lee had the luxury of being a focused woman, all scented fantasy and cunning compliments. She worked for Jack in an area where the payoff mattered to him. She made him look like a star in the office, doing his research, alerting him to the unexploded land mines of office politics. How could a "mom" compete with that?

She picked up the silver-framed photograph of Devon and Whitney. She remembered the day it was taken, the time when they had gone swimming with the dolphins in the Florida Keys. Devon had been nervous and Whitney had made fun of her, and later, when they had stopped for a burger, Devon had revenged herself by squirting the French's mustard right in his eye. An hour later the devils, turned angels, had posed for the picture. Carol smiled as she remembered. God, they had needed her then. But they didn't need her now. They were off to college, totally self-absorbed and walled away in their own lives of rock, rap, and fantasy, with their boyfriends and girlfriends and their vast, exciting future. She loved them with all her heart; but despite that, in some way, she couldn't help identifying them with her cheating husband. She knew it was irrational, but they had been such an integral part of the old dream that had blown up in her face. She put the picture down. Then, on an impulse, she turned on a tape of carols and walked over to the window, throwing open the glass doors. She shivered as the cold air and the strains of "Silent Night," Devon's favorite, washed over her.

She had told Jack that she wanted a divorce, but even as she had said the dread word she had felt the beginnings of remorse. He had looked so sad, so crestfallen, so deeply ashamed, if not at his infidelity, then at his inefficiency in failing to cover it up. This still was the Jack that Carol loved. Could anything make that love go away? Right now the anger and the sense of betrayal said, "yes." But she couldn't help thinking of the lonely road that stretched out before her. Who would look after her in the brave new world that she faced? Who would pay the bills, and who would care when she got sick? What would the empty bed feel like? How would she handle the sound of the silence? Who would be her friends when the country club was gone? The answers came back. Carol would be in control of her own destiny. Carol would be responsible for Carol. But where was Carol? Who was she?

Carol clenched her fists. Righteous anger at Jack's betrayal had given her the strength to leave him, but how long would anger last? Unable to imagine life without her, Jack had made a desperate attempt to keep her. He had promised to get rid of Page Lee and take Carol on a long holiday. They would mend the break. He had always loved her. He depended on her. It had taken the threat of losing her to make him see how very much he needed her. Carol had bent in the storm of emotion that Jack had unleashed, but when the wind died down she had been left standing. She had been adamant. She had made the decision to leave him.

Christmas would be the ultimate test. She had decided to go to the desert, to the legendary Hacienda Inn, to take the first fledgling steps into her new world. She had left on Christmas Eve, stayed the night in a local hotel, and contrived to spend most of Christmas Day traveling, blotting out its meaning with movement. Now, on the day after Christmas, she was confronted for the first time by the brand-new life she had planned, and already it scared the wits out of her. In the luxury of the beautiful retreat, she found it easier to look back than to look forward. She had escaped to find herself, but all she could think of were the memories: Devon with the mumps, her little face fat as a chipmunk's as she wept in misery. Whitney taking a bow at the play, smiling and so much a part of it all, only thirteen but already amazingly good-looking. And Jack, the old Jack, the young Jack, dancing and laughing with her and loving her as the "Blue Danube" played and the world went away.

Carol reached out and closed the doors on the desert and turned back into the room, her eyes misty with tears. She took a deep breath. It was dinnertime. She was going to have to get used to the loneliness.

Three

"I think you're simply *gorgeous.*"

"Gorgeous" was Camille's new word, and Tessa laughed as her daughter peered seriously over her shoulder into the mirror.

"Well, thank you, darling. That's a very sweet thing to say."

Tessa was certainly a beauty in the English sense, her nose aquiline, her pale, perfect skin a translucent carpet about big round eyes that looked innocent or guilty according to the mind-set of the observer. It was a face of paradoxes, soft yet strong, the determined chin seeming to contradict the delicate, sensitive mouth. Her hair was uncompromisingly short, severe, a warning that Tessa was a modern woman despite the aura of elegance that enveloped her.

"Do you miss the jewelry, Mummy?" Camille's face at her shoulder had gone sly.

Tessa smiled slowly. She checked her earlobes, pierced but minus her Cartier earrings, which the creditors had taken. Her neck was devoid of pearls. No diamond brooch adorned the simple black Givenchy she was wearing for dinner.

"I only miss Daddy," she said simply.

"What do you miss *most* about Daddy?"

Camille came around to the front of her, and leaned against her mother, a perfect clone in her black velvet dress.

Tessa put her arms around her daughter and rocked her from side to side. She bent down and nuzzled her face in Camille's hair, breathing the delicious scent of warm, clean child.

"Oh, I don't know, darling. Everything, really."

She sighed at the enormity of the question she had been asked. Everything. It was true, but it didn't do justice to the patchwork quilt of little memories that added up to Pete . . . the lock of blond hair that fell across his forehead despite all attempts to keep it in place; the way he slept, one arm flung out as if pointing the way to some new and future excitement.

"You know what I miss most, Mummy? You know how he used to say he was going to kiss me till I was sick, and I'd pretend to run away and then he'd catch me . . . I'd sort of let him . . . and he'd kiss me and kiss me, but I'd never be sick, would I, Mummy? I never even felt sick."

"Oh, darling. Poor Daddy, poor, poor Daddy."

"Do you think Daddy's missing Christmas?"

Tessa felt her eyes fill with tears. She fought the emotion. She had to be strong for her daughter, for herself, too. Christmas Day in the Hacienda Inn had been a nightmare—visions of Pete had hung over the halfhearted festivities like ghosts at the feast. The contrasts were almost too much to bear. In the wonderland that had been their marriage, Christmases had been magic. There had been mountains of gifts beneath the outsize tree that Pete had always insisted on decorating himself, cursing the lights that never worked, piling on glitter and ornaments and fake snow until the fabulous kitsch tree was an interior designer's vision of hell. But mostly there had been laughter, endless storms of mirth and happiness, as they had loved one another and Camille. Yesterday, Camille had had only one present, a talking doll's house, and lunch, while lovely, had been room service because Tessa could not face the public dining room. A tear began to trickle down her cheek. She didn't know if she was more sorry for herself or for Camille and the future she would face without a father. It was difficult to organize the hierarchy of horror.

"Don't cry, Mummy. You'll spoil your makeup, and Grandpa said that Pitt-Rivers never cried."

"No. You're right. It wasn't allowed when Mummy was a

child. Nobody was that keen on laughter, either. But we're not Pitt-Riverses anymore. We're Andersens, because we belong to Daddy, and he made the rules, not Grandpa."

"Daddy allowed us to cry, didn't he, Mummy?"

"Yes, he did, darling. But we never wanted to cry around Daddy. That's the difference, you see. It's one of the funny things about life. You only need rules against crying when there's something to cry about."

"I *think* I see."

Tessa wiped the tear from her cheek and allowed herself to remember. Pete Andersen had blown into her life with hurricane force, and she had fallen in love with him before she had learned his name. It had been the way he laughed. The humor had taken over his whole being, and the fabulous sound of his happiness had filled her heart with wild hope. She had been standing near the bar at a ball in Skye, and she had heard him before she had seen him. Tessa had turned around, and he had turned at the same time. His eyes had still been creased by laughter when they had met hers. She had felt the magic instantly, and had vibrated with sudden excitement. His smile had vanished as he watched her, and then it had been replaced by a look that locked into her. Nobody had introduced them. He had walked up to her and asked her to dance. She had consulted her dance program, and of course it had been full of Scotsmen—her brother's friends, her cousins, and the odd old Etonian or Harrovian from London. She had pulled out her pencil, and with a smile of the purest happiness she had scratched out the lot. Then she and Pete had danced all evening.

It had been a revelation. Pete said things, thought things, and believed things that Tessa had never heard before. He did not believe that life was predetermined. Nor did he believe in the sacred status quo. Most amazing of all, he did not believe in the past. He talked always of the future and of *changing* things, and he exhibited a strange and bracing emotion that Tessa had hardly ever experienced . . . enthusiasm. Further, he was that weirdest of weird animals, an optimist. In her milieu, optimists were written off as naive simpletons who had no awareness of destiny, no appreciation of the ineluctable process of decay from womb to grave that was called life. In short, he was an American, and strangely, far from laughing at him, Tessa only wanted to laugh with him. And she had, for ten wonderful years, until the laughter had turned to tears.

Tessa stood up and took her daughter's hand.

"Come on, darling," she said. "It's time for dinner."

Four

The headwaiter watched them coming. He was French, and Tessa's aristocratic deportment preceded her. The simple black dress was haute couture, probably St. Laurent or Givenchy, and the absence of jewelry hinted that she was rich, with no need to impress. She walked calmly toward what was always a mildly threatening situation, a woman wanting a table in a grand restaurant. She didn't hurry. Confidence was her keynote, and that meant a good table, not the Siberia by the kitchen doors to which single women were usually banished. However, there was a problem. She came with a child. The child looked as presentable as her mother, but children were restless diners. They ran about, they whined, they interfered with the imposing theater of a great restaurant like this one at the Hacienda Inn.

He sidled away from the lectern as mother and child approached.

"Good evening, madame," he said, bowing slightly.

"Good evening," said Tessa. Camille looked up at him, smiling sweetly, unaware that she was death to a good table.

"For two, madame, and you are staying with us, no?" He had taken in the platinum wedding band.

"Yes, for two, please. We arrived on Christmas Eve. I'm Mrs. Andersen."

"Why, certainly. Would you follow me, please." He swept up two menus and set off across a room of empty tables. Dinner started at seven and Camille's bedtime was nine. It suited Tessa to eat early.

"Here we are, madame, mademoiselle." The waiter pulled back a chair for Tessa. She stood still, not moving to take her seat.

"I don't think we will be happy back here," said Tessa simply. "We'd rather sit over there by the window."

She turned around without waiting for an answer and walked toward the window. She didn't stop or pause to see how her remark had been received.

The maitre d' wondered for an instant about invoking "booked tables." He didn't wonder for long. The nation that had invented fait accompli had just been presented with one. Tessa had reached the window.

"This will be fine," she said. She turned as the chastened waiter caught up with her, and gave him an icy smile. She did not move. He hurried forward and pulled out the chair for her. Then he did the same for Camille.

He picked up Tessa's napkin, opened it with a flourish, and laid it in her lap.

"*Bon appétit,* madame, mademoiselle," he muttered, backing away from the table as if taking leave of some medieval potentate to whom one was not permitted to show a back. From the lectern, he surveyed the damage. Rachel Richardson's table had been appropriated and Rachel Richardson was their celebrity guest. Luckily the one next to it was all but identical, and available. He hoped Ms. Richardson did not have a career woman's dislike of children.

Tessa looked around the room. It was adobe, understated, almost monastic. The stucco walls were white, sweeping along rounded lines to fluid corners and washing between wooden beams. A big fire burned, one that could have roasted a pig on a spit. Above it was a rough wooden mantel, covered with mistletoe and holly for Christmas. On either side of the fireplace, large terra-cotta earthenware urns guarded the flames, and fire irons as big as shovels rested on a wrought-iron platform in front of it. The floor, worn and pitted, was of faded Mexican tile from which the glaze had long since been rubbed away. Most of the tables, oak and big, were placed far apart, and Spanish chairs of dark wood and brown leather were arranged around them. On every table a trio of thick candles burned, and on the walls there were candles too, held in black iron holders caked with melted wax. It was a dark, romantic room, old and comfortable with itself. Tessa felt at home in it.

"Okay, darling. What would you like to eat? Are you hungry?"

"What can we afford, Mummy?"

Tessa smiled. "While we're here, sweetheart, we can have anything we want. Next week, when we go to New York, then we start economizing. This is our holiday. Are you hungry?"

"What's 'economizing'?"

"Worrying about what we can afford."

Tessa looked at Camille lovingly. There was so much of Pete in her. She looked such fun, a tight little parcel of energy and joy wrapped up in a beautiful exterior.

"You know, really, we're rich because we still have each other," said Camille suddenly. She reached across the table and laid her hand on Tessa's, because she could see something bad happening in her mother's eyes.

"Don't worry, Mummy," she said, squeezing her hand. "We'll be all right."

"Of course we will, darling. But what a beautiful thing to say."

"Can I get you a drink before your dinner, madame?"

The waiter poured iced water as he asked his question.

"I'll have a glass of Chardonnay," said Tessa. "And a Shirley Temple for my daughter."

"May I please have an extra cherry?" said Camille sweetly.

"I'm sure we can arrange that, miss."

Tessa picked up the menu. The Hacienda Inn was a present from her brother, Bob, with whom they had been staying at his home near Inverness. Ten days, all expenses paid, at the fabulous spa retreat, so that his sister could get herself together for the ordeal that would be New York.

"Well, I'm certainly not going to have smoked salmon," said Tessa firmly. In Scotland they had eaten little else.

"I think I would like to start with some soup," said Camille in her most grown-up voice. Her American accent was beginning to fade. Now she sounded a little like her English aunt, Miranda.

"They seem to have asparagus, and lentils, oh and a vichyssoise. You like that."

"Oh, yes, goody. That please, Mummy. And then some ice cream with hot chocolate sauce."

"You ought to have some chicken or some fish in between," said Tessa without conviction. "Oh, never mind. Have just what you like. We're in America." She laughed. Americans believed in children. The British didn't. It was perhaps the most startling difference between the two nationalities. Americans had wonderful childhoods and spent the rest of their lives trying to return to them. The British, few unscathed by the treatment they received when they were young, spent lifetimes attempting to recover. In England and in Scotland, you ate your greens, broccoli included. In the U.S.A., you aimed straight for carbohydrates.

The woman who walked through the door now, Tessa recognized instantly. It was Rachel Richardson. Tessa watched her often. American TV was short on in-depth analysis of important issues. It was a gap that Richardson fought to fill. She was bright, and yet personable, too. That was rare. Jeane Kirkpatrick-type intellectuals tended to be sandpaper abrasive. The maitre d' was bent at the waist as he welcomed her. Rachel's eyes shot toward Tessa. The maitre d's eyes followed hers. They exchanged words. Rachel nodded. She looked up at Tessa again, and then the pair of them set off across the room toward her. Tessa took her in. She walked fast, looking neither to right nor left, seemingly unaware of the newly arrived diners who peered up at her, hoping to catch her eye. She was self-confident, but there was threat in the jut of her jaw and determination in her eye. She was not relaxed about her power.

Just before they reached Tessa's table, they veered off, and with much ceremony Rachel was seated at the next table. The maitre d' had his back to Tessa. She heard Rachel say in a soft voice, "No problem at all. I love children."

Camille swiveled in her chair to check out the newcomer. Rachel smiled at her.

"Hello," said Camille.

"Hello," said Rachel.

"I'm having vichyssoise and ice cream. What are you having?"

"Darling, I'm sure the lady isn't interested in what you're going to eat . . ."

"That sounds delicious," said Rachel, laughing. "I wish I was allowed to eat like that."

"You mean your mummy won't let you?" said Camille, hitching herself around in her chair more fully, lost in the business of making a new friend.

"My waistline won't let me."

Tessa laughed.

"You're not fat," said Camille. "You're thin, like Mummy."

"Your daughter has a glittering future," said Rachel with a laugh, as she picked up the menu.

"Are you ready to order, madame?" The waiter hovered by Tessa.

Quite suddenly, Tessa was hungry and looking forward to a leisurely meal, one with an appetizer, a salad, an entrée, and even perhaps a pudding or what Americans called a dessert, a word that would in Britain have branded one a hopeless outsider. She ordered tuna carpaccio, veal marsala, then vichyssoise and ice cream for Camille, the ice cream to arrive at the same time as Tessa's veal.

She looked up. The room was filling rapidly. There was a line of people at the maitre d's lectern waiting to be seated. At the front of the line was another woman alone. Tessa couldn't help noticing her. She stood still, her head high, and she looked straight in front of her. Tessa could imagine what she was thinking. She was about to be offered a table at the back of beyond, and she was wondering whether or not she would have the energy to make a fuss about it. She wore a simple blue dress, neither stylish nor out of fashion, and it was clear that clothes were not her point. The maitre d' greeted her, consulted his book, and then scanned the room. His eyes wandered to the trio of tables by the window, and then to the table at which he had originally tried and failed to seat Tessa. Doubt reigned for a brief second before the decision was made. He bade the newcomer to follow him, and he set off across the room, placing her at the table on Rachel Richardson's left.

Tessa watched Rachel smile in welcome. So there they were, thought Tessa. Three women at the three best tables, and not a pair of pants in sight.

She came out of her reverie to hear her daughter going straight to the bottom line. Tessa had mentioned to Camille that Rachel Richardson had her own television show.

"Mummy says you're a star," Camille was saying. "Are you?"

Again Rachel laughed. She put down the menu. On her left, Carol, who had heard the remark, laughed too.

"I don't know about star, but I do get to be on TV quite a bit."

She turned toward the little girl as she spoke, as if making the decision to immerse herself in a research project. After all, children loomed large on her agenda, and she knew next to nothing about them. The little girl was really cute, totally unself-conscious, with no bratlike vibrations. The persona of the mother backed up that impression . . . very British, cool, reserved.

"My husband and I were big fans," said Tessa simply.

"Oh, thank you," said Rachel. Where is the husband? she thought. Not divorced, from the way she referred to him. Widowed?

"Daddy's dead," said Camille. "He disappeared from his boat and nobody ever found him."

Rachel was seldom thrown a ball she couldn't catch. This one was fast and curved and it dipped down suddenly as it reached her.

"Oh, dear," she said. It was hardly an adequate response.

"Camille!" said Tessa. "That's enough!"

"Well, he is," Camille replied. "And he did."

"I'm so sorry," said Tessa.

"Don't be," said Rachel quickly. "I wish we were all as straightforward as children. I'd be out of a job, though." Again she turned to Camille. "I'm Rachel," she said. "And what's your name?"

"Oh," said Tessa. "I should have introduced us. I'm Tessa Andersen and this is my daughter, Camille."

Andersen, thought Rachel quickly. Ah! Could it be that one? It wasn't the moment to ask.

"How are you enjoying the Hacienda Inn, Camille?"

"Oh, it's fun. I spent all day riding and reading and painting. Mummy ran about and got massaged and covered in mud. She says really it should have been the other way around."

A few feet away, Carol McCabe listened to the conversation. She had recognized Rachel instantly, and before the little girl had started to talk to her she had been thinking about the television star. Here they sat so close together, yet in other ways they were miles apart. Carol felt like the severed half of a Siamese twin, uncomfortable, lonely, and ill at ease at her table for one. She hadn't liked walking into the restaurant alone, and she didn't like the thought of ordering for herself. She wasn't frightened of it. It just felt wrong. Rachel, she saw, had brought a book to read. But Carol had nothing to distract her, nothing to do with her eyes except let them wander this way and that, catching the eyes of others and looking away in embarrassment. The waiter had not come for her order. She was being neglected, and yet she felt it was too early to make a fuss. Two women sitting so near, and yet the world separated them.

Carol was setting out on a journey that Rachel Richardson had begun perhaps twenty-five years ago. Rachel had given her life to a career, and now she had the payoff. She was famous, successful, and everyone in the restaurant knew who she was and admired her. Rachel sat there, calm and confident in her solitude because at a snap of her fingers it could be banished and her life filled with interesting people hanging on her every word. Her self-confidence would be real because she had earned the right to like herself with the sweat of her brow and the power of her brains.

In contrast, Carol had saved all her power for family, and now family had blown her out into the unknown like a circus performer from the barrel of a gun. And where the hell was her net? It was week one of the rest of her life, and in twenty-five years, the time it had taken Rachel to scale the peaks, Carol would be sixty-five years old. She sipped her water and cursed Jack for turning her life upside down, but even as she did so she remembered that there had been times when she had fantasized about being right where she was now. She remembered to allow herself to be excited by the control. She was in command. She could get up and walk out of the restaurant. She could get drunk. She could pack and drive to the airport. Nobody had a call on her time. No one was there to judge her, to ask for a favor, to shame her through guilt into this course of behavior or that one. And yet, what if you were the conductor and you could dream up no song to conduct? What if the dreadful truth was that Carol McCabe had spent her life in the service of others because she hadn't the guts or the know-how to get a life of her own.

"Mummy says you're a star." Carol had smiled when she'd heard it. It was the sort of thing Devon would have said, precocious, utterly unfazed by adult ideas of what was and was not appropriate. Carol was also a mother, and as such, an expert in the fiendishly difficult job of raising children. It was late in the day. The little girl would be tired and her blood sugar low. Camille might be angelic right now; in half an hour she could well be out of control. Carol noticed the way Rachel reacted to her, intrigued, fascinated, seeing only the fun and oblivious of the hard work. But then why should Rachel know about children? She enjoyed joking with presidents and senators, with movie stars and intellectuals, free from worry about fevers in the night.

At last the waiter was there. Carol ordered quickly, not caring what she ate and missing Jack's masterful way with waiters. "And my wife will have the sole . . . ," he would say, and Carol would feel the tiny thrill of pride that she was "my wife." It had been like a title. The happy memory faded as she wondered what he had said to the waiter in the Manhattan restaurants he had taken the snake to. "And my lover will have the sauté of camel's eyelashes. My mistress will try the lark's tongue paté. The passion of my life would like a little more of the pomegranate sorbet."

The waiter had gone. Now she tried to catch his eye to ask for a glass of wine. He hovered out of reach, seemingly determined not to notice her as he poured water for people at a nearby table. Carol raised her hand ineffectively and then let it drop.

"Shall I get him for you?" asked the voice at her elbow.

It was Camille, roving now, her soup finished.

As if he had heard her, the waiter deigned to notice that Carol needed him.

"I think he's coming, but thank you for asking."

"May I have a glass of Chardonnay?" she said.

"You know, I've noticed," said Camille, "that women drink white wine and men like red wine. Does your husband drink red wine?"

"How do you know I have a husband?" said Carol with a faint smile.

"Nearly all women do, you know, when they grow up."

Carol was aware of Rachel Richardson looking up from her book and catching the conversation.

"But not all women," said Carol. "Some women are very talented and wise and they don't get married at all. They go out and achieve things and make the world a better place."

Camille wrinkled up her face in disapproval.

"But that means they can't have babies. Everyone wants those." She was quite definite about it. She wound a lock of hair around her forefinger and looked up at Carol, head to one side.

"She's got a point, you know," said Rachel suddenly, entering the conversation with a laugh.

Camille looked around delightedly. She'd got them all involved. Tessa called out, "Is she bothering you?"

"Not at all, she's delightful." Carol leaned forward and caught Tessa's eyes, well aware of how conscious a mother was of her children's behavior in public.

"Have you got babies?" said Camille, turning back to Rachel.

"Not yet, but I hope to. I have to find a husband first."

It was an unexpected remark. Both Tessa and Carol were surprised by it. Both could imagine Rachel hoping for lots of things, a Senate seat, a Pulitzer, another six-figure contract . . . but babies were not on the list. And the thought of her having to "find" a husband was little short of bizarre. She was the sort of woman whose bedroom would be full of blood-red roses.

"I think lots of men would like to be your husband," said Camille, putting the thoughts of the other two women into words.

"And she said I was thin earlier," said Rachel. "I don't suppose she's up for adoption."

The three women laughed. The conversation was becoming general, with Camille as the catalyst.

"Darling, your ice cream has arrived," said Tessa, dangling the most effective bait.

"Goodbye," said Camille brightly as she scampered back to home base.

Camille had made Carol feel better. She had one like that at home, one who had been like that, anyway. The pride of creation surged through her. Devon and Whitney had been the work of a lifetime. But even as she felt it, she heard the past tense in her mind. Had been. Her lifetime wasn't over, but the child-raising that had been her twenty-four-hour-a-day job was. Once again, the extraordinary challenge hovered over her, full of promise and threat. Becoming Georgia, her heroine. Becoming someone like Rachel Richardson, so confident and so free. Becoming herself. She took another sip of Chardonnay as strange feelings of excitement and fear bubbled inside her.

She turned to Rachel.

"Did you mean that . . . about having children, getting married?" she said, astounded at her presumption.

"Yes, absolutely. Big step, no? The whole idea terrifies me."

"Kids are magic. It's the husbands that are the problem," said Carol with a little laugh.

"Is the problem getting them, training them, or keeping them?" asked Rachel with a smile.

"I had a problem with 'b' and flunked 'c,' but I did the leaving."

"Not an easy thing to do, I imagine, especially with children."

Rachel the reporter slipped effortlessly into information-gathering mode. It was second nature to her.

"Luckily, the kids aren't kids anymore. They're off to college. You know, they call for cash from time to time."

"God, yes, I imagine they do. I hadn't gotten much past babies in my mind." Rachel was quiet for a second, seemingly trying to embrace the odd idea that babies changed into miniature adults.

"Babies are great when you get over thinking they're going to die on you," said Carol.

"Listen, I'm Rachel. I feel I've known you for ages."

"Yes, I see your show all the time and I love it. I'm Carol McCabe."

"I used to love it," said Rachel with a little shake of her head.

"God, I imagine it must be the most wonderful life, just the best, meeting all those amazing people."

"You know what, Carol? Every single one of them is trying to peddle something: an image, a lie, a book, a movie, political ideas, sex. TV is a great-big con game. The moment the cameras start to turn, the actors start to act, and whether they are politicians, sportsmen, intellectuals, or bricklayers, they're all actors on TV. The mice become lions, the lions mice. The sincere shallow and devious. Sometimes I think I haven't met a genuine person in the last twenty-five years. I see it as my role to cut away the bullshit, and by the end of the hour I'm lucky if I've merely sponged away the surface grease."

Carol was astounded at the disillusionment in Rachel's tone.

"I never thought of it like that."

"It's worse. You know, all these guys who do TV are pros. If I ask you a question, you think about it and try to give a truthful answer. On TV rule number one is 'never answer the question.' Seconds and minutes are valuable free advertising worth thousands of dollars. So they mouth the lines they want to deliver no matter what you ask them. They have a script, sentences and whole paragraphs that they've churned out hundreds of times in speeches, in front of mirrors, on the other shows they've done. That's why the *Oprah*-type shows are so popular. Real people make fools of themselves and let it all hang out because they've got nothing to sell, no agenda, and they simply don't know how the game is played."

"But you're so good at probing and getting people to admit things. I mean, I saw you with the President and, you know, when he told you the thing that irritated him about his wife, the wiping down the basin in the bathroom thing and making him feel like a slob, I mean that was pretty real . . ."

"But hardly crucial, was it? Nothing much compared to admitting he underestimated the cost of the health care plan, or that he overstated a tax loss. He threw me a little bone, and it made him seem warm and genuine, the sort of guy people could relate to. It was PR as usual. And the subplot is this. If I push and push and get nasty and mean and come up with a whole load of incriminating evidence and stick it to them on camera, they slip and slide away and they never come back. And their friends never come back. And pretty soon not a guest in the world will come anywhere near my show except the over-the-top, whacked-out publicity junkies that I don't want anyway. It's catch-22. Interfere with the act major-league and you blow yourself out of the water and die a heroine."

"But the investigative pieces must be fascinating," said Carol, unwilling to abandon totally her glamorous idea of Rachel's job.

"They have their moments, but mostly it's a legal minefield. You spend twice as much time with the lawyers as you do on the story. The air is thick with writs and injunctions and bluster and threats, and our legal people crawl all over the office. They tell me what I can or can't say, whether it's true or false or vital to the story, whatever. The final product is a compromise built on a pile of concessions, watered down 'facts,' and surrendered principles. And the next day everyone's forgotten about the whole thing anyway."

"It doesn't sound like quite as much fun as it looks," admitted Carol with regret.

"I'd trade it all for a real family," said Rachel.

"It looks like we're heading in opposite directions," said Carol. "I'm just trading in a family for a life of making it on my own."

"You *are?* . . . Look, Carol, why don't you come over here and have dinner with me?" Rachel had made the decision quickly.

"Are you sure?" said Carol. And then, "I'd love to. How nice."

She stood up and looked around for an instant, wondering if she should alert the maitre d' to her table change. The hell with it, she decided. Rachel stood up as she approached. She held out her hand. Carol took it. It was weird. Carol McCabe had just started a new life, and here she was having dinner à deux with Rachel Richardson.

"What were you drinking?" asked Rachel conspiratorially.

"I've just finished a glass of Chardonnay."

"Great. Let's get a really good bottle and you can tell me all about families from hell, and I'll tell you about the torture of life as a career woman, and we can drink too much and be beastly about everyone."

"God, that's *exactly* what I feel like doing. How wonderful," said Carol. She felt like rubbing her hands. Could she possibly tell Rachel about Jack and his office snake? About the treachery and treason, and the sudden death of the "perfect" marriage that had only been perfect when seen through Carol's distorting lens?

At the next table Camille put down her spoon, the huge plate of ice cream demolished. She let out a monster yawn and stretched. It had been a long day. In the room was a great big TV. It was Sunday. At eight o'clock it would be *The Simpsons*.

"Mummy, what time is it?"

"It's five to eight, darling."

"Mummy?" There was a pause, a wheedling tone, big round eyes. A pretty-please question with a cherry on top was coming up.

"Yeees, darling." Tessa was wary, waiting for it.

"Mummy"—cunning now, legalistic, impeccably logical—"it's been a really long day, riding and all that stuff, and now that I've eaten I feel really tired. Would you mind very much, *darling* Mummy, if I went back to the room and got into bed and watched TV for a bit?"

"Because *The Simpsons* are on," said Tessa with an indulgent smile.

"How did you know?"

"Mummy knows everything. And what about me? Do I have to eat all alone?"

At the age of eight there was an answer for everything.

"You can have dinner with the two nice ladies next door," said Camille.

"Come on, niff-noff, I'll walk you back to the room. Are you sure you won't mind being alone for a bit?"

"Mummy, it's a *hotel*. I can pick up the phone and talk to room service anytime. And I can get them to page you in the restaurant. And I can . . ."

"Oh, my," said Tessa. She stood up and reached for Camille's hand. "Let's get you all snug and cozy for *The Simpsons*. That's the best plan, isn't it?"

"Bedtime?" said Rachel, looking up.

"She's tired. I'm going to take her to the room and then come back and finish my dinner," said Tessa with a laugh. "Bart Simpson is going to baby-sit."

"Listen, when you get back, why don't you join us?"

"Yes, do," said Carol.

"There you are, Mummy," said Camille. "You won't be alone after all."

"Thank you. That would be fun," said Tessa quickly. "I'll see you in a minute."

She walked toward the door of the restaurant, Camille's hand in hers.

Rachel and Carol watched them go.

"God, what a cute little girl," said Rachel.

"They're wonderful at that age," said Carol. "Everything they say surprises you. They're incredibly grown up in bursts and then they're tiny children again. And when tiredness strikes, they turn into monsters." She had slipped into the role of surrogate Dr. Spock, perhaps because she felt it was her only area of expertise. Perhaps it was.

"How old are yours?"

"Seventeen and eighteen, Devon and Whitney. I guess they'll always be 'the children.' I just remember bath times and hissy fits, time-outs and cuddles, and now they're spouting politics and social values as if we've never heard of them."

"Still 'we'?" said Rachel. Earlier Carol had said she was trading in a family. That had sounded like a brave way of referring to a divorce.

"We? Oh, yes, Jack and I. It hasn't been very long," she said.

"Is it the end of the line for you guys, then? God, I don't have the right to ask you things like that. Forgive me. I hardly know you." Rachel laughed, putting out her hand to touch Carol's arm in a gesture of reassurance. "I'm just a bossy journalist who doesn't have much in the way of social graces."

"Me neither," laughed Carol. "Sometimes I don't think I should be allowed out alone. I've absolutely no idea how to behave. I've been married for an eternity and there are just loads of things that I don't do anymore, like sit in restaurants and order dinner by myself and handle waiters. I'm dreading working out the tip. But actually, it's great to talk to someone you don't know. I suppose that's why people go to those shrinks who sit behind their head and aren't supposed to judge them."

"Jesus, waiters are like falling off logs. You just tell them what to do. But *husbands,* now that's heavy lifting. I mean, my life revolves exclusively around me and my work. Every second is spoken for. What if they *want* something, like food or conversation, or sex . . . ?" Rachel tailed off as she contemplated the enormity of the compromise that marriage must be, and Carol laughed at her confusion.

"Oh, boy, I begin to see the dimensions of the problem." It was amazing. They were opposites; at least they had opposite lives. Carol had had no life apart from her husband. Rachel couldn't imagine where a husband would fit into a schedule that had no room for one.

"Hang on," said Rachel. "I'll do my waiter bit." She held up her hand. In seconds, two waiters were at the table.

"The lady at the next table, Mrs. Andersen, will be joining us. As you can see, we will now be three. Can you arrange things? Oh, and if you could bring me a bottle of that Firestone Chardonnay, that would be fine. Thank you."

The trumpet of Rachel's command had a certain note. The waiters went to work instantly. Carol could imagine researchers jumping to order and muttering, "How high?"

"Listen," said Rachel. "Before Tessa Andersen joins us, you ought to know she has a bit of a problem. The little girl said her father was dead. I think he died quite recently and in rather tragic circumstances."

"How awful. That's terrible," said Carol.

"There was a businessman called Peter Andersen, married to a British woman, who disappeared from his boat in Florida. People reckoned it was suicide. He had financial problems and left a pile of debt. He could easily be her husband." Rachel the journalist had an encyclopedic knowledge of such things.

"And I thought I had problems," said Carol.

"Me, too," said Rachel. "Here she comes."

Tessa strode toward the table. She walked like a model, very straight, her head held high. In the simple black dress, and with the gamine haircut, she looked the height of fashion. Camille was taken care of, tucked up in bed with a package of cookies and an apple juice from the minibar. Tessa would check her later. In the meantime, she was looking forward to meeting Rachel Richardson properly and the woman called Carol, who had been sweet with Camille. She loved her daughter with all her heart, but at the end of a long day it was nice to have an adult break.

A waiter drew back her chair, and Tessa saw that her place had been reset. Her main course had been put on hold while she took Camille to their room, and she was hungry.

"How long are you all staying?" said Rachel as Tessa sat down. "I've got five days. I start a spa regimen tomorrow. So this is my last pig-out."

"We're staying for five nights, too," said Tessa. "I'm going to be using the spa, but not like a full-time thing. You know, a massage here, a facial there. Camille's crazy about horses, and the girl who organizes the riding seems to have taken to her. So I'll get some time to myself, thank God."

"I was hoping to stay another week," said Carol. "Painting, mainly, but also looking for somewhere to rent in Santa Fe. I'm going to use the spa like Tessa . . . I'm into aerobics, and I'm longing to try a mud bath."

"Well," said Rachel, rubbing her hands together, "three perfect strangers meet by chance in a restaurant for dinner. We should drink to something. What?"

"How about to women, friendship, and new directions," said Carol.

"I like that," said Tessa. "Women sticking together. Helping each other out. Men have been doing it for thousands of years. It's how they get to run things."

"That is so true," Rachel agreed. "All men are in an unspoken conspiracy to hold onto their power. We've got to learn that from them. United we stand."

They raised their glasses. "To women and friendship," they chorused.

"I've got another one," said Rachel. "What about to dreams, and making them come true?"

"I like it," said Carol. "And not being disappointed by the dream when you get it. Sometimes I'm frightened that my dreams *will* come true."

"Pretty soon we'll need an attorney to draft these toasts," said Tessa.

"Please, no lawyers," said Rachel. "They make my life a misery."

Carol lifted her glass. "I'll drink to that. An attorney sure messed up mine."

"But you know something?" said Rachel. A reflective tone was creeping into her voice. "I can't help feeling that somewhere out there is at least one good man."

Five

Charles headed toward the sunset, as if to lose himself in the red sky. By his side, bundled up against the cold, Harry Wardlow watched his friend. In their earlier conversation, he had squeezed the words out of Charles like drops of blood. Had describing his pain been good for him? Like any card-carrying resident of Manhattan, Harry believed in the culture of psychoanalysis. He had faith in the latter-day religion. Hurt should be released as words on the wind, that it might fly away. Charles was from another school. He mistrusted speech. Emotion was dangerous. Once set free, feelings did not disappear. They made you weak when you most needed to be strong.

"It helps to talk about it," said Harry gently. "Charles, my poor, dear friend. You must let it out. Get rid of it or it will destroy you. It's been over a year. Rose wouldn't have wanted you to suffer like this. Would you have wanted her to, if you had died?"

Charles looked straight ahead. Harry knew he was hiding tears in his eyes.

"But, Harry, you knew her. You knew us. You knew our life. How can you let go of the past, your memories, all the things that made you happy? We'd walk together like this every evening. I mean, I mean . . . she's walking beside us now, isn't she? Over there, in the darkness. A bit distant to preserve her damned independence, and all the time searching for things in the desert, rocks, sticks, flowers. We'd talk and be together, yet separate, and she'd search. I'm sorry, Harry—" His voice caught in the cold air of the desert evening. "She's still all I can think about."

Charles stopped for a minute, unable to walk on. He looked around wildly, searching for the searcher he knew he would never see again. Fifteen years of loving, and it was the little things, always the little things. He remembered the way she rubbed a silk scarf between her thumb and forefinger when she was preoccupied; the violin concerto by Mendelssohn in E minor that she played when she was sad; the plates from Italy, colorful and garish, that were all she had salvaged from her childhood. He had those things now, her scarf, her haunting music, her plates, arranged in sacred memory in his bedroom . . . but Rose, killed by cancer, he did not have. Now he wiped away tears.

Harry reached out and gripped his arm.

"I'm so sorry, Charles. I'm so sorry."

Beneath his fingers Harry could feel the sudden surge of strength as his friend fought against the despair. He watched as Charles looked up to the star-spangled sky. He could imagine his prayer. Then Charles took another step forward into the darkness. He shook himself, as if to cast out demons. Together, in silence, they walked toward the old barn, its single light beckoning.

Charles pressed down on the latch of the carved door.

"No keys?"

"No thieves," said Charles, glad that he could manage the smile.

"We city slickers can never understand that."

"Out here, we know the animals by name."

"But you forget the names of the people," Harry said, laughing. It was a long-standing joke. Harry knew everybody. Names were his life. Charles couldn't wait to forget them. He had never needed acquaintances. He and Rose had been a unit far more self-contained than most married couples, despite the fact that on Rose's insistence, they had never actually married. Now

Charles was paying for his neglect of people. Still, he had Harry, thank God. They had been friends for so many years, despite their being opposites. Charles, Catholic, a dreamer, an introverted mystic, had only one real love besides the woman he mourned. He loved the desert in which he and his ancestors had lived since before the founding of America. He loved the Indians, the animals, the cactus, and the fierce heat of summer, the clean cold of winter, the blood-red sunsets, and the simplicity of a life in which survival alone was a worthy goal. In contrast, Harry, a creature of the city, was a people person, popular and ambitious in a world of materialism made acceptable by the commodity in which it dealt . . . art. In this attraction of opposites an abiding friendship had flourished. Charles usually preferred the company of women. He loved them and felt at ease with them. But in Harry, a confirmed bachelor of his own age, he had a friend in whom he could confide.

"I find rattlesnakes a little more predictable than people," said Charles, this time with an actual laugh. He opened the door and flicked on the light. It was a simple room, large and uncluttered, as Rose had liked it. Her canvases were still stacked against the whitewashed wall. A single ox's skull, bleached by the sun, hung on the wall in homage to Georgia O'Keeffe. On an easel in the center of the room, beneath the skylight, was Rose's last work-in-progress.

Charles walked over to it, in control of himself now. The intense sadness, like a passing sickness, was over, although he knew it would come again.

"What was she painting?" asked Harry.

"The sound of a coyote at dusk."

The abstraction stared back at them, vibrant and stark, like the howl of the hungry animal that had inspired it. It was grays, browns, and desert colors, but the brilliant orange of the desert sunset was featured.

"It's very strong," he said. "Like Rose, like the desert, like a wild animal's hunger."

"I think so, too," said Charles.

"Are you going to leave the room like this?"

"I hadn't thought what to do with it."

Harry took a deep breath. This had to be done. "It's been a year, Charles. You need to meet somebody else. Not anybody like Rose. But somebody. Soon. You have to paint again, live again, even love again. That sounds crazy to you now, but it's sense, common sense. All the clichés are true. Time heals wounds. Life must go on. You loved your mother, I know how much. Yet she died, and you found Rose. You didn't forget your mother or your childhood. You have it with you now. It's part of you. But you can't let your past control your future. You can't live backward. You have to let it go. You have to look forward. You can't just exist. You have to become."

Charles wandered over to the picture window and stared out into the blackness.

"I know all that," he said. "Everybody does. It's true what you say. Rose would say it. But I don't feel it. I try, but I can't. I force myself to eat, to walk, to speak. I go through the motions, but that's all I can do. Maybe one day I'll wake up and there'll be a point to it all. But it hasn't happened, and I feel that it won't happen." He turned back toward his friend. His voice shook with the frustration of it all.

"Do you keep any drink out here?" said Harry.

"What? Oh, yes, I think so. Rose used to keep a bottle of Hine in the kitchen. Would that be all right?"

"Perfect. It's not often I feel like a drink, but when I do, the urge is uncontrollable."

"So even Mr. Wisdom isn't always in charge of his feelings," said Charles. He walked to the corner area with its range, sink, and single cupboard. There were two brandy balloons in there. They would be dusty now, but the memory of Rose's lips would be on them. He took a deep breath and opened the cupboard door. He reached up and took the glasses down, not wanting to wipe them, and not wiping them. He reached for the bottle, and held it as if holding Rose's hand, and he remembered the spirits the fiery liquid had summoned as they had talked into the night . . . of art and painting and the impossibility of draining the last drops from life in the shortness of the time they had left together. She had spoken then of the loneliness he would face, aware of her own death and not denying it.

As he poured the brandy they had shared, he heard her voice across the years.

"I'll seem to be gone, my darling, but I'll never leave you. I will be there in the desert. You will hear me in the howl of the coyote that I'll paint for you. I'll smile at you from the cactus flowers and I'll watch over you from the mountains. I will always be with you, my darling, in the dust and moonbeams, and when it's your time I will greet you in the heaven that will be the wedding we never had."

He had proposed to her then, falling to one knee and asking her to be his wife with the desperation of someone who knew that he was soon to lose the woman he adored. She had accepted him, and he had taken off the ring his father had given him and put it on her finger, and he had felt the wild joy that was already circled by a line of doom. The very next day, in the early morning, Rose had difficulty breathing. The doctor had come and taken her to the hospital. Within a week she had died.

Charles walked to the sofa and sat down, leaning back against the pillows and stretching out his legs. The light from the lamp caught him from the side and above, illuminating the moody, brooding eyes set deep in a brow furrowed by sadness. Harry watched him, noticing once again the force, the presence, of Charles Ford. His black hair rushed away from his temples, abundant and straight, and his mahogany-brown skin, stained by the sun, spoke of the Mexican and the Spaniard in him, the genes diluted by the blood of England, France, and an America far older than Independence. His upper body was taut and V-shaped beneath the faded denim shirt, and his forearms showed the anatomy of his muscles as they tapered to hands that seemed graceful and sensitive in contrast to his rugged appearance.

He sipped the cognac, swirling it in the balloon glass, peering into it as if seeing the memories there. "You know," he said at last, and his voice seemed to come from far away in time and place, "when I was twelve, my father would take me out into the desert for a whole week at a time. He'd have one of the men take us out there in a pickup truck and drop us miles from anywhere. We would take a blanket and one water bottle and a knife. Nothing else. We'd eat insects and lizards, and he taught me how to suck water from a cactus and make a fire from sunlight on a knife blade. And at night he'd tell me stories of the Indians and their spirits, and about gods and nature and the irrelevance of death. I never thought I could be happier than at those times, or sadder than when he died. But I was both, and he was wrong about the irrelevance of death."

He tapped his foot against the carpet, a tiny gesture that in Charles Ford's body language revealed his frustration, even his anger. He had loved his father and mother and Rose, and they had gone. They had deserted him, and there was rage inside him all mixed up with despair.

"But Charles, you can't just hang around here forever and rot. I mean, your painting. You've got to start again. It'll be therapy. You just have to start something, anything. Stick the paint on the canvas and the ideas will come."

There was genuine angst in Harry's plea. He was not only Charles's friend. He was the owner of the avant-garde Manhattan gallery that sold his paintings under exclusive contract. Charles had never been one of his most prolific painters, nor one of the Wardlow Gallery's major stars, but Harry was convinced that he had a rare talent. In years past he had encouraged Charles to increase his output, but Charles had painted for his own satisfaction rather than for money or success. Or perhaps, all along, he had painted for Rose . . . to please her? . . . to compete with her? . . . because since her death he had painted nothing at all.

Charles waved away art with a dismissive movement of his hand. "Maybe there'll be a time for that one day. I don't know. I honestly don't care. What is paint? What is canvas? What the hell is the use of words?"

"Oh, yes," said Harry, enlisting sarcasm as an ally. "And what is God, and heaven, and what is Rose, and your parents looking down on you and seeing a stranger indulging himself in self-pity?"

Harry held his breath. He saw fire flash in Charles's eyes like the flame of a campfire in the shadows, suddenly flickering to life. Charles turned toward him.

"Be careful, H," he said quietly. It was a warning not a threat, but Harry didn't regret his words. All this Christmas period they had been building to this moment.

Charles stood up suddenly. He walked slowly to the painting on its easel and looked at it. Harry knew he was hearing the howl of the coyote at dusk, and that it was Rose's voice speaking to him. She was telling him what Harry had just told him. And *that* was the use of words.

At last, he turned away from the canvas and back toward his friend.

"I'm sorry, H. You're right. I've got to go forward. Somehow I've got to begin again, but I don't know how to do it."

Suddenly he looked haggard, as he dared to deal with the problem of life without Rose. There could be no replacement for her. The sunshine had walked beside her.

Harry felt the moment. He knew exactly what Charles needed. He needed to learn to love again, to find a woman, to have a wife and raise a family. Charles had always wanted to be a father, but Rose had been unable to have children. He had dreamed of a boy, of teaching him the ways of the wild desert as his own father had taught him, of having an heir to carry on the ancient *estancia* and link the past and the present to the endless future.

"Charles, trust me. I know what you need. You have to get away from this place with all its memories. I know it sounds like hell, but come with me back to Manhattan. You have the loft. Stay there for a few days. Meet people, see things, hang out at the gallery. Let me arrange your life."

"Oh, H, you and your mighty Rolodex. You know how long

it takes me to get to know someone. Years. And I run out of patience in minutes, if not seconds. I care about what people think in a world that is only interested in what they do."

"Look, Charles, I haven't mentioned this before, but this might be the moment. You know who Matt Harding is?"

"Yes, the information superhighwayman."

"Precisely—and a collector. He's a client."

"Good for you, H. Unto them that hath . . ."

"The point is, he's interested in your work. The paintings I have in stock."

"Oh?" said Charles. "Which ones?"

"All of them really, but mainly the Indians. You know, the one with the Indian in the back of the pickup truck against the foot of the mountain. He's crazy for that one."

"Well, sell it to him, H."

"It's a little more difficult than that. He's one of those collectors that like to be involved, you know, meet the artist socially, discuss his artistic motivations. You know the deal."

"H, you *know* I don't do that."

"Shit, Charles, Francis Bacon did it. He puked all over Baron Lambert's shoes and the old boy was absolutely *thrilled*. Thought it was absolutely the right sort of behavior from a tip-top artist. You don't have to be polite, you can just growl and grunt, and he'll probably think you're magnificent, uncompromising, remote. People like Harding don't want to buy anything that wants to be bought. You know that. And he's influential. His collection is far better than good. We could probably double your price if he takes several."

"So that's why you want me up in Manhattan. To prance around Harding's drawing room like some tame prima donna? No, H, I don't mean that. I know you're really trying to help."

Harry Wardlow shot a glance of pure exasperation at the ceiling. How could you help someone who would not be helped? He had done his best.

But at the precise moment that Harry was beginning to lose patience, Charles capitulated.

"Okay, okay, H, I'll do it, if only to keep you from nagging me to death. I'll come up to Manhattan."

"Great! You won't regret it," said Harry.

"What were you thinking of doing this evening?" said Charles, retreating as if by instinct from people-rich New York.

"No plans. That's the beauty of staying with you. A book by the fire. Then bed, I suspect."

"I thought I might drive over to the Hacienda Inn. Do you want to come?"

"No, I think I'll pass. How's it going over there? I have lots of friends who think it's magnificent. I keep boasting that I know you, and they say you're never around."

"I slip in and out. A drink at the bar, a walk around, and I'm gone. It's far more revealing than the formal tour, with everyone on their best behavior until you've gone."

Charles remembered the days when the Hacienda Inn had been a ghost ranch. On the northern borders of the Ford property near Santa Fe, it had been built by his great-grandmother, but after her death it fell into decay. For a child it had been a magical, mysterious place, fun by day, and deliciously spooky in the desert dusk. Charles had learned every inch of its adobe ruins. He had stepped on a rusty nail in the broken-down corral, gotten stuck in the chimney, and sprained an ankle in a fall from the rotted roof. All those pains were sweet memories now of the far-off land of simple childhood, when emotions were nothing more than tears, honest rage, and shouted laughter beneath the bright sun and the phosphorescent moon. For many years he had been badgered by an up-market hotel company that specialized in small, exclusive developments. They had wanted to buy the "ghost" property and turn it into a superb hotel and build a spa next door. A couple of years before, they had capitulated to his demand that he be given right of refusal over any development plans, and when he saw the drawings he was so impressed that he had sold them the land and invested some of his own money in the project.

In the desolate months following Rose's death, unable to

paint and in need of occupational therapy, Charles had taken an active interest in the place, but now his visits were less frequent.

Charles stood up. "Okay, H, I'd better get going. If you're gone to bed by the time I get back, I'll see you at lunchtime."

He drained the brandy, and Harry did, too. Then he took both glasses back to the sink, rinsed them, and stowed them away in the cupboard where they lived. He felt strangely elated. Perhaps talk did help after all.

They walked back to the ranch house together in near silence. Things had somehow changed. There were plans. There would be movement. But, as he bid his friend a second good night, Charles couldn't quite work out why he felt so excited.

Six

The bright desert sun tempered the crisp freshness of the air, and the mud cuddled Rachel's body. She moved her hands through the glutinous mess, marveling at the strangely familiar consistency. Had it been like this in the womb? Was this what it had felt like in the primordial soup? If so, then progress sucked. She looked up at the cloudless sky and watched a red-tailed hawk drifting on the thermal currents against the sapphire blue. She looked down at the bubbling mud that covered her body, and then across at Tessa lying next to her in an identical open-air mosaic-tiled bath.

"I can't work out whether I'm dying or being born," she whispered. "Either way, it's heaven."

Tessa turned toward her. Her face was caked in a mask of mud. Her eyes, headlamps in the muddy darkness, were the only bits of her face that could laugh.

"It's impossible to talk without breaking this thing," she mumbled.

The attendant hovered near them, watching carefully for the signs of claustrophobia that some people showed in the mud baths. She dipped a thermometer into the bubbling mess, wiped it clean, and read it. "Ninety-eight degrees," she said, half to herself.

Body temperature, thought Tessa. No wonder it was so comfortable. The skin on her face was taut; everywhere else she was slippery, yet buoyant. The mud covered her and cushioned her, diminishing her body. Her limbs and her insides were no longer bombarding her with messages, distracting her with their aches, pains, and vague discomforts. It was as if her body had gone away and her mind had been left to its own devices. I think, therefore I am.

"Why does this feel so good?" said Rachel.

"I was reading about it at breakfast. It's to do with mineral salts and the texture of the mud. On the face, it's passive exercise for the skin. It tones the muscles by stretching them as it dries."

"But the skin doesn't have muscles," said Rachel.

"Well, there are apparently these things called erector pili muscles. They're the ones that make the hair stand on end when you're frightened. And there are layers of fasciae that can contract and relax . . ."

"That's fascinating, Tess."

"Then there was a whole load of stuff about the importance of mud to the Pueblo Indians. You know, their making their adobe houses out of it, because that's what 'adobe' means. When it rained in the desert it was a big deal, so mud became magical to them. They believed mud had healing powers. Maybe it does. I feel quite wonderful."

"Me, too." Rachel rearranged her head on the wooden platform with its cunningly placed triangle of white cotton towels. She breathed the vitalizing ozone-and-sage-tinted air and the strangely clean and wholesome smell of the liquid dirt in which she lay.

"Do you know, I think I'm actually beginning to unwind. I'm not very good at that," she said.

Tessa was drifting, too. She thought of Camille. By now, she would be busy reorganizing the riding school. At eight, Camille was self-sufficient, and never happier than when she was out there putting her charm and energy to work ruling the world.

"What have you got next, Rachel?" she whispered dreamily.

"Yoga, I think. But I'm not going to make it. This is too exhausting. I had no idea doing nothing was so tiring. Have you got anything?"

"I'm going down to the pool. They've got mineral water-falls—hot, cold, and tepid—and there are jets that pummel you underwater at the same time. The blurb said it was great for stress in the back and shoulders."

"Oh, that sounds wonderful. Can I join you?"

"Sure, I'd love it."

Tessa was relaxing. The mud was working its magic. She felt close to Rachel. She liked her. Then she remembered a remark that Rachel had made at the first dinner they had shared. Camille had asked Rachel if she had babies. "Not yet, but I hope to. I have to find a husband first." Rachel's answer had surprised Tessa. Now she felt she knew Rachel well enough to ask about it.

"Rachel . . . I hope you don't mind my asking this . . . but how is it you never married?"

"Never fell in love," said Rachel with a laugh. "My friends tell me love is a minor detail, but I always felt it was kind of important."

"Never?"

"Well, I don't *think* so. I mean, I've had boyfriends, relationships. I've sort of *cared* about guys, minded when things went wrong. Is that it?"

"Absolutely not," said Tessa, laughing. "You know it when you feel it. It's so certain, so strong. It happens in a single second and you remember that second for the rest of your life. It's absolutely overpowering. It's a moment of magic, and it never fades. For instance, when I met Pete, it was as if I had come alive for the first time. Until that moment, I'd been like some zombie, undead, walking the world, being there but not really being there . . . I don't know how else to explain it."

"And now?" said Rachel gently.

"And now I still have the memory of it. But my man has gone, and it hurts like hell."

Rachel heard the catch in Tessa's voice. She reached over and touched her hand. Tessa gave a brave laugh. "But anyway, Rachel, we've got to find someone absolutely wonderful for you."

"Oh, I don't know," said Rachel. "Maybe I just want a baby,

goddamn it, and some romance to go along with it. Is that too much to ask of life? What was it the song said? 'Love is all you need'?"

"Love has been the best thing in my life so far," said Tessa, shifting in the warm mud. "But I suppose your career must be incredibly fulfilling."

"Yes, it *is* good. It's great at times. Of course it is," said Rachel, as if reassuring herself. "Except when Steve, my egomaniac producer, forces me to sacrifice my principles to the mighty ratings-god. Sometimes I feel my whole life is at the mercy of a group of invisible channel-surfing couch potatoes."

They laughed together, and then, once again, the silence and the mud settled around them, wrapping them in womblike peace.

It was a time for sharing secrets.

"You know, Tess, there *is* a man in my life at the moment. Have you ever heard of Matt Harding?"

"The media mogul Matt Harding?"

"Yes. In fact, he's asked me to marry him, several times, and I keep saying, 'maybe.' It's basically why I'm here. I've promised to give him my final answer soon."

"Good Lord, Rachel. You kept that one quiet, didn't you. Here I am telling you all about magic moments, and you knew about them all the time. That's wonderful! Matt Harding is so good-looking. I read a *Vanity Fair* article about him the other day. He sounded just fabulous."

"Yes, he is," said Rachel. "I mean, it is wonderful. I've known him forever. In fact, he was the one who got me started in television. He's a very special man, and he's sweet and kind, when he isn't doing killer deals. You should see my room—the roses don't leave much oxygen for me. I can't think why I haven't said yes," she added.

"Well, why haven't you?" said Tessa.

"Have you ever thought of doing a TV interview show?" said Rachel with a rueful smile. "You ask the difficult questions." She paused. "Why haven't I said yes? I guess I've been doing what I'm doing right this second, failing to face up to things.

Putting off decisions." She took a deep breath. "I suppose the bottom line is that I *really* want to be in love with him, but I just don't feel the magic that we've been talking about. It all seems to be happening a bit more in the head than in the heart, but maybe magic simply doesn't happen for everyone . . . and it's not meant for me."

"Tell me about him," said Tessa.

"Well, he's brilliant, of course, and powerful, and very rich. He's been married twice, and he has three grown-up children. Of course you know how he's positioned himself to control a huge section of the information superhighway, with the cable, the wireless licenses . . ." Rachel petered out. Tessa was nodding politely, waiting for a punch line that she had not yet delivered. For one of the very few times in her life, Rachel was failing to carry her audience with her.

Quite suddenly, irritation flashed through her. Then, as suddenly, her anger faded. Tessa wasn't a Martian. Tessa was a real person, far more real in a way than Rachel was. Tessa had a different intelligence and different understanding of life's priorities. Tessa was not obsessed by money or power. People like Tessa and Carol dealt in love and warmth, children and families. And Rachel wanted to be in Tessa and Carol's world, and out of hers. That was what this was all about. She tried again.

"Everything he says interests me. I'm never bored when he's around. He has this incredible memory for people's names and . . . and he loves my cat. Vesper has always hated my other guys . . ." Again, Rachel tapered off.

"He sounds really nice," said Tessa determinedly. "And does he want lots of children?" she added with sudden enthusiasm.

"Well, he says of course if I want them I can have them. But he's already done that side of things. He isn't against children. He says as long as I don't give up my job, he doesn't mind what the hell I do."

Tessa's silence was Rachel's reward.

"I guess it isn't the magic we were talking about, is it?" said

Rachel at last. "Hardly the affair to remember that becomes the unforgettable marriage."

"You'll find him," said Tessa quietly. "He exists. He's out there somewhere . . . and he's looking for you. And when you meet him, you'll recognize each other and the world will become super real, and you'll just know."

The attendant's voice cut into the conversation.

"Time's up, ladies."

The attendant, joined by another, marched forward with fresh towels. Tessa and Rachel staggered from the slippery mud. Soon they were swathed in crisp cotton and being led to a wooden-floored shower area where coiled hosepipes waited.

"I wouldn't want the laundry bills in this place," said Rachel.

"Don't they just throw the towels away?" said Tessa.

It seemed a reasonable question at the Hacienda Inn. True luxury was the total absence of economy. Nobody thought about saving money. Two guests meant two attendants when one would have been enough. It was fun being hosed down together. They giggled like schoolgirls, twisting and turning as the powerful jets pounded them. Then they tingled deliciously as they were rubbed down with loofahs until their rejuvenated skin glowed. Being naked in the bracing open air seemed as natural as breathing, and Rachel and Tessa's worries washed away with the muddy water as it gurgled through the wooden slats beneath their feet.

Now they were wrapped in vast terry dressing gowns bearing the crest of the Hacienda Inn. On Rachel's was pinned the printed itinerary of the day's spa program, packed with activities.

"I haven't been this busy in years," said Tessa with a laugh.

They walked out of what was known as the mud house, a square adobe courtyard built with the mud bricks that the Spaniards had taught the Indians to make in the days when Santa Fe had been a far-flung outpost of the Spanish empire. The two women meandered along a tiled walkway flanked by cactus and serenaded by cicadas. The sun was warming up. They passed through an ancient gate in a high stone wall, and there was the pool complex, deserted, the chaises laid out with piles of towels.

An attendant hovered with a basket of suntan creams, screens, moisturizers, and lip glosses.

"Shall I prepare two chaises?"

"Yes, please," said Rachel. "We're going to do the waterfalls."

"I've just realized," said Tessa. "I haven't got bathing things."

The Hacienda Inn had thought of that, too. There were neat piles of swimsuits in a variety of sizes.

"Whoever dreamed up this place had a lot of style," said Tessa.

"I think so, too."

"Who does own it?"

"A company called Rosewood. The spa is run by the management team that operates the Doral in Miami. But there are other investors. A rancher who lives around here has a big investment, I heard."

They climbed into bathing suits.

"Rachel," said Tessa suddenly. "I imagine you know almost everything about anything. Do you know about Pete . . . and what happened?"

Rachel took a deep breath. She had been expecting this.

"The headline stuff. The boat in the Bahamas. The business failing. I knew pretty much immediately that you were *the* Tessa Andersen."

Rachel had thought a lot about those headlines since first meeting Tessa. Peter Andersen, a charismatic entrepreneur, had founded a highly successful chain of theme restaurants called the Heavenly Sports Cafés. His empire and his fortune had crumbled in debt and disaster, and then he had disappeared from his boat in the Bermuda Triangle, leaving mystery and chaos behind. Rachel had very briefly considered doing a piece on it, but Steve had overruled her in the early stages of program development. Now it seemed that Tessa wanted to talk about it.

"Do you want to tell me about it?" Rachel said.

"Yes," said Tessa. "I think I'd like to." She took a deep breath, and then blurted it out. "The trouble with me is that my husband disappeared, and I'm trying to come to terms with the fact that he's dead, and I'm trying to believe that he didn't commit suicide, and we were really rich . . . and now it turns out there isn't any money at all."

"Wow," said Rachel softly. Tessa had gone straight to the bottom line.

When she continued, Tessa's voice was strangely detached. "I mean, I'd known that there were all sorts of problems with the business. There was competition from the Hard Rock Cafés, Planet Hollywood, and the Harley-Davidson people. The movie studios like Warners' and Disney and everyone else were going into theme restaurants. The banks were nervous, the recession was biting, the stock was falling. But that was just the way things were sometimes. It was tough in the beginning, and at lots of other times." She paused. "Pete had this boat—a fishing boat, which he kept in Florida, down in Palm Beach, actually." Again she paused, as all the memories flooded back. "It was called *Camille.*"

"A big boat?" asked Rachel.

"No, fifty feet. Pete used to drive it himself. Camille was the first mate. She had a hat that said that."

Tessa stared away into the room. Camille had loved that boat, but Tessa had never really liked fishing—all the blood, the smells, the hours bobbing on the ocean.

"One day he said he was going to fly down and slip over to the Bahamas. He said he needed to do some thinking, and fishing would help. There was nothing odd about that. It was like Pete—spontaneous, spur-of-the-moment. It was one of the things I loved about him. They found the boat in the Gulf Stream," said Tessa. "Pete wasn't on it. Nobody was. I've never seen him again."

There was a silence.

"He went fishing without anyone to help him?" said Rachel.

"Yes. That was odd. There was a young guy he usually took with him to help out. And apparently, Pete never got in touch with Karen, the dockmaster in Palm Beach. He always did that—told her, I mean, where he was going, when to expect him back. It's part of what experienced boaters do."

"Had he been fishing?" said Rachel, always the journalist.

"No, not really. No lines out. Outriggers not rigged, no ballyhoo on board—that's bait. And he hadn't taken his passport, and you need one for the Bahamas."

"Were there signs that he had been on the boat?"

"Yes. His briefcase. His glasses. His fingerprints on a can of beer."

"But no evidence of anyone else."

Tessa turned to look at her, as if in a trance. "You mean what they call foul play?" she said.

"Yes," said Rachel. "It *was* the Bermuda Triangle."

"No, no evidence of anyone else." How many times had Tessa been through all this? In her mind. With the Coast Guard. With her brother. With the people from the SEC. "Pete kept a boat gun in case of pirates. That's a problem in the out-islands, drug smugglers hijacking boats for cocaine runs and killing the crew. But he had radar. It was on. He would have been aware of any boat approaching. There was no sign of a struggle. The engines were turned off. The boat was just drifting in the Stream. Pete wasn't on it."

"He just disappeared," said Rachel. "And you don't know what happened to him."

Tessa simply nodded. There were all sorts of levels of knowledge.

"He didn't leave any . . . message?"

"You mean like a suicide note? No," said Tessa. "And he didn't seem depressed. Everybody asked that. But Pete was never depressed. That was another thing I loved about him."

Rachel waited. There was so much more to this story . . . the bit Rachel knew . . . the god-awful financial mess that Pete had walked out on. He had borrowed a ton of money to shore up his sagging business. He had signed personal guarantees for the loans. Everything he possessed had been mortgaged. There was nothing left.

Tessa held her head high.

"He left us," she said. "And he left us with nothing. Zip.

Zilch. Far less than zero. The banks took everything. There was nothing to sell. I had signed papers making over everything to him. He was always the cockeyed optimist. He thought it was just a matter of time before things turned around."

Rachel winced. How could anyone love a man like that? He had left his wife and daughter destitute. He had killed himself in an act of total selfishness to escape the consequences of the mess he had made. Or had he disappeared and deserted them, and was now living in South America with money stolen from the company? She felt the anger and the scorn build inside her, but there was no way she would let it out. Tessa was still in love with him.

"I still love him, you know," said Tessa, subconsciously reading Rachel's thoughts. "But as the months go by, sometimes I feel desperately let down by him."

"When exactly was it?" said Rachel.

"A year next week," said Tessa.

"You must miss him so much."

"I do, but mainly I *did*. In the beginning it was so awful. I was numb. I'd walk around for hours and not know where I was or how I'd got there. I felt dead inside. I couldn't do anything, not even cry. Then time passes and it's different—still as bad, but different, more real. The practical things are coming back, and sometimes I can judge Pete as well as love him. Now I have to get my life together, and I have to find a future for Camille."

"Have you got a job?" said Rachel.

"I took my real estate exams, and I have a job lined up at Sotheby's in New York. It starts in a few days. Believe it or not, I've never had a job before, and the prospect terrifies me." Tessa laughed bravely.

"God, and I've never not had one," said Rachel. They laughed together. But Rachel couldn't let it go. She had an agenda—the removal of the rose-tinted spectacles through which Tessa saw Pete. Tessa seemed somehow to sense Rachel's purpose.

"But if something terrible *did* happen out there in the Gulf

Stream, something completely beyond Pete's control, it wouldn't have been his fault, would it?"

"Is that what *you* think, Tess?" Turn the question back on the questioner. It was the old shrink's trick.

"Sometimes I don't know what to think. I used to know. But as time passes, I seem to know less. He was a gambler. He was an optimist. He was spontaneous. He didn't *worry* about things. Those were the bits of him I loved. They were what made him different from all the gloomy Englishmen I was supposed to marry. I keep thinking that if I loved all those things when everything was going well, then how can I stop when things go badly. I mean, how can I blame him for being the man I married and adored?"

"Wasn't there even an insurance policy, Tess?" said Rachel gently.

"No."

Tessa felt the emotions bubbling up inside her. She was tired of standing up for Pete. She had exhausted her expertise in that area, and there wasn't a distant cousin or the remotest acquaintance in England or Scotland who hadn't tried some version of "I told you so." But somehow, with Rachel it was different. Rachel was an American. She understood people like Pete. And she was a bright, clever woman who had seen loads of life and knew how to dig beneath the surface and ferret out the facts. Rachel wasn't blaming anyone. She was letting Tessa do it. It was like psychotherapy, painful but compelling.

"You're saying he should have left us something."

"I just asked, Tessa."

"Well, he didn't, and he should have. I *do* blame him for that. It was stupid . . . if it wasn't cruel."

Rachel heard the subterranean anger. It rumbled like a far-off storm. One day it would arrive with all its force, and the fond memories of Pete Andersen would be blown away forever.

"Are you very worried about Sotheby's?" Rachel, with her reporter's intuition, had heard Tessa's earlier panic. Tessa had downplayed her fears of the New York career world, the most vicious workplace jungle on the planet. But if she wanted to swim with sharks, Tessa would have to learn survival techniques. Rachel could help her to a point, but from then on, Tessa Andersen would have to change. She couldn't go on being charming and childlike, gracious and generous. She would have to start to want—to need—to win, and to go on winning.

"I'm terrified. I've never sold a thing, let alone an apartment." She laughed disarmingly.

"And you've got somewhere to stay?"

"Yes, a one-bedroom on Madison. It's a rent-controlled place that a friend kept for their chauffeur. Luckily, they sacked the chauffeur." She laughed bravely as they walked out of the changing room into the bright sunshine. "I suppose I'm pretty lucky to get such a good place for next to nothing."

Saved by friends, thought Rachel. Tessa was relying on connections that would run out far sooner than later if she couldn't hack it. In Manhattan, few people had the time or the inclination to give second chances.

As if reading Rachel's thoughts, Tessa said, "How did you get started in television?"

Rachel smiled as she remembered.

"Do you believe weathergirl?"

"Weathergirl!" Tessa turned to look at her, laughing.

"Yup. And I had a bachelor's in communications from Smith, and a master's in history. I went to WNBC in Chicago and met this station manager guy called Matt Harding—yes, *the* Matt Harding, my Matt Harding, only he wasn't *the* Matt Harding then—and he said I wasn't pretty enough to be in front of the camera."

"He said that? To your face?"

"Oh yes, he did. And then he invited me out to dinner. I said, 'No, I'm not pretty enough to go out to dinner with you, and you're for sure not bright enough to go out to dinner with me.' It was a great start."

"But that's terrible."

"No. It wasn't personal. He was right. He was just doing his job. I *wasn't* pretty enough. In those days everybody thought you had to be a knockout to do the weather."

"But you got to do it anyway?"

"Yes, and I didn't know cumulus from stratus or a cyclone from a tornado. But boy, did I find out! On the first night I said, 'It'll be getting late early this evening.' And I also said, 'The high today was forty-nine degrees and the current temperature is fifty-one.' Matt tried to sack me, and I said that when I was famous I would start every print interview by saying he was the one who tried to sabotage my career. I can still remember the expression on his face when I said that. Isn't it funny how you can remember expressions?"

"Tried to sack you. Wants to marry you. A man of contradictions, Matt Harding," said Tessa.

"Not really. There are things I don't understand about romance, maybe, Tess, but there are things you don't begin to understand about business. Things change. Strategy has to change to take advantage of that, or you lose, and that's what everyone's trying to avoid. In business, you have to keep reinventing yourself, women especially. Matt was a master at that. Still is. I wasn't so bad at it myself. When you're successful at something, everyone jumps on the bandwagon and copies you, does it cheaper, quicker, better, with a new spin. If you stand still, you disappear. Matt wanted a weathergirl with teeth and tits, but I was able to persuade him that personality could sell soap too, and that the women liked me and they do the buying. Now he wants to marry me because I'm huge and trendy, and this year I'm really hot. Good for him.

"When you get to Sotheby's, you'll have to remember that. You'll have to use your friends mercilessly. You'll have to poach listings from the nice girl who was so kind to you that first week, and you'll have to push and push to close, even when the buyer doesn't want to and you know the house is a piece of overpriced shit. I used to work for Barbara Walters on *20/20*, and some of the other girls didn't like her because she never used to remember their birthdays and sometimes she forgot to say thank you for some hard work, and she could be abrupt. But I didn't even see that. It went over my head. I just saw a consummate pro, the drive, the ambition, a woman cracking nuts and making it in a man's world. I watched and I learned and I worshiped, and I wouldn't have cared if she'd used my skirt to wipe her shoes. And funnily enough, she *did* remember my birthday, and *I'd* forgotten it. She gave me a cushion that said 'Aiming high is not enough. You have to become the bullet.' The other girls didn't talk to me for weeks."

"But you don't seem like that, Rachel. You seem gentle, and very friendly."

"Try competing with me for a story," said Rachel, laughing. "Anyway, I've just been in the magic mud."

"I don't think I'd like to compete with you for anything! Let's hope I never have to," said Tessa.

She laughed too, but she had seen the sharp edges of Rachel Richardson. Rachel had shown them to her as a kindness. She was trying to teach her that amateurishness and gentility would have little place in her new world, but the hardness lingered. They had moved a little apart. Tessa's trials were just beginning, but at the same time, if Rachel had been remotely serious about romance, babies, and normal family life, she, too, had one hell of a lot of learning to do. Tessa might have to learn cunning, manipulation, and ruthlessness. Rachel would have to brush up on trust, patience, and selflessness.

They had arrived at the chaises. They flopped down on the carefully laid out towels, one rolled in a long pillow to put beneath the neck, another arranged in a square to support the lower back, a third providing a pillow for the legs.

"Everybody has something, Tess. You have so many assets. There's a quiet strength about you. You're incredibly confident. It beams out from you in waves. You can turn that into anything. People are just sucked toward confidence. It makes them feel safe. I got mine through achievement. Maybe you got yours in your genes, or in your upbringing somehow. I don't know, but trust me, you have it, and it's cash in the bank and career success if you just give it a chance to work. I mean, that maitre d' gave you my goddamn table. He said you'd insisted on having it, and did one of those French What-could-I-do? things with his shoulders and hands. I can think of senators who wouldn't have pulled that one off."

"Well, he tried to put me near the door to the kitchen and I just hate that," said Tessa.

Rachel laughed. "That's what I mean," she said. "You should hear yourself. Try it on the clients next month. 'Listen, I've come all this way out to Southampton to show you this house and I had a lot to do today. The least you can do is buy the damn place.' It's all in the telling. The way you'd say it, it would probably work." Rachel propped herself up on the chaise. She was getting the hang of this relaxation business. You lay around all day and chatted about anything that came into your mind, and people brought you things, tidied your towels, and worried about whether you were completely and utterly happy at every moment. You soaked up the sun, telephone didn't ring, the outside world didn't intrude, and there were no business decisions to make.

The pool, one of three at the Hacienda Inn, was a pool with a view. A curved adobe wall lined its edge at one end, and beyond the low wall the vista stretched for miles to the mountains, across brown, parched desert hungry for the water that existed in such profusion for the delight of the guests of the Hacienda Inn. That, too, was luxury. There was plenty amidst shortage, the latter enhancing enjoyment of the former. The extraordinary comfort of the Hacienda Inn was in this way amplified by the fierce wildness that surrounded it. A pile of outsize boulders formed the other end of the pool. Water cascaded down them in three distinct streams, which were captured in three separate but interconnected "baths," themselves hewn from the natural rock. The main body of the pool was separate from these grottoes, but you had to swim it to reach them.

Rachel and Tessa lowered themselves into the heated pool and swam toward the waterfalls of the rock face. Each "bath" was fitted with a seat that held two people comfortably and was situated so that the stream of water descended directly onto your neck and shoulders if you sat upright.

Side by side, Tessa and Rachel sat beneath the hot waterfall as the heavy torrent massaged away their stress.

"Oh, God," moaned Rachel, turning her head from side to side. "This is better than sex. Even better than chocolate."

"What's sex?" Tessa laughed.

"Sex," said Rachel, "is what everybody's surprised everyone else has so little of."

They were having fun again. The earlier seriousness had gone. Tomorrow could look after itself. Now they could just enjoy the delicious comforts of the Hacienda Inn.

"Are you going to the make-up demonstration tomorrow night? It should be fun," said Tessa, writhing beneath the warm jet of water.

"Yes, why not. My make-up girl works for Steve, my dreadful producer. Between them, they decide what I look like, if you can believe that. I'd like some killer ideas to use against them. Let's persuade Carol to come, too."

"Sounds great to me."

The splashing water cascaded down. Tessa looked out to the desert across the smooth waters of the pool. There was a rider out there in the distance on a white horse.

She pointed at him and turned to Rachel.

"Do you think he's a fabulously rich guy who discovered a gold mine? Or maybe he carved a few hundred thousand acres of cattle ranch out of the wilderness after murdering all the sheep farmers."

"I think you're fantasizing again, Tess, and fantasies can get a girl into big trouble."

Tessa ignored Rachel's advice.

"Well, whoever he is, he looks romantic on that horse," she said. "Maybe he's that rich rancher who owns part of this place. Perhaps I'll just marry him, and then I won't have to worry about having a career after all."

"That's not such a bad idea," said Rachel.

Seven

Charles stared into the fire. He sat slumped in the big chair, his legs stretched out, his shoulders hunched, as he fought off the black mood that was threatening him. He missed Harry, who had gone back to New York the previous evening. Once again the loneliness was closing in. He looked at his watch. It was nine o'clock. Maybe he should go over to the Inn to check that everything was running smoothly. He stood. Yes, that was what he needed. He would take a horse. The ride through the desert would cheer him up.

In the stable he saddled the mare quickly, calming her as she snorted her pleasure at this unexpected visit. The steam from her breath sprung from her nostrils into cold air rich with the smell of hay, horse, and old Spanish leather. He left her briefly to pull on long riding boots, a cape lined with fur, and gloves of soft brown leather. He wound a scarf around his neck, adjusting it so that it covered his mouth to his nose. Then he turned and led the mare out onto the cobbled courtyard, her hooves clicking comfortingly in the still of the windless night. The sky was bright with the fullness of the moon, but some sense told him that it would snow before morning and that tomorrow the desert would be carpeted in white, the cedars covered with icicles, and in the shadows the snow would be colored a vivid blue.

He mounted in the moonbeams, silver bars crossing his blackness, and he turned the mare toward the trail she knew by heart. He checked the stars, which he could steer by but did not need, and the mare soon found the rhythm of the familiar track, easily dodging the prairie dog holes and loose stones. Soon the cedar trees towered above them. In the distance, the lights of Santa Fe glowed like a sunset delayed.

Out here, the animals that he respected watched him. There would be bobcats and coyotes, jackrabbits and cottontails, their glistening eyes bright in the gloom as they sensed a fellow animal at home in their world. Charles Ford threw back his head and looked up at the stars, to the heaven where Rose was watching him, as she had promised to, and he felt for the first time not sorrow but peace at the order of things and faith in the mystery of God's unknowable purpose. He breathed deeply taking in the scent of the cedars and the perfumed oil of the sagebrush, and quickened his pace, touching the mare's flanks with his booted heels.

The Hacienda Inn, slung low on the mesa near the foothills of the mountain, was lit from above by the moon and below from the quiet lights of its rooms. Charles reined in the mare, slowing his pace as he approached. He was exhilarated from the brisk ride in the dark night. It had been timeless, a man on a horse in the desert, alone in the moon shadows. There had been nothing between him and his past, no intrusion of modernity to complicate and confuse a relationship with nature that was as old as the snowcapped mountain that looked down on him.

He walked the mare through the gates and up the winding drive, turning off to the right to the stable block. The night watchman loomed from the side of the building, recognizing him instantly.

"Good evening, Mr. Ford. Lovely night for a ride."

"Good evening, Willie. It is indeed."

He dismounted, handing the reins to the servant. "I won't be long. An hour at the most. My stable's free, isn't it?"

"Always, sir. Of course."

He walked away toward the main entrance of the Inn, the lights of the building illuminating him.

His black cape streamed behind him and his black-booted

feet hurried him forward, his upper body bent in the direction
of his progress. The scarf at his neck flowed in his slipstream
like a dark red banner, and he looked like a messenger from
another age. .

Rachel hurried along the corridor from the ladies' room to
the library, where she had arranged to meet Tessa and Carol.
She was late, and she was looking forward to the fireside meeting. Her two brand-new friends were an unexpected bonus to a
holiday she was thoroughly enjoying.

Damn! She had taken the wrong turn. She was heading back
to the lobby. As she entered it, the man turned his whole body
toward her. A black cape swung in the air like a bullfighter's,
floating, unwinding, hanging in space as if suspended by some
mysterious force. He stared straight at her, his dark, brooding
eyes boring into Rachel's. His hair was matted by wind, and his
mouth, angry, dangerous, raced across an absolutely certain jaw.
She noticed black boots, scuffed and old, a sleeveless jacket of
soft leather, and a mahogany neck framed by a soft blue denim
shirt. He had come from God knew where, for God knew what,
and Rachel stopped short and stared back at him. She heard
herself take a deep, long breath.

"I'm sorry," she said, and her voice was the voice of a stranger.
She wondered what she was sorry for. She didn't feel at all sorry.

"Are you talking to me?" he said. It wasn't said crossly. Yet
it wasn't said with overwhelming courtesy either.

"I'm not quite sure," she said, and she managed a confused
smile and a small laugh.

"Am I in your way?" he said. He did not stand aside, although
he was not really blocking her way.

She tore her eyes away from his, turned her head, and focused
randomly on the clerk at the reception desk, with his silly little
glasses and a tie whose knot was half a size too large. The
grandfather clock said ten-thirty—not quite—and the Christmas
tree on the desk had a fairy in a gold dress on top of it.

She didn't want to walk past the mysterious stranger, but she had to. And he had to let her. There was nothing else to be done. He hadn't recognized her as Rachel Richardson. She was certain of that.

"No, no, not at all," she said in belated answer to his question, turning back toward him. Still she didn't move. Still he did not.

His cape was off now and across his arm. He wound up the blood-red scarf that had been around his neck.

"It's cold out there," he said. And he smiled. Humanity surged into his face. As Rachel saw it, she was both relieved and disappointed. He had been absolutely elemental, timeless and without place. Now he was almost a person, and so once again—-nearly—was she.

"You look as if you have been riding a horse," she said.

"I *have* been riding a horse." He reached up and tugged at his ear, and Rachel knew there was no reason for the gesture except shyness. He looked away, but then, quickly, he looked back again at her, grabbing her eyes with his, forcefully, almost hungrily.

"Is there anywhere," said Rachel, to whom questions were all but second nature, "to ride to or from at this time of night?"

He was in his forties, early forties, she managed to think. He was . . . well, it was simply irrelevant that he was attractive.

"My home," he said. Rachel thought of silent movies. This man was black and white, bright and dark, and words were not his point.

There was nothing more to say. There was only more to think and much more to feel.

She sidled around him like a boat around a dangerous but beautiful island. She said, "Goodbye," over her shoulder, but he didn't answer as she left the lobby.

Rachel walked slowly toward the library. This was ridiculous. She had been sensitized by the conversation with Tessa earlier. She was like a child frightened in the dark after being primed by ghost stories. These silly emotions were the result of exposure to a couple of charming women who felt too much and thought too little. She had been dreaming of magic, and now, like some suggestible sheep, she had gone straight out and experienced some to order.

Rachel *tried* to tell herself that, but she did not succeed. She had felt magic. There was no denying it. She walked into the library and threaded her way through the armchairs toward the fireplace. She knew that there was something wrong with her face. It was glowing with heat. She saw Carol turn toward her, and then, in slow motion, Tessa's head swung around, too. She could see in their eyes the reflection of her expression. Somehow they knew something had happened.

"Ohmigod," said Carol. "How can anything that tastes so wicked be so good for you?"

They all felt that. They sat back in their chairs beneath the crystal chandelier in the rotunda of the spa that in the evening was the restaurant, and marveled at the extraordinary cuisine. They were full to the brim, and their taste buds vibrated, but the facts could not be ignored. None of them had racked up more than a thousand calories. They knew that, because the menu listed the calories of each dish, and laid out beside the silver cutlery and Royal Worcester china was a little black calculator for guests of the Hacienda Inn.

Cantaloupe wrapped in prosciutto, the soft, sweet texture of the melon playing deliciously off the salty, silken ham from Parma in Italy. It had weighed in at 115 calories, and Rachel's casserole of veal and mushrooms, thick with softened cloves of garlic and with a cup of white wine, had been barely three times that. She had finished with a sunburst of figs, the green fig laid open in four quarters, with a cluster of bright red cranberries in its midst, the whole on a bed of sliced oranges and covered with an orange sauce.

Rachel raised her fruit juice cocktail. "To the chef," she said. "When I came in here I prayed, 'Lord, make me good but not yet.' Now I think I'll just be good right away."

They drank to the chef. The Hacienda Inn was serious about

its pleasure and about its healthfulness. But revising eating habits was an attractive proposition only if eating could remain pleasurable. The spa dinner had proved that it could.

"Tomato omelette with basil and olive oil, baby lamb's kidneys in a mustard sauce, fruit salad of kiwi, star fruit, mangoes, and peaches. I mean, you'd think you could get fat just looking at it. I don't suppose they've left the noughts off the calorie counts, some sort of printer's error?" said Tessa.

"Could be," said Carol. "I can hardly move, but then I haven't done anything all day except paint. You two have been rushing from massages to saunas to aromatherapy wraps like ants on speed."

"Thanks a bunch," laughed Rachel. "I think an 'ant on speed' is a first for me. Pretty accurate, though. How's the painting going, Carol? What exactly do you paint? I mean, what style?"

"I think of it as broody, moody landscapes, full of mystical messages about the effect of nature on our lives. Jack used to say they were 'pretty' and 'decorative,' as if it was like a needlework thing, a little hobby for the little woman."

"He was just threatened by your painting," said Rachel. "But he's not here. You're here. Your paintings are what you think they are. Other people's opinions change from year to year, minute to minute, but if you keep on pleasing yourself, one day you'll find that everyone believes in you. Not forever, mind you, but for a time."

"It's like the Ricky Nelson song, 'You can't please everyone, so you have to please yourself,'" agreed Tessa.

"Jack called again today," said Carol.

"How did you handle it?" asked Tessa.

"Good, I think. I told him about you two. He was incredibly—rather pathetically—impressed . . . a bit like the husband in *Enchanted April*. You know, surprised that anyone like Rachel would be interested in his wife. He didn't actually say it, but I could hear him thinking it between the lines. He kept on saying, 'But what did you talk about?' as if I wouldn't have anything to say to you. I just said, 'Oh, I told her about us and she was completely in favor of women taking control of their lives and not putting up with shit from men, especially husbands.' He really thinks you're bright, and he went very, very quiet."

"Well, he does sound sensible," said Rachel, making the joke to keep it light.

The lightness, however, had faded. Neither Tessa nor Rachel had liked to ask about the details of the breakdown of Carol's marriage. Now, both felt that they were about to emerge.

"Isn't it funny how love can blow up in your face?" said Carol suddenly. "Or it can be taken away from you, like with Tessa. Maybe it's safer to go for success, like you, Rachel. That way the harder you work, at least you benefit. The trouble with love is that you can give it everything and walk away with absolutely nothing except a failed marriage, an empty bank account, and a couple of selfish teenagers. Perhaps that was my problem . . . I loved too much, and I kept nothing back for myself."

"How did it all go wrong, Carol?" asked Tessa.

"The trouble was, I didn't know it had. I simply didn't recognize the danger signs."

"Your husband was unfaithful." The word needed to be said, thought Rachel.

"Yes, he was. But that doesn't really do justice to what he did. 'Unfaithful' is just totally inadequate. I mean, you'd have to understand what we had, what I felt about him, the sort of marriage we had." Carol could feel the tears building in her eyes. It was difficult to describe how close they had been.

"Is he really sorry about it?" said Rachel.

"Yes, he's sorry. He's on the phone all the time, rambling on about forgiveness and second honeymoons . . . but . . . it's just over."

"Isn't that where time comes in?" said Rachel. "Right now you want to murder him, but months pass and the pain fades, and then one day you laugh about it . . . In a few years," she added quickly.

"No," said Tessa slowly. "I could never have forgiven Pete if he'd done that to me. I can't imagine it. But if he had, then

I would never have forgiven him. I had too much of myself invested in him."

"That's *it*," said Carol. "That's precisely it. I gave him me. All of me. I had nothing in reserve for a situation like this. That was why it was so magical, because there were no doubts."

"I completely understand," said Tessa. "It's not infidelity. It's the murder of your soul. It's the crunching up of the essence of you by the only person in the world that you trusted with it."

"Heavens," said Rachel. "Obviously, I have one hell of a lot to learn." Her relationships so far had always taken place with one eye on the exit.

"It sounds as if you have pretty big decisions to make," said Rachel, turning to Carol.

"I thought I'd made them," said Carol. "But the trouble with decisions is that you have to keep remaking them. This afternoon I was painting, and I just got completely lost in the work and it was wonderful. And then it stopped, and all the worries and doubts came crowding back in again, and then Jack called, and he's so brilliant at talking, and suddenly I didn't know what I wanted to do anymore. It would be so easy to go back and be horrid to him and wounded. But I know that would just be wrong. I'm so angry inside. I'm just burning up with this *fury*, like I want to kill him, really kill him, and the hideous creature that he was . . . with . . ."

Carol tried to laugh through the painful emotion. Rachel and Tessa listened. Carol was the table's sole expert on infidelity.

"I can't imagine what I would feel if Pete had done something like that," said Tessa. "I think," she concluded, "that I would have gotten incredibly ill."

"I was, at first. It's funny you should say that. The first feelings were physical. I was sick. I actually threw up several times. I kept feeling faint."

"You did?" Rachel said in astonishment. How could a mere man achieve that kind of power?

"God, how awful," said Tessa. "What did he actually do? How did you find out?"

Carol's expression was grim as she continued. "My son knew. He told me. And I didn't believe him at first, but bit by bit the puzzle came together. I started with the credit card receipts, oddly enough, and then air ticket stubs with . . . his friend's . . . name on them." She paused. Her voice had taken on a dreamlike quality as she dared to remember the detective she had been, numb with shock, consumed with a slow-burning rage that had built inside her.

"It's amazing," said Carol, "how careless he was. It was as if he simply didn't care whether I knew or not. I went through the phone bills and I found a number that had been called hundreds of times. It was her apartment in the city. There were calls late at night from our home, sometimes for two hours at a time. He must have slipped out of bed, out of our bed, and called her when I was asleep. And then I found letters."

"Oh, shit," said Tessa.

"Where?" said Rachel.

"In a file marked 'Capital-Gains Tax, 1992.' Can you believe," she said, "that he hadn't even bothered to lock the cabinet? Sometimes I think that's the most unkind thing of all."

"Were they love letters?" Tessa wanted to close her eyes.

"Not really. Not what I'd call love letters. They were kind of mechanical letters, written by two attorneys, because that's what she was, a junior attorney at his firm. They said things like 'It felt really funny and very exciting to do it in your bed. I think the guilt made it better . . .' Something like that."

"That's very bad," said Rachel. "That is really nasty."

Carol droned on, the monotone some small protection against the tragedy.

"The children knew, I think, and Whitney knew for sure when he saw them kissing. And the children shouldn't have been exposed to it. That was one of the worst parts. And then, of course, there were all the so-called friends who hadn't told me, 'for my own good' and because they felt sure it would 'blow over.' They had quite a few gory details, as you can imagine. 'Well, darling, as you know now, I might as well tell you that Warren thought

Jack had gone too far when he saw them fiddling with each other's feet under the table at one of your dinner parties.' "

"What happened when you confronted him with it?" said Rachel.

"Guess what? Big surprise! An attorney? A man? He denied it. He had an answer for everything, until I showed him the letters."

Carol's eyes filled with tears as she remembered her feelings at that moment. Jack, the hero. Jack, the hypocrite. In a millisecond he had gone from one to the other before her eyes. She could see the shame break over him, the defeat, the fear. "Oh, dear," he had said. And then he had repeated it. And he had sighed. "Oh, dear."

"You know," said Carol, "men never give like a woman gives. I put all my eggs in the basket that was Jack and the children. I didn't mind. I didn't feel resentful. I wanted to, because it was all so wonderful. And our house, you should have seen it . . . it was perfect. I mean, my orchids, the potpourri I made, and this fabulous garden. For all those years I hardly thought of myself, and when I did I felt guilty and I stopped. But I knew I was giving up myself. I was happy to do it, but I was aware of it. I have this thing, I can really paint, and I used to love it. I could have made a career out of it, but I just didn't. There wasn't time. Jack and the kids wanted all my time. So, deep down inside I had this little dream of painting one day, like Georgia O'Keeffe, in the desert. That was my fantasy at those endless ballgames and dinner parties. Somehow it survived, and when ninety-nine percent of me exploded into complete nothingness, there was just this one percent left. That's all I've got right now. Believe it or not, that's why I'm here in this ridiculous dining room in this ridiculous hotel, boring you all rigid, because I thought I'd go to the desert and paint and take a shot at becoming Georgia. Don't laugh, because it's true."

"I think that's the bravest thing I've ever heard," said Tessa. "You've left him. You've made the decision. And you've done so without having anything arranged, no man, no life, just the unknown. I mean, if you'd had someone to go to, you know, like some man who'd loved you for years or you'd secretly fantasized about . . . that would be different. Or if you'd had a career as a painter or anything, and some kind of alternative life . . . But just to go, just to come here, and just to, I mean, just to *start,* is incredibly strong."

"It is," said Rachel. "It's feminist, too. It's heroic."

"You mustn't go back to him," said Tessa suddenly. The feeling of Carol's pain had reached inside her and become her own.

"I know," said Carol.

"I don't think you should either," said Rachel.

She was surprised by the change in her own attitude. Was she beginning to understand the strange world of feelings, in which infidelity was the automatic end of magical relationships that had been constructed out of trust and blind faith? For Rachel, sex and men were sideshows to the main event that was her career. Men came and went. They represented strategic alliances, transient pleasures. For Carol and Tessa, however, they were the firm foundations on which their whole lives were built.

"It's funny, isn't it, Rachel," said Carol, "that in a way we're both at a crossroads. But we're heading in different directions. I'm a bit like you, but also the opposite of you. You want family life, and family life has just blown up in my face. You're sick of career and success, and I'm just starting out along that track. We both want what has just turned sour for the other."

Rachel couldn't help but see the undercurrents. She and Tessa and Carol, between them, all roughly the same age, around forty, epitomized the problems of women everywhere, perhaps of people everywhere. What path to take? What sacrifices to make? How to deal with loss? How to find the magic of love? How to survive success? How to find the courage to live your dreams? Now, she answered Carol:

"So we should be uniquely positioned to help each other . . ." She hesitated, thinking hard. "You teach me how to love and survive family life, and I show you the upside and downside of making it out there in the big, wicked world."

"My main problem," said Carol, "is that I don't really know how to be alone, and yet somehow loneliness is what I feel I need."

"You are so right," said Tessa. "I can't stand the loneliness. Luckily, I have Camille, but it's not the same. I hate being without Pete. I loathe all that silence and wondering what the hell the point is of doing anything."

"Loneliness is easy," said Rachel. "It's seductive. It's selfish. Loneliness is all me, me, me, until you're walled off from everything and everyone, and everything makes you irritated. I've had enough of it. I'm bored with it. Not because it's difficult. But because it's far too easy."

"I really admire people who can be self-sufficient," said Carol. "That's what I love about Georgia O'Keeffe. She lived entirely, not for herself but for her work. Things that got in the way of her paintings were just cast off, possessions, friends, lovers, whatever."

"But you know what everyone says about careers not loving you back," said Rachel.

"Sometimes husbands don't, too," said Carol.

"The thing you have to have," Rachel continued, "to make it on your own, is focus. And the thing to guard against is fantasy. Becoming Georgia sounds like fantasy. Getting paint onto canvas, day in, day out, is focus. All action. Hold the thought."

"And the way to fall in love is to relax and lose all focus. And the thing to guard against is reality. All thought and fantasy. Hold the action," said Carol.

They all laughed.

"How is Jack coping without you?" said Tessa. "Could you tell on the telephone?"

"Not very well. The maid quit. And the gardener sounds as if he's on the way out. I was pretty close to both of them. Oh, and he said that he'd met you, Tess. You didn't mention that."

"I met your husband?" said Tessa. "I don't think so."

Tessa was aware of Rachel's head turning toward her lazily, like a tank turret. Carol was looking at her hard. What had the guy been called? McCabe? Jack McCabe? It meant nothing at all to her.

"You met Carol's husband, Tess? How fascinating! So now we have an independent character witness. Tell. Tell," said Rachel, a half smile playing around her lips.

"I'm not tremendously good with names," said Tessa. She felt the blush beginning. This was tricky ground. She didn't remember Jack McCabe, the great love of Carol's life. Magic for some was clearly not magic for others. Was that in some way rude, a blasé, if inadvertent, comment on the lack of memorability of Carol's husband? And yet, to remember meeting him and not to say would be sly, as if she had something to hide . . . as if, perhaps, she had flirted with the adulterer.

Carol was scrutinizing her. It was clear that she expected people to remember her husband. A part of her would be wondering if Tessa was lying. And if so, why?

"He said it was at a business party. His firm was representing some people your husband was negotiating with. He said he remembers that you were very beautiful, very stylish, Tess, so it was you for sure. I guess Jack gets some things right."

Carol couldn't help the compliment, but there were other feelings in there. She noticed that Tessa was blushing.

"God, I met so many people at those parties," said Tessa. Jack McCabe. A lawyer. Hell, they were all lawyers. It sounded rude, dismissive. "I'm really surprised he remembered if I don't," she added. She wasn't at all sure whether that made it better or worse.

"How disappointing," said Rachel.

"I wonder if I'd have remembered Pete," said Carol.

"Yes," said Tessa with a nervous laugh.

They'd all have remembered Matt, thought Rachel, and then immediately wondered if they would. A silence descended. Every woman thought her own man was special—that was lesson one. Lesson two was that not everyone agreed with her diagnosis. In the silence, Rachel wondered if anyone would have forgotten Charles Ford, whose name and brief history she had pieced to-

gether from casual conversations with spa employees. No. There
was the sun rising tomorrow, and there was that. Both were cer-
tainties.

"Anyway," said Carol, "he said you discussed British politics. The similarities between the Republicans and the Conser-
vatives, and the differences between Democrats and Laborites.
You obviously made quite an impression on him, for him to
remember the conversation." Accusation hovered in the air:
Surely you remember my Jack. And if you do, why on earth
are you concealing it? You made an impression on him. It's
inconceivable that he made absolutely none on you.

"I have people on my shows that I don't remember when I
meet them again," said Rachel. She felt the need to make the
remark, although it was totally untrue.

"Yes, I do remember him, now you say that," said Tessa,
relief rushing out with the words. "He was tall, and he wore a
spotted tie and he had a nice laugh. It was about two years ago.
I remember him quite well. I just didn't remember his name."

Carol laughed, somehow relieved too.

Tessa's memories were coming together fast now. "He said
'Laborites,' and I said nobody called them that in Britain. We
call them Socialists. He was rather charming—in fact, very
charming—and he had blond hair. Yes, blond," said Tessa, sitting
back in her chair, proud of herself.

Was he coming on to you? thought Carol suddenly. It was
still so raw, that jealousy just beneath the surface. Had Page
Lee been part of a pattern? It had been two years ago, and Jack's
affair had been well under way, yet he had been busy being
charming to beautiful women at cocktail parties. For a second
she allowed herself to imagine Tessa and him together, not then,
but now. Jack and Tessa. What an asset she would be at the
partners' dinners. She could hear the wives talking in the pow-
der room: "Jack really fell on his feet, didn't he? For a moment
there, after Carol left him, I didn't think he was going to make
it. But this one has such style, even though she hasn't got any
money. I didn't recognize the drawing room . . . and the flow-

ers . . . and Jack seems besotted by her little girl. It's always the children that are the main hurdle to be jumped . . ." She blocked out the ridiculous thought. Tessa was far too sophisticated and cosmopolitan for semidetached suburban Jack McCabe. But he could give her the security, the home for Camille, and when he became the managing partner, she would be the managing partner's wife. She tried to remind herself how ridiculous all this was. Jack was history. She was her own future. And yet, and yet, the thought patterns died hard. Memories were the hardest habits of all to break.

Rachel watched Carol. She knew what she was thinking. Carol was sizing up Tessa as a rival, despite the fact that she liked her. Jack still had power over her, and perhaps in the dark corners of her mind he always would. How pretty she was. She lacked Tessa's unique good looks, but she had all the attributes of the homecoming beauty queens who had been the bane of Rachel's boy-free childhood. Big eyes, small nose, high cheekbones, smooth skin. Minimal crow's-feet. Aerobicized body. For a second, Rachel remembered the pain that girls like Carol had once caused her. Homecoming had meant long evenings in bleak movies, hiding away from the world. The boys had been terrified of her single-minded determination to become "someone," and although most of the time she had despised their thoughtless focus on fun, there were times when she had envied the popularity of the Carol McCabes. Only this Carol McCabe was more than that. She had struck out on her own to pursue half-remembered dreams. So she was a brave artist, perhaps like Charles Ford, a saddened, brave artist, struggling to create once more after happiness was sucked from his life by the death of his lover.

With a shock, Rachel realized what her unconscious mind was doing. She was putting Charles and Carol together as Carol was putting Jack and Tessa together. Carol was a soon-to-be-single artist, soon to be living in Santa Fe, and she had lost the one she loved as had Charles Ford. They would have much in common. Together, they could discuss the line of the horizon, the depth of the shadows, the mystery of the desert, that both were drawn to. Together, they could discuss the hopelessness of a loveless future, comforting each other . . .

"Well," she said, brutally suppressing the unwelcome thoughts. "Are you both ready for my surprise?"

"What surprise?" they chorused.

"A private make-over session with Alonsa Pirello, make-up artist to the stars."

"You're joking," said Tessa.

"What do you mean?" said Carol, smiling.

Rachel looked at her watch. "In ten minutes' time, in the beauty salon, I have arranged a special session with Pirello, just the three of us. My treat."

"Your nose shouldn't be more than five percent of the total area of your face," said Alonsa Pirello, as if issuing an edict direct from the Creator.

Tessa peered into the looking glass, which these days the British upper classes were allowed to call a mirror. "Are you sure that wasn't fifteen percent?" she said hopefully.

"That's a classical nose, Tessa," said Carol. "You're the exception that proves the rule."

"Nonsense," said Tessa. "How do you lose a nose without cutting it off to spite your face?"

Alonsa materialized at Tessa's shoulder. "You have a long, thin nose, so you can widen it by putting highlighter along both sides and blending it in. You can shorten it by applying contour shadow to its base and then blending that in."

"I don't need a nose job?"

"Don't be ridiculous, Tess," said Rachel.

"Certainly not now, but noses droop with time. You might want the tip raised in twenty years," said Alonsa.

"In twenty years I'll settle for the blooming lid to be lowered," laughed Tessa.

"I've got a great idea," said Carol. "Why not have everything done *after* you die, but, like, *everything* . . . and then lie in state like Lenin and have everyone traipse past you marveling at how great you look. They'd talk about it for years and you wouldn't have to worry about the pain and expense."

Alonsa didn't like that, or the general laughter that followed it.

"Now, you, Carol, have a lovely face. Very much *standard* good looks. Conventional. Aren't you lucky? But you'll see that if you draw an imaginary line joining the center of your nose tip, the crest of your upper lip, and the center of your chin, you have a fault of midline symmetry."

"Oh dear, poor Carol," said Rachel, mock serious. "So sad. A fault in midline symmetry."

"It was the first thing I noticed about you," said Tessa, taking up the game. "That poor, sad thing," I said to myself, "I wonder how she's struggled through life with that terrible facial fault. It made me feel quite giddy just looking at you."

"Don't make me laugh," said Rachel, "or my mascara will run and I'll be left with eyes like a ferret's. I've only just increased the damn things from dimes to nickels."

Alonsa slunk along the counter, bright with its barrage of lights, to her star customer, the one who was paying. She didn't care if she never saw the other two again, but Rachel Richardson could open doors for her.

"Your eyes are beautiful, Rachel. Just remember to use the eyelash curler *before* the mascara, and bend the lashes at three different points. Don't crimp in one spot. Actually, you might want to try an eyelash perm and have them tinted. It would save you bags of time."

"I don't want to save time," said Rachel. "Being in Make-up is the only time I get to think."

"But for your social engagements," persisted the make-up artist. She clattered across the pink marble floor of the beauty salon, opened specially for this session. Her cheekbones looked like they were suffering from vertigo, and Carol could swear that she'd done a Dietrich and had her molars taken out to accentuate them. She was terminally thin, and she couldn't stand still. To Carol, she looked like a whippet on speed.

"Oh, God, social engagements," said Rachel, waving them away as if they didn't exist. "Slap it on and try to remember to take it off. Then you're ahead."

Pirello twirled about, shaking her head from side to side as she emitted a little tut-tut noise and a brittle laugh.

"That's always my policy," agreed Carol.

Alonsa turned on the lesser mortal. Rachel Richardson could get away with frivolity about makeup. Not this one.

"Oh, but it shouldn't be. It shouldn't be," she cooed cruelly. "Rachel has so much . . . energy in her face. But you need to lift those cheekbones up, up, up." She darted at Carol with a highlighter, holding it as if it were an offensive weapon. Briskly, she dabbed a couple of spots on the ledges of Carol's cheekbones, starting below and outside the corners of her eyes, and angling diagonally toward the tops of her ears. She blended them in with lightning movements of her thumbs. "There. That gives you a bit of bone structure. Less like a pudding."

"A what?" Carol laughed incredulously. Rachel and Tessa, mouths open, smiling broadly, watched the fun.

"Oh, that is so much better, Carol," said Rachel. "Now you're a pudding with structure, more like a tiered dessert."

"But with a fault line, lopsided, Leaning Tower of Pisa pie," said Tessa, laughing. Carol, too, was beginning to lose it.

"Don't laugh, Carol, or the crow will land."

Alonsa Pirello determinedly ignored the fun that was being poked at her. "Now, brown contour shadow to the hollow of the cheek . . . mid-eye toward middle of ear . . . and there you have it, and blend like mad."

As if by magic, Carol's cheekbones had appeared.

"That's very impressive," she said, her laughter fading. "Where were you when I needed you?"

"God, you look like a cover girl, Carol," said Tessa.

"And you look like a princess."

Tessa did.

"Now with Tessa," said Pirello, warming to the new and more flattering conversational trend, "we had to counteract her blue undertones, which made her skin appear a little pink, with a pale green color-corrector. We put it on with a wedge-shaped latex sponge *before* the foundation. Then we took away the tiredness under the eyes with concealer. Dot it on with a small brush and then blend, but never rub it in. Same with the creases from the nostrils to the outer corners of the mouth, and the marionette lines at the outer edges of the mouth. We reduced the jaw a little by shading the actual jawline itself and then blending below it, and we fixed the nose. Isn't she beautiful?"

"So are we finished?" said Rachel. "I feel like a femme fatale. Where the hell can I go to practice with this brand-new face?"

They all stood up, shed the pink overalls, and peered at themselves in the mirror.

"I think that men are the one thing that the Hacienda Inn forgot to provide," said Carol.

"Probably part of the grand plan. Fewer distractions," said Tessa.

"Mmmmmm," said Rachel, in minimal agreement.

They wandered down the grand marble staircase of the spa. It was a moment strong with feminine solidarity. It was as if they were one, not three, a team far stronger than the sum of its parts. Did men feel like this around the campfire on their hunting trips? To Rachel, it felt strange, but very good.

"You know," she said, "this time has been really important to me. Meeting you both. Talking like we've talked. I simply don't have these kinds of conversations."

"Me, neither," said Tessa. Carol nodded in agreement. They were all wondering where things went from here. There was an inescapable feeling that some sort of ending was near.

"So we'll see each other around," said Rachel. She felt relieved. "It sounds silly, but you know I think we all need a bit of help in totally different ways. The odd thing is that each of us seems to be an expert in an area where one of us is deficient."

She threw out the idea, only vaguely aware of what she was getting at.

"That's right," said Tessa. "I mean, I need desperately to get hold of some money, and Carol needs the strength and courage to make a new life, and Rachel . . . well, you need . . ."

"To learn how to fall in love," said Carol, as they all laughed.

"And that's not a problem," said Tessa as Carol nodded vigorously. "That's a joy."

"Bullshit," laughed Rachel. "I'm the one with the real problem. All you two need is cash and success. Anyone can get those. It just takes hard work. I have to discover these weird things called emotions."

"I guess we really could help each other," said Carol.

"You know, it's funny," said Rachel, "I've always had trouble trusting women as friends, ever since a girl called Ruth pinched the producer I was dating and got him to give her the job I wanted. I just have the feeling that men are more loyal."

"I trusted women all the way," said Carol. "I had loads of friends. Then, when this Jack thing happened, I got the feeling they were all kind of pleased about it. And you know, none of my girlfriends told me, and they knew, right from the beginning."

"Does that mean that whatever we say now, in the end we'll let each other down?" said Tessa.

"No," said Rachel. "Let's agree now to help each other. We'll keep in touch and be there for each other, just like the damned men do."

As they walked abreast down the stairs, the three women linked hands as if on some unspoken command. They looked at each other and smiled. They had been strangers, but they were strangers no more. They were friends who would help each other.

Eight

Rachel woke, and before she opened her eyes she knew it was time to go. She had had enough. She had escaped. She had relaxed. Now she had to get on with her life. Still with her eyes closed, she reached for the telephone. Like everything else at the Hacienda Inn, even the leaving was easy. When at last she opened her eyes, she was already booked on a flight to New York. She had barely three quarters of an hour before the limo would take her to the airport.

She showered in a hurry, marveling at the way her mind had made the decision while she slept. Perhaps that was the true miracle of a spa visit. It healed you, but it didn't hang on to you—like a good mother. She pulled on her clothes and then emptied drawers into suitcases, not bothering to fold things. As she did so, she thought of Carol and Tessa. Warm feelings rushed through her with the memories, Tessa wallowing in the mud, Carol graceful and hardworking in the step aerobics. They were both so normal, so ordinary, that she felt protective of them. Over the last few days they had grown close. It was rare to make real friends at this stage of life, but she felt she could say anything to them and it would not be taken wrongly, because each genuinely wanted the best for the other and each knew it. That was the acid-test of friendship. She looked at her watch. It was seven-thirty, and she should say goodbye, although she hated goodbyes. But it was early for Tessa. She would leave a note for her at reception to be delivered to her room. She dialed

Carol's room, but there was no answer. Okay, she had done her best. Already, New York was filling Rachel's mind. She hurried around the room, scooping up things she had forgotten, and then headed down to the lobby.

She paid her bill at the reception desk as they gave her details of her flight. The car was waiting outside. She dashed off a note to Tessa and another to Carol. As she hurried across the lobby, she stopped briefly and remembered. A cape was floating in the air, a hand was pulling at an ear, and Rachel knew with absolute certainty that she would be meeting Charles Ford again.

Nine

Tessa drifted back from uneasy dreams. The anxiety covered her mind like a blanket, worst of all in this moment of darkness before opening her eyes. The dream fragments lingered, losing their reality slowly as she wandered into wakefulness. Pete and her brother had been having a fight. "You're not fit to look after her," her brother had shouted. Pete had looked so sad, and then he had changed into a man on a white horse in the desert, like the one Tessa had seen with Rachel.

Tessa opened her eyes, and there, inches from her own, was Camille's face. Camille, the bed hog, had managed to push her to the edge of the king-size bed. Tessa felt the dream and the anxiety subside. Her daughter looked so happy while she slept, her limbs thrown everywhere, like a kitten. Tessa lay still for fear of waking her. It had been a fabulous few days since meeting Rachel and Carol, but now, suddenly, the guilt was coming on strong. Okay, so the Hacienda Inn was her brother's gift, but wasn't this fiddling while Rome burned? To anybody in their twenties, with a trust fund and no responsibilities, being a Sotheby's realtor would be an exciting challenge, but Tessa *had* to make it a success. The alternatives were too horrible to contemplate.

Camille stirred, as if pricked by her thoughts. Don't wake, darling, Tessa thought. Sleep a little more in your dreamland, far from reality and grown-ups.

Tessa couldn't escape the worst case scenario. After a few

agonizing months, during which she demonstrated to the world that she couldn't sell water to a man dying of thirst, Sotheby's would let her go. What then? A clerk in a store? A secretary who couldn't type or do shorthand but could mess up making filtered coffee? In her mind's eye, Tessa drifted down through the female job hierarchy, and before long she was out there in the street panhandling with Camille by her side, big eyes reproaching her, cold and hungry, but never blaming her because of her sweet nature. What would a woman do then?

She sat up in bed as panic plucked at her. Then she saw that someone had pushed an envelope beneath her door. She got up carefully, to avoid waking Camille. She walked over, picked up the envelope, and tore it open. Then she moved to the window and pushed the note behind the drapes to read it.

Darling Tessa,

I woke this morning with an irresistible urge to get back to my life in New York. So I am gone without saying goodbye, because I didn't want to disturb Camille so early.

Tess, I know how worried you are about the future, and mere words can't make the worry go away. But I know you and Camille will be wonderfully all right, because I recognize the strength in both of you. I wish I was as strong. All you need is to believe in yourself as much as I believe in you.

I haven't mentioned this before, but I have had some sort of magical experience here . . . something like you talked about with Pete, and Carol with Jack. I kept it to myself because it was probably just gas or something . . . but who knows?!? Anyway, I have learned from you both that it is what you feel that matters and not what you think. I always thought it was the other way around.

So good luck, Tess, and may God go with you, because for sure I will. If there is ever anything, *anything,* that I can do to help in New York, you have only to ask. You know how to get hold of me, and I will always be there for you.

Your new best friend,
Rachel Richardson

Tessa wiped the tear away from her eye. She couldn't remember when she had had a more lovely letter.

"Who is it from?" said the sleepy voice from the bed.

"It's from Rachel."

"I like Rachel. Why is she writing you a letter?"

"She's gone, darling. Back to New York."

"Oh, no. But she didn't say goodbye."

"She's saying it in this letter."

"But we'll see her when we get to New York, won't we?"

"Yes, of course."

Tessa moved back toward the bed. Camille peered at her suspiciously.

"Are you all right, Mummy?"

"Yes, darling, of course I am. It's just that it was such a sweet letter and sometimes sweet things make you sad."

"Sweet things don't make me sad. They make me very happy," said Camille with absolute certainty.

"You know, darling, I think that we should think about getting back to New York, too," said Tessa.

Ten

Carol opened her eyes slightly, and the early morning light filtered through, brightening an already bright mood. The Hacienda Inn and the two new friends she had made were working wonders on her psyche. At last she was feeling things, things about *her* and *her* life. It might be a roller coaster, but it was *her* roller coaster, not Jack's, not the children's. What an extraordinary few days it had been.

She jumped up and walked to the window. It was a perfect day. She threw back the sliding doors and the desert air rushed in. It was six-thirty, and about forty-five degrees. It was a wonderful day for painting. Carol ordered some coffee from room service and headed for the bathroom.

She had dressed by the time the coffee came, and she threw it down quickly, anxious to get off. She ticked off the inventory: paint, easel, a couple of canvases, brushes, palette. Oh, God, the beauty of freedom. This day was all for her. She hurried out to the rental car and stowed her kit in the trunk with the couple of canvases she had already painted. Did she need anything else? Not really. There was enough turpentine and rags. Oh, yes, sunglasses. She ran back and grabbed a pair.

She was way past the main gates of the Hacienda Inn when she remembered she had left the map on the bedside table. For a second she wondered whether to go back for it. No. She could remember the direction she had to go. And there wouldn't be too many tracks in the desert. Carol drove on, away from Santa

Fe and toward the distant mountain with its ponderosa pines and bare aspen trees. She wound down the windows and reveled in the fierce light and bracing air, the browns and the grays and the brilliant blue of the cloudless sky. Dream on, Carol McCabe, dream on, she thought, feeling once again like the teenage queen she had been when first she had met Jack.

After she had been driving for an hour, the tarmacked road tapered off. Finally it ended, and three dirt tracks provided three different choices. She took the left one. She remembered that the map had been clear about that. On either side, sagebrush stretched away in the rocky flatness. She passed a stream flanked by clumps of willows. An adobe house nestled in their shadows. Then the landscape was bleak again, white-winged doves taking off from the side of the track as she drove by.

Carol marveled at the fierce remoteness of the place. It was so stark, a blank background for invention. Life here would be about survival, about just being. Here in the desert Carol would strip away the surface layers and find the roots that nourished her.

She took a left turn. From then on, the tracks diverged all over the place. Carol picked at random. She had not found the place she was looking for, the one the locals had told her about, and she had been driving for nearly two hours. It was supposed to be only an hour and a half away. Damn! She was lost, but she didn't care. She was alone and in charge. And if she couldn't find anything to paint today, there would be tomorrow, and the rest of her life, for painting.

Then she saw it. A few feet from the track, beneath a cedar tree, was the picked carcass of an ox. Its bones were bleached by the sun, stark and elemental. It was death in the desert. The complicated had been made simple and clean by the unforgiving heat and the ceaseless activity of the silent predators who waited, endlessly. Here was the rawness of life in symbolism. An animal had died, that other animals might find sustenance, and soon these white bones themselves would be nitrogen for tiny flowers that would bloom in the desert spring. Carol stopped the car. The skeleton was pure Georgia, the skulls she painted, the bones she used as ornaments at Ghost Ranch. O'Keeffe had loved to start with the magnificent dead, the end and also the beginning of the circle of life that spun through eternity for the amusement of God in his heaven.

The bones had drawn Carol's attention, but they alone were not a subject she could handle. Now, as she looked out around her, she saw the painting. The carcass could be a point of reference in the foreground, but to the right and left of it were clumps of cactus whose interesting shapes, fingers poking askew toward the sky, cast long shadows across the scrub from the still-oblique angle of the sun. In the middle and the distance was the mountain rising to a snowcapped crown in what would be the center of her painting. It would be a difficult but rewarding exercise in chiaroscuro, the artist's technique of arranging light and shade to create form. The perspectives and depth of field were not easy. It would be important but difficult to prevent the dead ox from stealing the eye of the observer.

Carol stopped the car and turned off the engine. The silence rushed down and surrounded her as she got out and looked about. She felt strangely at peace. She was going to create beauty, to fulfill not others, but herself. Nature existed at that moment for her alone, and she was grateful for it. She made sizing motions with her thumb, organizing the perspective, and all the time her excitement was mounting as she could feel the potential of the picture. The first step would be sketches. She hurried back to the car and found her sketch pad, some pencils, and an eraser.

Back at the skeleton, she made the first lines, organizing the picture she wanted into sections as she had been taught, starting with the straight line geometry as a prelude to the flowing lines that would eventually capture her unique version of reality. She sat down and began to draw. In a few minutes she was lost in the work. She had no thought of bobcats, snakes, scorpions, or any of the other desert hazards that existed to plague the unwary. She was focused inward. The world had gone away. There was just her vision, and the minutes and then the hours drifted by in the magic process of creation. Carol was dimly aware of the passage of time and of the rarity of this moment. There was a time like this in art, in writing, in composing, when an external force seemed to control all action. There was no effort involved, no decision-making, just a rushing flow of movement—and the sketches. Now, other angles, other perspectives, suggested themselves, and the pages turned and the pencil slid over the paper. Carol watched in wonder as the beauty stared back at her, hers, yet hardly hers, because the process had been so effortless. It was almost as if someone, or something, was working through her.

Again she looked at her watch. It was two P.M. She should take some photographs and then make a start on the oil. She might never be able to find this place again, so she should lay down as much of the base as possible. Later, she could work from color photos and the sketches to fill in the rest. She had to finish the groundwork well before evening. Time passed as she set up the easel and mixed the paints on the palette. Then, once again, the automatic pilot appeared on cue to guide her hand and eye. Time speeded up.

Carol felt the chill on her shoulders. She shivered and looked around. The sun was low in the sky, its light oblique and beautiful, far less warm now. She should stop. The moment the sun sank, so would the temperature. She had only a skimpy sweater. When darkness fell, the air would begin to freeze. She packed up her things, not wanting to leave but knowing that she had to. Then, quickly, she took some photographs and it was over. It had been a magnificent day. She looked back one last time at the scene that had inspired her.

She turned on the engine and revved the motor of the rented car. It was funny how you relied on machinery. She checked the gauges, just to be grown up like Jack. Oil pressure fine. No overheating. Gasoline on . . . Empty. Red light in dash showing low fuel. Oh, no! The panic hit hard. She tapped on the fuel gauge. Nothing changed. The red light glowed solidly. It was not blinking on and off. She tried to remember when she had last filled up. An *age* ago. She could remember the face of the old Mexican through the windshield as he wiped it down. Carol cut the engine and tried to think. What the hell should she do? She had driven for about two hours to get to wherever she was. How long had the stupid light been on? Suddenly she felt thirsty; but she hadn't brought a drink. She had sunglasses, but no water in the desert. Oh, Carol, oh, Carol, you stupid, irresponsible *idiot*.

She should try to go back. You never knew how long you could go on Empty. No. It was better to stay where she was. While she could keep the engine running, the battery would recharge. When night fell, she would be able to keep the headlights on. In the desert they could be seen for miles. But night was hours away, and that was defeatist thinking. She should try to head for home, but she wasn't sure exactly which direction "home" was. She tried to laugh it out of her mind. What would Jack think! She could hear him tut-tutting and polishing his Boy Scout lecture on preparation. She wished he was here now. Would this become the pattern? Hating him when the going was smooth. Missing him the moment things got rough. The hell with it, she had to make a decision. Carol McCabe, decision maker. Along with the territory of freedom went the freedom to screw up.

Irritated now, she jammed the car into reverse and did a three-point turn on the track until she was heading in the direction she had come. High in the bright blue sky, a vulture hovered on what breeze it could find. Again she pressed down on the throttle. At that precise moment the engine died. Panic rippled across her stomach and then faded. She pressed the starter. The engine coughed into life, expired a second time, and was dead. She sat still. Then she leaned her head forward onto her hands and tried to think. The important thing was not to panic.

She went over the options. Stay by the car. Set off on foot to find help. Make a fire. In bright daylight? No, better to wait till night. But how did she start a fire? She had neither matches nor a lighter. Did rubbing two sticks together work? Once again, she thought of Jack and Whitney. They were always going camping. This would be an adventure to them. She could see them now, rushing about, competing with each other to come up with the brilliant, lifesaving solutions.

She wound up the windows of the car and checked that everything was turned off so as to preserve the battery's precious power. The sun and its heat were fading fast. She could actually feel the temperature dropping, and still it was far from dusk. She looked out across the mesa. Clouds were drifting down from the distant mountains, and the blue of the sky seemed to be thickening to metallic. She had the heater, but how long would the battery power the heater without an engine to recharge it? She looked around the car. There was no blanket. Nothing at all for warmth. Maybe while it was still light she should set off down the track and try to find an Indian adobe like the one she had passed. No. She shouldn't leave the relative safety of the car, its lights, and its *horn*. She pressed down on it, but the honk was disappointingly slight in the vast silence of the desert. What was the code for SOS? Dash-dash-dash, dot-dot-dot, dash-dash-dash. Or should the dots and the dashes be reversed? Did the desert Indians know Morse? Shit, she had to do something. She jumped out of the car and began collecting brush and twigs for a fire.

She assembled a small pile of debris by the car and then twisted off the rearview mirror to use as a glass to concentrate the sunlight that remained. She could imagine Jack muttering about the cost of the damage to the rental car. She tried to focus the sun's light on the twigs, but there wasn't enough of it, and when she tested the laser beam of light she had created, it could hardly warm her finger, let alone start a fire. Didn't you have to have a magnifying glass? Oh, God, this was awful. It was so pathetic. It was like every caricature of every helpless woman throughout the ages, useless outside the kitchen and the drawing room, no good with the barbecue, always trying to find a man to program the VCR. She kicked at the pile of potential firewood in irritation and climbed back in the car. She felt safe inside it, because at night there would be animals out there, and the car was womblike. The truth stared at her. Carol McCabe was not safe outside suburbia, was not destined to lead her own life, was fit only to be an appendage to other people's lives, people who could really cope. It was those thoughts that hit her hardest. No, no, she would get through this somehow! She must.

Carol made a decision. She would wait until dark. Then, throughout the night until the battery died, she would alternately honk the horn and flash the lights. There were two or three hours till darkness. So she climbed into the back seat, closed her eyes, and tried to go to sleep. Surprisingly, she succeeded.

She was awakened by the cold. She opened her eyes in the pitch darkness and gasped in the freezing air. For a second she didn't know where she was. She was numb already, and by the light of the moon she could see her breath steaming inside the car, although all the windows were closed. And there was something else. The windshield was already covered by a thin mist of what at first Carol thought was frost. It wasn't. It was snow. She wound the window down and the flakes swam down from the hazy night sky, big and beautiful . . . and deadly. She wound the window up once more. She clambered into the front seat, shivering with cold, and honked the horn. The sound was muffled, softened to meaninglessness by the thin layer of snow that already covered the mesa and by the thickness of the mist that swirled around the car. She flicked on the headlights, but they were lost in the whiteness.

She turned on the heater and at last there was relief. The car warmed. She turned it off. As quickly, the car cooled. Damn! It had been a mistake to go to sleep. She should have kept moving. It was only eight o'clock. It would be thirteen hours before sunlight warmed the morning. And it was while that thought flew around in her mind that Carol came face to face with reality: It was entirely possible that she would not survive this night.

She curled up in a small ball because she didn't know what else to do, and she prayed. She closed her eyes and asked God to save her, and all the time, a refrain in her thoughts, there were the children.

She remembered Devon in the waiting room at the dentist's,

sitting apprehensively in the huge chair that had been made to look like a tooth to charm the children as they awaited their fate. She had been so brave with the injection, lying there, her little body rigid with fear, but not crying while the dentist worked on her. Later, Carol remembered creeping around in the dark with the money from the tooth fairy and the little leather bottle that Jack kept the children's teeth in. Like a typical lawyer, he wrapped them in bits of paper with a "W" for Whitney and a "D" for Devon, and the date the teeth had fallen out. Carol smiled as she shivered. She had always thought that if ever there was a fire, that would be the thing she would save from the house once Jack and the children were safe—the little leather case with their teeth in it.

She felt a tear grow in her eye. Maybe she wouldn't see any of them again. Ever. She tried to remember the last moment she had seen them, the last words they had said. "I love you, Mom," Whitney had said, hugging her at the airport. She remembered looking back at him as she went through the gate, the lock of loose hair, greasy of course, covering one of his eyes. He'd had a yellow Walkman hooked on his belt, the headphones hanging over it, and on the way home she knew he'd be lost in some street-band paradise, a no-man's-land of sound and nothingness in the precarious present of a teenager. Devon had squeezed her hand and said, "Come home soon, Mom," with a little smile that hinted that she thought "soon" would be next week rather than the never that now loomed as a possibility. She'd had her navel pierced the week before because her heroine, Christy Turlington, had done it. Devon's chief worry had been about her belly button going septic rather than the strange fight her parents seemed to be having about the infidelity thing. Dear, brave Devon had always wanted to be a doctor. At the age of six she would place her friends behind the TV set and fiddle with the knobs till the picture went fuzzy, in the pretense that it was an X-ray machine. Carol could see their little heads with their apprehensive expressions poking over the top of the television as Devon issued brisk orders.

Carol's eyes were full of tears in the dark car in the white desert. Once again, she honked the horn in the SOS she hoped she remembered, and she flashed the headlights again in Morse code. She turned on the heater for a little longer this time, huddling in the front seat near the vents where the warm air came out. For a couple of hours she kept it up, bringing herself back from the brink of hypothermia and then sinking toward it again. Then the battery was gone. No more light. No more sound. No more heat. She checked the luminous dial of her watch. It was midnight.

She knew she shouldn't sleep. She would simply never wake up. The numbness encircled her from the edges. She couldn't feel her fingers and hands, or her toes and feet. She couldn't move her face to form an expression, and it seemed that even her frosty breath was diminished as her temperature cooled.

She made another sudden decision. She would get out and walk till she dropped. She pushed open the car door and the icy blast hit her. It was colder by far outside. But her decision was made. Inside, there was certain slow death before dawn. Outside, there was a faster ending, but one that contained within it a tiny seed of hope. She stumbled out into the snow. She could make out the track from the position of the car, and she started down it, staggering as her numb feet tried to find and keep her balance.

In front of her, lit by the moon, was the virgin snow she trod. She noticed the fresh track of a large animal . . . a coyote? a bobcat? . . . and she thought back to that very afternoon when she had been so happy in the desert, painting, and she thought of the skeleton in the foreground that soon she could become. She staggered on, not upset by the thought, in some way comforted by it. Dust to dust. The return to nature. She would become a thing of stark beauty in a landscape that had seen humans come and go for thousands of years.

She lay down in the snow, her head against the carpet of white, and she curled into the shape of the fetus she once had been. It was over.

Then she heard the sound. It was like a drumbeat coming

from the earth, vibrating into her consciousness. She could hear it clearly in the silence. It was not a car. There was no light in the darkness. But it was something, and it was getting louder. She sat up and tried to focus, and then she saw it. A shadow loomed, rushing up on her, a vast wild animal that would crash into her and devour her. She raised her hand to fend it off, and she tried to shout through numbed lips. She looked up to see a horse standing over her, breath steaming from its nostrils, sweat and snow mixed on its neck. Behind the twisting head of the horse was the shape of a dark horseman. The wide brim of his hat was covered with snow. His face was hidden in its shadow, and beneath, a red scarf was wound tightly around his mouth and chin. He vaulted from the saddle, hurried toward her, and knelt down beside her as she tried to sit up for him. She didn't know who he was, alone on a horse in the middle of the desert on this snow-swept night. He could be friend or foe, rich man, poor man, beggar man, thief, but Carol was past caring.

"Are you all right?" he said, his voice urgent. She nodded and tried to speak.

"Cold. Help me!" she managed, as if it needed saying. He took off his cape and wrapped it around her.

"Don't worry," he said. "You're going to be all right. You're safe now. I promise. Can you feel your feet and hands?" She shook her head. He unwound his scarf, and she looked up into his eyes as he leaned over her. He was friend. That Carol could see. Worry was all over his face, and concern.

"Out of gas," murmured Carol.

"I heard your horn," he said. "I've been looking for you for hours."

"Thank you."

She felt herself drifting away, moving sideways, felt herself caught by his strong arms as she slipped into unconsciousness.

Eleven

Later, in the dark, Carol woke, and there was a night-light burning in the corner of the room. A man was sitting on the end of the bed, staring at her, looking intense and worried and strange, yet comforting. His eyes were set deep and his hair was wild, but he seemed very trustworthy, and even more than that. So she closed her eyes again and went away from him. She woke again later, *crinkled* as she turned in the bed, and found that she had been wrapped in tinfoil. But she was too tired to try to escape it, and she fell back to sleep until dawn's edges showed around the corners of the damask curtains. For the first time in what seemed like an age she was awake and herself.

She was alone in a vast four-poster bed between linen sheets. The foil had gone and she was warm, blissfully warm. She peered around the room in the semigloom of early morning. It was a big room, full of what looked like dark old furniture, chests and armoires, and paintings everywhere with ornate mahogany frames. Her watch said seven-thirty. Where on earth was she? How had she traveled from the edge of death to this luxury through no conscious effort of her own? As if to answer her questions, there was a gentle knock on the door.

"Come in," she said.

The door opened and a maid, dressed in black except for a starched white apron, stood in the doorway.

"Oh, señora. I am so pleased. You are awake and well. How you feel after such a terrible night?"

"Where am I?" said Carol. And then, "I feel just fine."

"This is ranch of Mr. Charles Ford. El señor found you freezing in the desert."

"He rescued me," said Carol. It was half fact stated to herself, half question.

"Si, señora. He hear your horn. He out riding and he find you, bring you back here. Dr. Rodriguez, he come and check you over in the night. He say you okay. You just rest."

"I've been very stupid," said Carol.

"No stupid. Who care? You all right, señora. That what matter. You hungry?"

God yes, that was what she was, incredibly, ravenously hungry.

"Yes, actually I am," said Carol.

"I bring you breakfast. Oatmeal. Juice. Eggs. Big selection."

Carol made as if to get out of bed.

"No, you stay there. I bring. Miss Rose eat breakfast in bed. Always, Miss Rose. You wait." She was gone.

Carol tried to make sense of it. Mr. Charles Ford, of the brooding eyes and the wild hair, had saved her life. This was his ranch, with servants and antique furniture. She was lying in "Miss Rose's" bed. Who was she, who always ate her breakfast in it?

Carol threw back the covers and moved gingerly to the edge of the bed. Then she stood up. She was wearing a nightdress, someone's nightdress. Rose's? It was soft and silken and very fine, the stitching, couture. She walked to the window and drew back the drapes. Bright sunlight flooded the room. She was not prepared for the view. It took her breath away. The desert was white to the foothills of the distant mountain, and the vista unfolded across acres of fenced paddock in which horses frolicked in the sun and the as-yet unmelted snow. There was a stable block in the Mexican style; it looked hundreds of years old. Beyond it were courtyards and walkways that might have been transported unchanged from Seville or Granada, with statues faded by the sun, and fountains, waterfalls, and ponds shaded by the snow-laden branches of cedar trees.

Carol turned back toward the room, and its classic glory struck her. It was a bedroom from a distant age. The walls were covered with oils in heavy frames, many of them seemingly by painters of the Spanish court like Goya and Velázquez. There were ornate chests, beautifully carved from dark oak, and chairs of damask; a sofa in faded red, its back held to its arms by coils of golden rope. There were tables everywhere, and on the tables were photographs in ornate silver frames, tarnished not at all, but apparently polished daily, loved and looked after. There were freesias on the sofa table, and pots of hyacinth and narcissus, and the whole room smelled sweetly of them. Carol picked up a picture and then another, and soon the theme was apparent. They were pictures of Charles Ford and a beautiful woman, painting at an easel, on horseback, walking together. They held hands and they held eyes in the photographs, and they were lovers through a period of what looked like several years as age subtly changed them. This was Rose. There was no doubt about it.

Carol walked back to the bed. That was the moment she saw it. Above the bed was a huge oil, beautifully painted, of a girl in her twenties. She wore a dress that Scarlett might have worn on a day that Rhett was visiting, and the expression in her eyes carried that feeling, too. Character and vitality blazed from the canvas and dominated the room that had been hers. Carol could feel her presence. She almost felt the need to introduce herself. She felt like an intruder here, in Rose's room, but for some weird reason, Carol McCabe could not get rid of the idea that she had embarked on an adventure, an adventure that would last for the rest of her life.

Breakfast came with magnificent ceremony. There were two maids now, in identical uniforms, and they wheeled a large trolley into the room, laden with spotless white damask, silver dishes, and more flowers. There was a device that burned beneath the silver tureens to keep them warm, and there were pots of what looked like coffee and milk in old and intricately worked silver.

"Welcome to our *estancia*," said the maid who had knocked initially. "Mr. Ford, he say he hope you will join him for lunch at one, if you feeling very well. He gone to Santa Fe. Dr. Rodriguez, he come at eleven. You ring after breakfast and I draw you a bath. I am Rosita, the head housemaid." She performed a minuscule curtsey, as did her companion. Carol didn't know where to begin.

"I'd love to lunch with Mr. Ford," she said, "but after this breakfast I don't think I'll be able to eat anything." They both giggled as they withdrew, exchanging glances. Somehow, it had been the right sort of thing to say. Carol could hardly believe she was in America. "The head housemaid." Her bath "drawn." She vaguely remembered them saying things like that in *Upstairs, Downstairs* on television. Here she was in the middle of Andalusia, and the coffeepot alone was older than the founding fathers.

As she continued her thoughts, the telephone by her bed rang. For a second she wondered if she should pick it up. Then she did.

"Hello," she said tentatively.

"Good morning," said a man's voice. It was gruff, formal. He didn't say who he was. It was as if he expected her to know. And she did know.

"Good morning," she said.

"How are you feeling?"

"Fine, thank you. I don't know what to say . . . how to thank you . . . you saved . . . I mean . . ."

"You draw very well," he said, cutting through her confusion. "I'll see you at lunch."

"Yes, oh, how did you . . ."

But he had put down the telephone. Last night she had ridden in this man's arms, semiconscious, numb from cold, warmed only by the heat of his body. He had sat at the end of her bed and watched her in the night. He had saved her life.

Carol lay back on the sheets and took a very deep breath. Above her head, Rose looked down on her.

Twelve

Carol walked down the stairs feeling like the star of *Sunset Boulevard*. They were that kind of stairs. She could all but hear the cries of "Lights, camera, action." But instead of a phalanx of press photographers waiting at the bottom for her, there was one lone man dressed in black. The butler. He was stooped and yet, oddly, he gave the impression of being at attention. Carol had the distinct feeling that he had been waiting for her all morning.

"Good morning, señora," he said as Carol descended flanked by ancient ancestors, her feet sinking in the deep pile of the stair carpet. She was aware of flowers everywhere, narcissus and hyacinths, freesias and jonquils in old Chinese vases. Old wood, fresh flowers, and from somewhere in the depths of the house, the sound of a grandfather clock striking what must be twelve.

"Good morning," she said.

"I am José, butler to Mr. Ford," he said. "I trust you are feeling better. Dr. Rodriguez seemed very pleased."

"Thank you, I am," said Carol as she reached the bottom step.

"Then perhaps I can show you to the morning room. Mr. Charles is back from town and will be with you shortly."

He set off at a snail's pace across the hall, and Carol's artistic eye noted the harmonious merger of the different styles of decoration. The adobe Santa Fe influence melded happily with classic European furniture of the baroque tradition, Empire, Regency, and William and Mary pieces, some of the bookcases laden with leather volumes, others with exquisite porcelain lit subtly from behind. The room was dark, needing light even in the middle of the day, a reminder that heat was the enemy here in the desert as much as the cold that Carol had barely survived.

The morning room was different. Bathed in light, its French windows looked out over a broad vista. Lawns and cedar trees were arranged in some formality before the landscape surrendered to the desert scrub and raced away for miles to the foothills of the distant mountain.

"May I bring you something, a glass of sherry perhaps, or something soft? I think we have most . . ."

A glass of sherry. It sounded so British, but of course sherry was from Jerez de la Frontera. The British were merely popularizers of the drink.

"I think a glass of sherry sounds magnificent," said Carol. "Who is that lady?" she said suddenly. She knew, of course. The painting was of Rose.

"Ah, that's Miss Rose," said José. His old face relaxed in a smile as he said her name. "Miss Rose was the mistress of this house for many years, until she died just over a year ago. A very wonderful lady. An artist, ma'am. Like Mr. Charles."

"She was very beautiful," said Carol.

"Oh, yes, a great beauty. A lady. It was an honor to serve her."

"I feel so stupid, disrupting the whole household with my crazy behavior," said Carol. "I'm from the East. I don't know much about the desert, as you can see."

He smiled again, a slow, understanding smile. "The desert is a hard enemy and a loyal friend," he said. "It takes years to get to know it. You didn't disrupt us. It is exciting for us to have a visitor."

"Have you worked for Mr. Charles for a long time?" said Carol.

"Oh, yes. I served his father. When he was very young, we were good friends. I taught him to ride, you know."

"Then in a way I owe you my life, too," said Carol.

"Destiny. Fate. In the desert we believe in such things," he said, smiling gently as he walked away to get her glass of sherry.

Carol went to the window and stared out over the mesa. It was so beautiful, but it had so nearly taken her life.

"The doctor says you are in perfect health," said the voice behind her. She spun around. He stood there, framed in the doorway of the morning room, in jeans and a navy-blue sweater. Behind him were the dark shadows of the hallway, but from the front he was bathed in sunlight. It was an extraordinary sensation to see him. This man had saved her life. She had been dimly aware of his arms around her as they had ridden through the night. Now he was here, and she was awake and desperately grateful and curious in a way that she had never been before.

"Oh, Mr. Ford, I don't know where to begin. What can I say to thank you for what you did . . . ?"

He walked toward her, watching her closely as she struggled for words.

"Nonsense," he said. "You saved yourself. You were very wise. I saw the lights. I heard the horn. Light and sound travel for miles in the desert. It may seem a small thing, but SOS is three short, three long, three short. But I got the basic message."

"How did you know that I drew?" she said.

"Because this morning I had your car brought back from the desert and I found your drawings in it."

"I'm glad you liked them," said Carol, aware that she was fishing.

He walked to a table and picked up a magazine, seemed to look at it, and then threw it down with a gesture of impatience. He was quite fierce, but Carol didn't find him remotely frightening. There was something incredibly attractive about him. He was ill at ease, but not through weakness. Small talk was just not what he did. Carol knew it instinctively.

"That carcass that was in the foreground of your landscape would have interested Georgia O'Keeffe," he said suddenly. "She lived near here, at Ghost Ranch."

"Did you *know* her?" said Carol. It seemed almost impossible that anyone had.

"Yes," he said. "When I was a child I spent quite a lot of time with her. I liked her. Many didn't."

"What was she like?" said Carol. "She's a heroine of mine. In fact, she's one of the reasons I'm here."

"Really." He looked away. "What was she like? Oh, I don't know. Different. Unpredictable. Talked to children as if they were grown up. I like that. I liked most things about her. I liked her painting."

"I think she was the most admirable woman," said Carol. "I admire the way she chose her life, every bit of it, and did what she wanted and not what other people wanted. And she cared about art more than anything and hadn't any time for things and possessions."

He turned once again to face her, a quizzical expression on his face.

"Is that what you think, Carol McCabe?" His face had softened into an almost smile.

"Yes, it is."

"Well, it's what I think, too."

"Oh."

"So you came to the desert to be a painter," he said, taking off on an aimless journey around the room, as if standing in one place were acutely uncomfortable.

"More or less."

"Which?" he said, out to the right of her and still moving. She turned to follow him with her eyes.

"Which what?"

"Which. More, or less?"

"More. Yes, actually it's odd, but I have a dream about living in the desert and becoming an artist. It probably sounds stupid to you, especially after last night."

He had nearly vanished behind her.

"No such thing as a stupid dream. We must all have dreams to follow."

Carol stopped trying to follow him. He was now invisible behind her.

"What is your dream?" she said.

Silence.

"Life has killed the dream I dreamed."

He emerged on her other side, creeping into the corner of her vision.

"That sounds very sad," she said.

"Or very self-indulgent," he said, peering at her closely as he walked past to complete his circuit.

"And the dream you dreamed was to do with Rose?"

He stopped dead.

"You have been talking to José," he said. There was no accusation in his voice.

"I think your house has been talking to me. I'm not even sure that Rose hasn't been talking to me. She's everywhere, isn't she? In the smell of the flowers, in the sunlight, in the chimes of the clock."

"*You* can feel that?" he said. His eyes misted over as he spoke.

"Yes."

"Would you like to see where she worked, where she painted?"

He blurted it out. The words sprang from him as if coiled on a spring.

"Yes, I would."

"Come with me."

He opened the French windows and the desert air rushed in, warmed by the sun, fresh and invigorating. "This way." He walked away fast.

"Where will you live in the desert?" he said.

She hurried to keep up with him.

"That's what I came here to find out. I was staying at the Hacienda Inn, and I was going to look for a place. You see, I've just . . . well, my marriage has broken up and I . . ."

"New life," he said simply, shooting a sidelong glance at her.

"Yes, new life. Not a very good start, I'm afraid."

"I wonder."

He didn't look at her as he said it.

The barn was a few hundred yards off to the right, by the copse of trees. Was that where Rose had painted? Why did she care?

"You're serious about painting?" he said.

"Very."

"That's the thing to hang on to, then."

"Have you hung on to it?"

"No."

There was a long pause. Then, "It seems I'm better at preaching than practicing. You ask difficult questions."

"Perhaps my loss and your loss are not so very different," said Carol.

They walked on in silence until they reached the door of the barn.

He turned to her then, before he opened it, and there was an extraordinary look on his face.

"This is Rose's studio," he said. "I've not shown it to a woman before."

Thirteen

In stark contrast to Rose's comfortable studio, which Carol had been shown before lunch, Charles's was a huge room, fiercely white, cold, and quiet.

He walked into the room, his loafers making no sound at all on the painted white boards of the floor. The silence of a monastery enveloped them. Carol felt that breaking it would be difficult. She followed him, and the impressions piled up in a mind already working overtime on processing emotions. The work that was done here was harder than any manual labor. There was no pleasure in this room. Instead, there were piles of quiet, invisible pain. She tiptoed across pools of angst, and felt the cobwebs of doubt and fear pluck at her.

"My room," he said. He flicked out a hand to embrace it, and half turned toward her. His voice echoed bitterly in the cavernous studio.

"Yes," she agreed. It was. It could have belonged to nobody else. The moment he had entered the door of "his room," the charming Charles Ford of lunchtime had disappeared. He had been replaced by someone else. She sensed that immediately.

"You work here?" she asked, unnecessarily.

"I don't work here," he said. Again, there was bitterness, almost anger. "This is the place I don't work." He repeated it as if to punish himself. An easel in the center of the studio stared back at them. The blankness of the canvas it bore mocked him. His shoulders sagged as he beheld it.

"It's just a canvas," she said gently.

He turned more fully to her, his face twisted in anguish. She was talking on a deeper level. That meant he could, too. He tried to smile, but he couldn't.

"Have you ever seen anything so cruel?" he said with a harsh laugh. He meant the canvas.

"Isn't the enemy in you?"

"It is a mirror to me," he said, determined not to avoid a single whiplash of his endless penance.

"How long?"

"A year and two months."

"Nothing? Or nothing that worked for you?"

"Nothing. Not a line. Not a brush stroke. Not even a vision of a painting."

He walked in front of her, moving past her quickly, like a bird flitting across the windshield of a moving car.

"Why?" She stopped. It was not the time for a "why" question. Every minute of every day he would have asked that. He looked at her as he passed, disappointed, forgiving her, moving on. "Block," she said, as if by saying it she was isolating the enemy. "It serves a purpose. It protects us from failure." She remembered a psychology book. Viktor Frankl? Paradoxical intention? You were supposed to remove the barrier to failure by willing the actual failure you dreaded. Then, the barrier dismantled, the block disappeared.

But he knew that one. Perhaps all the ones.

"I forbid myself to paint," he said, hovering tantalizingly on the edge of her field of vision. "Rather than struggling to paint. And then"—he snapped his fingers in the quiet room—"abracadabra, I can paint." He paused. "Doesn't work. Tried it."

"I'm sorry," she said. "I've never had that. I had to make time for painting. I almost had to hide it. Like a bottle under the bed."

He laughed harshly.

"Maybe I should try family life," he said.

She turned and looked at him. He was peering at her as if she were a strange wild animal that he was seeing for the first time.

"I think" she said, "that creative block chooses not to live in suburban families." There was accusation in her remark as well as humor. It prefers it here in this great big studio amidst the pretensions and the self-indulgence, far from the Cocoa Puffs and the bedroom slippers, was the hidden implication.

"You're very beautiful," he said suddenly. There was a fierceness about the way he said it. He wanted to surprise her, to punish her for daring to judge him, and he wanted to tell the truth.

"Oh," said Carol. She hadn't expected that. There was no possible answer. She knew she was supposed to be unsettled by his statement, and she was. For a single second she felt fear, but a delicious variety of fear. He was elemental, as he had been in the desert snow when he saved her life. That bleak place was his natural habitat, which made him at one with the coyote and the fierce bobcat, with the Apache and the other Indians.

There was a couch against a wall, a daybed with a Navajo blanket cast across it. She could picture him lying there, his hand over his face, blocking out the light, as the hours passed and the moments came and went, the calls to creation unheard or unanswered.

"Not as beautiful as Rose," she said, as cruel suddenly as the canvas in the room's center.

"The *devil* with Rose," he barked suddenly, and he slapped his hand against his thigh very hard, showing how deeply she had touched him.

"Is your block the penance you do for losing her? Did you feel her death was your fault, that not marrying her was?"

"Oh *spare* me the pop psychology . . ." He sprayed out his exasperation at her, but Carol didn't mind because she knew she was close to the core of him. She was only surprised at how very badly she wanted to be there. Then, as suddenly, he relented. "I'm sorry," he said. "I am not behaving as a gentleman should. I'm very sorry." He ran his hand through his thick hair, and Carol could see him unraveling in front of her, could see him trying in vain to stop the process. He turned his head from that way to this to escape some invisible noose.

"Yes. It is all about Rose. I was happy then. I don't know why it all . . ." He trailed off.

"Would you like to see some of my paintings?" he said, suddenly changing the subject. He folded his arms across his chest in a gesture of asserting control.

"Yes. Very much."

They were stacked in racks along the wall of the studio. He hurried toward them, to the safety of work finished.

"I'm astonished when I look at them now. They seem so clever. I say to myself, how could anybody have been so brilliant to paint so well? I did them, but it doesn't feel like I did them. That's why I needn't be modest about them. These are Charles Ford's paintings, and he was one hell of an artist while he lived."

He opened the pile at the middle, and Carol peered in to see what he had made. It was the head of an Indian. Almost before she recognized that, she was sucked into the mysterious depth of the eyes. The ancient man was staring at her through the ages, and she stared back. She could feel his disdain, his distance, his pride, his world-weary self-confidence. His hair was gray but flecked with white, and he wore a simple turquoise-colored headband stained with sweat, which offset the bronze dignity of his face. The canvas, colored brown, was the backdrop, and the face lived amidst the arid brown as its owner lived amidst the weathered mud of the pueblo.

"Oh, Charles!" she said simply.

He moved as if to show her another, but she signaled him not to. The painting was too good to leave.

"You like it," he said without the question mark.

She simply nodded, looking at him as if for the first time. Now his agony made sense. He was a very great artist. To be cut off from this expressive power would be as bad as lost sight, lost vision, lost love. She had believed him because of the intensity of his feelings. Now she believed him because she knew where they came from.

"I don't know what to say," she said. "I mean . . . I mean . . . I wanted to be an artist, but this, this . . ." She shook her head in disbelief. "You can paint like this, and you haven't painted for a year and two months?"

He said nothing. He watched her quizzically, seeing her irritation spring from jealousy to color her cheeks. Carol McCabe was beautiful, inside and out—she had slid into the meaning of the picture with the ease that she had slid inside his wounded psyche. He had been in emotional hiding and she had found him. He had just met this woman, he had saved her life, but Charles knew already that he didn't want to let her go.

"You'll paint again," she said suddenly. She put out her hand and took his, and she led him across the room like one might lead a small child, with kindly firmness. The table that held the paint, brushes, and palettes was against a wall. She let go of his hand and reached for a tube of black acrylic. She squeezed it onto a brush, a great big, black gob of goo like the devil's toothpaste. Holding it in her left hand, she reached again for his, and she led him to the canvas. It was only then that he realized what she was going to do. She handed him the brush, and she said quite simply, "Put the paint on the canvas."

He laughed at the stupidity of it.

"That's not how it works," he said, smiling broadly.

"Put it on," she said. "Flick it on. Stick it on. Jam it on. Put it on the canvas, it doesn't matter how."

"Of course it matters how." His smile was gone. "That's the whole point. If you can't see that . . ."

"*Do* it!" She raised her voice to him.

"Don't you see, I *can't* do it. That's the problem. I have nothing to paint. I have nothing to say."

"Charles!"

He tried to explain patiently. "This is not a mechanical thing, Carol. This is too important to play games with. I can't produce ugliness. That would be unbearable. It would be far worse than nothing."

She moved like lightning. She grabbed his hand before he

could resist. Pushing the brush into it, she circled his fist with
hers, and she heaved the whole at the empty canvas. His hand
shot forward. The brush crushed against the canvas and sawed
down it, leaving a jagged and uneven stroke of black on the
pristine white.

"What the *hell* are you doing . . . !" He tore away from her
and from the canvas in horror. His eyes, open wide, ran from
the dirty streak to the brush in his hand that had done the deed.
His mark was on the canvas. His black was on the white. He
had *painted* it there. He dropped the brush and it fell on the
white floor, leaving a spray of acrylic where it landed.

Her lips were parted in triumph. She was breathing fast.

"It's a start," she said, and she smiled at him, not afraid of
the fury she knew she had unleashed.

He looked at her, at the canvas, at the mess on the floor. He
was trying to make sense of it. It should mean nothing, but it
didn't mean nothing. He had assaulted the sneering blankness.
He had made war on the emptiness in his soul. She had made
him do it. The bitch had taken away his excuses. Now he had
only himself to blame. The mark on the canvas proved it. For
the first time in his life two totally conflicting emotions bubbled
up inside him, mixed so completely that the one could not be
separated from the other. One was the purest elation. The other
was the whitest rage.

He took a step toward her, and she didn't recoil from him.
She stood her ground before his fury and his joy. Her eyes were
wide with excitement. He reached out for her, taking her
roughly by the shoulder and behind the neck. She made no move
to resist him.

"*Damn* you!" he said. His voice throbbed with anger, and
his eyes were adrenaline wide. He pulled her toward him, and
he thrust himself at her, and he kissed her. It was a ferocious
kiss, shorn of delicacy and tenderness. He just took her, helping
himself to her, and his lips ground against hers with no thought
for her pleasure or her pain. It was unmistakably a punishment.
And yet, too, it was a breaking down of the dikes of his passion.

Pinned tight against him, her heart heaving with a wild and alien joy, Carol could feel what was happening. The river of Charles Ford, long dammed, was flowing once more.

She felt the fire leave him. He drew back from her and there was confusion, but not sorrow, on his face.

He still held her, his fingers tight on her shoulder, his eyes burning into hers.

"You must stay here," he said, his voice shaking with conviction. "You can paint here in the desert. You will use Rose's studio. We will help each other."

And then he turned, before she could answer, and walked away from her, shaking his head from side to side. She could not see his expression.

But Carol knew something of what he felt because she, too, was feeling it. Charles Ford had saved her life, but she had set him free.

Fourteen

Rachel reached forward and pressed the button of the intercom on her desk. Jake, her assistant, answered.

"Jake, can you get in here with a pad?"

In seconds, he was there.

"Jake, can you find out all you can for me about one Charles Ford, a painter who lives in Santa Fe?"

Half an hour later Jake dropped a sheaf of laser-printed pages onto her desk with a thud. All he said, as he did so was "Mmmmmm!" Then he was gone, and Rachel was alone with her stranger. There was a part of her that dreaded what she might find. But she leaned forward and began to read.

Fifteen

"It's quite pretty," said Camille. "Not gorgeous, but pretty." She strutted about, craning her neck in a pantomime of inspection. "Oh, goody, a garden." She darted toward the window and looked out over the patch of green three floors below. The rusty fire escape that led to it looked to Tessa like not so much an exit as a potential entrance to the flotsam and jetsam of the New York night. She fought back all negative thoughts. Camille seemed happy. What else mattered?

"Can I go down to the garden now, Mummy? Please, pretty please? If I don't nag all day?"

"Later, sweetheart. Let's look at the rest first."

There wasn't much of the rest: a kitchenette ran off the main room, as did a bedroom and a bathroom. That was it.

"Where do I sleep?" said Camille, who had entered the territorial stage. "Presumably, I have to sleep with you, *right,* Mummy?"

"Right, darling. We won't always have to live in a place as small as this. Soon, when I can afford it, we'll get something bigger."

Camille nodded gravely.

"First of all, we'll have to do a bit of cleaning. And I think some flowers would help, don't you?" said Tessa.

"I could pick some in the garden." Camille's voice was cunning and tenacious. The garden remained an objective.

"I can't see any really nice ones in the garden," said Tessa, walking to the window and looking down at the patch of weeds and sparse grass. "No, we'll buy some on the street."

"But we have to look after money, or it won't look after us."

"Right, darling, but when I start work, we'll have money."

"I hope I like public school. I don't mind not going to Brearley, 'cause Mrs. Snead was really *mean* and kind of *weird*." She paused. "Well, if I don't like it, I'll just have to put up with it. There are worse things."

"Darling, you are so grown up for your age. You're such a big, good, brave girl." Tessa leaned down and hugged her, and Camille cuddled in, pleased.

"Remember when we would all cuddle in like this, Daddy and you and me, and we'd all say 'I love you' at the same time?" said Camille. "Let's say it now and close our eyes and hear Daddy saying it and feel him cuddling in with us, okay?"

Tessa closed her eyes. "I love you," she said. She could feel the tears forming behind her lids. Then Camille's little voice was saying, "I love you," and Tessa was trying, trying oh so very hard to feel Pete's arms and hear his voice, but she couldn't.

"Did you hear him? Did you hear? I did. I did. And I felt him, too," said Camille, opening her eyes. "What's the matter, Mummy?"

The tears came pouring down. Nothing would stop the damn things.

"Oh, sweetheart, my baby. It's nothing. It's just that I miss him so much. So much, and I know you do too, but you're just braver than me."

"I cry buckets at night," said Camille.

"Oh, darling! Do you? Why don't you wake me up?"

" 'Cause then we'd just cry together," said Camille with a cheerful laugh. "Even though Pitt-Rivers never cry."

It had the desired effect. Tessa dried her eyes and smiled through the mist. Camille had cheered her up on purpose. What a girl she had brought up. Now it was time for action to banish dreary thoughts.

"Come on," she said, "let's start on this kitchen."

"Okay," said Camille. "I get to squirt the stuff about like Felisa used to. This is like being at the fishing lodge, everyone pitching in, isn't it?"

"Sort of," said Tessa. The small apartment was not the fishing lodge in Scotland, with its crackling log fires and huge armchairs so comfortable they made staying awake in them almost impossible. There were no stags' heads on the walls, no tackle rooms full of damp clothes warming by the water heater. There was no raucous laughter and deflating of pomposity as her friends and cousins cut each other down without mercy, and Pete, laughing loudest and giving far better than he got, as he ribbed the English as the great unwashed and for their terminal cheapness. Bathing was a source of much merriment. Americans showered at least twice a day. The British soaked in a tub maybe three times a week. "You know, you could fit England into Florida," Pete would say, "but the rest of America wouldn't be able to stand the smell." It had all been such fun.

Camille squirted the Fantastik, and Tessa started scrubbing the kitchen countertops. The apartment was small, but she was lucky to have it. One of Tessa's friends had kept it when she had married her investment-banking fortune. On Madison, it was rent controlled and in a prime location, but it was still a one-bedroom walk-up. Tessa had been offered it for free, but had insisted on paying for it.

Tessa was glad to be back in New York. She felt she had been putting her life on hold for quite long enough. She had left a note under Carol's door, telling her to keep in touch, and she and Camille had caught the noon plane to Manhattan.

"What are those little black things?" said Camille accusingly. "They look like tiny mouse doo-doo." She was peering into the black hole that was the space beneath the sink.

"I think they're roach droppings, darling. Don't worry. We'll get rid of them in no time. We'll call the exterminator."

"Swarzabeggar?"

"No, darling," said Tessa, laughing, "not Arnie. The little

guy with the nozzle that squirts. You know, Mr. Blobs, or whatever you used to call him."

"Oh, goody, will Mr. Blobs come here?"

"Well, if not him, then his friend will." Tessa smiled grimly.

"It'll be fun not having staff," said Camille. "Just being us. Cleaning is fun, isn't it?"

"Anything is, if you let it be," said Tessa truthfully. It was so odd. All her life she had been materially looked after, even at the same time she had been emotionally deprived. Now the absence of material things was almost a relief, but her separation from Pete, who had given her all the love and warmth she had never had, was unbearable. What you had as a child you never cared about losing. You took it for granted. What you didn't have as a child you clung to with every fiber of your being. Money and Pete had gone, but only Pete was missed.

"When is Aunt Cornelia coming round to pick me up?" said Camille.

"First thing in the morning. What are you going to wear?"

"My velvet skirt, frilly shirt, and blue cardie. You know Aunt Cornelia, she's so proper!" Camille made a little pout with her lips to indicate disapproval.

"Well, she is 'proper' and *very* Manhattan. But that's nice sometimes, to dress up and pretend that one is very posh and grand. It's like make-believe."

"I think," said Camille, changing the subject, "that I shall leave the roach doo-doo for Mr. Blobs when he comes."

"I think," said Tessa, "that is a pretty good idea."

Sixteen

Tessa leaned against the door as it closed behind her. God, Cornelia was tiring. She could hear her on the stairs, rattling on to Camille, "Now, darling, you mustn't mind living here in this . . . place . . . for a little while. You know you could have stayed with me, but your mother wanted to be here, can't think why . . . But anyway . . ."

"But I like it," Camille was replying. "It's a neat place and it has a garden . . ."

The sounds drifted out of earshot, and Tessa was grateful to be alone. For about thirty seconds! She wandered back into the room and sat down on the sofa. The walls needed something on them, some of Camille's drawings, anything, really. She leaned back as the quietness closed in on her. She felt herself going down, and she had to stay up. She needed to get out. She remembered the bookstore down below on Madison. Yes, that would be good. She would browse through some books and try to lose herself in them. It would be a way to give perspective to her own problems.

She walked down the stairs in the dusty gloom. On the street outside, New York hit her. There was life on Madison, or a version of it, well-heeled and hurrying to luncheons and appointments, to galleries and leg waxes, to sleek shops and expensive food places, where money could be exercised at the same time as little dogs on long leashes. Tessa stood there for a second or two, adjusting to the cold and the brightness. New Yorkers didn't avoid

her eyes. They peered deeply into them, questioning her, puzzled
by her, sensing the strangeness inside the outward familiarity.
She could tell the art people from the brokers, the attorneys from
the merely rich and underemployed. It was all there to see, the
rakish cuts of the overcoats of the dealers, the boxlike squares
of the middle-aged preppies, the Burberrys of the safety-seeking
middle managers. A couple of models stalked by, eyes straight
ahead, dangling their portfolios and trying to make up in their
haughty walks for the humiliations that would be heaped on them
at the go-sees they headed for.

Had they all had a good Christmas? Had they all cuddled up
with their significant others and wished each other well as they
looked forward to a new year together? Tessa turned right, and
in seconds she was pushing through the door of the Madison
Avenue Bookshop.

She had always loved the store. It was small and intimate,
and the people who worked there knew and loved books. As
always, Tessa found herself drawn to the art section. Her eyes
flicked over the displays and settled on a coffee-table book
whose severe black-and-white cover consisted of a photograph
of the famous glass house, the seminal creation of architect
Philip Johnson. The book, titled *The Glass House,* was obviously selling well. It was the only survivor of what had clearly
been a pile of a dozen or so. Tessa picked it up. Scotland, so
rich in old architecture, had never made the successful passage
to the new. It was one of the things she loved about America,
about Manhattan in particular. It was so brave and forward-
looking, daring in its buildings. Here was Johnson's Glass
House, oriental in its simplicity, devoid of the clutter of life that
confused purpose and blurred focus in Europe.

Tessa turned the pages. As always, God was in the detail, the
supreme artistic talent, whose greatness was evident as much
in what was left out as in what was included.

As she looked at the book, Tessa became aware of someone
hovering at her shoulder. She did not turn around, and the figure
shifted, giving off an aura of impatience that although not seen

was quite easily felt. As if to emphasize his presence, the stranger coughed.

Tessa turned. He stood there looking straight at her, not bothering to deflect his stare. Neither did she. She arched her eyes in question. He was beautifully dressed in a lightweight suit of charcoal gray, double-breasted and unbuttoned. His cotton shirt looked like a Turnbull and Asser, but overall his appearance was classic French rather than classic English, as far as the clothes were concerned. He was very good-looking, she had time to think; distinguished, patrician, and richly suntanned. If there were elements of both French and English in his clothes, his face was that of a Spanish aristocrat, haughty, proud, and featuring interesting dark eyes.

"I was wondering," he said, "if you were going to buy that book, as it appears to be the last one. If not, then I would like to buy it myself."

"I haven't decided yet," said Tessa.

"Ah," he replied. A silence descended. They continued to stare at each other. More information had been exchanged. Despite his European appearance, he was American. He had spoken precisely, his tone clipped in his effort to appear polite when he probably didn't feel polite. Tessa sensed that he was not a great people-lover, this elegant stranger, and that he was used to having his own way.

"You're English," he said.

Tessa looked away from him, not answering. She continued to study the book in her hand. It was intended as a rebuke for deficiencies in his earlier attitude. But he had interested her. This wasn't the end of the conversation. Both knew that.

"I visited the Glass House once," he said.

She looked up. It was a good line.

"You did?"

"Yes, it was very fine. A winter's day. Snow on the fields. A gray sky. The best conditions, really, I suppose."

She liked the diffidence. He spoke as a poet or an artist might speak, aware of light and color, of peripheral things that meant something. A parvenu would have started out on the architect. "I know him. He's a friend of mine. I have lots of grand, interesting friends" would have been the message. But this man addressed the beauty. She didn't doubt he knew Johnson, but for him the Glass House was what was interesting.

"It's so beautifully thought through . . . Eames, the Barcelona table, Mies van der Rohe, even the Kandinsky. It's like a poem, not a word out of place," said Tessa, flicking through the pages of the book.

"Yes," he said. He took a step forward and began to look at the book over her shoulder. He was closer now, on the edge of her territory. "Neutra, Wright, the ghosts are there. You stand inside and yet you are outside. The boundaries between house and nature evaporate. I like that."

"I agree. In Scotland, the boundaries are castle walls, and the last thing those are is blurred. And it's the same here in Manhattan. The doormen guard the gates. Boundaries are vital. They are about survival. I think that's what I like about the Glass House. It's to do with freedom from fear. The outside isn't a threat, it's a treat."

"Is that where you come from, Scotland?"

"My family does. I've been here for about ten years now."

"Manhattan?"

"And Southampton . . . mainly. I've just moved into an apartment on Madison with my daughter."

It had flowed forward fast, and Tessa was amazed at how much she had said.

Charles looked at her carefully. She was cool and patrician, with the translucent skin that her class had patented, and big, soft eyes. Her chin was far from Hapsburg, hinting that at some stage her ancestors had taken onboard some less rarefied blood to add backbone to the genes. Her hair was cut short and she hadn't bothered with makeup, which made her a rarity on Madison and, with her bone structure, a delightful-looking one. She stood straight, like someone who had been taught the value of standing up for herself, and Charles could sense Viking strength in her. She hadn't bothered with her clothes, blue jeans and an outsize sweater that looked like a hand-me-down from a boisterous elder brother. She wore sneakers, or what the British called gym shoes, and in any other bookshop except this one, the salespeople would have watched her like a hawk, not understanding that outward appearances in Europe meant absolutely nothing. Over there, who you were and what you had been was telegraphed in a secret language that took a lifetime to learn. It was on this level that Charles and Tessa now spoke.

"Listen," said Tessa, suddenly closing the book and thrusting it at him. "You have it. I wasn't actually going to buy it. I was just browsing."

"No. Really. I don't want to influence you at all. I mean, I suppose I was a little rude earlier. I apologize." He seemed surprised by what he had just said. "Yes," he repeated firmly, "I apologize."

"You weren't rude," said Tessa with a laugh. "I suspect you are not used to being kept waiting. Nothing wrong with that."

"And you, perhaps, are not used to being hurried up," he said, smiling himself. "Nothing wrong with that, either."

Both paused. It was a strange moment. They had paid each other the compliment of being like each other. Both had high self-respect. They were not opposites. They were similars.

"Why do I get the feeling that you are an artist?"

He cocked his head to one side. He wasn't wearing a beret and smock.

"Because I am?" he answered with a short laugh.

"A painter?"

"Right again."

"What sorts of things do you paint? What I really mean is, in what style do you paint?"

He reached up into the shelves and took down a copy of a book. It was *The Paintings of Charles Ford*. He thrust it at her.

"These are mine," he said. "Actually, the book is out of print, but they keep it in here because I'm such a good customer. It's probably the simplest way to answer your question."

Tessa took it, impressed.

His paintings were good, very good. Indians mostly, Indians poor but at peace in the deserts of Arizona or New Mexico. Some were in headdresses, resplendent and proud as once they must have been. Most were in everyday clothes, their faces alone the mark of their ancestry, as they merely existed, sitting on a chair at the edge of a dusty porch, walking amidst the sagebrush, turning to watch the painter as the sun caught them in profile. There was an overpowering sense of melancholy in the paintings that had transferred itself to the glossy reproductions. Tessa could feel the hardship of these people's lives and much, much more. There was an otherworldliness that lurked between the lines of their weather-beaten faces. They were here, but they were not really *here.* They lived, too, among spirits, haunting and timeless, walking with ancestors on grassy prairies by the edge of rivers, surrounded by the buffalo. Somehow, Charles Ford had reached into their secret world and captured it on canvas.

She looked up at him, a new interest on her face.

"You love them, don't you, and the desert? It's as if you're one of them. They look at you like that. An honorary Indian. Is that what you are, Charles Ford?"

He laughed openly, throwing back his head. White teeth flashed against the darkness of his skin.

"Yes. Yes, I suppose I am. Perhaps that's exactly what I am."

Tessa smiled. "I can identify with that. In Scotland where I lived, there were people on the estate whose families had worked there since the sixteen hundreds and even earlier, gillies, keepers, thatchers. I loved being with them. All my childhood I hung out with them, and they knew things about the land and the animals and the fish that seemed to spring from their genes or their souls or something. They could sense the salmon and feel the grouse, and smell weather on the wind. They weren't educated, but they had a wisdom that was timeless. The English came and employed them and lorded it over them, from dukes and earls in their castles to doctors and solicitors in the villages. But they were all rubbish compared to the real natives. They were just foreigners, just conquerors. The natives never left, because they were part of nature and to leave it would be to lose a part of themselves."

She saw the strange intensity creeping into his eyes. "What made you leave?" he said at last.

"I fell in love."

"Ah, love," said Charles. "I know about that, too."

Tessa said nothing. She sensed what was coming, sensed, too, how difficult this would be for him.

He paused, and then coughed once, turning his head away as he cleared a throat that didn't need to be cleared.

"I was on my way to the Franz Kline show at the Guggenheim when I dropped by here," he said. "I don't suppose you'd like to come with me. I wouldn't ask, but I feel you're the sort of person who would have no problem saying no, thank you."

"Yes, please," said Tessa.

Seventeen

"They seem easy to do," said Tessa. "But that's true of a lot of difficult things."

She peered at the Kline. Every single one of the thirty-five paintings at the Guggenheim retrospective displayed the artist's uncompromising black-on-white color scheme.

"A single line of black on a white canvas can be a leap of faith," said Charles. He paused and took a deep breath. "It depends on your personal demons."

Tessa turned to look at him. It was the first time that anything he'd said had appeared odd to her. What did he mean . . . personal demons? A black line was a black line. What did it have to do with a leap of faith? Her expression said she didn't understand. His said he wasn't going to explain.

"Kline was interesting. He influenced his contemporaries de Kooning and Pollock. And his successors Rauschenberg and Twombly. If you're enjoying this as much as I am, we could go on to the Met and see the Twombly show."

He turned toward her. Tessa looked back at him and smiled.

"It's fun. I'd enjoy that. It's like an art history lesson."

"Oh, dear," said Charles. "For God's sake, stop me if I lecture. I'm never quite sure what I like, but I know quite a bit about art."

She laughed at his reversal of the popular saying.

"I don't believe you. I imagine you know exactly what you like. And even more, exactly what you don't like."

"So you think I'm opinionated?" He smiled. He was, of course, but not about art anymore.

"I'd say that," said Tessa, as they walked on to the next gritty abstraction, titled *Untitled, 1957.* She twirled around to face him when she reached it. "I'd say you'd be a hard person to argue with."

She smiled, aware that she was flirting with him, and wanting to. He was so straight and honest and direct. Somehow that made her want to wind him up just a little. Why? It would be fun to find out. He was very attractive. Very. She liked the clothes he wore, the old and highly polished shoes, the classic build of his suit, the faded but spotlessly clean tie. Nothing about him was new, and paradoxically, that made him more original.

"And you an easy person, by implication?" he said. "I don't think so." He liked the way her eyes sparkled. He very much liked her short, sculpted hair and the way it emphasized the fineness of her bone structure. She was too stylish to be British, and too vivacious. She was more French in those respects. Perhaps living with an American had saved her.

"I don't know very much about you," she said, changing the pace and casting a disdainful expression at the Expressionist canvas. She turned back to him at the end of her sentence, emphasizing it.

"Nor I about you," he replied.

"You answer my questions with questions?"

"I answer your facts with facts. Your remark wasn't a question."

"Touché," said Tessa, smiling broadly.

"Are we jousting?"

Of course they were, and they both laughed because this was "getting to know you" and it couldn't, and shouldn't, be hurried. It was exciting here at the beginning, perhaps the most exciting time of all. Everything was new. Everything was discovery. It was like finding an enormously long Christmas stocking stuffed full of knowledge, and perhaps in its toe, a key . . . a key to intimacy. Or so Tessa thought as she walked beside him past Kline's concrete abstractions.

"Okay," she said. "Let's recap. What do I know about you? I know you are an artist, and you like old things and beautiful things, you don't like to be kept waiting . . . and you know about love. Is that quite a lot, or quite a little?"

"What do you mean, I know about love?" he said, tipping his head to one side.

"You said you did. In the bookshop."

"I did?"

"Yes. I said the reason I came to America was that I fell in love, and you said, 'I know about love, too.' "

"Mmmmm. I see I shall have to be careful what I say around you."

"In case you give too much of yourself away?" Tessa laughed, pleased by the conversation. He liked her. She knew that now. And it was mutual. She wanted to spend more time with him. She had agreed to go to the Met. Now she hoped he would ask her to lunch.

"Okay, okay, let's see what I know about you. You're Scottish, and you have lived in America for ten years. You love the countryside. You are extraordinarily perceptive, have great taste and style, have a daughter . . . and . . . and, well, to tell the absolute truth, you are very beautiful."

The blush rushed up from Tessa's feet. By the time the warm tide had reached her stomach, her face was bracing for its arrival. She only had time to open her mouth before the sunburst exploded on her cheeks.

"Oh!" she said. And then, "What a charming thing to say. Thank you."

Tessa reached out and touched his arm. He did not withdraw it. Her fingers lingered for just a second, and then she took them away.

"Do you suppose we might be done with Franz Kline?" he said. He forced himself to move away from his feelings and toward seemingly safer actions.

"I think we might," said Tessa. She liked the way he expressed himself.

They walked out through the domed lobby of the Guggenheim, and soon they were back on Madison in the fresh cold, amidst the reds and greens of the Christmas aftermath. As they passed the window of the Madison Avenue Bookshop, they both looked in. Was it already "the place where it all began"? Tessa was thinking that, and then she tried not to because of Pete. Was Charles Ford, who knew about love, also thinking of someone else? He looked at her and smiled at her secret thoughts. Where was the husband who had fathered the daughter? Where the daughter? Where the homes in Manhattan and Southampton?

"That's where I live," said Tessa. "In there." She pointed at the door next to the bookshop. Charles stopped suddenly. There were five bells beside it. Inside, on the floor at the bottom of a dingy staircase, was a pile of circulars and junk mail.

"Here?" he said, his mind racing. Why here? He could have sworn this Scottish woman came from a family of landed gentry. Southampton? The Glass House? Something didn't make sense.

"Would you mind if we had some coffee?" she said. "I need warming up."

In her apartment?

No, she didn't mean that. Of course she didn't. When he nodded, she steered him into the Madison Avenue Café, right on her doorstep. They sat down and ordered cappuccino and espresso.

"Do you have a job?" he said. She was a mystery, a refined mystery of the very best kind. Charles Ford stirred his coffee and thought of the dramatic acceleration of his life. Until recently, he had existed in suspended animation, his life a hostage to the past, his future a dark and distant planet. Then there had been the mysterious woman in the lobby of the Hacienda Inn. Next he had found Carol in the desert, and she had drawn his unwilling hand across the canvas. He had kissed Carol in gratitude, in fury, and yes, in the strangest passion, and the curtain had gone up on his life and his play had begun once again. Here was New York, the second scene. Tessa sat across from him, and already he had told her she was beautiful and Rose had not interfered. Nor had Rose cried "Stop" when he had kissed Carol McCabe, for some oddly urgent reason that still he could not fully understand.

"I start work at Sotheby's next week. Real estate, not art." Tessa answered the question he had almost forgotten he'd asked.

"You're a realtor?"

"Not yet. I've taken my exams. Sotheby's has given me a job as an associate. I work under a broker."

"They pay you a salary? I was never quite sure how that worked."

"No. They give me an office, actually more of a cubicle, and the use of a secretary, telephones, et cetera. I split the six percent commission with them fifty-fifty."

"Sounds good. Independence," he said. She didn't look as if she was in sales. But then, she wasn't—yet. It was difficult to see how she would be good at it. She was very, very straight-forward, a million miles from *Glengarry Glen Ross*.

"The trouble is, there's no security. If I don't sell anything, I don't earn anything. I'm rather nervous about it, actually."

He could hear the British understatement. Suddenly his desire to protect her was strong.

"I imagine getting around the city must be expensive."

"A fortune! I mean, say you show six apartments in a morning and you have to pay for the taxis. It could be fifty dollars. More. Some of the associates hire limos when they think they have a really hot client. The old pros say not to do that, because you can never tell who's a time-waster or who is a bona fide buyer."

She sipped at her coffee. "How about you? Is art a full-time job?" She looked at him over the rim of her cup.

"Not exactly. I'm with Wardlow, but I've had a bit of difficulty producing lately," he said, borrowing her nation's under-statement. "I live in the desert outside Santa Fe. I have a cattle ranch."

"That's amazing. I just got back from Santa Fe last night. I was staying at the Hacienda Inn."

"No!" said Charles, wondering at the coincidence.

"You must know it."

"I used to own it. Still do. Part of it."

"You *own* part of the Hacienda Inn?"

"Yes, I sold it to a development company called Rosewood, and retained a share. Did you enjoy yourself?"

Tessa now knew a whole lot more about Charles Ford, honorary Indian. He was also Charles Ford, multimillionaire. He must be the rich rancher that Rachel had told her about in the mud bath.

"Very, very much," said Tessa. "I think it's one of the most stylish places on earth."

"Coming from you, that is praise indeed."

It was the second compliment he had paid her. The second direct one, anyway.

"I was staying there with my daughter. Did you know Rachel Richardson was staying there?"

"The TV person? Yes, I think they mentioned it."

"We made friends. She is really sweet."

"I thought she had a reputation for being a pretty tough nut."

"Well, she probably does have that side to her. Luckily, she never showed it to me. I'm surprised I never saw you there, if you live nearby."

"I dart in and out at odd times when nobody is around."

"What a pity," said Tessa.

"But we met anyway."

"Oh, yes, we did."

Tessa wondered at her brazenness. What the hell was happening here? Where was the guilt? Was Pete fading? Damn! She didn't want him to fade. The memories of him were all she had.

"Are you married?" he said, as if he could read her thoughts.

"My husband died. A year ago." She didn't pause for long. "Are you?"

"No. I lived with someone. For many, many years. She died, too. I'm sorry about your husband. It's hell, isn't it?"

"Yes," she said with a bittersweet smile. "And I'm sorry, too, about your . . . your friend."

"So, same sort of boat," he said. "Not easy."

But getting easier, apparently. The thought was completely inescapable. Both Tessa and Charles shared it.

"What is the hardest part for you?" said Tessa, resting her chin on her hands. She liked him more and more.

"Sharing things. Having a brave companion for the road. I haven't been able to paint since she died."

"That must be terrible."

"I hadn't realized how important it was to me. I took it for granted. If you can't lose yourself in something, you experience too much of yourself. You have to be able to escape the intolerable clutches of reality."

"Not blocked poetically," she said with a small laugh, smiling her encouragement at him across the red Formica.

He smiled back. "And what is the most difficult part for you?"

"Being broke," she said simply. "And not being used to that. Having no mechanism to cope with it. My husband left a financial nightmare, and I have to sort out some kind of future for my daughter."

"I was wondering about Southampton and the place in Manhattan," he said carefully.

"In contrast to my rent-controlled flat on Madison?" she said, making it easier for him.

"And I whine on about creative block," he said. "Being poor must be intolerable. I wouldn't know how to begin." It was only partially true. In the desert he could live on almost nothing for the rest of his life if he chose, but then it would be a choice, and he had no child.

He looked at her, a new respect in his eyes. He knew she would win through, if not at Sotheby's, then somewhere, somehow. The thoughts rolled on, impelled by her big round eyes across the table and by the memory of her hand touching his arm earlier. Her face was alive with resilience and energy. He could see her at the other end of his dining-room table, talking easily to José about the silver. He could see her at the Sheraton desk in the morning room, organizing the menu with the cook, the flowers with the housekeeper.

"I don't think creative block is a self-indulgence," said Tessa.

"It must be difficult for a non-artist to understand," he replied.

She felt him back away from her. She wasn't an artist. Somehow, she knew the woman who had died was.

"What do you think your friend would have wanted for you?"

"My happiness?" he tried. It was the obvious answer, but not the correct one.

"That's what we'd hope, isn't it? But taking into account human nature, I have the odd feeling that Pete would want me to grieve for him for the longest time. Never remarry. Never fall in love again."

"And perhaps wallowing in grief is our gift to the dead. The last thing we do for them is to grant their last wish."

"Maybe. Maybe your block is that. Possibly you feel your friend might have liked that . . . your not being able to paint without her. Her meaning that much to you. So you sacrifice your creative talent on her funeral pyre, like the wives of an old Indian maharajah."

He laughed out loud. "Oh, Tessa, it's such a pleasure to talk to you. I haven't met anyone like you for what seems like a lifetime. You're like my Spanish cousins, like the stories about my grandmother. She was English. Do you think we're related?" He laughed.

"Related? Almost certainly closer than six degrees of separation," she said. "What was your grandmother's name?"

"Manners."

"No, I think the Mannerses steered pretty clear of Scotland. The Welsh borders were more their stamping ground."

"Well, perhaps that's a good thing."

"A good thing we're not related?" She didn't let it go. "It would have been nice to have been cousins, wouldn't it?"

Her head was cocked to one side.

"But then we couldn't get married," he said simply, surprising himself as much as Tessa.

He laughed, so she had to laugh too, but she was blushing again.

"Listen," he said. "Do you feel strong enough for Twombly?"

She felt strong enough for nearly anything, stronger than she had felt in a year.

Was that her future sitting across the table from her, and Camille's future?

He got up and she did, too.

They hailed a cab, and for a time, side by side in its back seat, they were quiet.

"Tessa," he said.

"Charles."

He paused, as if he was going to say something difficult.

"Look, I hope you are going to understand this, but, well, I have this loft downtown, and it's quite a substantial one . . ."

She turned toward him. He looked away.

"Since Rose died, it has a lot of memories, sad memories, and I've been thinking of selling it. What I was thinking was, if you start at Sotheby's next week, perhaps you could be my realtor."

"Your realtor?"

"Yes," he said with a laugh. "That's what you'll be, believe it or not, when you start at Sotheby's. A realtor."

Tessa's mind was suddenly in chaos.

"I know. Well, I suppose I know. Gosh. Isn't that wonderful or something? I'm sorry, I don't know what to say. Perhaps I have to say no, because we don't know each other well enough, or because I know you feel sorry for me."

"I think most realtors would say yes," he said gently. "It's worth a million two."

"Charles, I can't take that. That would be over thirty thousand dollars in commission." She felt the excitement bubble inside her. Her math abilities seemed to have survived the surprise.

"It wouldn't be charity, Tessa. You'd sell the apartment. It's called work. You're entitled to get paid for it." He was smiling broadly. He wouldn't have expected anything else from her.

"But I have no experience. You need a real professional. There must be lots in the office."

Again he laughed. "Tessa. Tessa. This is America. Now, repeat after me: 'You'll never regret this decision, Mr. Ford. You have chosen the hardest-working, most competent realtor in Manhattan, and I will have your apartment sold for you in no time. I happen to have the papers here for a year's exclusive, which I would very much like you to sign right away.'"

She laughed back at him, because suddenly she knew she could accept, and it made a vast and wonderful difference to her life. She had a listing, a million-dollar listing, and she hadn't officially started work yet.

"Oh, Charles, what a fabulous thing to do for a perfect stranger. That is *so* kind. It'll make all the difference. I'll walk in with a listing. I'll be bringing something with me." Tessa went quiet. "Do you suppose, because I got the listing before I joined them, I could ask them to take a bit less than three percent commission?"

"What I think," said Charles, his eyes widening at Tessa's sudden and unexpected business savvy, "is that you're going to learn this game a great deal faster than you thought."

Eighteen

"Ms. Richardson. How wonderful to see you again. A happy New Year to you. Mr. Harding arrived a few minutes ago. He is at your usual table."

Mario, the maitre d' at Le Cirque, led Rachel through the restaurant. The craning necks of the lunchers waved like corn on every side. "Their" table was tucked away in the back of the room, not at all in the fashionable section. They liked it that way, far from the beaten track of the professional table-hoppers.

He stood to greet her, his arm reaching out around her waist. His lips brushed the side of hers in a gesture that said this was no casual relationship. He was tall for a tycoon, and lean. His face exuded the quiet strength of a timeless frontiersman, mining merely a different form of gold. Rachel noticed the effect he was having on women at nearby tables. They were mesmerized by the charisma of his naked power.

"How was Santa Fe?" he said, as they sat down. "Boring as hell, no? Like Christmas in Connecticut without you, and just my children and their dull wives and duller children. God only knows why He invented families."

He stopped short as if he had let slip the details of a merger deal to an outsider. Quickly, he changed the subject. Rachel believed in happy families, never having had one of her own.

"You certainly came back soon enough," he added quickly.

"Yeah," said Rachel. "I guess I've forgotten how to relax."

"Ha! That's my girl," he said. "Same with me. Stick me on

a yacht in the islands, give me a rum punch, hand me a test line with a black-fin tuna at the end of it, and all I can think of is business and closing the deal. Sometimes I feel like Nixon felt . . . I get up in the morning to confound my enemies."

"Aren't couples supposed to be opposites?" said Rachel, moving toward the point of the lunch—her point, not Matt's.

"Listen, darling. You're a woman and I'm a man. Isn't that opposite enough?" He had heard her underlying message. Beneath the confident, extrovert exterior, Matt Harding was a sensitive man. He could read feelings as well as balance sheets.

"I wonder, Matt. I mean, shouldn't one of us be able to relax? Shouldn't one of us love the idea of families? Shouldn't one of us be able to think about something other than work and confounding our enemies?"

He sensed philosophy edging its way into the conversation. Philosophy, as always, was a disguise for the discussion of personal emotion.

"Am I hearing discouraging words?" he said with a careful smile. He was on to her.

"I don't know, Matt. A year or two ago, I was happy with who I was, where I was going. But just lately I've begun to reassess. I may want to be a new Rachel, like the new Nixon, to use your analogy. A mellower Rachel. A more feminine Rachel. I really want to have a family, a real family, an American family with apple pies and babies and all the trimmings. You've had family, and you were never big on it. You know, Southampton and all your dull children and grandchildren . . ."

Matt cursed inwardly. All his life he had extolled the virtues of a tight mouth, in business and in everything. Now he had shot himself in the foot.

"Rachel, Rachel, I'm not against family. Some of my best friends have families. There I go again. It's the way I joke. It's my sense of humor. Okay, so family isn't my priority. *You* are my priority. You, Rachel." His voice deepened. He leaned closer across the table. "Rachel, I want you to be my wife."

Rachel tried to feel the excitement. Where were the chills,

the sweating palms, the beating heart? Oh shit! Where were feelings when she needed them? Why couldn't they be summoned to order? Suddenly, she was back in the lobby of the Hacienda Inn, and the *memories* of those feelings were far stronger than anything she was getting now. Okay, she was flattered. It felt good to be wanted. She liked and admired Matt.

"I don't know, Matt," she said.

"So you keep telling me." She heard the edge to his voice. Matt Harding was a big man. A strong man. He would not hang around her indefinitely. Sooner or later he would take her at her word. Rachel's intellect looked at that, and she felt fleeting doubt—maybe she was passing up reality for the illusion of romance. How many women had faced a similar dilemma throughout history? Should she take the bird in hand or hang on for the prince who might never come? Should she settle for security or follow her heart? She had experienced a kind of magic, but had it really been magic, or simply the creation of the chaotic mind of a drowning woman reaching out for anyone to keep her romantic dreams afloat?

Matt was so good-looking, so certain, so decent beneath the image of the swashbuckling, take-no-prisoners businessman. Suddenly she thought back to Chicago, to the cold and the hunger. Rats scratched through the night, and Rachel would hear the traps snapping shut on them as they went for the peanut butter, excitement at winning that small victory obliterated by the thought of having to dispose of their mangled corpses in the morning. And all the time the books, great piles of them devoured beneath a light of insufficient strength, as an escape route to the better world that she had promised herself and had found. Here, across the table, was this successful, attractive man who wanted her. Damn it, his ex-wives were among the richest women in America. Rachel knew that money didn't bring happiness, but even so, she knew that refusing his proposal was not a step that any woman of forty should take lightly.

"So what's new from the world of high finance? I heard Malone was after your cable interests."

"Where did you hear that from?" he said with a smile, pretending to study his menu. "Not *Barron's* or the *Wall Street Journal.*"

"Sounds like a confirmation. You know I never reveal my sources."

He laughed. "Off the record, and not a Connie Chung 'off the record,' he is."

"Mmmm. Malone's tough. I bet he wants to steal them."

"Yeah, he's tough, but then I've been around, too."

"Does it make sense to get out of cable now that the Republicans will probably ease up on price regulations?"

"Okay, wisewoman, here's the situation. I have big plans for the cable, and having Malone bid for it just establishes a price. I won't sell to him. Have you heard of RadioComm?"

"Vaguely. Didn't they buy up all the taxicab-communications wavelengths nationwide?"

"Damn right they did. They have seventy-five percent of the country covered. There's a new technology that can convert the old taxi bands to state-of-the-art digital, and they got FCC approval to go ahead. Motorola has developed it. If the Radio-Comm wavelengths were converted—and it would cost a couple of billion—you'd have a nationwide cellular phone system just like that." He snapped his fingers. There was fire in his eyes.

"Are you going after RadioComm?"

"Not directly." He was whispering now. "But CableCo wants my cable properties, and CableCo has fifty-one percent of RadioComm. I'm going to swap one for the other."

"But then you have to find two billion to convert the RadioComm wavelengths."

"Motorola will do the conversion, make the phones, provide the equipment. It's a big, simple deal for them, they say. They're on the edge of committing in exchange for an equity participation in RadioComm. I would end up with a nationwide cellular-phone network for no cash down. McCaw Cellular sold out to a Baby Bell for twelve billion, and they won't have either my market penetration or my futuristic technology"

"So you get to control a twelve-billion-dollar-plus cellular business in return for your cable interests and whatever you have to give Motorola in RadioComm stock."

"Pretty close. Malone thinks the cable is worth three billion. I give Motorola two billion in RadioComm stock in exchange for their handling the technical side of things. Then I control a maybe fourteen-billion-dollar company."

"So you make two billion. Why doesn't CableCo go to Motorola direct? Then *they* make the two billion."

"Because they aren't me," said Matt. "Motorola doesn't want to play with little people like CableCo. CableCo wants to stick with what they know best, which is cable. I'm the only guy in a position to slip through the window of oppurtunity. RadioComm and Motorola know that there will be all sorts of problems down the line, regulations, the FCC, finding a brand-name partner like Sprint to market the deal. I can smooth the path. That's why I get the two billion. Even if I never seem to get the girl."

She had to laugh at him, with him. He had made his two billion before the soup, or so it seemed. How many women were there who would not be impressed by that? Not many lunching in Le Cirque today.

"You're a tough one, Matt," she said. "Tough and shrewd and very, very clever."

"You, too, Rachel," he said, returning the compliment, not quite sure that it was a compliment.

"I don't think I'm that tough," said Rachel. She smiled wryly. She hadn't wanted her remark back.

"Remember the Davidson story?" said Matt simply.

The shock hit Rachel like a flash from the past. She was sucked from the present, from the fashionable restaurant with its monkey motif, pink tablecloths, and pinker, prosperous patrons. The time machine of memory took her away.

The assignment editor sat at the filthy desk, and the newspaper cuttings and wire copy piled up in front of him with the

*empty coffee cups and cigarette butts. Rachel put her hands on
the metal tabletop to steady herself as she looked down at him
through bleary eyes. She was so tired it hurt. Her muscles
ached, and her head, and bits of her she was not usually aware
of, all way past aspirin.*

*"Fucking flu," he said. "Sometimes I think there's a virus
specific to journalists. How come you don't get it?"*

*"No virus would want to live in here," said Rachel with feel-
ing.*

*"Ha, ha," he said. "You'll need your sense of humor on this
one."*

*He adjusted his glasses and read the handwritten note from
the dispatcher. "Just came in. Hot as hell. It's an ill wind . . ."*

*Oh, yeah, thought Rachel. An RTA downtown, or the confer-
ence at the Marriott with all those dull dermatologists. A numb-
ing boredom of B-rolls and background interviews.*

*"Someone took a chain saw to a schoolgirl in the woods at
the bottom of Fourteenth Street. Bits everywhere. A genuine
Maalox moment."*

Rachel was wide awake. The pain had gone.

"Is it on the wires?"

*"Nope. Tip-off from a friend who owes me in the P.D. You've
got maybe an hour's lead time on the oppo. Could be a na-
tional."*

*Rachel felt the surge of adrenaline. As always, the clock was
ticking. It was three hours to deadline for NBC Nightly News.
Her mind whirred. Nightly wouldn't do any old murder. But a
chain saw on a schoolgirl! She was acutely aware that her
human feelings were on hold. To her, this was not a cold-blooded
murder. It was news, and a scoop, courtesy of the flu and the
fact that she listened to this broken-down old newsman with the
hot information on his desk when he bellyached on and on about
the wife who made his miserable life even more of a misery. It
was her big moment. She could have her own segment on the
NBC Nightly News: This is Rachel Richardson for WLCN-TV
in Chicago . . .*

"Sure about the chain saw?"

"Left at the crime scene. Took her legs off. Screwed her. Lopped off both hands, head. She was thirteen."

"Name?"

"Jane Davidson. You'd better get on down there with a crew. Captain Hodges knows you're coming. He'll expect you to puke."

"Can I take Freddie for sound and Paul for camera?" she said.

"Take anyone you can find, babe . . . and good luck."

She hurried back to her cubicle. Three hours. A chain saw. A schoolgirl. It was almost enough, but not quite. It was touch-and-go she'd get Nightly. *She needed an angle. She picked up a telephone book, acutely aware that the crime scene would be cooling as the minutes ticked away and that the other stations would have this in the next half hour. There were lots of David-sons. Twenty-four, to be precise. But one of them lived on 14th Street. She picked up the telephone and dialed the number.*

The girl's mother actually picked it up. Herself. Rachel knew from the stunned silence at the other end of the line that she was through to the right person. She didn't think about what she was doing. She was on automatic pilot. A girl had died horribly, and it was her story, her own baby, and it was going out on Nightly *under her byline in just under three hours' time. She was vaguely aware of Matt standing at her shoulder as she talked fast into the telephone.*

"Mrs. Davidson? Is this the Mrs. Davidson whose daughter . . ."

"They killed my little girl," said Mrs. Davidson. She sounded matter-of-fact. She was still in shock.

"Look my name is Rachel Richardson. I'm a reporter for WLCN-TV here in Chicago. I know this is an impossibly terrible time for you, but I'd like you to hear me out . . ."

She caught Matt's eye. He looked away. His gesture said all sorts of things that Rachel couldn't allow herself to face. She heard herself talking into the mouthpiece as if her whole life

*depended on what she said. "Sometimes it helps to talk about
things . . . we have to catch this man . . . widest possible publicity for this dreadful man's crime . . . you can help others who
have felt the way you feel . . ." and on and on and on into the
ear of the deeply damaged Mrs. Davidson. All the time, the
refrain had gone around and around in her head, I want this
interview. I need this interview for* Nightly. *God give me this
scoop and I'll never ask for anything again.*

She put the telephone down and let out a sigh of relief.

"You get her?" said Matt.

"Yup," said Rachel, avoiding his eyes.

"Dirty work, but someone's got to do it."

*She didn't answer him. She couldn't answer him. There wasn't
time for thought or finer feelings. She made another couple of
calls. She sent a crew to the crime scene and she lined up another for the Davidson interview. Then she called the executive
producer's office at* Nightly *and told him what she had. He
passed her down the chain of command to the domestic-news
producer.*

*"Sounds good," said the domestic guy. "Chain saw and a
young girl, plus the sexual assault. We have dead Israeli soldiers
in a bus in the Middle East, but not much else. If you can get
an interview with the mother and tears, plus a picture of the
girl, you'd have a good chance for, say, two, maybe two and a
half minutes. So write it for both time spans. I'll alert the news
editor."*

*She had entered a pact with the devil for those few seconds
on* Nightly. *She had invaded the home of a woman whose life
had been hideously plunged into tragedy, and she had assaulted
her with the same callousness as the murderer had her child.
She had made sure the Davidson woman's face had filled the
viewfinder as the tears had rolled down her cheeks and the mascara had run, and her dyed blond hair had stuck to the sweat on
her face. She had walked from the room bearing the photograph
of the smiling, bucktoothed girl from the top of the TV and she
had lingered in the doorway and looked back at her own personal*

crime scene. Then she had looked at her watch, and all her finer feelings were placed in storage for later.

She had huddled by the WLCN van and scribbled the story that would go with the interview. The B-roll of the crime scene would already be on the way back to the station. "One, two, three." She had tested for sound level, and then the cameraman had switched on the lights and adjusted the lens on his CP-16.

"Richardson reporting. Davidson murder story. Mother's interview. Counting down, five, four, three, two, one . . . Today, Mrs. Marilyn Davidson, the mother of Jane Davidson, was overcome with grief as she talked to me about the brutal murder of her thirteen-year-old daughter . . ."

It was nearly over. The magazine was off the camera, the film unloaded into the can and sealed with gaffer's tape. Later, back at the station, the film edited and cleaned, the final steps were taken as the minutes ticked away to deadline. The precious film was loaded into the feed window to the Nightly *control room. Feed bars and tone. Film winding through the projector. Numbers show on leader. Countdown. "Today, Mrs. Marilyn Davidson . . . Rachel Richardson, WLCN-TV, Chicago." Rachel held her breath.* Nightly *was evaluating. Minutes later,* Nightly *gave technical buy. Nail-biting time. Then, what she needed to hear: "Nightly gives editorial buy." She was on. She'd done it, and all for just a little piece of her soul.*

"Hello," said Matt. "Hello!" in Billy Crystal style.

Rachel came out of the memory. "Oh," she said. "Sorry, I was miles away."

"Back in Chicago."

"Yes. That was a shitty thing I did that night. With the Davidson woman."

"But it got you the NBC correspondent job, and in the New York office. That was motoring for my weathergirl."

"Yup, it did, didn't it? Stepping-stones, I guess. I just wish the stepping-stones hadn't had to be dead bodies."

"I didn't want you to go then. I don't want you to go now," he said simply.

"I haven't gone. I'm here, aren't I?"

Rachel was still trying to shake the memories. Where had her humanity gone that night? If there had been an execution, would she have asked them to wait while the crew loaded the camera? She didn't need to be so ruthless now. That was one of the luxuries of success. But you didn't get there without dirty hands. She took a deep breath.

"And what may I get for you, madam?" said the waiter in welcome diversion.

She ordered the flattened poached salmon in the cheese and champagne sauce, and then some rognons de veau. Matt had the same, and asked for a bottle of Musigny Comte Georges de Vogüé '61. Rachel had ordered it once herself and knew that it was priced at $675 a bottle. Life with Matt would be very far from humble.

"We had some good times," said Matt with a smile. "It wasn't all blue murder. You remember Mariel Murray, and that night she got drunk on the air?"

Rachel laughed. "And I sat in for her, and you could hear her screaming off the set, 'The bitch can't read diddly squat! The bitch can't read diddly squat!' Every time I read a monitor now, my subconscious is listening for poor old Mariel. I wonder what happened to her." Rachel shook her head and laughed at the memory of a situation that hadn't seemed remotely funny at the time.

"She married a policeman. I would never speed in the city limits after I fired her," said Matt.

"You tried to fire me."

"And now I'm trying to marry you."

"Well, you did give me my start in TV." Rachel laughed to show it was a joke, but, like all jokes, it had a serious side. She did feel enormously grateful to Matt. There hadn't been a stage in her career when he had not been there for her, at NBC, working for Barbara on *20/20*, the interlude as a speechwriter in the

Reagan White House. His business career had taken off not long after she had left WLCN and Chicago for the glories of New York and Rockefeller Plaza, and Matt had zoomed into the business spotlight while she had painstakingly put together her career in TV journalism. Occasionally, they had met and talked, and he had given her advice and even intervened a couple of times when office politics turned against her. But it hadn't been until she had her own show and become *the* Rachel Richardson that he had wanted to swap his role in her life from trusted mentor and benefactor to husband.

She didn't hold that against him. What you did changed who you were. More important, it changed who you wanted to be, and, of course, it changed who wanted you.

"So what was the Hacienda Inn like?" said Matt, persevering with his earlier question.

"Oh, you know, spa-di-da. Once you've had one guava-and-passion-fruit body-bath, you've had them all."

"Actually, it's supposed to be quite an interesting place. Part-owned by an interesting guy. Charles Ford. You wouldn't have seen him down there. He's something of a recluse. A painter. Damn good one. Sells through Wardlow. I've been trying to get him to meet up with me for months, but he's not interested. I want to get some of his stuff, but I like to meet the artist first, see if they've got staying power. Maybe I should get you to sniff him out for me—Rachel, what's the matter?"

"Nothing," said Rachel far too quickly.

But something was. All the feelings she had waited for when Matt had told her he wanted to marry her were happening now. Charles's name had released that emotion. She felt herself flush a deep beet-red.

She babbled on. "It's just that I've remembered something. Steve asked me to look into something and I completely forgot. I *promised*. He'll be furious." Rachel had surprised herself. She didn't lie. That one had slipped out all by itself.

"I'm glad my art-collector sob story caught your interest so thoroughly," said Matt with a smile to say he didn't mind, that he accepted that Rachel's career would always be number one, and that he wanted it that way.

The blush was fading. Rachel took a deep breath.

"You want to get to a phone now?"

"Yes, I should."

The idea came to her suddenly. She had to get out of this lunch. During it, she had experienced a moment of truth. The mere mention of Charles Ford's name had let loose a torrent of feeling, yet the latest in the long line of Matt's marriage proposals had left her untouched by emotion. She needed time to think, and she needed it right now.

"Look, Matt, I'm afraid a telephone call isn't going to cut it. I *could* sort things out on the phone, but not very well. Would you mind terribly if I went back to the office and we did this another day?"

He looked stricken.

"You know how you like me to be professional," she said quickly, reaching out to touch his hand. "Isn't that part of what you love about me?"

He nodded. It was.

"Darling, of course, go. I would, if a deal crisis blew up. I'm just disappointed, that's all."

Rachel got up, and Matt stood, too. He walked her to the door. Mario hovered, looking worried.

"Another time, Mario. Ms. Richardson's business calls."

"Ah, very busy, Ms. Richardson," said Mario, relieved.

On the sidewalk, she kissed him goodbye before clambering into a taxi. "I'm so sorry, Matt," she said.

"No problem. No problem," he replied. But he couldn't escape the thought. Something strange had happened to Rachel at the Hacienda Inn.

Nineteen

Charles Ford walked into the bookshop. For a second he worried that someone else might have bought it. Nobody had. *The Glass House* sat on the table where Tessa had left it. He picked it up and flicked through it as they had done together. The memories felt good. He went to the front and paid for it.

"Wonderful book, Mr. Ford," said the salesclerk.

"Yes, yes," he agreed absentmindedly.

He was thinking about the inscription.

He took the book from the bag and laid it on the counter.

"May I borrow a pen?" he asked.

The title page stared up at him.

"To Tessa," he wrote. That was the easy part.

"Who is both brave and beautiful. Yours, Charles Ford." That wasn't so difficult either.

He closed the book.

He had intended to ring the doorbell of her building, but when he tried the door, it was open. He walked up the dusty stairs to the third floor apartment marked "Tessa Andersen." He rang the bell. There was no answer. He propped the book against the door and retreated. He felt strangely elated, a little furtive. It reminded him of younger days, days of unpredictability, when people were exciting events that happened to you rather than mannered rituals, security, or irritation.

On Madison, the cold wind blew over him and the people hurried by. He felt movement in his life. At home, at the ranch, an artist was painting in Rose's studio. And somewhere out there was a courageous woman of great beauty who would return to a book she had wanted. And there had been another one, stranger than the others but more fleeting, a woman in the night who had stood there in the lobby of the Hacienda Inn and watched him in a way that he had never been watched before.

The memory of that brief encounter lingered on. Why? Something in her expression. Some intense vitality, some peculiar promise that had been impossible to ignore. Three women, each special, all beautiful.

For the first time in a long, long time, Charles felt alive.

Twenty

"Okay, ladies, gentlemen. *Richardson Show* editorial meeting. Counting down, four, three, two, one. And . . . Good morning, everyone . . ."

Rachel was in a playful mood. She often was when Steve was away on vacation, although, paradoxically, she missed his brilliant if acerbic observations. She looked down the old wood table that pretended to signify a boardroom. Out there in televisionland, they wouldn't believe how ordinary it all was, the threadbare green carpet, the notice boards on the wall shedding a dandruff of brightly colored messages and memos, the utilitarian chairs. The team around the table didn't look like much: a gaggle of secretaries nursing their steaming Styrofoam cups of coffee and dreaming of boyfriends and manicures? Oh, no! These were the cutting-edge production assistants, researchers, and bookers who made *The Rachel Richardson Show* the success it was, and today they had a guest.

"I want to introduce Celeste Ritter from *People* magazine. She is going to be sitting in on our operations for the next day or two so that she can write a brilliantly kind puff piece profiling . . . *moi.*" Rachel laughed as she struck a pose.

"Isn't sarcasm supposed to be the lowest form of wit?" said Jake with a smile. He was allowed to get away with remarks like that.

There was general laughter, touched with an edge of nervousness. *People* reporters had a reputation for stitching up celebrities. Rachel remembered the incredible furor when *People*'s Cheryl McCall had covered the Barbara Walters special on Willie Nelson. An insider at *Time* had leaked the poisonous article to Barbara and she had wheeled in *Time*'s head honcho, her friend Henry Grunwald, to try, unsuccessfully, to suppress the story.

Now Rachel paraphrased the famous and controversial commandment laid on President-elect Jimmy Carter by her *20/20* mentor when she had interviewed him.

"Be wise with us, Celeste, be good to us."

"I'll be fair," said the journalist, aware that it was a mildly discouraging word.

"Anyway," said Rachel more briskly. "We just get on with business as usual and Celeste scribbles away in the background."

Knowing glances were exchanged. Hard news journalists of the old school, like Rachel, had little time for gossipy magazines like *People* or the journalists who worked for them.

"I want to discuss our art program. Jenny, you were keeping it warm, weren't you? We had those two hotshot artists from Holly Solomon. Pritikin and Prntkin, or whatever."

"Sue Etkin and Izhar Patkin."

"I *knew* that," said Rachel with a laugh. She did. "Well, I think the time is now, or at least the time is soon. Art is hotting up. Warhol's *Shot Red Marilyn* resold for three point six million. That's a few hundred thousand less than it made in 1989 at the height of the art market. The old Reagan materialist artists are making records again: Basquiat, Clemente, and all the usual suspects. I think we should do a state-of-the-art-market piece, singling out the ones to watch, taking the pulse of the gallery scene, et cetera."

"You don't think it's a bit elitist?" said Mary, the assistant producer.

"All human life is here," said Rachel. "That's the point of my show. If you go slavishly for ratings, you end up in the gutter with everyone else. Maybe we all *are* in the gutter, but at least some of us are looking at the stars."

She glanced over at the *People* girl. Good, she was writing that down.

"It probably needs something of an angle," said Jake gently.

That was what Steve would have said, thought Rachel. Only he would have added, "How do you think we can keep boredom to a minimum on this one?"

"I think so, too," she said.

There was a point to all this.

"I suppose some of you have heard of Charles Ford . . . ," she went on, looking down at the blank yellow legal pad in front of her.

"I have," said Jake with a slow smile. He knew her so well.

". . . He's a very fine, well respected figurative artist, a bit of a recluse. Lives and works near Santa Fe. He's with Wardlow, and Wardlow thinks he's really good. The point is, he's mainstream. That makes him a contrast to the other two, but he's still thought trendy among the cognoscenti, although he would hate the idea of being thought trendy."

She looked up. They looked back at her: Yes? Go on. There were I-haven't-got-the-point-yet expressions on their faces.

She stopped short. Somehow, she had imagined the Charles Ford name would have had the same effect on them as uttering it had on her. Only Jake seemed to be aware of the undercurrents.

"Well, anyway, he appears to be suffering from creative block. I thought that would be an interesting thing to explore in an interview. To some extent we all suffer from it. What to write in a letter. How to say something in a speech. How to make up a bedtime story for a child. Painters and novelists might represent creative block in capital letters, but it's every man and woman's problem, too."

"And one hell of a lot of people do creative work, even if it's a regular type of job, an ad copywriter, a journalist against a deadline, a graphic designer," said Jake, pitching in.

The *People* reporter looked up. "Would you mind my asking how you heard about Ford's block? I imagine it's not something an artist shouts about from the rooftops."

Mmmmm. Shrewdini, thought Rachel.

"We don't reveal our sources, do we?" she said.

Wardlow had told Matt Harding, and he had told Rachel.

"So, basically, I thought we could get Etkin and Patkin on film painting their pictures, then do some B-rolls at a gallery opening, say Solomon or Wardlow. We do some live interviews about what's happening in the art market and I cap it with an in-depth one-on-one with Ford. I get into his block and what caused it . . . The death of his girlfriend, I think. That should throw off quite a bit of emotion. So the show is about what's happening, what's new and now, how to turn a buck by investing in these up-and-comers. There's glamour at a gallery party with lots of pretty, interesting people and some meaty motivation stuff with psychic pain to round it off. You know the pitch: you might think being a painter is easy, but underneath, it's hard as hell, like staying on top in our business."

"You thinking a half hour?" said Mary.

"Yes. I don't think it would hold the hour."

"Well, Sue and Izhar are standing by," said Jenny. "The galleries are thrilled and will fit in with any plans we have. Solomon says they'll put on a private show for us of the in-house work they have for both artists. That way you can see it personally, Rachel. I knew you'd like to do that. We have mountains of reviews for you to go through. And we've taped pre-interviews with the artists. Of course, we have nothing on Ford yet, because he's only just entered the equation. Do you want me to start work on him?"

"I have quite a bit on him," said Rachel, trying to keep her expression neutral. "Jake did a computer profile and got all the clippings together. He has a reputation for being a bit tricky, mediawise. Contact him through Wardlow, and be nonspecific. Would he be interested in doing a program about the art market today, his opinions on art, his work . . . very general stuff. No mention at all of block, okay?"

"Shall I tell him who the other artists are?"

"Not finalized yet. He might not like them."

"When are you aiming for this?" said Jake.

"Let's get Ford first." Rachel stood up. "Look, there are a ton of other things, and I'd like to get back to them, but I promised Celeste a bit of time alone. Can you carry on without me? Then Celeste and I can roam around and do some work. Jenny, you get onto Ford right away, okay? If he doesn't buy it, I'll handle it myself. Just do your best."

The *People* reporter stood up, too.

"Sounds like you make all the decisions," she said as they walked out.

"Steve Bloch, my exec producer, is on vacation," said Rachel. "He's a co-equal, to put it mildly. Actually, I miss him when he's gone. I need the foil to play against. He keeps me sharp."

"Creative tension?"

"Yup. Absolute power can corrupt one's Nielsens. Steve is like the guy at the back of the chariot at a Roman triumph, muttering 'Remember thou art but a woman.' Only he isn't quite as reverent as that."

"In case of disagreement, it must be useful to have Matt Harding on one's side," said Celeste, sliding into it.

"I'm professional enough to keep my private life and my work life separate," said Rachel. There was an edge to her voice. Oh, yes. Charles Ford. Oh, for sure, Ms. Professional!

"But wasn't Matt part of your work life in the early days?"

"Yes, he was manager at the station in Chicago where I started as weathergirl *with* my M.A. from Smith. He was negotiating to buy the station in those days. We started around the same time."

"But went in different directions?"

"We sure did," said Rachel.

"Here," said Rachel. "Meet the control room. It's pretty quiet in here at this time of the morning." She was right. The room was empty, but the banks of TV screens were switched on. Each screen displayed a different angle and a different focal length of an eerily empty set.

She flopped down in a chair. The reporter did the same.

"Yours was a pretty traditional ascent up the ladder until you branched out with this show?"

"Yup. I was on my way to *Evening News* anchor person, and then I got waylaid. I got lucky with a murder when I was reporting for Matt's station, and I bypassed the traditional domestic bureau job and went straight to NBC in New York. Then I did my statutory Washington bit, but as a Reagan speechwriter rather than covering State, White House, or the Pentagon. I did Paris and London, and then Barbara made me an offer I couldn't refuse, and that was *20/20.*"

"Reagan speechwriter sounds weird."

"It was wonderful. I had this office in the old executive building, first floor, corner, room 115. I could see the Washington Monument, the Jefferson Memorial, and the Corcoran Gallery out of my window. I had a pass to the White House Mess, courtesy of an affair with a lawyer at OMB," she laughed, wide open, not caring what she gave away about her personal life. "You know, you could pick up a really good steak dinner for under five bucks, and everyone who was anyone in Washington used to eat there."

"What about Barbara Walters? That must have been a learning experience." The *People* reporter rolled her eyes upward.

"Oh, yes, Barbara. She was the pioneer. She fought all our battles for us. The men lined up to do her down: Reasoner, Morley Safer, Chancellor, Brinkley, Cronkite. Even Connie Chung put the boot in on her. But she got them back. Because the public loved to watch her, and the public, thank God, are never wrong, especially about television."

"Walters had her own style of interviewing, with all those open-ended 'If you could be anybody in history, who would you be?'-type questions. Yours is distinct, too. How would you characterize it?" said Celeste.

"You can't really categorize it, but I'll tell you the vital ingredients. Number one: Be prepared. Know the subject inside out. That was a lesson from Barbara. I always try to do some research myself, however many research assistants are working on a show.

That gives me 'attack.' You have to have good eye contact, and you have to listen. That's vital. You have to be interested. Let people talk about themselves and find the subject on which they are expert. Everyone's an expert on something. Newt Gingrich is an amateur zoologist. He just loves to talk about animals and often says that he would have liked to be the director of a zoo. You don't expect a right-wing Republican to be interested in that. What else? Okay. Ask lots of 'why' questions, and never, ever, ask a question that can be answered yes or no. Never ask, 'Was that the first time you confronted failure?' Instead, you have to say, 'What did it feel like to fail?' Or better, 'Why do you think you failed?' 'Why' questions are what it's all about."

"What is the most important thing?"

"To like people. Or to find something about each person to like. I think that's the key. I love people. I think it comes across. People will forgive you anything if you have love in your heart. You can ask the toughest questions and they will answer them. They won't hold it against you if you are warm and you have enthusiasm, curiosity, and are able to laugh, especially at yourself. I constantly reveal bits of myself, private bits of myself, on the screen. I'm asking others to do it, so I set an example. It's part of being yourself and not being ashamed of yourself. Self-respect is contagious. It puts people at ease. Look at Oprah's empathy. She says she was an abused child, she lets rip with her weight problem, she goes on about Steadman and her girlfriends. She's *accessible*. She's like a friend. That's why she is the biggest star on television and it's why she deserves to be."

"Does it help to choose good guests?"

"Oh, yes, it does. The best guests are passionate, articulate, funny, and have a great big chip on their shoulders."

"A chip?"

"Yes. People like Von Bülow, dark and mysterious yet charming and urbane. Beatty, tricky as hell but fascinating. Dolly Parton, with her hatred of her own cartoon image. Guests are the key. They can make or break you. I once had a plane crash survivor, and nobody told me he was deaf. I broke the 'Never let them see you sweat' rule that time! Sammy Davis did me up with monosyllables one night, and I never found out why. And do you know, Warren always brings his own lighting man? Well, he looked like a million dollars, but his tungsten spillover lit me like a horror movie. See Rachel's crow's-feet! Fall into the hollow craters of her eyes! Cackle in the creases of her laugh lines!"

Rachel laughed happily at the memory. There was a knock on the door. It was Jenny, whose job it had been to deliver Charles Ford.

"I talked to him in Santa Fe," she said. She looked a little pale. "He said no way."

"That's all?"

"He sort of explained why."

"Why?"

"Well, lots of stuff about the painting saying it all; words confusing the issue; TV shows always having their own point of view and to hell with what the guest wants or thinks."

"Was he rude?"

"I don't *think* so," said Jenny. "Not quite."

"But rather brusque."

"Very!"

"Well, thanks for trying. I'll get to work on it myself."

"What will you do?" said Celeste after Jenny had gone.

"Oh, soft-soap him. Allay his fears, whatever they are."

"And then do the show you want to do anyway, whether he likes it or not."

"Isn't that the way you do your journalism? Is there another way I don't know about?"

"No. I was just asking," said Celeste with the innocence of an asp. She changed the subject. "What happens when career comes up against personal life? That must happen sometimes. With Matt Harding, maybe."

"Career wins," said Rachel without hesitation. But suddenly she was not so sure.

Her mind was drifting away from this interview.

The reporter brought her back.

"What would you say your show's format is? It seems pretty eclectic, hard to pin down."

"It's meant to be. That's the format. Basically, the show is Rachel Richardson. It's not an audience show, an interview show, a roundtable conference thing, or a *20/20, 60 Minutes* film-clip magazine. It's all of them, and none of them. I use the format that best fits the subject. I might walk from a hard-nosed one-on-one interview with a politician to an audience discussing something like marital infidelity, but *not* lesbian deadbeat dads. I'm the thread that links the one with the other. God knows why it works, but it does. At least nobody can say it's derivative. I just try new things and watch the ratings, and so far most everything seems to work."

"It certainly seems . . ."

"Look, Celeste, would you mind if we wrapped this up for now? There's a couple of things I need to do pretty urgently."

"No problem, Rachel. Thanks for the time. It was great. Lots of good insights. Good luck with the Ford guy."

Was there a hint of a smile around the reporter's mouth when she said that?

A couple of things! Right!

In her office, Rachel hitched her feet up onto the desk, while the switchboard found Wardlow's number.

"Harry? Rachel Richardson. How are you? No, not since Tina Brown's thing. Oh, quiet. Quiet. Listen, have you heard that we're trying to get your Charles Ford for a show we're doing on up-to-the-minute art?"

"He just called me from Santa Fe. Said he'd said no. That's my Charles, I'm afraid. You don't know him, do you? I'm afraid he won't play the game. Drives me crazy. But that's it."

"It was silly of me to have put a booker onto it. The thing is, it would only be good for him. I just want to say he's hot. And I wanted to B-roll a gallery opening of yours and have you say a few words about the state of the downtown art market, since you're the guru down there. It would be just you and Holly Solomon and a couple of her artists. Good company, no?"

"Ah, Rachel, the persuasive charms of an intelligent and beautiful woman . . ."

"Are lost on you, dear. Don't remind me."

"Listen, I'd love you to send a crew down here anytime."

"But I want Charles Ford."

"Has to be Charles Ford? Not Effingham or Koller? They're both coming on strong. Very interesting. Very articulate. More accessible, dear."

"No, I've set my heart on Ford."

"You like his Indians?"

"Yes. Very much."

"Do you mind my asking why?" God, he was shrewd. So was she.

"Because, although they are figurative, they capture the spirituality of the subject matter. The Indians sweeping the road in the later works transcend their surroundings. They are as proud and majestic as the earlier ones with their headdresses and all the period grandeur. I think Ford can put feeling into faces in a way no other painter can match. There is a mysticism, an abstraction about his work, and yet he paints reality in a way that people can understand."

"Goodness, would you be interested in having a go at writing my catalogues?"

"Listen, sweetheart, I've done speeches for Reagan. I can do T-shirts. I can do your catalogues."

"So it does sound as if it has to be Ford."

"Oh, yes, it does.".

"How's Matt Harding?"

"Fine. How's about I get to do Ford?"

"Well, yes, mmmmm, let me see what the calendar looks like. Ah, yes. Well, it just so happens that I am having a mixed show on the fourteenth, and Charles will be coming to that. He has work in the show, and I've been quite successful at prizing him out of his shell recently."

"He's a definite?"

"He promised."

"So I can come down with a crew and do my thing?"

"Yes, you can. That would be very fine."

"And I get to buttonhole Charles Ford?"

"Don't say I talked to you about it, okay? You can have a go at him, but I'm not promising he'll deliver."

"Oh, I expect he will," said Rachel, as the rush of excitement ran through her. "They usually do."

Twenty-one

Tessa could hear the phone ringing from the bottom of the stairs.

"Oh, *shit*," she said. Her arms were full of the endless shopping that was the great downside of being disorganized in New York. The trouble was, she distinctly remembered forgetting to switch on the answering machine. She started to run. Tessa hit the top landing. The telephone warbled on. Whoever it was wanted to speak to her badly. She dropped the shopping. Damn! When she eventually opened the Cokes, they would go off like fire extinguishers.

She opened the door and ran for the phone. And, of course, it stopped. But Tessa didn't. She put one foot on Camille's miniature wheelbarrow and the other foot continued as if nothing had happened. Camille, you are dead meat, she had time to think as she sailed through the air and landed on the floor with a resounding crash. She slid for two feet and ended up on her back, inches from the suddenly silent telephone. Tessa laughed. She hadn't hurt herself, but the lesson had been learned. Those who didn't usually run for telephones should never start.

The telephone rang again.

She reached up, still lying on the floor, and picked it up.

"Could I speak with Ms. Tessa Andersen?"

A business call. "Speaking."

"I have Mr. George Westchester for you. Please hold the line."

Damn, thought Tessa, what did he want? He ran Sotheby's

Realty. That made him technically her boss. She waited. Still the line remained quiet. She looked at her watch. It was three forty-five. He would just have returned from his boozy lunch.

At last there was a voice on the line.

"Tessa? George. Sorry for hanging you about. How are you?"

"Well. Looking forward to Monday."

"Yes." He coughed. "It was about Monday that I wanted to talk to you. I've been having a few words with my directors, and frankly, I've run into some feelings that I hadn't really anticipated."

"Like what, George?"

Slowly, Tessa picked herself up from the floor. This already had the sound of a conversation that shouldn't be taken lying down.

"Well, basically, it's vis-à-vis Pete, and Pete's, er . . . Pete's . . . well, his legacy."

"His 'legacy' meaning that there was money missing from the company."

"Precisely."

"It hasn't exactly been a secret," said Tessa. She could feel the anger rising in her. She knew what was coming.

"Of course not, and for me, personally, it's hardly an issue. Not a big issue. These things happen. There but for fortune . . . However, it seems I have misjudged other people's reactions. I need hardly tell you that real estate is a confidence business."

"Nobody accused *me* of anything," said Tessa.

"Of course they didn't. And nobody is, Tessa. It's just that . . . well, there's a feeling that it reflects . . . that it doesn't reflect too brilliantly on Sotheby's to hire you when Pete possibly . . . Well . . . you know what I mean."

"George, Pete has been gone for a year. He's dead. I've been doing this course for six months. I've got my license. All that time I had this job. I start work next week. Are you trying to tell me you don't want me after all?"

"It's not me, Tessa. You know that. It's just that I misjudged the prevailing opinion. I should have taken soundings earlier. I just didn't anticipate this opposition."

"Can't you override it, if it's not something you're worried about? Aren't you the headman there?"

Tessa could feel the sarcasm filtering into her words. Westchester was British, but Rugby, not Eton. Brooks, not Whites. It was rumored that at Cambridge he'd been at Sidney Sussex, a college that didn't count.

"It's n-not really up to m-me," stuttered Westchester.

"Listen, George, I can put up with anything but bullshit. Do I start on Monday or not? Yes or no?"

"Um, well, it's . . . I'm afraid it's sort of no."

"Well, then, sort of goodbye," said Tessa, and she banged the telephone down.

Tessa thought for a minute. She could either cry or do something. The idea occurred to her immediately. She remembered the last night at the Inn. Rachel Richardson's words came back to her. "We'll be there for each other just like the damned men are." She picked up the phone. She would soon find out if female networking was a reality.

In seconds, she was through to Rachel Richardson.

"Rachel, it's Tessa."

"Tess! Goodness, how great to hear from you! The Hacienda Inn seems like light-years away. I felt terrible about running out without saying goodbye, but I just had this uncontrollable feeling that I'd had enough. I just had to get back to work."

"I felt exactly the same way. I left that morning, and since then I've been running around like a blue-assed fly trying to get things together."

"Me, too. How's it going? How's Camille?"

"Oh, she's wonderful, as always. Otherwise, things are a bit of a mess."

"Like how? Are you all right?" Rachel picked up on Tessa's subdued mood.

"Yup. I just had a piece of bad news."

"What?"

"I just talked to Westchester, the head guy at Sotheby's. He's fired me even before I started."

"Why? He can't do that."

"Oh, Pete, and the collapse of the business. He says his directors think it's bad for the firm's image to hire the wife of somebody who left a mess like that. You know, the guilt-by-association thing."

Rachel paused for a second. "That's George Westchester, isn't it?"

"Yes, the bastard. He had six months to practice his bloody hypocrisy, and the common little man waits until now. I was absolutely counting on the job."

"Did you have an employment contract . . . anything in writing?"

"No. Just a gentleman's agreement."

"A verbal contract," said Rachel, half to herself. It would be difficult to prove. And incredibly expensive. Litigation was a no-no.

Sotheby's. What did she have on Sotheby's? Wait a minute . . . Yes, that might do it.

"Listen, Tessa. Give me an hour or so. I'll get back to you. Don't give up on it just yet. I'll call you back in an hour. Okay. Love ya. Keep your pecker up."

Damn it to hell. Tessa flopped down on the sofa. She had never expected this to be easy, but she hadn't expected this kind of difficulty.

Suddenly, she remembered Camille. She was staying over with Sissy. She picked up the phone. The Polks' social secretary answered.

"Oh, Mrs. Andersen. I'm so glad you called. Mrs. Polk asked me to call and find out if Camille could stay again tonight. Sissy and she are having such a blast, and Nanny says they're playing really well together."

"Is Mrs. Polk there?" said Tessa. It was good news that Camille hadn't strangled anyone or, more important, broken any of the famous Polk Ming.

"I'm afraid she had to go to the hairdresser."

"What about Nanny?"

"I'll put you through to the nursery."

"This is Nanny Polk," said Nanny in firm British tones. Tessa relaxed. This was a proper nanny. Tessa had never talked to her before, but already she knew her better than most of the friends she had made in America.

"Oh, hello, Nanny. I'm Mrs. Andersen, Camille's mummy. How are they getting on?"

"Oh, hello, Mrs. Andersen. Very well indeed. No tears. No tantrums. And they ate their plates clean like good little girls."

Manners and appetites. There wasn't much else to report in an English nursery. She could picture the room— its pastel pinks, the toys and dolls lined up like soldiers on a battlefield, everything in its place, the warm baby-oiled air thick with peace and security. Nanny would be in a uniform. She would be fifty-five if she was a day, and kindness and strictness would exist in equal proportions in every bone of her body. The funny thing was, the children loved the discipline. It made them feel safe and wanted.

"Would you like to have a word with her, Mrs. Andersen? She's painting a beautiful picture for you. Sunflowers, I think they are."

"Yes, please, Nanny."

"Mummy! Mummy! Can I stay tonight? Please, Mummy, oh, please say yes."

"Yes, darling, of course you can. Are you being a good girl? Are you doing what Nanny tells you?"

"Yes. Yes, and Mummy, Nanny taught us how to bake a cake, and how to cut out *gorgeous* gingerbread men; and tonight we're going to put on a play for Sissy's mummy, and I get to be a ballerina and Sissy is the prince, I think, or Nanny is. I'm not quite sure about that."

Tessa could feel the happiness down the line. It was all but tangible.

"Darling, can I have another word with Nanny?"

" 'Bye, Mummy. I love you lots and lots and lots, all the grains of sand on the beach."

"Mrs. Andersen?"

"Oh, Nanny, thank you so much for looking after Camille and having her for another night. She sounds as if she's having a wonderful time."

"She's a very well behaved little girl, and considerate of others." In nannyspeak, that was the ultimate praise.

"I'll call in the morning. 'Bye, Nanny."

"Bye-bye, Mrs. Andersen."

Tessa put down the phone.

Camille was safe and happy, but her own world had just fallen apart.

Twenty-two

George Westchester's digestive system was recovering from the unpleasant business of firing Tessa Andersen shortly before hiring her. He had eaten well at the Four Seasons, and treated himself to a couple of after-lunch Kümmels on the rocks. Those, with the chicken Kiev and the telephone conversation, had given him heartburn. Now he felt a little better. Possibly he wouldn't need the Pepto-Bismol after all.

He settled back in the leather chair behind the big polished partners desk, and he wondered if he closed his eyes he might catch twenty minutes of sleep. That would set him up tremendously well for the rest of the day.

His secretary had other ideas.

"Sir, I have a producer from *The Rachel Richardson Show* on the line for you. Are you in?"

Only just, thought Westchester. Shit. What do they want?

"Put him through."

"I have a Jennifer DiMaio for you. She's the senior research coordinator and assistant producer."

"Is she?" said Westchester, deeply unimpressed.

"George Westchester speaking," he said. "And how can I help one of my favorite television programs?"

"Thank you," said DiMaio briskly. "Mr. Westchester, perhaps you can help us. We are researching a couple of quite different programs, and you might be of help in each of them. First, you are obviously aware of the continuing weakness of

the art market. Things are getting better, but they're not back
to the good old days of the late eighties."

"Yes, I would agree with that. Not my area of expertise, of
course. I run the real estate operation."

"Precisely. Well, you must also be aware that Sotheby's and
Christie's have gone into the banking business to some extent
by advancing loans to potential clients to buy works of art at
auction. That is, the house gets a buyer's commission and a
seller's commission on a picture that might not otherwise have
sold. Also, of course, they receive interest on the loan and they
take an introduction fee for making it. They take a charge over
the painting as security for their loan."

Westchester paused. It was accepted practice, but it had been
criticized by some as involving a conflict of interest.

"Now, we have learned that in some cases, your firm has
advanced up to one hundred percent of the value of pictures
bought, and has asked their clients to pledge additional security
for the loans. That additional security has been, in several cases
we are aware of, real estate."

Westchester felt the trouble beginning in the pit of his stomach. There was a thunderous rumble, and a great rush of regur-
gitated wind hurried into the back of his mouth.

"What we wanted to discuss with you was the valuation of
that real estate—what those valuations were, who did them, and
what was the charge for those valuations. Could I have your
comments thus far?" said DiMaio, as if administering the coup
de grâce.

"That," said Westchester, his voice half strangled by his own
flatulence, "would be private business information."

"Not after it's aired on *The Rachel Richardson Show,* it won't
be," said DiMaio.

"Just one moment," said Westchester. Sotheby's art business
and its real estate operation had traditionally been separated by
a Chinese wall to avoid conflict of interest. Recently, his real
estate operation had been valuing the properties of potential art
buyers and charging a commission for doing so. This had en-

abled them to come up with collateral for loans and to pay top dollar for art, thus supporting the art market and restoring much-needed momentum to art sales. It was a questionable practice, but an enormously profitable one.

"You have chapter and verse on this?" he continued cautiously.

"Affidavits," said DiMaio.

"Oh, dear," said Westchester. "At this point I'd better say no more, but refer you to my attorneys . . ."

"That may not be necessary," said DiMaio. "I'd like you to have a word with Rachel herself."

Westchester cleared his throat and tried to clear his mind. He should never have had that second Kümmel.

"Rachel Richardson speaking."

"I'm a great admirer . . ."

"The other leg is this," said Rachel, talking fast, as if to some lesser species. "We always have a program on the burner about women in the workplace, and how they get victimized, underpaid, harassed, not given time off to have children, you name it. Now, I have just had a call from Tessa Andersen. You know her, yes?"

"Yes, a very unfortunate and delicate situation—"

She cut him off at the knees.

"To do with the good name and reputation of your firm."

"Exactly. For myself, I have no objections—"

"And that good name and reputation would not be greatly added to by publication of the items that Ms. DiMaio has just been talking to you about."

There it was. The deal. In America there always was one. Westchester had lived in the U.S. long enough to know that.

"So if, ah, some way could be found to reinstate Ms. Andersen, then possibly a way could be found not to publicize the alleged . . . business—"

"You've got it," said Rachel.

"Can I get back to you, Ms. Richardson?"

"I'll give you two hours."

"Thank you," he said. Rachel had hung up on him.

He pulled out a big red handkerchief and mopped his brow. He didn't need two hours. He didn't need two minutes. Tessa Andersen had just got her job back.

Twenty-three

The snow flaked down on the windshield of Rachel's limo as it nosed down Mercer Street. Outside the Wardlow Gallery, the high-end cars deposited high-end people onto a sidewalk already snow white, and they scurried up the steps into the warmth. It was raw here, Rachel had time to think . . . the alleyways stinking of tomcats, the gutters overflowing with detritus from the day's hustle, piles of unwanted newspapers bundled and rotting on street corners. A grill in the street hissed steam, and from the four floors of the brightly lit gallery, noisy laughter and conversation merged with the sounds of a reggae band. Rachel saw the van in which her crew had arrived earlier. Good. They would be hard at work inside. Rachel would be free to concentrate on the main event, finding Charles Ford. She checked herself in her compact. She looked okay, but maybe she was wearing a tad too little makeup. She was pale. He would be dark from the desert. God, how quickly New York devoured a tan. It made ghosts of everyone. The driver pulled up outside the gallery. She got out and stood at the bottom of the steps. Was he in there already? Almost certainly. She was late, as she had intended to be. She took a deep breath, aware of the drama she was creating, and wanting it to be dramatic. She knew it was ridiculous. Here was Rachel Richardson, one of the most experienced journalists in America, feeling just like a school-girl. But the so-called ridiculous felt weirdly wonderful, and, of course, that was what it was all about.

Jenny stood at the top of the steps to the gallery, waiting for her.

"Hi, Jen, how's it going?"

"Fabulous. Wardlow's done a fashion as art-type thing. Lots of Ritts and Weber photographs, and a load of great-looking girls. Wardlow says it's a performance exhibit. He makes a pretty good case. It's great for us. Very visual. Nice tension between the bohemians and the suits. We've got a ton of B-roll."

"Great, Jen. Where's Charles Ford? Did he show?"

"Yes, actually, I did," said a voice at her shoulder.

She spun around. He stood there, wrapped against the cold in a classic navy-blue double-breasted coat. A brown cashmere scarf was wrapped tightly around his neck. His head moved back as he saw her, instant recognition in his deep-set eyes.

"I know you," he said.

Rachel had little time to recover from the shock of seeing him, and from the realization that already she had given away her reason for being there.

"It was a brief meeting," she said. "How clever of you to remember."

"You were in the lobby at the Inn," he added. He seemed to be trying to make sense of it. "Who are you? How did you know I was going to be here?" Then he answered his own question. "I know who you are. You're Rachel Richardson." He paused. "The famous person."

She laughed with relief. What a funny thing for someone to say. He seemed as confused as she. For some reason, that was good.

At the top of the stairs, Jenny wondered what was happening. This was apparently the Charles Ford they wanted for the show. Why was there so much embarrassment in the chill night air? Why was Rachel blushing? Where had her legendary control gone?

"Is that what I am, the famous person? Then you must be the rich, reclusive artist who refused to appear on my show."

He half smiled, like a sly wolf. He was regaining his com-
posure.

"I think I get the picture," he said. "You want me for some
chat show about art. I said no, and you're not the sort of person
who takes no for an answer. You found out I was going to be
here, and here you are."

"Is that devious of me?"

She smiled warily. This could go either way. Her stomach
felt deliciously strange. He looked more human than he had in
the Hacienda Inn, but just as exciting.

"I imagine successful journalists have to be devious."

"Look," she said. "Can we sort of actually *meet?*" She thrust
out a gloved hand at him. "I'm Rachel Richardson. And you're
Charles Ford. I hope we haven't gotten off to a disastrous start."

He took her hand in his black-leather-gloved one. He held it
firmly while looking into her eyes.

"No," he said, shaking his head in emphasis. His eyes roamed
over her face. He seemed to be taking a complicated inventory
of her visible anatomy.

He didn't let go of her hand. She didn't try to take it back.
She wished that they weren't both wearing gloves. His eyes
continued to devour her. She had to laugh at the openness of
it. He seemed hardly socialized at all, a most potent form of
charm. For a single second she wondered if he might pick her
up, put her over his shoulder, and simply carry her away to his
waiting horse.

"Is my lipstick smudged or something?" she said.

"No. Why? Oh, you mean I'm staring, am I?"

At the top of the stairs Jenny said, "I'll catch you inside,
Rachel," and fled.

Rachel was neither surprised nor sorry to see her go.

With the hand that wasn't holding hers, Charles reached up
and tugged at his ear. Then he let go of her hand.

He gestured toward the retreating production assistant.

"Are you going inside with your friend?" he said.

"Are *you* going inside? It was you I came to see."

"Not the art?

"No, you." She felt amazingly brave.

The conversation had turned full circle. Rachel experienced a strong feeling of surreality.

He looked up at the window of the gallery. Conversation and loud laughter floated through it. There were men in expensive suits, women in short dresses. Waiters dispensed champagne. It looked like all the parties through all the ages. Rachel followed his eyes. The sense of déjà vu all over again was strong. Parties seemed like ancient history. Suddenly, she didn't care if she never went to another one. Did he feel that too? Both of them stood motionless at the bottom of the steps. Neither made any move toward the gallery.

"I haven't seen your show," he said suddenly. There was a hint of hostility in his statement, as if she was getting too close to him and he felt the necessity to push her away.

"I forgive you," she said, smiling.

"I'm sure it's very good. I've heard that." He seemed immediately to regret any hint of aggression.

"But not good enough to appear on."

He didn't answer her. His eyes left her face and darted at her body, down and up again, almost in the blink of an eye.

Again, he looked up at the party people in the window.

"Before we both plunge into that mêlée, would you take a walk with me?" he said.

"Yes," she said. It was clear he liked to make decisions. So did she.

They walked slowly and in silence. She turned to look at him and smiled. He shot a glance at her and then looked away. The sounds of their footsteps were muffled by the settling snow. The party noises receded. They passed a door laden with graffiti. He stopped suddenly.

"There. That says it." He pointed to a flyer with the discouraging message "Shoot all artists."

"Do you approve of that? Sounds suicidal."

"Oh, I'm not really painting nowadays. I'm more of a lapsed artist."

"Like a priest with the doubts?"

"Exactly like that." He laughed briskly to cover deeper feelings that would not be so funny.

Rachel the interviewer heard the pain. Rachel the woman was touched by it.

"Block?"

"So Wardlow told you. It would be part of your research, I suppose."

"I squeezed it out of him with thumbscrews," she said.

"Why the interest in me?"

"You are a great artist. You are articulate, intelligent, and good-looking. And you have pain all around you, I sense. That makes you interesting to me." Her heart was thumping. They walked on.

"So says Rachel Richardson, star TV interviewer." He paused. "Or is that Rachel Richardson the human being talking?"

"Can't I be both?"

"You have to be one more than the other."

There was suddenly a playful air to him, as if he was making up the rules of a children's game.

"One more than the other . . ." She played for time. "Are we being truthful here?"

"I always find that more interesting," he said. "Don't you?"

She did. Always.

"Rachel Richardson . . . the woman."

"Ah."

She swallowed. She looked up and breathed deeply. The dime-size flakes drifted down, filtering the sodium glow from the street lamps. A yellow cab crawled by, hoping for trade.

He reached out to her and she stopped. His hand went to her face and he brushed a crystal of snow from the tip of her nose. She held her breath, transfixed by the moment of unexpected intimacy. The gesture wiped away all the former awkwardness of his words. Rachel felt the tenderness merge. Hers. His. She would remember this moment, and that gesture, forever.

"Thank you," she said, her voice small. Up ahead, a panhandler walked toward them. The street was deserted, but Rachel felt no fear, only wonder as the magic danced about her once again. She wanted to translate the closeness of action into the closeness of words.

"When we met that evening," she said, "I knew somehow it was important."

She walked on as she waited for his answer.

"Yes," he said. "I felt that, too."

"You did?"

He didn't say more. Perhaps, like her, it was impossible for him to analyze. They were both so grown up, so worldly-wise. The feelings they were on the edge of discussing seemed out of place in both their worlds.

The snow was heavier now. A cold wind raced down the street. Through the speckled blanket, the sign of the café swung in the breeze, lit from the top. It was a wine bar called Tanzis.

"Look," he said, "shall we go in there and have a drink? It won't be much quieter than Harry's party, but it'll be more private."

The doorway was narrow and opened to a small cubicle with a door on its other side. They pushed through it. Charles stood back. She brushed past him. Her shoulder touched his chest, ran along the inside of his outstretched arm. She felt the nearness of him through the layers of coats. They repeated the movement in the tiny space between the doors. She was all wrapped up against him, closer than in a waltz. She could smell his scent, feel the hardness of his body against hers.

Inside, it was warm and bright. A scrubbed pine bar ran along one wall, tables with red-checkered cloths along the other. There were Victorian stained glass windows and boxing prints on the walls. The atmosphere was casual but artistic, and the people mirrored it. It reminded Rachel of the Café Flore in the St. Germain—even the drunks looked like faded literary lions.

There were two empty stools at the crowded bar. To the right of the door where they stood was a rack for coats. She began to take hers off, and he helped her. It was only the top layer, but the gesture was somehow symbolic. He hung up her coat and then took off his. His dark, well-cut blue suit complemented her plain black cocktail dress.

They sat huddled together at the bar. She ordered a kir. He asked for a Beck's beer. His hands, shorn of their black gloves, were delicate and expressive. She wanted to feel them, and play with his fingers.

"This is nice," she said, smiling at him.

"It is, isn't it," he agreed. She put out her hand and touched his arm. He didn't move it away from her. Instead, he leaned it in against her hand. I like you, was what she meant. I like you much more than good manners can let me say. She knew that he liked her, too. But why? Rachel wanted to know.

Farther down the bar, a couple had slipped into recognition mode. The man was whispering to his girlfriend. His mouth formed the words "Rachel Richardson." Almost immediately, a fat man by the cash register noticed her too.

"Perhaps *not* more private than Harry's party," said Charles Rachel was used to her celebrity, but to him it was a novelty to be remarked upon. Quite suddenly, she had part of the answer to her "why" question. Charles Ford liked the fact that she was successful. He liked that she was a meritocrat. Aristocrats often did. He had, perhaps, played at life. For Rachel, a woman trying to make it in a man's world, he knew life was a deadly serious business. He respected her tenacity, and the odds she faced.

He turned to her. His expression said it was a difficult question that he had to ask.

"I don't want to sound presumptuous," he said, "but was your art program conceived with me in mind?"

Rachel took a deep breath. Would he like the truth?

"There was the bare bones of a show. Let's just say it would probably have remained a skeleton without your flesh and blood."

"I see," he said with a slow smile, sipping his beer. "So, in a way, it's my responsibility whether it lives or remains in limbo."

"Yes. You're Dr. Frankenstein. It would be unkind of you to let it hang in zombie-esque undeadness."

"Not a person who gives up."

"Never."

"A person who gets what she wants?"

"Always."

"And who she wants?"

"She hasn't really wanted people." She watched him over the rim of her champagne glass.

"Do you think one day she might?"

"Yes."

He held up his glass. "A toast," he said. "To the day you get the person you want."

Rachel smiled into the excitement and raised her glass.

"To the day the person I want agrees to appear on my TV show."

"Is it job before everything in Rachel Richardson's world?"

"It used to be."

"Then who am I, with my trivial desires for privacy, to stand in the way of your career?"

He had agreed to do her show, because she had said that he might be more important to her than it. He had sensed a beginning. She did, too. To symbolize it, she reached out and touched his fingers—fingers she had so badly wanted to touch. He folded her hand into his and squeezed it, and the feelings exploded inside Rachel, warm and wonderful, as she knew they were supposed to be.

Twenty-four

The blackboard dominated the office. At its head, in bold white capitals, was the working title of the show—"SMART ART." Beneath it, in smaller cursive, was the subtitle "The State-of-the-Art-Market." The board was divided into five columns. "Rachel Intro," "Solomon/Wardlow IV," "Etkin-Patkin," "Gallery Party," "Charles Ford." The last column remained empty. Now it was being filled.

Rachel sat on the desk, her feet dangling. She sipped a cup of coffee. Jenny, just back from Santa Fe, stood by the blackboard with the chalk. The final interview with Charles Ford might last no longer than ten minutes. Nobody would know just how much research had gone into it.

"Okay," said Rachel. "Write 'background.' "

Jenny did as she was told.

"So, Jen, you researched the family. I've read your notes. His maternal ancestors arrived with the Spanish in 1610, so they were here before the Pilgrim Fathers pitched up at Plymouth Rock. That's pretty early, no?"

"I guess so, except the Navajo had been there for four hundred years."

"Okay, and then the del Castillo ancestors scratched about for a couple of hundred years trying not to get killed by the Comanches, and then big brother United States beat up on Mexico in 1848 and Santa Fe became part of the New Mexico territory. Were the del Castillos big wheels by then?"

"Beginning to be. The old Santa Fe trail got its railroad in 1880, and from then on it was boom time. The del Castillos, who were originally aristocrats from Córdoba in Andalusia, married into the settlers. They started to accumulate land on a grand scale, but they were artists, too. An ancestor had an exhibition in the Palace of Governors in 1890."

Rachel stared into the blackness of her coffee. Last night was so close. The bare facts of the history fleshed out the man and filled in the shadows in his character. He had come from such a very old world, such an ancient culture. It was no wonder he carried it with him, that unease in the midst of the plastic transience of today's America.

"So how come the Ford, Charles?"

They sat close at the mercifully small table in the back room at Tanzis. He had suggested eating there when they finished their drinks, and she had gratefully accepted. She kept her voice low, because the people on either side were so close.

"My father was an East Coast misfit, I suppose. A romantic. A poet. He didn't want to race yachts at Newport and sit around in clubs in New York. So he joined Will Shuster's Santa Fe art colony in the late 1920s instead of going to college. They were known as 'the five nuts in adobe huts.' The family was suitably appalled, which was probably the main reason he did it. Anyway, he loved it, and then he met my mother, Maria del Castillo, who was half English because my grandfather had married an Englishwoman, and they fell in love, and that was how I came about."

She looked across the table at him, desperately pleased that he had "come about." It sounded so romantic. Spaniards, Mexicans, English, American robber barons—the Ford money and the del Castillos' ancient landholdings had merged. No wonder Charles was rich. But it was so much more than that . . . the art, the closeness to the landscape, a family who had carved their lives from the rocks and the soil and who had never followed rules they had not invented themselves.

"So your father was in the forefront of the artists' invasion?"

"Yes, O'Keeffe, D. H. Lawrence, and the other famous ones. But it's more than that. New Mexico makes artists, or it finds the artist in all of us. The landscape speaks to you at a deeper level of being. Didn't you find that?"

He watched her closely across the table. Rachel felt it was a test of sorts.

"I don't think there is much of the artist in me," she said.

He laughed, throwing back his head, genuinely amused.

"Thank God for an honest woman. Artists are very self-obsessed. Often not very kind. Often arrogant. Sometimes not very wise."

"Is that a self-description?" said Rachel. *"It doesn't sound at all like the you I'm getting to know."*

"But then you don't know me very well yet."

His hand lay on the table inches from hers. She had an overwhelming desire to touch it, as she had earlier.

"Sometimes I wonder if we ever get to know anyone, even ourselves, perhaps especially ourselves. I don't even know what I really want," said Rachel.

His eyes were strangely alive. He was listening to her, hard. This was not small talk. With Charles Ford, perhaps nothing ever was.

"You know, the Pueblo Indians have a ritual called the Buffalo Dance, in which the Buffalo Mother symbolizes the mother of all large animals. In Pueblo legends, the Buffalo Mother appears to young men during their vision quests. She gives them a task and three days to perform it. In one legend, she asks Freud's question . . . way before Freud even thought of it: 'What do women really want?' "

"Is there an answer?"

"The freedom to be true to themselves."

"Oh," said Rachel. Her formidable brain was working on it. How did one know who one's self was? Weren't you a different person from year to year, week to week, minute to minute? And what the hell was truth?

"I can hear your brain whirring," he said, smiling. "All those clever thoughts. Why not just try feeling it, like the Indians."

She laughed. She remembered the philosophy course at Smith. It had been taught by atheists with a blind faith in their own brilliance. It had been taught by people who thought feelings were the things you had when you were having sex.

"You see," he said. "That's what you want, isn't it? The freedom to follow your heart?"

"Does it apply to men, too?"

"You know, I think what men want is a person to be true to them, and then, trusting, they are free to be true to that person."

"Like with Rose?"

"So much research, Rachel. But yes, like with Rose. Like with a son. Like with a daughter."

The carafe of red wine was on the table, the bread broken on the tablecloth. It was warm in here, and cozy, and Rachel was beginning to realize what it might feel like to be true to herself.

"What did you get from Wardlow at lunch?" said Jenny, bringing Rachel back into the here and now.

"What? Oh, Wardlow. Oh, I got Rose, basically."

"Shall I write that down under 'background'?"

"No! I mean, yes . . . Rose," she said. Rachel felt the tension. Career versus Charles Ford. The one had enabled her to meet the other. Now they were pulling in opposite directions. She felt it strongly, but there was nothing she could do about it. This was research. This was the vital element in the interview. It was this process that had propelled her to fame. Rose was the key to Charles Ford. Rose was her rival. It would be Rose that would release the emotion on TV where it belonged.

"Rose was an artist, the older woman, strong, didn't believe in marriage. Wanted to retain her independence," said Rachel, forcing herself to be professional.

"Feminist type," said Jen.

Rachel ignored her. She was thinking of her lunch with Harry Wardlow. Rachel had known that Wardlow's weakness was very fine claret. A Pétrus '61 had opened the floodgates on Rose. She had had the devil of a job persuading the Four Seasons to part with it.

Rachel continued. "Rose couldn't have children. They lived as recluses. Lived for each other. Fifteen years. Then breast cancer, and she died quickly."

"Producing devastation and block," said Jen. Under "Rose" she wrote "Block." "Presumably, the grief caused the block."

"Presumably," said Rachel, her mind beginning to wander. Grief caused block, she imagined. But didn't grief fade? There were all sorts of stages of grief: Denial. Mourning. Resolution. Why had Charles Ford been blocked for so long? There was something else. Her instinct said so. Rose Abernathy. Funny second name. Distinctive. From a small town in Delaware. What was it called? Rapids? River? Waterfall! That was it. Waterfall, Delaware. She jumped off the desk.

"I've just thought of something, Jen," she said.

Back in her office, she did what she had done so long ago in Chicago. Long distance information gave her what she wanted. There was only one Abernathy, a "John," listed in Waterfall, Delaware.

John Abernathy had heard of Rachel Richardson. Courtly and charming on the phone, he said that he watched a lot of television since he didn't get out much nowadays, and yes, he was Rose's father, the Rose who had died. Rachel told him about Charles Ford and her program, and he was eager to help. Poor Charles. What a fine, fine man. Scarcely a day went by when he didn't think of him and how happy he had made his daughter. Charles and Rose had been so close, so in love with each other and their art. They had this little tradition. When each was starting a new painting, the other would be the first to touch the paint to the canvas . . . It was a symbol of their togetherness, in creation, in life. It might be just a line, or a spot, nothing

more, but then every canvas became, in a sense, a dual creation . . .

Rachel put down the telephone. Her hand shook. It had happened again. A simple phone call and an answered prayer. She
could hear her own question as the camera zoomed in for the
close-up on Charles Ford.

"I know that you and Rose had this tradition that you would
start each other's canvases. Is that why you find it impossible
to begin one now?"

She took a deep breath. His reaction would be great television, but would it be good karma?

Twenty-five

Harry Wardlow sat upright behind his desk as if his awkward body posture could in some way atone for what had happened. It hadn't been entirely his fault. But then, he hadn't been entirely blameless either.

On the cluttered desk in front of him was the final indignation. As yet, Charles didn't know about it.

"She's tenacious as hell," said Wardlow. "But if it makes it any better, you came across really well, I mean, you—"

"Listen, Harry," said Charles, his voice soft but cold as winter. "I was used. I was investigated, set up, wheeled out and manipulated. My most private feelings were pulled out of me by cunning and deceit. Then I was displayed in front of the mob for their casual enjoyment. They popped their corn and sucked their six-packs, and I was the emotional entertainment for them. See the artist hurting. Watch one of the 'haves' bleeding for a change. It was *Oprah* with long syllables. It was the most degrading thing that has ever happened to me."

"But Rachel is known for that, Charles," said Harry gently.

Charles's laugh was bitter.

"I realize that. It was why I turned down her program when the booker called me. But when I *met* her, she was . . . she was just different. She was real. I *liked* her. I mean, there was a warmth, and I thought, I actually thought, that she liked me. That's what makes it worse. That I could be so gullible."

He turned his head away and then back to Harry, his gesture saying that all this was too hard to believe.

"I was opening up, Harry, after the long sleep. I was beginning to live again. Rachel seemed to understand things. Can people fake that? Are they all actors out there? Is everyone a great, big, bloody *fake?*" He almost shouted the last word, hurling it like a gauntlet at his old friend.

"Charles, listen, the telephone has been ringing off the hook ever since that show aired. I've had calls from collectors I thought were dead. I've heard from dealers who I know for sure dream about *me* being dead. They all wanted to know about your work, Charles. It struck a chord. That interview has made you hot again. Just that one interview. Now, I know you don't care a—"

"—shit about all those people," said Charles, his eyes flashing as he finished Harry's sentence. "Who the hell cares about that? The paintings are the same, and sometimes people want them and they're fashionable, and sometimes they're not. I'm just mad that I dirtied myself in the process. I'm sorry, I'm desperately sorry, that I used Rose's name, and what Rose and I shared . . . those precious things . . . If you don't understand that about me, you understand nothing, Harry."

"I understand, Charles. I, of all people, understand." He stood up and walked around the desk. He laid his hand on Charles's shoulder. "I shouldn't have exposed you to that. I should have protected you."

It was the right approach.

"No, it was me, old friend. I've lived too long out of this world. It was a luxury I used to be able to afford. Maybe I've got to get back into it. Everyone else has to. Why not me?"

He thought of Tessa and Camille, as they faced their uncertain future. He thought of Carol, alone and frightened. There was life out there, and it was not easy, but there were rewards for overcoming difficulty.

"Did she call you?" said Harry. "Did she dare?"

"Oh, yes, she did." Charles smiled a rueful smile. "You know, I honestly think she thought she had done me a favor, getting me to emote in public. You know, like some cathartic verbal dump in front of some bloody shrink." He was furious, but there was laughter . . . incredulity . . . in the anger. How could anybody have the brazen effrontery to get him so wrong?

"What did she say?" Harry was trying to ally himself with the humor.

"Oh, 'You were great. I really enjoyed talking to you. I hope you enjoyed it as much as I did.' I let her prattle on and on, and then she picked up that she was more or less talking to herself."

"And? . . ."

"And then I said, 'Rachel Richardson, in all my life I don't think I have ever met a more deceitful and devious woman, and I hope and pray that I will never set eyes on you again.' "

"Ah," said Harry. "It may be that she got the message."

Harry looked at the desk. Now? Later? Get it over with? Or would it be overkill?

"Do you think?" Charles said. "I mean, Harry, is it possible that she really didn't think I'd mind what she did? I'd like to know. I'd really like to know."

His mind ran back. The arc lights were hot in the studio, the roses on the table that separated him from Rachel were blood red. Symbolic of the psychic blood that was about to be spilled, he remembered thinking. But it had been a joke in his mind. He was not prepared for the reality. She had led him in gently. She had been so charming, so flattering, as she had leaned in toward him, and he had noticed her breasts and how pretty they were behind the bottle-green dress.

"How proud you must be of these magnificent paintings."

He had seen them on the monitor, beaming out to the millions, and yes, he was proud of them, and yes, it felt good to be the center of so much charming attention. She had known what she was talking about. She had gone on about the mysticism of the southwestern Indian, the distant focus on the far-off place where the spirits roamed. It was in their eyes. Charles had seen it and recognized it, and it had been his great art to capture it in the canvases that once he had painted.

"What are you working on now?"

He had tried a platitude, but he couldn't lie, not even on television, that great medium of untruth and hyperbole, innuendo and PR bullshit.

"I haven't been able to work for some time."

"Oh, artist's block? Tell me about that."

It had been like a slippery slope. The setup. The relaxation. The getting used to the cameras off-set, the people wandering around in the darkness offstage. He had felt as if he was alone with her, as they had been alone in the back room at Tanzis, their hands close, touching, their thoughts in apparent harmony as they trusted each other. It had felt so warm and so easy.

"It's not something I like to talk about. It's a rather personal thing for a painter."

"I know that you were very much in love with someone who died a year ago. With Rose Abernathy."

Abernathy. The word had struck him across the face with the force of a whiplash. He had swallowed. He could feel the adrenaline now. It was pumping again with the memory—

"Yes."

Harry's voice broke into his thoughts, answering the question he had asked earlier.

"Different worlds, Charles. It's to do with different worlds. In her world, people like to be on TV. Tears are badges of courage. Dole's presidential bid began when he wept at Nixon's funeral. Women love it when a man gets sad, and women make up the audience of *The Rachel Richardson Show.* She's in tune with her audience. She's probably half in love with you herself by now, if she's capable of the emotion."

"Hah. She's capable of it, all right. She's head over heels in love—with herself and her miserable career, and with all those hideous people who need her to sell their soap and their rubbish to the great 'American people.' But yes, I agree with you. I think she really believes she didn't do a bad thing. She got to the truth, didn't she? And isn't truth in journalism the Holy Grail, no matter who gets hurt by it, and what feelings get trampled, and how out of context it is? The truth shall set you free. I tell you, it does a whole lot more than set me free. It makes me sick to the pit of my stomach."

He stood up and walked stiffly around the room. He looked at the pictures on the wall, singling out a particularly good Rembrandt drawing, as if it would in some way protect him from the evil spirits that assailed him.

But the pencil strokes of the master did not perform their function as a talisman. He was back there, hot now, beneath the all-revealing lights. He saw the red of the flowers. He saw the smile on the face of the woman who had conned him.

Abernathy. She had found old John in his backwater in Delaware. What had she prized from him? What profound and sacred secret was about to become a secret no more?

"Look, I'd really rather not . . . this is a private thing."

It had been too soon for anger. He had been sandbagged by her charm. He trusted her still, even now, when his brain said to trust no longer.

"You loved her very much, didn't you?"

"Yes." The monosyllable had shot out, and with it the surge of sorrow. Rose. He had loved her very much. It couldn't be denied. It mustn't ever be. Rachel's eyes had arched in question. She had wanted far more than "Yes."

"So perhaps not being able to work is to do with missing her?"

He could all but feel the camera zooming in on him. He did not look at the monitor, but he knew his face filled it. The sadness was overwhelming. It had exploded from his face, coursing over his features.

He had simply nodded, past speech. He had seen Rachel's face through the mist. Concern. Elation. Excitement. And something else that he couldn't quite fathom. She had paused and taken a deep breath and seemed to hesitate. But then she had plunged on, and she had hit him with her best shot, at the very moment when he was most vulnerable.

"Rose's father told me how you used to, as a symbolic gesture of your closeness, paint the first line of each other's pictures . . ."

The tears had sprung from his eyes then, and rolled down a face rigid with a terminal sadness. Rose at the canvas, the first stroke, always the first. Rose first and last. Half of him, the half that had died.

He had simply shaken his head in anguish and amazement. A feeling of derealization had washed over him, providing merciful release from the torment. There had been more questions, dimly remembered answers, but the feelings had at last been numbed. And then it had been over. Rachel had held on to his arm as he walked in a daze from the set, and he remembered taking her hand away from him, gently, and saying no more until he was gone from the hell he had exposed himself to, from the horror that she had arranged for him.

He had been silent while the memories rolled in action replay. Now Harry made his decision.

"I suppose you should see this," he said, and he picked up the magazine from his desk.

Charles looked at it absentmindedly. The *People* headline jumped from the page: BITTER AND SWEET. " 'Be Prepared' is Rachel Richardson's motto. Her guests had better watch out, too" was the subhead. The article's byline was "Celeste Ritter."

He started to read, but his eyes wandered down the page to the passage that Harry Wardlow had highlighted in yellow.

I sat in as Rachel and her team planned an upcoming show on the "state-of-the-art-market." They wanted reclusive figurative artist Charles Ford to appear as a guest. He was suffering from artistic block, Rachel had found out. It was agreed that getting him to do the show would be difficult, and that he was a private person who would be unwilling to discuss creative difficulties in front of an audience of millions. "Tell him anything he wants to hear. Just book him and leave the rest to me," said Rachel blithely. It was a fascinating insight into the sort of personality traits you need to breathe the rarefied air that the Rachel Richardsons of this world inhale.

Charles Ford stared at the words in silence. And then he flung the magazine away into the corner of the room as if it was Rachel Richardson herself. But still, he had the oddest feeling. He was going to see her again.

Twenty-six

The knocking on the door was not gentle. Carol put down the book. She was expecting nobody. There was nobody to expect. She got up and walked across the small apartment.

"Who is it?" she said.

"It's me."

She felt the surge of adrenaline. It was like a wave crashing on the beach.

He stood there in blue jeans, boots, and an old leather vest. He looked stormy against the bright blue of the cloudless Santa Fe sky.

"You moved out," he said. It was an accusation.

She smiled gently at the force of him.

"Yes," she said. "I had to."

"Because of what happened?" There was no apology. There had never been one. There had never needed to be one, Carol felt.

"Do you want to come in?"

"Oh. Yes," he said, as if aware for the first time that he was still outside at the top of the steps to her studio apartment.

He walked in—stalked in—looking around as if sizing up an enemy.

"This is your apartment," he said. Again his tone was almost aggressive, but it was also bemused. "They said you'd moved out," he repeated.

"No," said Carol, answering his question at last. "It wasn't anything to do with what happened. Nothing bad happened. Only good things happened. Do you like it?" she added.

"Like it? Yes, I suppose so. It's very light," he said, looking up into the shaft of brightness that arrowed down into the living area. His voice softened.

"I left without saying goodbye," he said. It sounded like an apology.

"I didn't mind," said Carol. They both stood there. It was formidably, and wonderfully, awkward. She could remember the force of his lips on hers. She wanted it to happen again. Now. It was pointless to deny it.

He looked haggard. New York, Carol somehow knew, had not been an unqualified success.

"Look," he said. "I'm sorry to come barging in here like this. I got back this morning and they said you'd gone, and . . . and . . . well, I had imagined you wouldn't be gone. That's all."

It was very, very far from all.

"Would you like some tea?" said Carol.

"If you have some."

She smiled again. He was so different from the other men she knew. He was like some magnificent, wild animal-man. He walked to the window and looked down on the square, over at the Mission church and the people outside. Carol continued to talk as she made the tea.

"You know why I left for the desert. It was to stand on my own two feet," she said. "I didn't do very well. I nearly killed myself. You saved me, and then you gave me shelter and the use of a studio and somewhere to live. It was wonderful, and so kind and hospitable, but that was the person I used to be. I was falling into the same old trap. Being dependent on someone. On you, instead of Jack." She took a deep breath. She poured water into the kettle and settled it on the range.

He simply nodded to show that he understood. He continued to stare out at the square.

She took herb tea from the cupboard. "This apartment reminds me of the place I had at college," she said, talking on into his silence. "It says 'freedom,' 'independence.' It says who I am, and who I can be. I can let it get dirty, or I can clean it till it sparkles. It exists for me, not me for it. And if I like, I can just walk away from it and never come back, or I can sit in here and lock the door, and the world can't touch me."

Again he nodded. "The desert is like that for me, and the ocean. I like to escape to big places. You, to small ones. But I understand escape."

"You sound as if you want to escape right now," said Carol.

He turned and looked at her. His expression said that her intuition could surprise him.

"Did you have a good time in New York?" she said.

"Nearly."

"But not quite."

"Not quite."

He walked to the chair where Carol had been sitting, and he slumped down in it. Carol's book lay on the floor. It was Hemingway's *Islands in the Stream*.

"Bimini," he said, "and a painter who escaped."

"Did you meet lots of people in New York?" said Carol, pouring the tea into a mug.

He twisted around and looked at her long and hard.

"I thought I was beginning to gain a little trust in people," he said. "I think you were responsible, a bit, for that."

"But trust was misplaced?"

"Oh, yes, it was," he said, with a small, bitter laugh. He noticed that she was steering things away from herself.

"But what about you and your new beginnings?" he said. "Is the work going well? Is being alone working out?"

"Some moments are easier than others. Work and loneliness."

She took the tea across to him. There was nowhere else to sit, so she sat on the floor. He started to get up.

"No, please," she said. "I like sitting on the floor. I always used to sit on the floor."

"Before you were a grown-up?"

"Yes," she laughed. "Before we all had to start pretending that we weren't children anymore."

"Will you come and visit me sometimes?" he said suddenly.

"Of course," she said. "And you can come here anytime. And we can have tea." She looked away and then back at him. "But why do I have the feeling that you are going away?"

"Because I am," he said.

She felt the sharp tug somewhere inside her. She liked him more than she had thought it possible to like anyone so soon after what had happened, but why was she holding back from that feeling? Why was she shutting him out? And he liked her, she knew that. Why was he going away?

"Do you mind my asking where?"

"To Europe."

"Do you mind my asking why?"

"Because sometimes America, Americans, are too raw."

"One particular American?"

He had met someone. In New York. She herself had opened him up to the experience, and it had not gone well. She felt jealousy collide with hope, but hope for what? Part of her was pulling toward him, another pushing him away.

"One. Maybe all. People want so much here. Perhaps too much. Great expectations. Greater disappointments."

"So the medicine for American optimism is European pessimism?" said Carol.

"Would you miss me?"

There was the earnestness again in his voice and in the expression on his face.

He was asking her a serious question. She could feel the intensity. He would not ask more directly. It was now or never. A simple yes, and maybe he would not go, and perhaps what had started in the studio would be merely the end of the beginning. Anything else, and it would be a rejection. There was nothing in between. Carol tried to think, and she tried to feel. Was it too soon? Was Jack still there in her life despite everything? Was this dark, brilliant man too strong for her?

"Would I miss you?" she said out loud. Both of them knew she was playing for time.

Twenty-seven

The Sotheby's building, low, like some bunker built with un-friendly airplanes in mind, had the virtue of closeness. It took Tessa five minutes walking on Madison to reach it. Today she felt better than she had in weeks. She was finally about to close a deal. She floated past Bemelman's Bar at the Carlyle on a cloud of optimism. She might drop in there later for a glass of post-closing champagne. And then what about a massage at Georgette Klinger across the street? It would be just like the old days. Tessa tried to smile as she pulled the coat around her and the freezing wind ripped along the sidewalk. But it was one of those days when cold-induced facial paralysis made smiling impossible, not that there was a lot of smiling done on this street. Madison Avenue was God's living proof that money did not bring happiness.

She strode into the marble lobby of Sotheby's, past the display windows of sumptuous Palm Beach homes and stunning Tuscan retreats. Her good mood went up with the wood-paneled eleva-tor to the offices. The two receptionists smiled as she entered. One stopped munching a chocolate to greet her. "Hello, Tess. Big day. Eleven o'clock. Hope you didn't forget."

"Forget?" laughed Tessa. "I've been up most of the night, in case I didn't wake up."

On the wall by the reception desk was a board listing the names of the eighty Sotheby's realtors. Three separate columns were headed respectively "Home," "Office," and "Other." She rubbed out the tick against her name in the "Home" column and chalked one under "Office."

"Don't forget my commission," said the receptionist.

It was only a joke. One of the few friendly realtors had given Tessa a useful tip on the day she had started: Be super nice to the receptionists. If they didn't like you they could sabotage the vital communications on which the business depended, leaving you stranded on lonely street corners when clients canceled at the last minute. More important, they could channel the walk-in trade your way. Tessa had taken the advice and had spent time nattering to the receptionists about the trials of life in New York and everything else. Then, one fine day, she had been rewarded by a tall dark stranger with a French accent. It was he who, today, would be closing on the United Nations Plaza apartment that Tessa had sold him. Even now, she could remember the excitement.

Day after day she had sat in her cubicle waiting for the telephone to ring as her frustration had mounted. Finally, when depression had bitten sufficiently hard, she had steeled herself to start ringing her friends. There had been lots of good intentions and halfhearted promises, but no hard business. Her friends all had realtors of their own, more experienced than she, and their plans were always vague because nothing ever *had* to be sold. It was always a question of *wondering* about the farm in Connecticut or the seaside cottage in Maine, and would it be more fun to have this house in Aspen now that the kids were so into skiing and the ski instructor was so cute? Charles Ford's downtown loft had not sold, despite her showing it at least once a week. It was one of the many downtown buildings restricted to bona fide artists only, and most people with $1.2 million to spend were neither poets nor painters! Art and money, it appeared, only went together when you spent the money on the art.

"Any packages?" asked Tessa, consulting the large book on the receptionist's desk that charted the inflow of courier mail. "Oh, great," she said, as the receptionist handed her the UPS parcel. "That's the layout on the Ford place."

"No action yet on that?" said the receptionist.

"Sniffers. No bids. Lofts are sticky as hell at the moment," said Tessa.

"The Countess Vittadini sold one," said the receptionist, striking a pose and putting on an Italian accent.

"Probably to one of her Mafia cousins," laughed Tessa. Mona Vittadini was loathed by everyone, but she racked up the sales. If, when they shook America, all the nuts and flakes ended up in California, the bogus titles stuck to New York.

Tessa ripped open the package as she headed for her cubicle. It had been a shock when she first saw the rabbit hutch that was her office. Somehow, she had imagined that Sotheby's realtors had attorney-type offices. Instead, Tessa had to huddle in a space that had room for not much more than a chair, a wooden shelf, and a telephone. Now she emptied the photographs of Charles Ford's loft layout onto the table. Relief flooded through her. The pictures had caught the feeling of space and light. And the arrangement of the photographs on the brochure was stylish. She read through the particulars, checked the measurements, and admired the blurb that had taken her a whole day to write. Best of all was her name on the glossy brochure . . . "Please contact Tessa Andersen." This would be a big help. She should get down there this evening and show it to Charles. He had left a message on her machine the previous evening. He would be arriving in town this very morning and could she contact him.

She felt the warm feeling. It was Charles Ford, the stranger, not all the old friends, who had helped her when she had so desperately needed a listing. But it was much more than that. It was the memories of him, the little things, the "honorary Indian" joke; the way he had watched her above the steaming cup of cappuccino; the time he had confessed to the childlike desire to scribble on one of Cy Twombly's "blackboard" paintings. He had left a copy of *The Glass House* outside her door, and she remembered the thrill of finding it there and the greater thrill of reading its intimate inscription. It sat there now, in pride of place on the coffee table in her apartment, a wonderful memento of a wonderful day.

He had not let her down. One of the very first calls she had received in this little cubicle had been from him.

"I suppose you'll need to measure, take some photographs, have me sign a listing agreement," he had said, and somehow the excitement of the done deal had paled beside the thrill of knowing that she would be seeing him again.

"Thank you for *The Glass House*," she had said. She had tried to contact him the moment she received it, but Charles Ford had proved to be a difficult man to reach on the telephone.

"Thank you for your charming thank-you note. The gallery sent it on to me."

"You are very welcome, kind sir. It was a sweet thing to do. I loved that book. Now, I like it even more."

"So when are you coming?"

"When am I invited?"

"The light is best in the mornings."

"Well, it just so happens my mornings are free this week." And every week, she had thought.

Tessa drifted off on the tide of memory.

"Pretend to like it." The sound bites from the Sotheby's sales and orientation program kept creeping into her mind, but Tessa didn't have to pretend. It was magnificent, the sort of space any artist, or anyone with an artist's spirit, would die for. Outside, Charles Ford's building had failed the "location, location, location" test . . . the standard fire escape on the dirty street; a tall building that looked like the warehouse it had been; the windows through which grand pianos could cheerfully have been slung. But inside, it was as full of soul as sunlight. He stood back and watched her first impression.

"Oh, Charles, it's beautiful. I knew it would be."

"How did you know?" he said with a smile. He was pleased

to see her. Already, he was playing with her in the delightful way that he did.

"Because people who dress well have good taste in homes," she said, turning around to challenge him, despite the presence of the lurking photographer and the man who would do the measuring.

"Thank you," he said. He moved forward to take her coat, and she shed it for him, aware of his closeness.

For a second they both stood there, smiling.

"Tell me what we have to do," he said at last.

Tessa picked up the clipboard with its copy of the listing agreement, and the manila folder with her homework.

She laughed. *"I don't have to tell you that this is my first listing,"* she said. *"Just console yourself with the fact that you'll have a hundred percent of my time."*

"Sounds like a good deal."

She blushed. *"I've got some things to go through. Sales of comparable properties from the computer to help decide on the asking price, what's to be included—obviously fixtures and fittings—how long are you prepared to wait to sell, things like that."*

"Mmmmm," he said. *"Sounds good. Why don't we take a lightning tour, and then the photographer can do his thing and we can get down to all those details."*

"You definitely want to go ahead with the listing? Oughtn't you to hear my sales pitch first?" said Tessa.

"Why do I feel I should sign the listing agreement before I hear the sales pitch? Anyway, consider it signed. Gentleman's agreement."

"Gentlewoman's agreement," said Tessa. She reached for his hand, and he for hers. Behind them, the photographer coughed.

He steered her toward the three mighty windows. The New York skyscape stretched into the distance. Smoky, gray light streamed into the whitewalled, teak-floored space.

"A room with a view," he said. *"Actually, it's even better from*

up there." He turned and pointed toward the gallery where the master bedroom would be.

"Better see it," said Tessa quickly.

He went before her up the wrought-iron spiral staircase. His blue jeans looked as soft as velvet. His dark blue velvet slippers were the kind that you could wear with a dinner jacket. He wore no socks. He was right about the view from the master bedroom, and specifically about the view from the master bed. They were way above the rooftops of the surrounding buildings. The bed was king-size. A cubist Picasso of what looked like a young girl hung above it. A modern lamp sat on the bedside table and a single book, The Paintings of Frida Kahlo. The polished teak shone in the brightness of massed, yet subtle, downlighters. There didn't seem to be anything else in the room at all, unless you counted the Pratesi bedcover in a geometrical design in shades of gray. Tessa walked to the balcony with its carved wooden railings. Below, her two colleagues mooched about moodily, awaiting the call to action.

"That's beautiful," she said, turning and pointing at the Picasso. But, somehow, in its Zen but strangely sumptuous simplicity, it all was. So was he.

He stood by the side of the bed. She stood at the end of it. It separated them, but it also joined them.

"He painted it the week after Desmoiselles d'Avignon."

"Did he?"

Beneath the black silk of her shirt, Tessa's body was talking to her. Her mouth was dry.

"Yes."

The atmosphere was suddenly parched and deliciously brittle, the sort of surroundings in which a single flame would become a conflagration.

"You sleep here," said Tessa, aware immediately that it was a ridiculous remark.

He did not smile at its silliness, because he knew the cause of her confusion. He knew it because he, too, felt it.

"Come here," he said.

She swallowed hard, but there was no wetness in her mouth. She had to go to him, and somehow that felt incredibly right.

She walked around the bed, her mouth parted, her breasts rising and falling against the sheer silk of her shirt. He opened his arms and she drifted into them as if into a waltz in a dream. He held her gently, and bending down, he kissed her. She turned her face up toward him. Her dry lips touched his, and she fanned his face with her shuddering breath as the passion engulfed her.

Tessa forced herself back into the present. She looked at her watch. It was ten after nine. She had plenty of time to get over to the closing. What should she do? The bleak options loomed in her mind. Cold calls were very un-Sotheby's, and cold doors were worse, although she knew some of the realtors who stooped to doorsteps. She had herself spent several long afternoons scouting the concierges at high-end condos for potential sellers. It had been a soul-destroying business that had produced nothing but blanks for her. Prospecting FS-BOs, newspaper listings of properties for sale by owners, hadn't been much more of a success. It was catch-22. Everyone wanted to know how much business you had done and how many properties you had listed, and Tessa had hardly made a start.

Thank God for the closing today. It was the break she needed. Her dapper walk-in Frenchman, courtesy of the receptionist, and Melissa Partridge's $800,000 UN Plaza apartment would produce $12,000 for her and Camille. The six percent commission on $800,000 would be split fifty-fifty with Sotheby's, and the remainder Tessa would share equally with Melissa. It wasn't the greatest deal in the world, but it was exactly twelve thousand times better than any she had done so far. She tried to tell herself that it was a slow market and that there were three-thousand-plus one-bedrooms cluttering the Upper East Side, but the truth was, there were producers in the office who were doing as well as ever. There was movement in $2 million-plus co-ops, and at least prices had stopped falling, although giveaway seller financing deals obscured the fragile state of business. The problem was she didn't have forever. Any minute now she could be asked to vacate her cubicle. Rachel had saved her once. She wouldn't be able to save her again.

She thanked God for today's closing, and for her exclusive on Charles's loft. The first she would sell at eleven o'clock today. If she could eventually sell the loft at a million-plus, she would have made $54,000 for Sotheby's in commission. That should keep her job safe, and clothes on Camille's back and food in her little tummy. The wave of sadness crept over Tessa. Camille was doing well at the public school, coming in at the top of her class in everything. But how different it was from Brearley. And what else would she be learning in that school? Tessa shuddered at the thought. Once again she thought of Charles Ford, of his lips against hers, of the answers that he could provide to the problems she faced. Then she thought of Pete, and there was a flash of tenderness that merged with a flash of anger that he had let them down so badly. You were supposed to forgive the dead. *De mortuis nil nisi bonum.* But the mess he had left was here and now.

Why hadn't Charles called? Neither of them had known how to handle the kiss that had seemingly come from nowhere, but which had meant something. Both had their own ghosts to confront, both had recognized it, and the business of taking instructions on the sale of his apartment had gone on somehow. She knew that he liked her, but perhaps he was not ready to get involved. She was hardly sure she was, although she was getting a bit more certain as the days passed and he didn't get in touch with her. Showing his apartment was a mechanical business. She had a key and the telephone number of the superintendent who looked after the building. She would call in advance. So far, Charles himself had not been there. She really wanted to see him again, but she didn't want to until he was ready.

Tessa whiled away the time, checking the new listings on the computer, reading articles on the state of the market and the likely course of the all-important interest rates. Then, it was time. She grabbed her bag, her folders, and her cellular phone, and bounced out of the office. This was what made it all worthwhile. She hailed a taxi on Madison and in no time she was in the lobby of the lawyer's office where the closing was scheduled.

She was early by about fifteen minutes. The secretary said, "They're mostly there already," in a way that sounded nonspecifically ominous. Tessa felt the sinking feeling. Oh, no! She knocked on the door. "Come in." Oh, yes. This was a funeral, not a wedding.

Melissa Partridge, her Sotheby's colleague, was pacing up and down. The seller's lawyer was sitting behind a vast desk fiddling with a pencil. The title insurance person sat in a corner. The seller in another. Of her own production, the neat French doctor, there was no sign at all.

"Where's Dr. DuPrès?" said Tessa, not waiting for the introductions.

"Not here," said Melissa nastily. "And not coming."

"Of course he is. It's early," said Tessa.

"His lawyer called. It's off," said the attorney. He looked irritated, but not overly so. Somehow, by someone, lawyers always got paid.

Tessa grabbed her cellular phone. She called the Pierre. The desk clerk was quite definite. "Dr. DuPrès checked out last night, ma'am. No forwarding address. The airport, ma'am. Yes, Kennedy."

"What did the lawyer say?" said Tessa. Her voice had sailed up an octave.

"The guy ran out. No messages. No nothing. How the hell did you qualify him?" said Melissa.

They all looked at her then. It was the right question.

"He had a credit reference from the Crédit Lyonnais. They're owned by the French government."

Melissa's eyes darted toward the heavens. "*And* a few characters from Marseille, apparently. Don't you know anything? What was his *American* testimonial?"

"I didn't ask for one. He was French," said Tessa.

"Dear God," said Melissa. "You make *that* sound like a reference."

There wasn't a lot more to say, but there was a great deal more to feel. The closing had remained open. Her baked-in-the-cake sale had been blown away. For a brief second, her ancient English hatred of all things French flared, but as soon it was gone. This was a hellish business full of cheats and liars and dreadful, slippery people. She shouldn't be anywhere near it. But immediately, she knew she had to go on. She made her apologies and left, as Melissa Partridge muttered darkly about limey amateurs and time-wasting frogs.

It was colder than hell on the street outside. As insult to injury, it was managing to rain rather than snow. It took her fifteen minutes to get a taxi. While she was climbing into it, soaked to the skin, she broke the heel on her shoe.

She collapsed back on the scuffed leather as the surly Lebanese pretended not to understand the word "Madison." She shivered, with fury, with the cold and the dampness, with the humiliation she had suffered. Any minute now, in the warmth of the cab, she would begin to steam. This wasn't living. This was living death. She took a deep breath and tried to hang on emotionally, but she felt like crying. She was wound tight as Scotch tape, rigid with frustration. Was this work? Was this what people had to get through to put bread on the table? Maybe men deserved to rule the world. This was not for the fainthearted.

Outside, the rain streamed down, driven almost horizontal by a wind that was chilling the temperature toward zero. She bent down and straightened the broken heel of her best Manolo Blahnik shoe. She prayed it could be stuck together somehow. She just didn't have the $200 to replace them. Damn! Damn! Damn! She simply hadn't expected it. DuPrès had been so charming. What particular perversion was it to wind everyone up for a closing and then walk away at the very last minute? There was no explanation and there would be none. That was the worst part of all. She would never know how to learn from the experience, except to "qualify" people more thoroughly—American bank references, credit agency reports, tax returns, personal references. Those things didn't eliminate problems, but they minimized them.

She thought of Camille in the public school reading out the flash cards as she learned her times tables. Poor little thing. She was blissfully unaware that her future had just been dented. Tessa clenched her fists. "Grit your teeth and say 'Scots Guards.' " That was what her brother and his old friends from the regiment used to say when times got tough. She imagined her great-grandfather leading the battalion, blowing the whistle as he took them over the top at the Somme into the machine-gun fire and all-but-certain death. It had seldom been all quiet on the western front, and there were Pitt-Riverses pushing up poppies to prove it. How they would have laughed at her silly reaction to a failed closing. To Death's men it wouldn't have the significance of a mosquito bite. You didn't have to look far in this life to find people worse off than yourself.

Her cellular phone rang. It was the Sotheby's receptionist who had given her DuPrès.

"Tess, I'm glad I caught you before the closing. I had a walk-in, a South American, Brazilian, I think. Very chic. Said he would be back at twelve. I mentioned you, and he said he liked the English. Wanted to see apartments in the five hundred thousand range. Any chance of you being back by then?"

Tessa thought fast. She needed to go to her apartment to change her shoes. But she kept a pair of comfortable yet scruffy ones at the office for when she wasn't going out. It was vital for her to get back into the saddle again immediately. Her family had always maintained that that was the best thing to do when you fell off the horse. She couldn't face mentioning the bad news about the closing.

"For sure," she said. "Thanks a billion."

"No problemo."

Tessa counted up the problems. She had to pick up Camille from school at three. There was no food in the fridge at the apartment. There was precious little money left in the bank account. The credit cards were pushing against their limits. She had to go straight to the office if somebody else wasn't to poach the Brazilian. That meant she would have to troll Manhattan apartments in shoes that weren't for showing. Would she be dry by then? Would it matter? Would anybody notice? She explained the new destination to the snarling driver. It was as if Tessa had changed the address from the North Pole to the South Pole while crossing the equator. The driver threw up both hands in exasperation, nearly causing an accident. The honking horns and the howls of abuse rang in Tessa's ears as she wondered if she had ever had a worse day.

"Put him in the conference room, will you, when he gets back, and maybe give him a cup of the good coffee. I think they like that in Brazil." She punched the End button, signing off.

When they arrived at Sotheby's, she shoved the money at the driver, not tipping him. Insults floated after her across the windswept sidewalk.

"What happened to you?" said the receptionist as Tessa hobbled in.

"Tell you later," said Tessa. "I need five minutes to get myself straight."

Five minutes later, she walked briskly into the conference room. It always reminded her of a VIP lounge at some supremely unimportant provincial airport. There were bilious shades of green, utilitarian furniture, and no windows. For some reason, the ashtray was permanently full of cigarette butts. The man who was sitting there stood up. He was sharp as a knife, sweet-smelling and suave, with patent-leather hair and an exuberant suntan. His teeth were bright white, and he would need to shave at least twice a day, maybe more.

He bent to kiss her hand as Tessa introduced herself, and he clearly noticed her shoes.

They exchanged cards. Alfonso Gamero's was engraved in elegant script, and bore neither address nor telephone number. That was very grand in the English tradition, but coming so soon after Dr. DuPrès, Tessa would have preferred something a little more commonplace and revealing.

She sat him down and began the sounding-out process that upmarket realtors use to probe their clients. What sort of apartment was he looking for? Did he want a prime location? If so, $700,000 would get him a one-bedroom in a first class building. Or would he sacrifice location for more square footage? Did he know New York? Was he single? How often would he be using the apartment? Señor Gamero said that he was an "investor." He took the view that Manhattan real estate had bottomed, and there was the business of getting his dollars into something solid. The Brazilian stock market had been very strong, but now with Mexico . . . well, it was time for a more defensive strategy. Emerging markets could . . . how do you say, "reenter," ha ha ha.

Tessa laughed. She rather liked him, but he was looking at her very intently—too intently.

What did he feel about the Upper West Side? He liked it. His wife loved the theater, but his wife would not be coming to New York very often, especially when he was on business. "I like to mix my business with pleasure," he said, his eyes twinkling, and then suddenly Tessa didn't like him so much. She wondered briefly whether to stop this then and there. She could "remember" a forgotten appointment and pass him on to some other hungry realtor. No! She had to plow on. He might buy. In this game you never knew which ones would, any more than Hollywood knew which movie would be a hit. It was a recognized truth of the realty business.

"So, a condo rather than a co-op?" she asked.

"Yes, I think that co-ops like a financial statement, do they not?"

"Yes," said Tessa. "A lot of foreigners aren't too keen on those. And the co-op boards can be tricky."

"Yes, a condo, I think. I would like very much for you to show me some."

"Well, I would be happy to do that. If you would give me a

day or two to do some research and make some calls, I can arrange some showings. What are your plans?"

"Oh," he said. "No. I have only this afternoon, and then I shall be coming back next week. But I need to see a few things now to get an idea of what the market is like."

Damn! Tessa thought fast. It shouldn't be impossible to line up two or three condos at short notice. The concierges usually had the keys, and the listing realtors sometimes allowed the introducing realtor to do the showings themselves. That wasn't such a big deal for small apartments. But she had to pick up Camille at three P.M. It was after twelve. Outside, New York was a soggy, half-frozen mess. Finding taxis would be a nightmare. She would have to show him at least three buildings . . . against the clock.

There was a knock on the door.

Paula Gilbert came in without waiting to be asked.

"Oh, sorry, Tessa. I didn't know you were back. I heard that Mr. Gamero was here. And I . . . I . . ." There was desperation in her voice and a steely glint in her eye. Paula was the hardest worker in the office. She would be happy to show this man apartments until the time came to drive him to the airport. If Tessa blinked, she would lose this Brazilian, whoever he was.

"I'm going to be showing him some apartments," said Tessa firmly, laying her claim.

"Oh," said Paula, still standing there, unwilling to give up. "Perhaps he'd like to see my Columbus Square Zeckendorf. I could come along with you."

"Paula, can I let you know, okay? I'm in conference here."

"Okay, okay," said Paula, retreating at last. The door closed behind her. Tessa felt the heat. This was an unbelievably competitive business. Gilbert would exchange teeth for a sale. And she would sink teeth for one. Were *her* credit cards bumping against *their* limits? Did she, too, have mouths to feed? Tessa thought of the Countess Vittadini and Melissa Partridge. Out there somewhere were the big producers already plotting her

downfall with the dreadful Westchester, using the botched closing as an excuse?

"Sorry about that," said Tessa. "Look, it's a little short notice,
but I think I can find some things for you to see that will give
you an idea of what's available. If you don't mind waiting here,
I'll make a few calls and see if we can get some keys and some
appointments."

He stood as she stood, courteous and well-mannered . . . but
there was something about his eyes . . .

Back in her cubicle, Tessa worked fast. She needed an overpriced piece of junk to show him first, then something good,
then something excellent. That was the best psychological approach. Never show someone more than three properties in a
day. It confused them. The City Spire building on West 56th
would do for the first apartment. It had an overpriced low-floor
unit with no view and a nasty interior. Then there was an okay
unit right across the road in the new Carnegie Hall Tower. It
had a great view, but was a bit cramped for the money. Finally,
perhaps, she should show him something in the Lincoln Tower.
She remembered there was a high unit that belonged to an architect who was hurting. It apparently showed well, and the
seller-financing deal was, reputedly, a dream—nothing down
and one under prime for a year. The Brazilian might cover his
costs on a rental and take the capital-appreciation ride for nothing. Jesus, if she had the credit history, she could do it herself.
Dream on, Tessa. She was into the City Spire in minutes.
Carnegie Hall Tower came with a selling realtor. The Lincoln
Tower unit was more difficult. She finally located the Corcoran
Group realtor in the middle of a massage, but she was able to
arrange for a key to be made available at the front desk.

They got a cab quite quickly on Madison. Tessa was aware
that she was breaking all the rules in real estate. She was going
to show three apartments she had never seen to a stranger who
was a totally unknown quantity. But she was desperate. He sat
close to her in the cab. He smelled strongly of some lemony
cologne and faintly of cigars. He lived, so he said, in Rio in a

penthouse apartment overlooking the better part of Ipanema.
And, of course, there was a ranch in the interior. Of course. He
didn't offer to pay as they pulled up outside the City Spire.

"Do you have a lot of friends in New York?" she asked.

"A few." It hadn't told her anything.

He didn't like the apartment. Neither did Tessa. It was a
chrome and glass nightmare with funny-colored lighting—
sound and fury signifying nothing. They walked to the Carnegie
Hall Tower on 57th Street. This was better, but it was impersonal
and lacking in style. The space was cramped. She let him walk
around it by himself. It was a trick she'd learned. People took
up room. Her own presence would make a small room seem
smaller. The realtor who was supposed to meet them had not
showed, leaving his apologies and a key at the front desk.
Gamero liked the view.

"I hope you are enjoying this as much as me," he said in the
tiny lobby, and he put his hand on her arm.

Tessa felt the rush of alarm. She stood back from him. He
smiled. They were alone in the empty apartment, way up on the
sixty-first floor. They could see most of Central Park and both
rivers, but nobody could see or hear them.

"I think you'll like the Lincoln Center place," said Tessa.

"I like the view in here." He had turned away from the view.
He was looking at Tessa. He was referring to her.

Oh, no! Surely not! Sotheby's. He looked rich. He had a
card . . . but with no address. Sr. Gamero from Brazil . . . the
walk-in from the cold, damp street.

"We'd better go," she said. "I have to pick my daughter up
from school." I have a daughter. I am not a single woman. I am
not available for the fun that goes with your business. She bran-
dished her cellular phone. I am in contact with the outside world.
We are not alone. We are in the middle of Manhattan, of civilization, in this up-market building in this up-market part of town.

"You are so beautiful. I like English women."

He took a step toward her. Across the marble floor, through
the picture window, rain swirled across the gray Manhattan sky.

Tessa had her back to the wall. The door was to her left, he stood to her right. On his face was that strange expression men wore when they were no longer in control of themselves. He had slipped the leash of manners and politeness. He was free. Tessa swallowed hard. This had never happened to her before. She didn't even know what "this" was.

"I have to leave," she heard herself say. She took a step toward the door. He took another step toward her. He put out his hand across her body, not touching her, but ordering her with his gesture to stay where she was.

Tessa was frozen in the moment. Rain smashed against the big window, borne on a gust of wind. Was this how it began . . . in the newspapers and in all those distant, far-off places where this happened to other women? She put out her hand to push his away, but he grabbed her wrist. His grip was firm. He was not hurting her, but he was telling her that he was in control and that it was male strength and not female words that counted.

"Let go of me," she half shouted. It had not reached the point of no return. It could still be stopped if the right words and gestures could be found. But what was right, for this man, at this moment? She felt the throb of panic. She tried to peel his fingers from her wrist, but his face was set now in a half smile, half leer. He was amused that she would try to stop him. He was away from his home in a strange land where nothing mattered. He was far from his wife and the laws that perhaps he respected, and the people that maybe he valued. He held both her wrists. He bore down on her. He plastered his body against hers, crudely and rudely. She felt his erection. It was hard and horrid against her upper leg, and extraordinary in this situation so devoid of passion and affection. She felt nausea reach up from her stomach and explode in bile at the back of her throat. He put his lips down on hers, and then there was the slippery wetness of his tongue, crude and lewd against her skin, slopping at her lips. Tessa didn't think. She acted. She opened her mouth wide, and she bit it. She bit it hard and long, and she did not let go even when her teeth met on either side of his tongue. She felt her mouth fill with his blood. She heard the weird gargle that was the noise he tried to make but couldn't make, the scream he could not scream. With her teeth sunk deep into the most tender part of him, she shook her head from side to side like a dog might shake a bone, and blood sprayed across the room and speckled on the whiteness of the walls of the Carnegie Hall Tower apartment. At the same time, she brought up her knee as she held his tongue in her teeth, and she smashed it against the disgusting, throbbing thing in his pants. Then she let go of him. He fell back from her in pain and shock. His hand rushed to his injured mouth as he tried to understand the terrible damage she had done to him. With his other hand he reached down to try to stop the other pain that his mouth could no longer express.

Tessa rushed for the door and opened it. She slammed it behind her as she ran from the apartment. She spat out a mouthful of his blood on the carpet of the corridor, and she ran for the fire escape. She hurried down the stairs for three floors as the adrenaline cloaked her in unreality. Then she calmed enough to find the elevator. She pressed the button. In no time there was the "ping" announcing its arrival. For a second, she felt panic once again. Could he be in it? But it was empty, and she glided down with her falling stomach to the safety of the Carnegie Hall Tower lobby.

They stood around in their uniforms, the pretty concierge and the men whose job it was to open doors and stand guard in this castle of civilization amidst the nameless dangers of New York. She didn't complain to them. She had brought this man to their place. She simply ran outside as they watched her and wondered who she was, and what was her hurry to get out into the rain and the cold. As Tessa burst out onto the sidewalk, her cellular phone began to ring. She stuffed it against her ear and pressed the button to receive.

"Yes," she panted.

"Tessa, it's Charles. Listen, I'm here at Kennedy and my flight leaves in a minute or two. I just called to say goodbye. I've decided to go to Europe. Madrid, for a bit. I wanted to tell you . . ."

"Oh, Charles, Charles," she gasped. "The most terrible thing . . ."

She couldn't go on. She was beginning to sob. It was all catching up with her. The traffic was piled up on 57th Street. There was a solid block along the westbound lane. She had made it to the middle of the road.

"Tess. Are you all right?"

"Yes, yes, I'm fine. I'm fine, but—"

Her cellular phone began to beep. Then it went dead. The lit-up message in the silly little window said "check batteries." Tessa stared at it in disbelief as she threaded her way through the parked cars to the sidewalk on the far side of the street.

"Charles? Charles?" But there was nobody there. The connection was broken.

The bicyclist courier on the racing bike streamed along the line of parked cars. His head was low, his lean body streamlined against the cold and wind. He wore goggles and a woollen hat, and an outfit that was made of black, shiny Lycra. He was traveling at twenty-five miles an hour when he hit Tessa, as, in a daze, she stepped up to the safety of the sidewalk that she never reached.

She felt the terrible blow on her shoulder and she knew that something awful was happening. The world slowed and the sky twirled as she fell backward through space. Her phone flew away from her, useless as her limbs, and she waited for the sounds that would signal that she had hit whatever she would hit. She wasn't braced for impact, she was simply a spectator at her own accident. The crack she now heard would be her head against the sidewalk. Sparks exploded in her mind, but still there was no pain, only a total numbness. She heard somebody shout. She was not moving now, and that stickiness by her ear would be her blood. Hang on, Tess. She felt hands holding her. "Are you all right?" said a man's voice. She didn't know, and she couldn't answer him.

"Don't move her," said somebody. "I'm a paramedic," said somebody else. "Oh, she's bleeding. Oh, she's bleeding," said a woman's voice that sounded panicky. Tessa felt herself slip-ping away, and half wanting to and half not wanting to. But she had to say something to all these people who were being so inconvenienced by her. So she just said, "Rachel Richardson," because those were the two words that came out of her mouth. Then she nose-dived into a warm, fuzzy darkness that was full of the sound of sirens.

Twenty-eight

"*Seventeen* stitches! God, how awful, Tess. And you *still* look better than I do."

Tessa did look good. The paleness suited her. She lay back against the fierce white sheets of the hospital bed like a princess.

"Luckily, it was all under the hair. Thank the Lord I didn't go face first."

Rachel paced back and forth at the end of the bed, unwilling to sit down. She didn't like hospitals. They were one of the few places that made her nervous.

"Listen, Rachel," said Tessa. "I haven't really had a chance to thank you for everything. I was pretty drowsy last time you came, but I just want to say how incredible you have been to me. Really, I mean, it's impossible to put into words."

"For a limey?" laughed Rachel. "They can do anything with words." She squeezed Tessa's toe through the sheets.

They had called her at work. Some paramedic had been walking down 57th Street. An Englishwoman had been hit by a bicycle and appeared to have a serious head injury. The only thing she'd said before passing out was, "Rachel Richardson." He was calling just in case it was "the" Rachel Richardson and she knew a blond Englishwoman by the name of Tessa Andersen. They'd found her name in her wallet.

Rachel hadn't hesitated. She and Jake had arrived on 57th Street before the ambulance. As always, she had immediately taken charge. She hadn't seen much of Tess since Santa Fe. Both had been too busy. But they'd talked a few times on the telephone, and it had been a pleasure to put George Westchester straight when he had attempted to renege on his agreement to hire Tess. Rachel had insisted on riding in the ambulance with the unconscious Tess, and while she did, she lined up a top neurologist and one of the best rooms at Lenox Hill. Sometimes even she was amazed at the power of her name, and of television. The neurologist had been in the E.R. to meet them. He had performed a thorough examination that had ruled out brain damage, and ordered a CAT scan to confirm his findings. Then he had given his pager number to the E.R. intern for when the CAT scan results came back. He had looked at Rachel as he did so, making sure that she realized he was giving this patient his top priority.

"Rachel, you know I haven't got any insurance, but my brother . . ."

"Forget it. It's all taken care of. When you're running Sotheby's and I get zapped, you do my accident, okay?"

They laughed together. This was the stuff of genuine friendship. Rachel had found the address of Camille's school in Tessa's Filofax. She herself had gone to pick up Camille and had taken her home to her own apartment for the night.

"How did you get on with Camille? It was so clever of you to find her."

"It was wonderful. She slept at the foot of my bed on a camp cot. And I read her politically correct bedtime stories, and then she read me one. I haven't slept so well in years." It was true. It had been wonderful playing mom. She'd even found some Froot Loops, Camille's favorite, in the back of the cupboard for breakfast.

"Dry run?" said Tessa with a laugh.

"Somehow, I don't think so. It's beginning to look a lot like Matt Harding after all. Diamonds as big as the Ritz, hold the Cinderella and Snow White."

"No knights on white chargers?"

Rachel smiled ruefully. "Almost, but not quite."

"Almost? Sounds interesting."

Rachel wondered if she could face telling Tess the story of Charles Ford. She opened her mouth to start it, but then, at the last moment, she couldn't face it. What was there to tell? That she had met a fine, sensitive man, a romantic, a man for every woman's dream, and that she had stuck him on TV and turned him into an emotional performing seal for the good of her show's ratings? She didn't feel proud of that. She wasn't cut out for the real, warm world of real, warm feelings. She was destined instead for the surrogate one, where emotions were sound bites and the saying to remember was "If they cry, they buy."

"Not very interesting. Believe me. I just proved to myself that I am what I am, and the rest is fantasy. Matt and I deserve each other."

"What was he like?" said Tessa.

"Like? Oh, I don't know. Yes, I do. He was admirable, a man who could love and feel and be loyal, and who expected those things in others. I . . . I . . . I think I'd rather not talk about him. He's gone. It's over."

Tessa watched her. Rachel had been touched by someone. That she knew. Later, perhaps, they could talk about it. Not now, apparently.

"What about you, Tess? Apart from fighting with cyclists, how have you been getting on? No tall dark strangers on the Sotheby's client list?"

Tessa winced. She hadn't told anybody about the events that had precipitated her accident. She didn't want to relive it in words. She didn't want the police to be involved, with all their horrible questions: "Did you in any way encourage him, Mrs. Andersen? What were you wearing at the time? Was it, if you don't mind my asking, a see-through blouse?" And then there was Sotheby's. A woman, a realtor, nearly raped by one of their clients? It wouldn't sound good. It would mark her. No woman emerged from a near-rape ordeal as a heroine. And how could she prove it? Gamero would be long gone. He probably wouldn't even have stayed to have his tongue stitched back together. Good! She'd got him there, and in the other place where it hurt. No, it was best to do nothing and say nothing, but to be more careful in the future. For a second, she felt a flash of anger. For every woman brave enough to report a sexual assault, there must be ten or more who said nothing for reasons not unlike hers. It was so unfair, but you couldn't ignore the harsh economics. With ten million in the bank, you could scream blue murder. With a bare cupboard, you bore it.

"Work's hell. I can't seem to get listings. I can't close the deals. But I'm going to do it. I'm going to make it happen. I *know* it will."

"Oh yes, it will, Tess, with that attitude." Rachel could almost see the determination. Certainly, she could feel it.

"Still Pete?"

"Yes, I guess. But I did meet someone. Not at all like your guy. Not sensitive, really, not much of a romantic, but very strong, and solid, and sort of . . . safe. I mean, he's almost English in lots of ways. And he's very, very rich, but he'd rather die than splash his money about. You know, reserved, and sophisticated and cultured."

"Where is he now?" said Rachel gently. It had to be asked.

"Oh, he's in Madrid. He doesn't know about all this. In fact, he called a few seconds before the bicycle hit me. He was just catching his plane."

"Do you know where he's staying in Madrid?"

"No, I don't. It's not that much of a thing. It's just, oh, well, he'd be the answer to a maiden's prayer right now." She laughed. "I suppose that's rather awful, isn't it?"

"It doesn't sound awful to me. It sounds like incredible common sense," said Rachel.

"It's funny," said Tessa. "You know, I came all the way to America to get away from my background, and then the only guy I meet who interests me at all has the same sort of background as me. Different, but basically the same."

"So you were 'similars.' My guy was an 'opposite,' " said Rachel.

"Opposites attract. Similars sit contentedly side by side," said Tessa.

She shifted in bed, and frowned as the drip needle shifted in her arm.

"What's in that drip?" said Rachel.

"Antibiotics. Apparently, sidewalks are dirty. I was always brought up to believe that dirt was good for you. Built up the immune system."

"You Brits," said Rachel with a laugh. "No wonder you have a reputation for never washing. Don't want to get rid of the 'goodness.' " She paused. "So, will you see your guy when he gets back from Madrid?"

"I hope so."

"Do you remember that night in the Hacienda Inn, when we all met? Wasn't that an amazing evening?" said Rachel.

"It certainly was. It seems as if it was years ago," said Tessa. "Have you heard from Carol? I got several postcards from her. She's found herself a studio, but she hasn't got the phone on yet. Probably doesn't want Jack irritating her. Oh, and she met a man she liked."

"Yes, I had a postcard, too. In fact it arrived only yesterday," said Rachel.

"What did she say? She hasn't gone back with that dreadful husband, has she?"

"No way. She's still in Santa Fe. In the apartment. And she talked about the mystery man!"

"Tell. Tell. What do you think he sounds like?"

"Nothing like ours, that's for sure. Neither your aristocrat nor my romantic. A tortured artist, no less. Perfect for Carol after all that suburbia, don't you think? Apparently, he's all stormy and unpredictable, and he's become her creative mentor. Sort of like a warm weather Heathcliff. I must say I never imagined people like that lived in Santa Fe."

"Goodness! That's exactly what he sounded like to me. How marvelous," said Tessa, clapping her hands and wincing with the pain of the movement. "Good for Carol. She deserves a bit of life. I'm so happy for her. Is it serious?"

"Impossible to say. Jack's coming to visit her next week. That should be a test of sorts."

"So, she got what she wanted. Her own studio in Santa Fe."

"Yup. Painting up a storm, and a gallery is interested, she says. I think she wins the 'dream' stakes. You, second. Me, a miserable third," said Rachel.

"Carol wanted independence. Yes, I guess she got it. You wanted romance, and it sounds as if you had a bit of it, and didn't like it. And I wanted security. Mmmmm. I think *I* come third," said Tessa

"Not after you marry your millionaire, you don't."

"But he's in Madrid."

"He'll be back."

"Yes," said Tessa, smiling broadly, "I have a feeling he will."

Twenty-nine

Carol looked at her watch. She was going to be late, and she didn't like to be late. She corrected herself in her mind. The old Carol didn't like to be late, because it put other people out and was impolite and thoughtless. The new Carol didn't mind being late. If other people didn't like her lateness, it was their problem. At least, Carol *tried* to think that. She didn't quite succeed, because she was about to be late for Jack.

She pushed down on the accelerator in a reflex action and then forced herself to slow down. Everything was still a test. The plane was due at eleven. He would have baggage. If she missed him at the gate, she would find him in the baggage area. Yes, that would be the right place to meet him. With the baggage. From the past. She would blow in without even apologizing, and she would be pleasant and calm. If he tried to suggest that she hadn't been on time, she would take his head off with a barrage of razor-sharp words. It was extraordinary the power he still had over her. History didn't go away. Jack was a factoid, and the children were facts. They were part of her life like her fingers and her feet, and they would always be. The question was, where would they be put? No longer on a pedestal on the mantel shelf.

She made the airport turn. He would be landing about now. She could picture him. The polo shirt, blue and somber. The Brooks Brothers beige pants, the Cole-Haan loafers in brown. He would have a jacket just in case, his brown tweed one, which he thought looked English, and he would carry his attaché case, of course, to prove that he was somebody with work to do even when he was on holiday. Where was Page Lee? Fuming at home, furious that the lover she had so nearly landed was making a play for his wife? Or perhaps she didn't know. Perhaps Jack the cheat had dreamed up a business trip for Page Lee, and now it was Carol's turn to play scarlet woman despite her wedding ring. Yes, maybe she should take him to bed to spite his mistress, and then ring Page Lee and tell her. Maybe . . .

Carol tried to clear her mind of all those hideous yesterday thoughts that centered around her old world and Jack. She had to move on, past revenge and jealousy, to the brand-new life she was already making. She thought of her studio, and of the wonderful, stimulating artistic battles she had already fought there as she struggled to shape her own style. She thought of the desert and of the inspiration it provided, and she thought of Charles Ford and the magical ranch where today she had gone to paint. He had insisted she treat it like home while he was away in Europe, and she had taken him at his word. She hadn't asked him to stay, even though she felt he would have stayed if she had. Something had held her back.

Now she missed him, and going out to the ranch was a way to be closer to him. Charles Ford seemed to be present in every corner of the old house, and the charming, gentle servants who had been told to treat her like an honored guest talked endlessly of him . . . the grooms, the housemaids, the old butler, and the Indians who tilled the fields. She knew him by proxy. And she knew him by feel, too. Half conscious in his arms, she had ridden through the night with him, and she had been put to bed in the room of the woman he had loved. And then, in that extraordinary catharsis in his studio, he had kissed her. He was powerful medicine, Charles Ford, a dark enigma wrapped in a puzzle, surrounded by a mystery. To the old butler, José, he was the little boy who loved the animals and communed with the horses, and who spoke Indian dialects and Spanish before he was fluent in English. The Indians called him "Cnawen," the one who understands all without listening. She had gotten to know tantalizing bits about him, but she knew she had hardly scratched his surface. How different he was from Jack, the divorce attorney with the silver tongue and the slippery morals.

She followed the signs to the parking area and her sense of foreboding grew. As an antidote she thought of the painting she was working on. She could see it now in the shaft of sun from the central skylight of her studio. It was a rose, open wide and in full bloom, and in the center of it was her own self-portrait. It was a wonderful painting, the best that she had done and a radical departure from her usual style. She wanted to give it to Charles. She had thought long and deep about the symbolism, but it was what she felt, and the new Carol had learned that to be true to yourself was what mattered. Yes, the rose was Rose. But Carol was not a replacement for Rose. She was a continuance. She knew Charles would understand it. He was Cnawen, the one to whom things were known without speech. She parked the car, and made an effort to remember where it was in the cavernous parking lot. Jack would not forgive her if she forgot. But screw Jack. Oh shit, why was he coming? Oh shit, why was she late?

She found her way to the baggage area and began looking around for the electric sign with his flight number.

"Carol! Carol!"

She spun around and there he was. Yellow polo, but otherwise as predicted. He put the attaché case down and held open his arms for her in the old way. Carol walked toward him.

"Hello, Jack," she said.

His hands fell to his sides.

"Hello, darling." He seemed subdued by the lack of warmth in her welcome.

She bent her head in his direction and allowed him a shot at her cheek. What did she feel? Cold, but frightened of him, oddly. She was fearful of the power he had always had over her. He could make her do things. He had always been able to do that, because she had always wanted so desperately to please the man she adored. Now, the adoration had gone, but the subtle feeling of subservience lingered like a bad habit that had to be broken.

"You look terrific," he said. "The desert suits you."

"Freedom suits me. I suppose I should thank you for letting me find that out."

Her hostility was a defense mechanism against his power. She knew that. So, it seemed, did he.

"It's over, you know," he said. "With Page Lee."

"I'm sorry for you," said Carol. "Because it's over with us, too."

"Let's not get into that right now," he said, trying to take control. "I've got to find my baggage. Where's the car? Is it close? Would it be a good idea for you to get it and drive to the entrance while I get my baggage? That way we save time."

"For what?" said Carol.

"Save time to save time," he said, looking at his watch. Somehow the gesture contained a rebuke for Carol's lateness.

She could feel him doing it to her. It had always been like this. She was being told what to do by this man who had fucked his lover in her bed. He had traveled all this way to her magic land with his silly briefcase, and he was already bossing her around like the hausfrau she had been pleased to be for the major part of her life. The fury bubbled inside her.

"You go get the car," she said. "It's a long walk. Here are the keys. It's a red Nissan. Four-D in the short-term block. The ticket is on the passenger's seat."

"It would be more efficient if you did, because you know the car and exactly where you left it, and . . . and I wouldn't be insured to drive," he said with his old attorney's sharpness.

"How about this?" said Carol. "You take a taxi to whatever hotel you're staying at, and you give me a call sometime and we'll meet for lunch."

He looked at her in amazement. This wasn't his Carol. Something had happened to her. A stranger was standing there, someone who looked like his wife but wasn't.

"I'll get the car," he said. "You'll probably recognize my suitcase. It's the old brown one."

"Fine," said Carol, handing him the car keys as if they were a tip for a bellboy. She felt the exhilaration inside. She had stood up to him. She had prevailed, and it felt very, very good. Paradoxically, her success in standing up to him softened her feelings toward him. He was just a great big boy, a bully and a fool who had lived too long without discipline.

She turned back to the baggage carousel that was spewing cases onto the conveyor belt. Jack's would be instantly recognizable and full of memories. How often she had packed that case for him. For holidays they had shared. For business trips that had turned out to have been trysts with Page Lee. Once again her stomach churned in anger, and the ambivalence flowed over her. What would be the outcome of his traveling to Santa Fe to see her? Would it be merely a lawyer's last futile appeal to the jury? Or was there a possibility that he would do or say something that would change her mind . . . and give him a second chance to ruin her life? No! No! What then would become of the painting of the rose in the studio and the embryonic Carol inside it . . . the brand-new person struggling to be born in the land of art and hope and mystery and excitement? There was the suitcase. She yanked it off the belt, lugged it outside, and sat on it by the curbside as she waited for him.

He wasn't long. He parked the car, dealt imperiously with an airport official who tried to move him on, and in no time his case was in the trunk and they were ready to go.

"I'll drive," he said.

"No," said Carol. "I'll drive. It's my car."

He smiled indulgently. "Do you know the way?" It was code for male dominance, female subservience.

"I expect I'll find it," said Carol. "It isn't the Sahara."

They got in in silence. Jack seemed to be aware that the case was difficult, the jury hostile, the judge cantankerous. But he had won cases under worse circumstances. You just had to work at it, prepare yourself, persevere.

"Where are you staying?"

"I thought I'd stay at the Hilton for the first night or two."

He stole a sly look at her as she pulled away from the curb. She looked great, better than the tearstained wreck who had caught the plane for Santa Fe all those months ago. In fact, better than the pre-Page Lee Carol. "The first night or two" was his code for "Before I move in with you."

"I don't know how much time I'll have available for seeing you," she said, as she took the exit to the city.

"Oh?" he said. "I thought this was sort of a breathing space for you to get your thoughts straight. I imagined my being here could help us work things out. What are you up to that makes you so busy?"

Without me, the kids, the cooking, the cleaning, the driving, the dinner parties, the garden, the household bills, the servicing of the cars, maintenance of the house, etc., was the unspoken coda to his question, she thought to herself.

"Painting," she said simply.

"Ah, painting," he said.

The old enemy.

"Sold any yet?" He tried not to make it sound patronizing, but he didn't succeed.

Carol was on the freeway. So was her tongue.

"No, and I don't have to on my share of the divorce proceedings. I live simply. I can actually do things for pleasure. *My* pleasure."

"Don't talk about divorce," he said. "That hasn't been decided. I don't want a divorce." He wasn't so confident now, and he wasn't supposed to be. For one of the very first times in her life, she felt superior to him. She didn't care that she hadn't a clue where the Hilton was. It would turn up somewhere.

"It's always what you want, isn't it, Jack? Well, you wanted Page Lee and you got her. I bet she's just great when you all go out together, Whitney and Devon and good old Page Lee, chipping in and being one of the regular guys."

He sat in silence through that one. Their group outings had

numbered three and would not number more. The children had
loathed Page Lee's pickiness and her bright insistence on bossing everyone around. They had wanted Boston Chicken. She
had wanted Pollo Tropical. "So much better for you." They had
wanted to see Schwarzenegger. She had wanted to see an art
movie. She had even corrected Whitney's grammar.

"It hasn't been the same without you," he said, his voice
quiet. "It's been lonely. Have you found that?"

"Yes, I have. At first it was difficult, but it gets easier each
day. Each month. The secret is to keep busy. That's what I've
found. I just paint and paint and I lose myself in it, and the day
flies by and I wonder where it's gone . . . and I'm even sorry
it's gone."

Again, he looked at her. She had changed enormously. It
hardly seemed possible.

"Where exactly is this place you're living, and who is this
rancher you keep talking about?"

The attorney spoke. Big changes equaled emotional changes.
They were most often brought about by romance. It was unthinkable that "his" Carol could survive so well for so long
without him, unless his place had been taken or was in the
process of being taken by someone else.

"He's called Charles Ford," she said, enjoying the sound of
his name. "He has eighty thousand acres, which I suppose is a
reasonable-size ranch. He's also a painter. One of the Ford family, but very old on his mother's side, from the French, the English, the Mexican . . ."

"Oh, a sort of half-breed." Jack couldn't help it. He was as
liberal as a New England attorney could be, but he had to pick
up on that. A painter and rancher with eighty thousand acres
so easily outranked a divorce lawyer in Connecticut—at least
"Mexican" evened the playing field a bit.

"I don't think I've ever heard you say anything racially preju-
diced before," she said.

"No, I didn't mean that." He backtracked.

"Well, he *is* a mixture, a marvelous, cultured mixture of

everything that's fine and noble in this world. He actually saved my life."

"He did *what?*"

She told him then, in great detail. He tried briefly to blame her for letting her car run out of gas, but went silent after she related that Charles had arrived on horseback and carried her through the freezing night to a fairy tale *estancia* with flickering candles and portraits of ancient ancestors on the wall, to a house smelling of gardenias and the wax of old wood.

She told him of Charles's offer of Rose's studio, and of her feeling unable to accept it. That was who he was, a gentleman full of old-world generosity, and he wanted nothing in return.

"We'll see," said Jack.

"He liked my painting. That's why he wanted me to have Rose's studio. Some people feel that way about art, you know, Jack. I do, for instance . . . the woman you lived with all those years. They look at a painting and they don't see dollar signs and sale rooms and insurance certificates. They don't think about fakes, and whether the air-conditioning is set right to protect the investment. They just see beauty or ugliness, and if beauty, it makes them feel good and happy. You haven't met a lot of people in your life like that, have you, Jack? And neither had I until I left you. But you should, you know. They're good for you, those people. They fill up emptiness. They put life in its proper context. I look at the stars down here, and the sunsets and the desert. I look and I accept. I don't keep thinking: this needs six-six-six fertilizer, or the sprinkler head needs adjusting, or the fruit trees need pruning. I just see and enjoy. You should try it sometime. And what was it you said . . . 'We'll see.' . . . Yes, we'll see. We'll just wait and see what happens."

"Are you in love with him?"

"Yes, I'm a little bit in love with the idea of him. Like with someone who has helped to make dreams come true. Like I was with you once, Jack. Because there was a time when you made my dreams come true."

She looked to see where her words had landed. He looked

stricken. He couldn't bear his wife, his possession, talking like that about another man, and a man like Charles Ford, who seemed in so many ways to outclass him. Jack's self-respect was a fragile thing. It needed bolstering from wherever it could find support, from the office, from Page Lee, from Carol, from the kids. He knew that in the scheme of things he didn't amount to much. He was an attorney in a suburb, a leech attached to the body of the litigation society. In China he would have starved, and in places like India, where most of the world's people lived. But artists and farmers were respected everywhere. One provided food for the soul, the other for the stomach. The world could live without neither. But lawyers profited from lawlessness. They were a measure in their quantity of a citizen's disrespect for his fellows.

"It's all right to be a painter and a dreamer if you've inherited a whole pile of money," he said bitterly.

"Life isn't easy for anyone," said Carol. "For the poor little rich kid or the poor little poor kid."

Carol was suddenly full of exhilaration behind the wheel. She was talking to Jack and she was winning, not because she was cleverer than he, or better with words . . . She was neither . . . but she was right. *That* was what made the difference.

He seemed to sense it, because for a long time he said nothing. When he spoke again, it was on more trivial, and safer, territory.

"Do you know where you're driving to?" He posed the question like an accusation.

"To a brilliant future," said Carol cheerfully, seeing right through the ploy. He was rather sweet now that she had the drop on him. So predictable. So easy to outsmart if you just had confidence on your side.

"What about the Hilton?" he said.

"You wanted to talk and we're talking, so why don't we drive around for a bit until we see a big sign that says 'Hilton.' I'm in no hurry."

He couldn't let it go.

"If you run out of gas here there won't be an artistic millionaire to save you."

"How do you know?" said Carol. "I didn't expect one to find me in the middle of the desert, in the middle of the night. In Santa Fe, chances are quite a bit higher."

He couldn't touch her. This was wonderful. She was actually glad he was there. She was enjoying this conversation that she had dreaded. What had changed her? Why did all his old tricks no longer work on her? It was as if she had seen the light on the road to some personal Damascus. Was a decision to leave as enlightening as that, the simple decision to take control of your life and go?

"You've made love to him," he said suddenly. "I can tell by the way you talk about him. That makes us equal. I made a mistake with Page Lee. I think we should make up and let bygones be bygones. I love you, Carol. And deep down you still love me. I can tell."

She laughed at him then. What a cheap, childish trick. A gentleman saves his wife's life and offers her a sanctuary in the desert to pursue her life's ambition, and somehow Jack manages to compare it to what he did with Page Lee.

"Charles Ford and I have *not* made love," she said. "Maybe one day we will. Maybe one day I will want him to."

"Please don't say that. I told you I've broken up with Page Lee."

"Well, good for you, you long-suffering martyr. House getting a bit dusty, is it? Meals out of the fridge? Sex not quite so hot when it's no longer illicit? Joined the bachelor club, have you, Jack? Dates and disappointments. AIDS and herpes and paperwork before sex. What a wonderful time it must be to be footloose and fancy free in the great big world, with the children off to college and nobody to police you but yourself. I bet the senior partner and his wife enjoy the catered dinner parties with the bimbo of the week. Can't you hear their conversation in the car on the way home? 'Pity about poor old Jack. Couldn't handle the midlife crisis. I wonder if he's really the man for the new Sony account. That nice Fred Nichols is so stable. Did you see the flowers tonight? And who was that awful girl he'd dug up? She must have been half his age, and she hadn't a clue what to do with the finger bowls.' "

"Don't be a bitch, Carol. It's not like you."

"No, it isn't, is it? It's a different Carol. One who tells the truth, Jack. What's the matter with my little scenario? It's not a pretty picture, but it's *true,* isn't it? And you know the thing about the truth, don't you, Jack? It sets you free. When you tell the truth, it means you're not afraid anymore. Lies are for the frightened people."

"I think we just passed the Hilton," he said. "Do you think we could drive to where you're living? Just so that I can see it."

"No way."

"Why not?"

"You want the truth?"

"I suppose so." He didn't sound certain.

"Because I don't want you to defile it. It's mine. I got it without you. I will live in it without you. I don't want memories of you wandering about, picking things up and putting them down. And saying the type of things you say."

"Oh, God," he said. He seemed to sag in the passenger's seat beside her. It was the moment he knew he had lost her.

She turned toward him, hearing his defeat. It was what she needed to hear before there could be any hope of absolution, and perhaps whatever he did, there would be none. But it was a prerequisite. She saw that his eyes were filling with tears. Poor Jack. Never in the whole of her life before had she felt sorry for him, but she did now. The Hilton—he hadn't even bothered to try to discover one of the funky, fabulous little inns, like the Territorial or the Grant Corner, that Santa Fe was famous for. He had no soul, and she had been too busy being in love with and in awe of him to notice. Now, he was lost without her, when they had both expected her to be lost without him. How strange life was, and how wonderfully unpredictable. Carol was in the driver's seat, figuratively and literally, and the road was life and she was steering.

Jack felt the misery burst over him. He tried to stop the tears, but they wouldn't be stopped. They became sobs that shook him. He had made such a mess of everything. He had felt invincible. There had been Page Lee, full of admiration for his letters and court performances. And there had been Carol, standing bathed in love-light when he returned home—the scented house, the delicious dinner, the tales of trivialities that he endured grandly, the progress report on the homefront where the battles were always won, and the enemies . . . leaking cisterns, brake linings, telephone repairmen . . . were always vanquished by his competent wife. Carol had been so right in her bitchiness. The senior partner was noticeably cooler toward Jack. Nichols was usurping his role as favorite son, and Page Lee, rejected at her moment of victory, had become his implacable enemy at the office. Each night he returned to the empty house and cursed the maid who had slacked off without Carol's supervision, and watched the garden go to seed, as he heated up the Stouffer's in the microwave and drank far more of the Chivas Regal than he should. Carol put her hand out and touched his knee. She felt the tenderness well up inside her. "Don't, Jack," she said. "Don't cry."

"I've made such a terrible mess, Carol," he sobbed.

"Yes, you did, darling," she said. "But maybe it's for the best. Maybe we're meant to move on and find ourselves, and grow and develop. Maybe you needed it, and I needed it. Perhaps Page Lee wasn't right, but someone else will be, and you'll find her."

He turned to her, the tracks of his tears wet on his face.

"I found her. It was you. It still is you."

Carol took a deep breath. She was free now. She had made the break with the past. The hardest part was over. She thought of her painting, of her studio, of her face peering out from the petals of the rose that surrounded it and perhaps inspired her.

"It's not just about what you did, Jack. I'm moving through that, the anger, the jealousy, the terrible sense of betrayal. I'm . . . how can I say this . . . I'm becoming me, Carol, not

Carol McCabe. I'm not even becoming Georgia anymore. I thought I had to escape and be someone else, but all I had to do was find the real me. It sounds metaphysical, but it means I can make decisions for myself. I don't have to think about you anymore, or even the kids, or anything. I guess it's called freedom."

"You can be free with me. Can't we be free together?"

She laughed, a bittersweet laugh.

"You were always free, Jack. That was clever of you. But you abused freedom, and now you're alone. Some people find freedom with others, some by being alone. Maybe you're the one and I'm the other. You don't find out until you try it."

She had backtracked and found the Hilton, and now they were there and the doorman was approaching, and this conversation would be ending soon.

"Will you come up and see my room?" he asked, almost like a child to a parent on being left at some new boarding school.

"No," said Carol. "Maybe we'll meet for dinner later, or lunch tomorrow."

So she dropped him off like a hitchhiker at a station, because she wanted to prove she could do it. Carol was surprised by the sudden realization of how much she still loved him as she watched him, dejected, at the curbside. But she watched him still as she drove away, an object in the rearview mirror that had appeared larger than it was.

Thirty

When Carol was painting out at the ranch, it had become a tradition that she would visit the house for midmorning coffee, and if Charles was there he would join her. Now, as she sat at the vast mahogany dining-room table, she thought of Jack at the Hilton, all alone like her, but somehow sad in his loneliness as she was strangely secure in hers.

José entered the room and bade her a respectful good morning.

"Good morning, José. Any news when Mr. Ford will be returning?" she said.

"None as yet, ma'am. A last-minute person, ma'am, Mr. Ford, like his father. We expect him when we see him."

He poured the coffee for her. "Mr. Ford" hung in the gardenia-scented air.

"What was his father like?" said Carol.

"Ah," said José, pleased to talk of a man he had clearly worshiped. "There never was a man quite like him. He could walk like the Indians, you know, and never make a sound."

"How amazing. How did he learn that?"

"Oh, the way he learned everything, ma'am. He learned from books, but mostly he learned from watching and listening, and he'd go out for weeks sometimes. Just walk away into the desert, and then one day he'd be back."

"His wife must have loved that."

"The señora understood him. He was a mystic, Mr. Ford. He

knew what you were thinking, and he was kind and good. Almost like a spirit himself. Words don't really describe what he was. You'd have had to know him."

"Does Mr. Charles take after him?"

"Oh Lord, yes, he does, ma'am. He's more, would you say, grounded, like his mother. But he has his father's mystical side. He knows the weather. He feels it in his bones. In this house we don't watch the television to find out what's going to happen. We ask the master. I can't remember him being wrong."

"Was he close to his father?"

"As close as anyone could be. But his father was a loner. He loved the desert more than people, although he was kind and good to us all. Mr. Charles lived for the times they would go to the desert together. But his mother was close to him, too. And he loves women, Mr. Charles."

He quieted suddenly, as if he had said too much. Carol wanted him to go on, but she knew not to press him.

A man who loved women. A mystical side to him. A man who could feel the weather in his bones. She thought of Jack, catching the early CNBC business report on cable at the Hilton. How were his Pacific Rim shares doing, his emerging markets gambles? Would he be working on his little laptop to find out how much he had won or lost before tackling *The New York Times*?

That morning, on waking, she had phoned home and talked to Devon and Whitney before they left for school.

Carol smiled at the memory of their good cheer and their excitement at returning to see their friends. Why did one ever worry about kids? Was it denial? Were they really worried to hell about their parents' marriage and just hiding it? Perhaps they hadn't even noticed. There had been arguments before. Perhaps they thought this was just another one. Or were they just so self-contained, selfish even, that divorce and the mental anguish that Carol and Jack were suffering was simply irrelevant to their MTV/girls/boys/cars life? Was that the American way, families slipping across the surface of the vast nation, colliding only at Thanksgivings and Christmases, with the only concern being which set of parents to spend which holiday with? Divorce was a way of life now. They gave kids little books to read titled *Going to Mommy's Wedding*.

Well, she was learning from the children of the careless society and focusing in on herself. All the same, Carol couldn't help feeling that there was something deeply wrong with it all.

She finished her coffee, got up, and walked out into the hallway. The kids were out of the equation. There was only her and Jack. One thing was certain. She would never return to her old life and her husband, unless it was on her terms. And Charles was a factor now. Did Jack have a rival? *He* had seemed to think so. Did she?

As she walked out of the house, Carol realized that her future might be more exciting than she had ever dreamed.

Thirty-one

Matt Harding looked as good as he had intended. His dinner jacket was painted onto his lean frame, and he wore a dark tan, of the kind Aristotle Onassis said no really successful person should be without. He stood in a corner of the vast sale room, and already it was turning into the center of Sotheby's party. Rachel stood by his side, the soon-to-be-signed superstar that would orbit, shining brightly, around the Matt Harding sun. He didn't seriously doubt that tonight Rachel's nos would become yeses. It was the sensible thing to do, and he had rarely met anyone as deeply and meaningfully sensible as Rachel.

"Are we going to look at the paintings?" said Rachel.

In the desperate nineties, the art market was trying everything to move the canvases, and this summer cocktail party was a stylish marketing ploy. The Riverhouse collection of German Expressionists was for sale, and it was as good as any in the world. So now the megabuck collectors, the hot dealers, and the perennials that were the sine qua non of any high-end Manhattan party had been invited to drink champagne and check out the exhibits prior to the sale in a few days' time.

Rachel felt uncomfortable, almost like an imposter. Matt was taking her for granted as his wife-to-be, and she was not granted. But on the other hand, she had tried extra hard tonight. Her dress was killer, her skirt Locklear short, and the punk Versace made her look far younger than she was.

"You go check it out, darling. I hate looking at art with people around. Distracts me. I'm only interested in a couple, the Munch of the girl screaming, and the Kandinsky self-portrait. They're going to hang them in my office next week so that I can make up my mind. Tell me what you think. Don't be long."

Rachel slipped away, glad to be by herself. Across the room, she saw the Munch that Matt was thinking of buying. A man was standing looking at it. Rachel went up and stood beside him. He turned away from the canvas and looked at her. She turned away from the canvas and looked at him. Their eyes met.

"Oh," she said.

"Ah," said he.

That was not good enough. Both knew that. They stood quite still. Rachel felt the blush rushing up from her neck.

"A strong painting," he said at last, tearing his eyes away from hers and back to the Munch.

He turned to her again. His eyes were as deep as they had been, but he was no longer a creature of the night, wild and feral, the black-and-indignant person brushed with mystery that he had been when first they met. He was the recognizable man of their second meeting, well dressed, urbane, sophisticated, looking at a painting of a screaming girl, one that he found "strong."

It was the same. It was happening all over again. Hyperreality surrounded her. The room with its chattering people had gone away. There was only him . . . and her.

He turned fully toward her now, the painting no longer a possible conversation piece. She had his total concentration. He stared at her hard.

"Hello, Rachel," he said.

"Hello, Charles."

"I didn't expect to see you here," he said. "I don't know why. I suppose you are everywhere."

He was trying to be cold. He wasn't entirely succeeding. Rachel, the interviewer, noticed it. Rachel, the woman, was disarrayed.

"You mean I crossed your mind? In an 'I expect Rachel Richardson won't be there' thought?"

Her brain was holding together. Wherever the emotions lived, in the heart, in the gut, she was a mess.

He couldn't help smiling.

"The famous interviewer speaks," he said.

"So you haven't forgiven me for that."

"What's to forgive?" he said with a dismissive wave of his hand that said "everything."

"Harry said he showed you the *People* piece, too."

She wanted everything out in the open. She was on automatic pilot. Her script was writing itself.

"Yes, he did."

"It was awful. It made me sound shallow and cheap."

"Yes, it did, didn't it. But I was brought up to believe that one shouldn't trust everything one reads in the press."

The irony was positively iron in its heaviness.

"I'm not. But I am ambitious, and I do put work first, and that's how I got where I am, and that's what you liked about me."

She stuck her chin out with the words, defiant, desperate. She wanted this man as much as she had ever wanted him, and he was almost a lost cause, almost . . . But he was still there. He had not walked away from her. He was talking to her. They were having a conversation, damn it. That must count for something.

"How on earth do you know that's what I liked about you?" he said with an incredulous laugh.

"Women's intuition," said Rachel, still defiant.

"Do honorary men possess women's intuition?"

Okay, so they were fighting. That was fine, too. Rachel felt herself getting angry. The relief from the other emotions was overwhelming.

"I'm not an honorary man. I'm an honored woman. Perhaps in your life only the men are allowed to achieve things."

"Anybody can conquer," he said. "Male or female. What is at issue is how low one is prepared to stoop to do so."

"Oh, is *that* what is at issue?" said Rachel. "Or is it just that aristocrats don't understand meritocrats? Maybe the silver spoon they stuck in your mouth at birth left you blind to the fact that the rest of us have to work for a living."

She saw the color spring to his cheeks.

"I merely object to being used as cannon fodder for your apparently insatiable ambition."

"Hello, there," said Matt Harding. It was impossible to say if he had heard the last sentence. He stood there beside them, in front of the Munch of the girl screaming, waiting to be introduced.

Rachel turned toward him in confusion. Matt didn't usually move around at parties. He stayed put and people came to him. Obviously, he had missed her. "Matt. This is Charles Ford. And this is Matt Harding," she said. It was the best she could do. The anger was fading. Perhaps it hadn't been a proper argument at all.

"Charles Ford. Charles Ford," boomed Harding. "Good Lord, speak of the devil. I thought you didn't go out. I thought I wasn't allowed to meet you. Trust you, Rachel, to dig up Charles Ford."

Charles took a step back from Harding. It was an involuntary gesture, but it said a lot.

"Hello, Mr. Harding," said Charles.

"Matt, Matt," said Matt, pushing out a hand and capturing Charles's with it. There was one-sided pumping and then the Ford hand was dragged away from him. "Now listen, Charles. Harry Wardlow has a lot of your stuff in his back room. And I love it. *Love* it. I keep telling him to fix it up for us to meet, and he gives me all this bullshit about you being a recluse, and then I find you myself, or rather my fiancée comes up with you."

Fiancée. The word pierced Rachel's heart like an arrow. She saw a look pass across the face of Charles Ford, like a scudding cloud across the sun. He shot a glance at her, and then turned back to Matt, who was droning on, unstoppable.

"I always like to meet my artists. Make a point of it. Look in their eyes. See the man behind the work. And now I get my chance . . ."

"I'm not your fiancée," said Rachel. She tried to keep her

voice calm. She smiled at Matt to try to soften the blow, and she shot a sidelong glance at Charles to see his reaction.

Charles Ford's eyes opened wider.

"I'm not your fiancée, Matt," she repeated.

He laughed incredulously. "There you are. You see? That's what happens when you take a woman at her word and don't buy her an engagement ring. Being cheap always costs you in the end. One of my mottoes."

Charles was looking at her, questioning her.

"How do you two know each other?" said Matt suddenly. Clearly, he had not heard about Rachel's interviewing Charles.

Charles looked at him, and then back at Rachel. She could see him make some kind of decision. It was in his eyes.

"We don't really know each other at all," he said. Then he turned, and without saying another word he walked away.

Matt watched him go.

"Funny guy," he said. He looked at Rachel, a quizzical expression on his face.

But Rachel was watching Charles's retreating figure. No! She didn't say the word, but it seemed that her soul was screaming it. Don't go. Not again. Not ever. She was acutely aware that this was madness, but it was the madness of which she had always dreamed. She had never felt more alive. Never more involved. To fight with him was better than all the love she had ever made with all the lovers. She couldn't remember when she had cared as much. She had to stop him from leaving, but there was no way to do so. He had gone.

"So you are not my fiancée," Matt said. "Or is it just not my fiancée in front of people, or people like, say, Charles Ford? Maybe we should get this cleared up once and for all?"

He was furious with her for making him look foolish in front of Ford. But he also realized something more important. He realized that it was the moment he had lost her. He knew now that Rachel had never been in love with him. He had chosen to believe that his desire for her, and the life he had to offer her, would be enough to win her. Now, he faced the truth. It was like the boardroom. There was always a precise moment when the deal was done or undone, and you recognized it. Often it was the smallest thing . . . a smile, a gesture, a clearing of the throat.

"Oh, Matt . . ." said Rachel. She looked at him. He stood there so strong and certain. He was perhaps one of the toughest people Rachel had ever met, because deep down he needed nobody. He was like her ten years ago. But Matt thought he needed her for some strange reason . . . maybe because she couldn't be had. Ten years ago he would have been perfect. But that was then and this was now.

He went on, as if talking to himself, forcing the change of subject.

"You know, it's funny, isn't it? If there was some woman screaming in the next-door hotel suite, you'd call the police. And if she was doing it for fun, you'd avoid her like the plague. But next week I'll pay a million bucks for this girl and her scream. Crazy world, really."

"Crazy can be wonderful," said Rachel.

"Rachel," he said suddenly, "let's go have dinner. I think you owe me that."

"Do we have to do any goodbyes?"

"No way. This is a business thing."

"Ohmigod, there's Tessa," said Rachel. They had reached the doorway.

"That's it, Rachel. We're gone. Call Tessa tomorrow." Matt's tone said his mind was made up. He'd had more than enough of the Sotheby's party.

But Rachel was standing stock still and the color was draining from her face, because Tessa was reaching out and touching the arm of a man who was smiling down at her . . . and that man was Charles Ford.

Thirty-two

Slowly but surely, it was all coming together for Tessa. She had learned that you had to prospect for clients like miners prospected for gold. So she forced herself again and again to make telephone calls to friends. It was a soul-destroying business, but the worst they could say was no. And when they did, which was nearly all the time, she said, "Fine." Now, she was learning to *think* "Fine." It was simply a question of percentages. An old pro in the office reckoned you got a listing for every hundred calls you made.

She had several listings now, because she had caught some people at the right time on the telephone . . . after rows with their present broker, at the expiration of exclusives, at moments of elation or despair. There had been nothing big yet, but the little ones added up.

She picked up the telephone and called Mary Sinclair. This would be her fifth call. Each time previously, she had reached the social secretary. Today, as luck or hard work would have it, the social secretary was off with a cold.

"Mary? It's Tessa Andersen."

"Hello, darling. How *are* you? I haven't seen you in ages. How lovely to hear from you."

Mary Sinclair, married to investment-banking money, had seldom been so friendly. It soon transpired why.

"You know, darling, I am *so* upset. You remember that terrible

Mamie Van Buren, the big wheel at the Meadows who lives next door and makes everyone's life miserable?"

"The one who looks like a basset hound?" said Tessa, taking the cue.

"Yes, she does, doesn't she? How *hilarious!* Goodness, Tessa, that's *exactly* what she looks like, doesn't she?" The Sinclair laugh pealed through the telephone.

It went from better to best. A few days before, Mamie Van Buren had accused Mary Sinclair of cheating at golf by moving her ball in the bunker.

"Well, anyway, darling, Fred has been talking about moving to the Vineyard for years. So we're putting Bridgehampton on the market. That's it. Mamie Van Buren can go jump in the lake."

"Do you want me to sell it for you?"

"Goodness. I'd forgotten. You're a realtor now, aren't you? Who are you with?"

"Sotheby's."

"Oh, I like Sotheby's. Yes, of course, why not? Fred wants to ask five and accept four and a half."

She was talking about $4.5 million, maybe more. If Tessa got an exclusive and sold it herself, her take-home commission would be $137,000.

Tessa had put down the telephone with a shaking hand. The Sinclair house by the lake at Bridgehampton was incredibly marketable. She put her head in her hands and thanked God.

The telephone rang.

"I have Rachel Richardson for Tessa Andersen."

"This is Tessa Andersen."

"Please hold."

While Tessa waited, she could scarcely control her excitement. It was fate that Rachel had chosen this minute to call. Rachel had made all this possible. Without Rachel's intervention with Westchester, Tessa wouldn't have had this job. And it had been Rachel who had picked up the pieces during and after her accident. The expenses of that alone could have sunk Tessa and Camille.

"Rachel, I'm so glad you called. I've just had the most amazing piece of luck. Mary Sinclair, you know, the Dillon, Read Sinclairs, has just given me their Bridgehampton house. Five million bucks. Exclusive. Can you believe it?"

"Well, isn't that great?" said Rachel. "Did you enjoy the party last night?"

Tessa picked up on the edge in Rachel's voice immediately.

"The Sotheby's thing? Were you there? I didn't see you."

"I saw you as I was leaving."

"Why didn't you say hello? I never saw you." Could Rachel have thought that Tessa ignored her on purpose? Was *that* what the attitude was about?

"I know you didn't. I was in a rush."

"Oh, what a pity . . ."

"Tessa, are you doing anything for lunch today? I need to talk to you."

"No, I'm not. Let's do that. Where would you like to go?"

Tessa could feel that something was wrong. What?

"Will Le Bilboquet be okay? My treat."

"How fabulous. Yes, please," said Tessa.

"Around quarter of one. You know where it is?"

"Perfect. Yes, I do. It's near me on Madison. Perhaps if you have a moment you can drop by my apartment afterward."

"That would be nice," said Rachel. The words were okay, but something was wrong with their tone.

"Is everything all right?" said Tessa.

"Yes, of course. Shouldn't it be?"

It didn't sound like Rachel at all. As she put down the telephone, there was a small cloud in the blue sky of Tessa's good mood.

Thirty-three

It had been a strange lunch, Tessa couldn't help feeling as they walked along Madison toward her apartment. On the surface everything had been friendly, but there had been tension in the air.

"Are you sure you have time for coffee?" said Tessa.

"Oh, yes, absolutely, and I'd love to see your apartment."

"With a bit of luck I won't have to live there much longer."

Rachel paused, as if making a decision. Then she took the plunge.

"Tess, you remember that night at the Hacienda Inn, when we all met . . . and how I said what I really wanted to do was to fall hopelessly in love, like for real, the whole romantic bit, nothing held back?"

"Yes, of course I remember."

Tessa stopped dead in the street. She had the sense that Rachel was about to say something that was difficult for her. Maybe that explained her weird mood.

Rachel stopped, too. "Look, Tess, I'm not much good at this, but the bottom line is . . . well, I did meet a man. At the Hacienda Inn, of all places. And I felt all those wonderful things we had discussed . . . the magic, the absolute knowledge that this was it. I didn't say anything then, because it seemed so unbelievable . . . that we would discuss something and then I would go straight out and experience it. I'm just not that suggestible. I'm just not." Rachel started to walk again.

Tessa said nothing, but she felt like laughing out loud. This was *so* unlike Rachel.

"Anyway," Rachel continued, "when I got back to New York, I found out more about him." She shot a sidelong glance at Tessa, who smiled encouragingly. "I just had to meet him again. Nobody seemed to know him, so I arranged it myself. I was doing this TV show, and I asked him to be on it. At first he didn't want to. Then, when I met him to discuss it, I persuaded him to do it."

"Sounds like the Rachel I've come to know and love," said Tessa with a laugh.

"Well, when I met him properly, we had dinner together . . . and . . . and I know this sounds crazy, but I fell in love with him. I was fascinated by him, totally blown away."

"That's incredible, Rachel."

They had arrived at the door of Tessa's apartment building.

"This is it," she said.

"Oh," said Rachel, still lost in her story. They walked up the stairs. Rachel went first. At the top, she turned to Tessa. "Here's where it gets complicated," she said. "I told you a bit about him in the hospital. Then you told me about someone you'd met. They sounded very different. Do you remember that?"

"Right," said Tessa, finding her keys. Rachel was watching her carefully, like she did sometimes on TV when she was maneuvering an interview subject into a corner.

"Yours was solid, very safe, sophisticated. We agreed he was a 'similar,' while mine was an 'opposite.' "

Tessa opened the door. She hadn't a clue what Rachel was getting at.

Rachel followed her.

Tessa waited for some kind of polite comment about the apartment. She had made it look nice, although she could never make it look big. But Rachel was miles away, lost in her own agenda.

"Let me take your coat," said Tessa. "Sit down. I'll make some coffee."

But Rachel remained standing. Tessa felt there was something a little ominous about that. She moved away to the kitchen area and emptied the dirty filter bag into the trash.

"So what went wrong with your man, after things had started out so well? I remember you telling me things hadn't worked out," said Tessa. She was intrigued. She sensed that some punch line was coming, and she hadn't a clue what it was going to be.

Perversely, Rachel changed the subject.

"You know, at the Hacienda Inn you said it was your dream to get yourself together financially and support Camille. I guess the money side of things is beginning to work out pretty well, with that big listing you just got."

"Yes, it took an age. But it's a beginning."

"So now it's just getting over Pete, and letting time heal the wounds."

"I suppose so," said Tessa with a laugh.

"So, in a way, you've achieved your objective."

Why was Rachel being so persistent?

"I've got quite a long way to go, actually," Tessa said. "But, yes, I've made a start."

"That's how I feel about my goal," said Rachel.

Tessa poured the coffee.

Somehow she felt that a cat-and-mouse game was being played. And she was not the cat.

"So you met this chap at the Hacienda Inn," said Tess. "Who is he, Rachel? Are we allowed to know his name? What was he doing at the Hacienda Inn? Trying to lose weight?"

Tessa took the coffee over to Rachel, who sat down at last on the sofa by the coffee table.

"Why on earth didn't you mention him? You do play your cards close to your chest, Rachel."

"Perhaps you do, too, Tessa."

"Me? Why? What do you mean?"

"His name is Charles Ford," said Rachel. Her eyes never left Tessa's.

Tessa couldn't stop the blush.

"Painter Charles Ford? New Mexico Charles Ford?" she said, her blush deepening.

"The Charles Ford you were talking to at the Sotheby's party last night."

"Oh, I seeeee . . . ," said Tessa.

"You looked like you were pretty friendly."

"With the man you've fallen in love with."

"Right on, Tessa."

"What an incredible coincidence," said Tessa, splaying her hands to show how odd fate was.

"Isn't it just," said Rachel. If she had had gloves on, she would be peeling them off.

"I had no idea you knew him. He never mentioned you."

In all the long, lingering conversations you've enjoyed with him, thought Rachel. Tessa knew him better than she did. That was obvious. She knew him well enough to touch his arm. Was her new friend already a rival with a head start? The green thoughts grew and grew. In vain, Rachel tried to control them. She told herself she had no claim on Charles. Quite apart from anything else, he despised her because of the insensitive way she had behaved toward him. But Charles Ford remained her fantasy, and Rachel had made it her life's work to turn her fantasies into reality. This one would be no exception. She had found her Cary Grant. Nobody was going to take him away from her.

"Tess, can we speak honestly about this? I mean, no holds barred, as friends?"

"Of course we can, Rachel."

"I need to know if you have any feelings for Charles. If he has any for you. You know what I'm saying. I mean, for a start, was he the man you were talking about in the hospital?"

Tessa sidestepped the question. "Rachel, look . . . I told you all about Pete."

"It's been a year and a half. Pete let you down. People forget. Life goes on. Would you mind if we started at the beginning?" said Rachel.

Tessa sat down on the arm of the sofa.

"The truth, the whole truth, and nothing but the truth?" asked Rachel.

"Of course," said Tessa, but in her mind she was already editing the story. Why?

She knew the answer. It was why men, not women, ruled the world. Women would stick together up to a point, but that point would be a man in whom they were both interested. The thought hit her hard. She *was* interested in Charles Ford. Rachel's antennae were on track, reading the situation more clearly than Tessa had even known. It was an attraction between two people who knew each other's ways because they had to some extent shared a common upbringing. She felt at ease with Charles, and the list was long of the things she liked about him. She liked his soft, subtle shirts with their mildly frayed collars. She liked his reticence and the way he held doors for women, and she liked the smell of his cologne, understated like himself. She liked that he was seemingly shy, yet strong and independent. And she liked the way he had kissed her. Tessa's eyes fell toward the table. The book he had given her sat on it. *That* she would not mention, nor the kiss. Everything, nearly everything, but those.

She went back to the kitchen, talking as she went, to get some cream. Somehow she didn't want to be staring directly into Rachel's eyes as she carried on this conversation. She told of the meeting in the bookshop. There was a book she had been browsing through, one that he had wanted, and so they had got to talking . . .

Tessa looked over her shoulder from time to time. Rachel was sitting on the edge of the sofa, totally focused on Tessa's words. She was like a sharp policeman, thought Tessa, listening for inconsistencies, watching for emotional displays, storing up a list of questions for later.

"He said he was going to the Franz Kline show at the Guggenheim and he asked me if I wanted to go. I was lonely. Camille had just gone to a sleepover. I was missing Pete. So I said yes. He was charming and kind. In fact, I thoroughly en-

joyed it. He knew an awful lot about painting, and then when
we'd seen the exhibition, we went on to see the Twombly one
at the Met, and then . . . we exchanged telephone numbers and
said goodbye."

Tessa advanced into the living room with the cream. So far
so good. *The Glass House* stared accusingly from the table.

"He didn't ask you for a drink or dinner or anything?" said
Rachel with a quizzical smile. She was embarrassed by this
conversation. Tessa was a friend and she was treating her as a
rival. But she had seen Tessa touch Charles, and Tessa wasn't
a toucher. The gesture had meant something, whether Tessa
knew it or not.

"No, he didn't. He just said goodbye and thanked me for
coming with him."

"But you saw him later?"

Tessa took a deep breath. This had to be admitted. "Yes, I
did, because you see, well, he was wanting to sell this loft that
he has downtown, and he asked me to sell it for him. Obviously,
I had to go down there to check it out."

"He gave you the listing on his apartment after picking you
up in a bookstore?" Rachel's face was a mask of disbelief.

"He did *not* 'pick me up in a bookstore,' any more than I
picked him up in a bookstore. We *met* in a bookshop, like two
civilized people. We went to a couple of art exhibitions. We
spent the day together. We had a cup of coffee. Believe it or
not, we *talked*. And we liked each other. He is a very charming,
very intelligent man. Yes, I suppose he took pity on me, and he
gave me the listing. But I do work at Sotheby's. It's not exactly
Century Twenty-one. It wasn't the most irresponsible thing in
the world to do."

Tessa felt on the defensive. It was beginning to irritate her.

"Why are you asking me questions like this? I thought you
said your relationship didn't work out. Why am I getting the
third degree? He's just a friend of mine."

"You looked like close friends last night," said Rachel, hardly
able to keep the accusation out of her voice. She was acutely

aware that she had no right to be having this conversation, but she had to have it anyway.

"Maybe it's all in your mind, Rachel," said Tessa gently but firmly.

"Maybe," said Rachel. "But anyway, you two never talked about me?"

"I might have. I can't honestly remember. I'm sure *he* never did. I don't know how well you know him, but he doesn't talk much about people. He talks about philosophy and art, and about spiritual things. That's one of the things I like about him."

Tessa was aware that this was something of a cut-down, but she couldn't help it.

Rachel heard it.

"I'm sorry, Tessa. You're right. I'm out of line. But it's like how you described that first meeting with Pete. That evening I met him at the Hacienda Inn was like poetry. I remember you telling us that Pete turned around and laughed, and you knew he was the guy. Well, Charles was *the* one. So please forgive me. I just can't stop thinking about him. It's sort of addictive to talk about him, to hear his name, to have some details. On one level I feel like a schoolgirl, and on another I feel a woman's mistrust for my feelings. Tess, I'm sorry. I'm not good at this. I don't know how to do it. I'm in 'obsession' with this guy I hardly know, and you seem to know him a million times better than I, and it sort of freaks me. I guess I'm jealous. And I've never been jealous, except of Oprah and maybe Barbara Walters. I have no right to ask you all these questions, but it *does* sound like some kind of pickup in the bookstore."

Tessa felt herself go cold inside. They'd already been through this.

"How *exactly* did you meet Charles?" she said. "Apart from the time at the Hacienda Inn?"

She saw the color rise in Rachel's cheeks.

"I told you, I met him professionally. I interviewed him on my show."

Tessa smiled. Charles and Rachel on TV couldn't possibly have been a success.

"I imagine that was where the magic died," she said simply.

"Yes," said Rachel. "It was a failure. I made a mistake, but it doesn't change what I feel. I have to know exactly what's going on with you two."

"Listen, Rachel. I don't have any feelings for Charles except that I like him, and I think he likes me. That's allowed, isn't it? Can't women and men merely like each other, or are you with Billy Crystal on that one?"

"Well, tell me precisely what you do feel about him. Do you think he's attractive, for instance?"

They were both upping the ante. The irritation was coming out.

"Yes, objectively, I think he's attractive. That doesn't mean I want to jump into bed with him. When you get to be genuinely in love with someone, Rachel, you'll find out that it sort of turns you off other men in a sexual sense."

"Don't patronize me, Tessa. I know what love is and what it isn't."

"I wonder," said Tessa coldly.

"And you think he feels the same about you? That you're attractive. But because of Rose he doesn't see you as a sex object?" said Rachel.

"I don't presume to climb inside his mind or anyone else's, Rachel. That's your job, not mine."

"Yes, it is my job, and I think you've got the hots for him." Rachel was angry now. She leaned back on the sofa and let Tessa have it.

"What a *disgusting* expression! Where did you get it, *Sassy* magazine? That seems to be where you're picking up your feminine psychology these days, Rachel."

"Sassy magazine!"

Rachel looked at Tessa in horror. She, Rachel Richardson, the intellectual queen of the airwaves. *Sassy!* She couldn't help it. She burst out laughing. It was too ridiculous. Tessa smiled.

"Sassy!" Rachel blurted out through her laughter, which was going ballistic. Tessa started to laugh, too. Rachel stood up, went over, and flung her arms around her friend.

"Tess, I'm sorry. You are right. It's teenager time. I'm sorry. There's romance and there's ridiculousness. I guess I went over the top. No fool like a middle-aged fool. They do desperate things in the Last Chance Saloon."

"Oh, Rachel, that's all right. Let's forget it."

Tessa, still in Rachel's arms, looked down at the table. *The Glass House* stared back. What were the true answers about Charles? Could she have an affair with him? Could she be unfaithful to Pete's memory? Oh, God, she honestly didn't know. Not right now, maybe, but later? She *could* imagine being married to him. There was no denying that. She could imagine herself and Camille all wrapped up in the warm blanket of Charles Ford's sophisticated security. She hadn't seen Charles since she had visited his apartment for the first time. The day, almost the moment, of her accident, he had gone to Europe for months, and only just returned. Last night, at the Sotheby's party, she had met him by chance and he had invited her downtown, this very evening, for a drink. Where might the drink lead? To dinner at a fashionable downtown restaurant, a fine wine chosen by a man who would know about fine wines and other fine things, a man who would never let down his wife and child, never risk the security of those he professed to love . . . ?

"So I don't have to worry about you."

"Not one little bit," said Tessa, taking a secret deep breath.

"You don't think I'm being ridiculous about all this?" said Rachel suddenly.

"Of course I don't, darling," said Tessa. "I think that if you felt the magic, he felt it too. I think that to work, to exist, it has to be mutual. Even if you fell out, there had to have been something there at the beginning." Tessa steeled herself to get the words out.

"You do?" said Rachel. "You really do?" Her smile was Tessa's reward.

"Yes, I do. And I think you should ring him up and get together with him. I think you should give things a chance to happen."

"Well, I just might take your advice," said Rachel. She paused. "Oh, Tess, I just wanted to clear something up. You didn't answer earlier when I asked you about the guy you told me about in the hospital. You know, the one who was in Spain. The one you said would be the answer to a maiden's prayer."

"Yes," said Tessa. She felt her stomach sinking. She had forgotten the famous Rachel Richardson photographic memory.

"Was that Charles?"

Tessa took a deep breath. "No. It was a Frenchman I met through work, but I don't see him anymore."

"Oh," said Rachel. She paused. "And another thing. Do you mind my asking . . . out of interest, what was the book you were reading when you met Charles in the store? The one he was interested in, too?"

Tessa swallowed hard.

"It's called *The Glass House,*" she said. Now she knew why Rachel Richardson was a superstar interviewer.

"Oh, this one," said Rachel, reaching forward and picking it up. "You have it out on your coffee table in pride of place."

Rachel opened the book.

"Well, actually . . . ," said Tessa.

But Rachel was already reading the inscription. "To Tessa, who is both brave and beautiful. Yours, Charles Ford."

"Sounds like a gift," said Rachel, borrowing British understatement.

Oh, God, it's going to start up again, thought Tessa.

"So we *are* rivals," said Rachel simply. "Rivals and friends. Well, I guess that has probably happened a time or two before."

Tessa sighed. "Okay, Rachel, perhaps I haven't been totally honest. Actually, there wasn't a Frenchman. It *was* Charles that I was talking about in the hospital when you were trying to tell me about the man you'd met. I do like him. I am attracted to him. What woman in her right mind wouldn't be? But frankly, nothing has happened. I don't think he's available. Not to me, anyway. Maybe he was to you. I've met him three times. That day in the bookshop, at his apartment when he gave me the listing, and last night at Sotheby's. That's it. I've shown his apartment, but he's never there. He's been away in Europe for ages, and he spends most of his time in Santa Fe, anyway. He hardly ever rings. He didn't send me a postcard from Spain, not that I'd have expected one from someone like him. He's just . . . I don't know, he's in his own world. He's in the past. He's all bound up with Rose. Yes, to be totally honest, he would make enormous sense for me right now. But I'm not even sure I would be ready for anything, even if he were, and he's not. That's where we are. Okay, so he thinks I'm brave and beautiful. Sometimes I think so, too."

"Thank you for being honest," said Rachel. She seemed quite calm. "I believe you. I sort of didn't before, but I do now. But I have to tell you this. I'm going to get him. That's the end of it. I don't give a damn if he likes it or not, he's going to be got."

Tessa laughed out loud. "A lot of people would say that men and women aren't things, and that they can't be had just by wanting. Why do I think you're the exception that proves the rule?"

"Are you going to stand in my way?" said Rachel.

"No," said Tessa. "I'm going to help you. After all, it's not one I owe you, it's two."

Thirty-four

Tessa went ahead. She looked back at Rachel and smiled encouragingly. The door at the top was to the highest loft.

They stood side by side outside it. There was no little hole in the door that allowed the owner to scan his prospective guests. The superintendent on the ground floor had waved Tessa through. She was the realtor. The other woman was presumably a prospective buyer.

"Shall I ring?" whispered Tessa with a nervous smile.

Rachel nodded.

They heard the bell ringing inside the loft. After about thirty seconds the door opened. He stood there, in blue jeans, bare feet, and a dark cashmere sweater. His apartment, highly polished floorboards as far as the eye could see, raced off behind him to vast picture windows. Rachel's heart nearly stopped as the flood of doubt hit her.

"Tessa," he said, smiling in welcome. Then he saw Rachel and his head flicked back in an exaggerated double take. He looked totally surprised. It was impossible to say whether the surprise was pleasant or unpleasant. He looked back at Tessa. His expression asked, "What the hell is going on?"

Tessa talked fast. "Listen, Charles. I can't stay. I've got to rush, but I brought along my best friend, Rachel Richardson. I just know she's got loads to say to you, and I know you've got to listen." She stepped back, turning her palms up in a sorry-about-this-but-it-had-to-be done gesture, turned on her heel, and fled.

Rachel took a step forward into the doorway. He did not block her progress. There was a faint smile on his face. Sarcasm? Could it possibly be the beginnings of some kind of amusement?

"Can I come in?" said Rachel. She took another step forward.

"It seems you are in already," he said.

He closed the door behind her.

Rachel turned to face him.

"Look," she said. "You have to hear what I have to say."

"Sounds like an order," he said. Again, he smiled.

She smiled, too, but only just. She had a speech ready. She had taken charge, but already she needed some help from him. He seemed to sense that.

"Would you mind if I sat down?" he said. "If it helps, you could sit, too," he added.

He walked to the sitting area. Two leather sofas by Mies van der Rohe sat opposite each other across a Barcelona table. Over in one corner of the vast space, a canvas sat on an outsize casel. In front of it was a paint-splattered stepladder. It was some sort of work-in-progress.

She walked quickly to one of the sofas and sat down on the edge of it. He sat down on the other one, far back, relaxed.

"Thank you," she said.

"You are welcome," he said, in a tone of voice not totally devoid of humor. She sensed he was actually enjoying this.

"Look, here's what I want to say. Please don't interrupt." She paused. He said nothing.

"It seems . . . ," she said. "It seems that I have decided that you are the man I want to be in my life. I don't know why, but I've felt it since that night I first met you at the Hacienda Inn." She took a deep breath.

"I think people call it love, or obsession, or fascination. I don't know what they call it, and frankly, I don't care. The bottom line is that I am going to have a relationship with you.

You are going to feel about me exactly what I feel about you. And when that happens, sooner or later, I imagine we'll get ourselves married."

She paused briefly, trying not to analyze his reaction in case it put her off saying the other things she needed to say.

"Now, I realize this is incredibly uncool and all those things. And it's frighteningly direct, and seems to be, well, taking things for granted. But it's the way I am. I have always been like this. So I might as well be me."

He opened his mouth to speak, but she held up her hand.

"Not yet. Okay, things have gotten off to a bad start, and it's my fault. I think you liked me, but I screwed up. I screwed up big, but the reason I screwed up big was the reason you liked me in the first place. I'm a damaged person. I was a neglected child. All my life I've had to battle and fight against incredible odds for love, for affection, for warmth, for food, for respect, for the attention that we call fame. It's second nature to me. Ring a bell and I come out of my corner fighting. I have to be perfect. I have to be the best. I have to win. All the time. Every time. Now you know why I say I'm damaged. I can't be out of control, because if I'm out of control I'll get flattened. That's the lesson I've learned from life, and I'm acutely aware that it's not the lesson that all the cozy, comfy rich people have learned.

"So when I wanted you, I got you on my TV show. And the moment you were on it, you became a part of it. You ceased to be a person, because of my insecurities. I *am* that show. It's me. If it fails, I fail. If it dies, I die. If nobody loves it, nobody loves me. I know that's pathetic. I know that intellectually, but emotionally I don't believe it. So you see, you just fed into my neuroses, into my paranoia. I forgot that you were a strong, decent human being who valued privacy and had sacred memories to keep warm and safe. I sold you down the river because that's who I am . . . who I was. But now I want a second chance. And this, believe it or not, is my apology. It's not a very good one, is it?"

"It's the best one, because it's so very obviously the truth," he said.

She felt the rush of something that was much stronger than relief.

"I think I can change," she said. "I know I can."

"I had no idea," he said. "I mean, really, no idea . . ."

"That I liked you?"

"That you felt as you apparently do."

"Well, you know now. And I'm glad you know."

His smile was warm now.

"I've never met anyone remotely like you before," he said. It was a compliment.

"That's what I felt when I met you."

"So we're from different planets, meeting in space." He laughed. He seemed to like the idea.

"Meeting in your loft," she said. "Which is about as big as space. And that night at the Hacienda Inn, you came in out of the dark like someone from another galaxy."

"A Spockian figure!" He laughed out loud.

"Would you like a glass of champagne?" he said suddenly. Rachel nodded. "Does that mean I'm forgiven?" she said.

"Yes," he said. He stood up. "It's easy, as one gets older," he said, "to become rather good at blaming others for one's own failures. I've been around. I've even heard of Rachel Richardson, the interviewer. Why should I expect you to treat me differently from anyone else? It's not your fault that I'm so vain and you're so good at your job. It's to your credit."

He padded over to the open-plan kitchen area. Rachel watched him, her heart thumping. She hadn't expected it to go as well as this. Now she almost regretted all the incredibly truthful things she had said. Most men would have run a mile. This one was pulling a bottle of dew-covered champagne from the Sub-Zero, and a couple of chilled flute glasses to go with it.

He brought them back to the table, set them down, and poured the wine.

"Is that your painting?" said Rachel. Somehow, she had to

reduce the intensity level of the conversation. Choosing the painting was not perhaps the best way to do that.

"Yes," he said.

"Do you mind if I take a look at it?"

"Please do," he said. Rachel stood up. It was far enough away across the huge room to require an escort. Would he walk with her, or stay where he was? Rachel was acutely aware that she had let herself in for some sort of test. She would have to say the right thing about the painting, whatever that was. He hovered by the sofa until she had committed herself to go to it alone. Then, at the last minute, he followed her across the floor.

The painting loomed up, its back revealing nothing. Around in front, she saw that it was only a quarter finished, if that, but it was an unfinished symphony in blue. A woman's face sprang from the exact center of the canvas with incredible force. Rachel actually took a step back, it was so powerful, and as she did, she felt his eyes boring into her. The background was blue and the face, too, was blue, the blues playing soft and low like a sad-faced Picasso lady from Bob Dylan lowlands.

Her words came quickly.

"It can't be finished, can it? There's nothing to add, and there's nothing to take away."

She could almost feel his relief. And then she could feel his excitement.

"You think that, too?" he said.

She turned toward him, and it began there, in earnest, for real.

"So that's Rose," said Rachel, staring into his eyes.

"Yes. That's her."

Suddenly, Rachel knew something was going to happen, something wonderful.

He took a step toward her, and she realized she had stopped breathing.

He took her in his arms and she melted into them, and he bent down and kissed her.

At last he drew back from her, and she stood there, lost in the dream, a smile of surprise across her face.

They said nothing, but both laughed in happiness. Then slowly and tenderly he took her hand, and he led her upstairs to the bedroom.

Thirty-five

He led her to the bed, like a bride to the altar. His hand held hers, gently, with reverence. He was in control, but there was so much love in him. She could feel it through his fingers, pulsing with the passion of her own rushing blood. She saw the bed with its geometrical gray-white cover, and she wanted to remember it forever, and the wonderful sacrament that she would now experience.

She could not control her breathing. Her breath rushed from her in shuddering increments that had nothing to do with oxygen or the lack of it. He turned her around and sat her down on the edge of the bed. He let go of her hand at last, but moved it forward to cup her chin and cheek in a gesture of total tenderness. She turned her head toward his fingers, capturing them against her hot skin between cheek and shoulder, and her chest reared and fell quicker, deeper, as the feelings grew. With his other hand, he touched her hair, running his fingers through it. She turned toward him, her head still to one side, and their eyes met. They smiled gently, almost carefully, in wonder at the intensity of the moment.

Then he let go of her and she sat back, both hands behind her, and she waited, already locked tight in the conspiracy of hearts. He knelt down between her legs and she widened them to make space for him, her lips parted, her nostrils flared. She could feel the wetness now, and the tautness in her nipples as the blood roared within her. Still, they were silent, and the sounds of the traffic far below was beautiful music in the background, as the city went on without them.

"Rachel," he said, his voice stretched with the tension. But he needed no answer. Her hooded eyes were all the permission he needed for what would happen now. He reached forward and undid the buttons of her blouse. She moved forward imperceptibly to help him, but her hands did not move. This was for him. She was his. He must reach to take her, and forever she would be had by him. In the alien subservience, the odd acquiescence, Rachel experienced the foothills of what would become the peaks of passion. He slipped her blouse from her shoulders, and the warmth of her skin met the cool air of the room and she shuddered, not in cold but in anticipation of the heat to come.

He reached behind her and freed her, and he stopped in wonder as the flimsy garment slipped away and her breasts were there for him alone. He touched them, first one, then the other, his fingers at her nipples, wondering at the tautness, the pulsing blood, the hard evidence of her lust for him. Again, he stared deep into her eyes, telling her about love with them, promising her that this was a communion of bodies, a commitment that would not be broken. She nodded in agreement with his unspoken thought, marveling at the closeness of communication they shared, here at the edge of intimacy.

He leaned forward and laid his head against her, nuzzling her. Then he turned and his mouth was on her breast. She threw back her head, and a moan sprang from her. He watched her as he took her breast in his mouth, and she felt her nipple expand in the delicious wetness, tight with an impossible tightness, throbbing against the velvet softness of his tongue. He licked at her gently, feeling her heart beat in the pointed tip of her breast. Then he moved his mouth away from her, because he could not wait for what must be, and she could not.

He reached for her skirt, and she lifted herself from the bed to help him as he slipped it upward to the milk whiteness where her thighs met the sheer blackness of silk bikini briefs. He breathed out hard, the lust hot on his breath, merging with the warmth of her. She arched backward, her mind racing as she tried to hang on to the body memories, fighting to hold the moment that lived only to be lost in the glory of the next. He reached for her panties. Slowly he drew them off, exposing her. Rachel groaned her ecstasy as the chill air touched her heat.

"Yes, Charles, yes," she said, her voice taut with the panic of desire. She had never wanted like this. It was new, like birth, the nuclear fusion of lust and love that made a mockery of each alone.

She closed her eyes and sensed rather than saw him freeing himself for her. There was no time for kisses. Later, through eternity, there would be time for those. But now she wanted her emptiness filled. She pushed back with her arms and slipped farther up the bed, and he rose with her, and in the darkness behind her closed eyes, the sensation was amplified. She felt him hard against the smooth skin of her thigh, and then slippery at the entrance of her. "Yes, yes," she moaned, as she waited for the happiness.

She opened her eyes now, and he lay hard against her, his head above hers, bathing her in the light of love that shone from his eyes. His mouth was parted. His breath came fast as hers. She thrust her hips against him, willing him to make the moment, yet understanding his delay as he battled to savor this firstness. He had centered his whole body in the part of him that would merge with her. Now, he launched himself into her, filling her with his love, and she cried out with delight.

At last Rachel was no longer alone. Here was completion, fulfillment, the abolition of emptiness. Now the two were one, joined in the embrace that would not be put asunder, in a promise of bodies that transcended vows and ceremony. This moment could never be taken from them.

He drew back like a wave ebbing on the beach, but, as soon, he flowed upward again, until the rhythm was established and she rode him, as he rode her. She held his hips and felt the power of his buttocks, as she tried to make sense of the motion and the million points of joy that it lanced into her body. Rachel surfed on the sea of bliss, wetter than the ocean. She wanted it to last forever, and she murmured her love to him, as, paradoxically, she willed the sweet conclusion.

It began in the back of his throat, a low moan of promise and threat. She felt it inside her, the intensification of the rhythm, slower, deeper, harder, the pause between thrust and withdrawal longer. And then he was still, and the moan grew in the stillness, and his sound reached to the core of her and sucked out her own. She felt her whole body poised with his on the cliff above the surging sea, and then it was time. He hovered at the brink of her, the last thrust, the coup de grâce of love. And then he came forward slowly, shuddering, shaking, and crying out sharply with the pain of ecstasy, and she fell apart around him. Her legs encircled him. Her hands clawed helplessly at him.

"I love you, I love you," she screamed.

And his own cry pierced her heart, as his own love poured into the molten mass of hers.

Thirty-six

In the warm aftermath of love, they sat side by side on the sofa, their hands intertwined. Wrapped in the terry-cloth robe he had found for her, Rachel felt a happiness she had never known before.

"What's going to happen to us, Charles?" Rachel looked up at him as she spoke. The moment was so wonderful, Rachel was filled with a sudden panic that it might end.

"Why don't we find out?" he said.

"What do you mean? A fortune-teller?"

"If you like. I can tell the future. Some of it, seen through the glass darkly."

"You're joking with me."

"No, I'm not."

He was totally matter-of-fact, and once again the mystery descended over him and the magic shrouded him.

"You, an astrologer? I somehow don't see you as that."

"But then you don't know me very well, do you, Rachel? You haven't had me under your microscope for long enough."

"No, I suppose I don't, but I want to."

"Well, if you want the future, we can ask the bones."

"The bones!" She smiled incredulously.

He stood up, walked to the bookshelves, and took down a red leather pouch from among a pile of leather-bound books. Back at the table he undid the leather thong that tied its neck, and emptied out a small pile of bones.

"What are they?"

"Bones."

"Of an animal?"

"Actually, of a newborn child."

"Oh, my God, you're joking."

"Not a very good joke, really, would it have been?" he said.

"But they should be buried."

"They can't be buried. The child was killed by its mother at birth. In Navajo lore it has not been born, and therefore it cannot be buried in hallowed ground. But it had life of sorts, and so it has use of sorts. Its bones can tell the future that it never had."

"That's awful. That's simply not civilized. I mean, they should be buried."

"Yes, according to our ways and our laws, but not according to the lores and customs of the Indians. This was an Indian child. It was subject, is subject, to their laws, not ours."

"But this is America. There are laws that pertain to everyone who lives here."

"Whose America? The Indians were here first. Whose country, Rachel? Whose laws?"

There was a fire in his eyes now, a flame burning that she had not seen before, and at once she knew that this was a part of him that was vital to the feelings she felt. This was the mystical side of Charles Ford. He was not like other men. Part of him was as old as history, as the Indians, making odd laws that would make strange sense, but only to the ear that could hear, to the eye that could see.

On the table were the bones of the Indian baby.

"The mother was possessed by the evil spirit," he said. "The medicine man would have said that. Our psychiatrists would have called it postpartum depressive illness and given her electro-convulsive shocks after fiddling around with her brain chemistry using pills. The Indians banished her to the desert and wouldn't allow her to live with the tribe. Maybe the devil tired of her, or maybe her brain biochemistry sorted itself out without medicine and electricity. And maybe she went to the towns and became a whore and died of consumption, and left her dead baby's bones here to tell our future."

There was a hardness about him now. Almost a viciousness. He was ridiculing so-called civilization and Rachel's unthinking acceptance of it. The Indians had their ways. It had been their country. Where in civilization was progress? In gas chambers, genocide, crime waves? In drug addiction and Third World hunger, in ethnic cleansing, pollution, and child abuse? Had laws about the burial of dead babies made any significant contribution to the development of mankind?

She looked at him in wonder, at the savagery beneath the suave exterior. He was like a fierce animal. He would take her soon, again, this creature, and it would be primeval in its force, frightening and amazing, and things would happen that she hardly dared to dream about. And it would happen in a future that was about to be told by an Indian baby's bones.

She said nothing as she watched him, but her lips were parted, and through them her breath came a little more quickly. She sat still, transfixed by the moment of passion, his, and hers as a response to it. He clutched the bones, his knuckles tight around a would-be human's dead hopes, about Rachel's dreams, too, for the extraordinary future they just might share. She could feel the heat of the heart of him. He was stripped of his urban persona. He was in the desert with the Indians, crouched in the wind amidst the dust by a flickering fire. They would have given him these bones and taught him to read them. For what favor? For what trust?

He lowered his head and spoke words she did not know, but she knew they were a prayer in the language of an Indian tribe.

His hand shot out in the silence that descended, and she saw the yellowed bones float out and up and down, clattering on the polished oak floor and then lying still. He stood up slowly. Then he lowered himself where they had landed, squatting easily, like an Indian would, and he studied them as Rachel waited. She felt it was a church. The sense of ritual was strong, and of things not of this world or time. He was being a fortune-teller, but it was very far from ridiculous. Instead, it was grand and solemn, and it was exciting, too.

He looked over to Rachel. "It is about us," he said. "It is important, but it is not smooth. It is not easy. There is betrayal."

"Betrayal?"

"Yes!" he said. "There is betrayal." He stared hard at a section of the bones, his eyes boring in on them, racking his memory for the learned-long-ago meanings. His father outside the tent in the desert dusk, framed by the cactus. The bones in the dust. A great love in his future.

"Whose betrayal?" said Rachel.

"It is not known," he said. His betrayal of Rose's spirit with this woman of achievement, with light behind her eyes and life in her heart? Hers of him, when and if he allowed himself the indulgence of loving again? His of her, when he had tired of her grounded ways, of her common sense and fierce, rational intelligence?

"What else is there?"

"There is a clash of spirits."

"You want to know how to do it, don't you?" he said, and he smiled gently. "But I can't tell you. It is for me to pass on to my son and to no one else, and he to his, and onward."

"Your son?" said Rachel.

"Yes."

He stood up.

"Do the bones say that you will have a son?" Her voice caught on the very last word, like a frock snagged on a bouquet of barbed wire.

He walked to her, and reached out and took her hand. Once more he led her away, to the stairs, and she went willingly with him.

Thirty-seven

Rachel was in trouble. It had been nearly a week since she had made love to Charles, and he hadn't called. The business of waiting for the telephone to ring had begun the very next day. It had not felt good, and as the minutes, hours, and days had ticked by at a snail's pace, it had gotten one hell of a lot worse. Rachel simply didn't know how to handle the alien feelings. She had called Tessa to find out how to deal with it, in the vague attempt to find out from someone who knew Charles just what was going on. Tessa was fiendishly busy, but she had made all the right encouraging noises. She, too, had not heard from Charles . . . or said she hadn't. In her state of paranoid insecurity, Rachel hardly believed her.

So Rachel threw herself into her work. However, it was aspirin for a broken heart, making little difference to the pain, and the endless speculation about just what had gone so horribly wrong.

Time after time, she set her mind to work on the problem. It seemed that in matters of romance there were never any hard answers, just open-ended speculation that stretched into the distance when it wasn't circling around on itself and biting its own tail. What were the facts? A few short days ago, she had spent the happiest and most ecstatic night of her life in the arms of the first man she had ever loved. The warm glow of sexual arousal spread through Rachel as she remembered. She could feel it in her nipples, between her legs, at the nape of her neck.

She had stood still as he had undressed her. She could feel his hands, so strong, so gentle, easing her short skirt up to her waist. She had looked down, and her body had seemed to be the body of a stranger, no longer hers, but belonging to him, her firm thighs white against black bikini briefs that were already soaked with her desire. And all the time, the musklike aroma of her longing had merged with the music of passion that had filled her mind.

Next morning, bathed in joy, she had left his apartment and had walked back through the early morning streets to hers. It had been miles, but they had passed in a hazy daze of love and lust. She had been joined to Charles. From this day forth. She hadn't bothered to think what the next step would be, when the next wonderful meeting. He would call later in the morning, she had presumed, to murmur his love over the phone. That very evening they would be together again, doing something, doing anything, and then all the time making love, with their bodies, with their minds.

Instead, there had been the sound of his silence. No flowers. No little messages. No damned calls. Why? Some men did that. A conquest, and then the disappearing act. But not Charles. He wasn't that kind of man. If Rachel knew anything, she knew that. Didn't she? How many times had she said, "You never know the mind of another." It was one of her articles of faith. But it didn't apply to Charles. No, no, it couldn't. She remembered the bones. They had talked of betrayal. But not so soon! There was hardly anything to betray, except one night of earth-shattering love.

It kept coming back to Rose. That was the most likely explanation. He had been stricken by guilt. Torn between loyalty to the old and his feelings for the new, Charles had chosen Rose. Yes, that was it.

Rachel had talked to Tessa a second time, three days into her ordeal. She had told her everything, and asked her advice. Tessa had reassured her. Charles would get in touch. There had to be a rational explanation for his delay. Tessa knew it. Rachel must

not panic. Rachel had to have faith. Everything would end wonderfully. Oh, yes, Ms. Friendship. Wonderful for whom? At the
end of the third day, Rachel had done what she should have
done on day one. She had called. The answer machine. The Ford
servants in Santa Fe, Wardlow's gallery, anyone, everyone. But
she had not gotten through to him. Surely, the whole thing could
not have been some clever Machiavellian scheme to pay her
back for the TV show. One thing was certain. Charles Ford was
not taking her calls. Not letting people through to her on the
telephone was a Rachel Richardson specialty. Now, she was
having it done to her, and it *stank.*

Jake was standing in the doorway.

"Everything cool?" he said.

He could see that it wasn't, and he knew why. Jake was one
of the few people on this earth whom Rachel could talk to, and
there was little he didn't know about Charles Ford and the chaos
he had created in her hectic but usually well ordered life.

"Same old, same old," said Rachel with a wry smile.

"It'll work out. Trust me," said Jake.

"How do you *know?*" said Rachel with a bitter laugh. "How
do you know he'll die a horrible, slow death?"

"I have one of my feelings that this one will have a happy
ending."

He walked over to her and massaged her shoulders as she sat
slumped at the desk.

"I got your passport back from the Cuban Embassy, all visa'd
up. If Castro says *si,* we can be there in a day."

"Fuck Castro," said Rachel.

Jake laughed, digging in deeper with his fingers.

"Work is balm for broken hearts," he said. "And you've got
to get over to the Plaza and do Benazir Bhutto. She survived
an arranged marriage *and* a hanged father. There's always someone worse off than yourself."

"Matt Harding would be a bit like an arranged marriage,"
said Rachel. "Oh, that feels good!"

"Okay," said Jake. "Time to go. If he calls, I'll put him through to the Plaza. Promise."

Rachel stood up. She wanted to go now. She had to get out of here. Maybe with a bit of luck she'd get mugged on the sidewalk, something physical that she could handle, rather than all these surging, uncontrollable feelings.

Thirty-eight

On the street outside, the warm, wet wind blew across Rachel's face and Manhattan hummed with humid life. Out here at least, normal life seemed to be in progress. But maybe it was all a brave charade. Maybe all of these people who thronged the street were walking around with bleeding hearts, all screwed up, and waiting for telephone calls of their own.

The car was there, wedged against the curb. The driver would be inside in the air-conditioned comfort. She tapped quickly on the window, opened the back door, and climbed into the cool darkness. She didn't even have to tell the guy where to go. That would all have been arranged beforehand. She put her head down and returned to her broodings as the car pulled away from the curb. The psychic pain was almost unbearable, but she, Rachel Richardson, was at the dead center of her universe. Nothing mattered but her feelings. Me . . . Me . . . Me. I . . . I . . . I. Was that the secret of all this? Was romance merely the ultimate self-trip in which nothing mattered except number one? She pushed the philosophical thought away. What conceivable interest could it have? It didn't pertain to her emotions. Therefore, it had no importance. I feel, therefore I am.

She tried to think about J.F.K. Jr., his political magazine, and tonight's interview, but the laser focus was soft and blurry. She couldn't concentrate. She looked out through the window. Funny way to get to the Plaza. Still, who cared? She remembered the time she'd gotten into the wrong car, and laughed at the memory. She'd discovered the mistake at the curbside when the driver, expecting a Japanese businessman, had gotten the shock of his life.

The car kept going, way down south. Uh-oh. A communications snafu. She tapped on the window to the front compartment. The driver made a left, toward the river. Nothing happened. She tapped harder. Still nothing.

"Hey, driver," she called. "Wake up. I want to talk. Where are we going? Hello! Hello!" Nothing. That was the moment when the first alarm bell sounded inside her. It rang softly but insistently, like a beeper on Low. The car was negotiating traffic. She pushed down on the door handle. Nothing. She tried the other one. No movement. Central locking. Back to the front compartment. She opened her lungs.

"Driver," she shouted. And then upped the decibels. "Driver!" she screamed.

The panic beeper was turning up its power now, and a red light was flashing while it vibrated in her stomach.

"Oh, God," said Rachel out loud. "I'm being kidnapped.

"No, you're not. You've just got a deaf driver, soon to join the ranks of the great unemployed," she said to herself.

Now they were heading out through the tunnel under the river to Long Island. She collapsed back against the cushions. That was it. She was a prisoner. She tried to think. Who? Why? What on earth for? This wasn't an American thing. She could hardly remember a famous person being kidnapped since Lindbergh. Then the journalist in her reasserted itself. If she got out of this, it would be one *hell* of a story, with a built-in exclusive. If. Fear came rushing in to dampen the sudden and totally transient thought of a scoop. Who was up there in front? Was he armed? Did it matter? She picked up the phone, knowing that it would not work, and it didn't. But she shouted into it anyway, pushing at the buttons.

"Is there anyone there?" she said, knowing as she spoke how ridiculous it was to do so.

"Yes," said a man's voice.

"What?" she said, shocked at the sound of it. Friend or foe?

"Who are you? What do you want?" she said. Instinctively, she knew she was talking to her captor.

"I want you, Rachel."

She recognized his voice instantly. It was the voice she had spent a week praying for. It was Charles Ford.

"Charles?" she said. Then, "Where are you?"

"Driving," he said.

"Look," she said. "I'm sorry, I'm having a bit of trouble. I'm here in this car in the tunnel, and I'm talking to you on the phone. You're driving it. What the hell is going on?"

Rachel didn't do confusion. She was doing it now.

"I've captured you," he said.

"You've *captured* me?" said Rachel. "Listen, Charles Ford, if you're driving, show me, goddamn it."

Had he gone crazy? Had she? What did he mean? Was this some sort of totally-over-the-top practical joke? What the hell did he mean, he wanted her? He'd had her, and the weird bastard hadn't called for a week, and now she was a prisoner in a car driving God knew where for God knew what.

"I will, after we've talked for a bit."

"You will *now!* This second, and you'll stop this car," she shouted.

"I won't," he said in a voice that meant it.

"Charles, what you are doing is against the law. Do you hear me? It's a felony. You can't kidnap me. It's not allowed. Are you a bit weird or something?"

"Maybe," he said. "I've decided that I'm in love with you."

"You *what?* You're in love with me and you don't call for a whole entire week. Do you think I'm stupid or something? In love with me? What is this shit?"

But it didn't feel like shit. "I've decided that I'm in love with you." It was so matter-of-fact. So intellectual. The conclusion reached after hours—hell, a whole week—of careful deliberation. On the one hand this, on the other hand that: "Yes, I think the inescapable conclusion is that I love her, therefore I shall kidnap her."

"I fell in love with you last week," he said. "When we made love, and before and during and afterward."

She paused. "You did?" she said. There were funny feelings all over her. Why, oh why, couldn't all this have been Monday?

"Yes. And so I hired a car and a plane, and I'm going to take you to the Mediterranean for a holiday on my boat."

"What, now?"

"Yes, now."

"But I can't. One, I don't want to. Two, if I did, I couldn't. I have interviews. Now take me back. I've got work to do. I'd have liked the Med and the boat and the plane and everything. But I'd have liked it last Monday, thank you very much. It's too late now. You blew it."

"I want an honest answer. One completely honest answer . . . actually two. Answer me these questions and I will turn this car around and take you back to your office."

"I don't have to make deals. I want to go back now . . . Okay, okay," she said, fighting back a smile. "You get two honest answers, and maybe a few more than that, and then you take me back to work. Deal?"

"Deal. One: If I had called you on Monday morning and asked you to come with me on an immediate holiday to the Mediterranean, would you have said yes?"

"I might have," said Rachel.

"The truth. Remember the deal."

"Okay, well, probably not. Because I have this schedule and there's the sweeps, and Steve, my producer, needs time to . . ."

"You wouldn't have come."

"Okay, no, I wouldn't have come because . . ."

"Second question. Would you have wanted to?"

She paused.

"Yes," she said simply.

"Precisely," he said. "Well, I knew the answers to those two questions, and I arranged it so you wouldn't be able to say no."

Rachel sighed. She remembered him so well. The week was gone. The bones were in the air. Their bodies were intertwined. Her heart was full of the most amazing love. And then there had been the betrayal, sooner by far than she had imagined possible. He hadn't called for an entire week.

But he had apparently been busy. A boat. A private plane. All was not as it seemed. He had wanted her after all, a big-time want that would not put up with the standard series of dinners, the quotient of parties attended, walks in the park, weekends, and funny little gifts, the whole thing lubricated with telephoned "Hello, darling"s and the invention of silly nicknames. He was a deep-end man, apparently. He had simply kidnapped her because he wouldn't take no for an answer. Wasn't that romantic? Didn't it define it?

"Charles, look, I mean, we could have gone on holiday. I could have arranged it. Not this week. But later in the summer, after the . . . I mean, I can't go. No clothes. Ah. No passport."

"They're in the trunk."

"They're in the *what?* You're joking, who *did* that?"

"Your assistant, Jake," he said. "And anything else you need can be bought in Monte Carlo, Portofino, Sardinia." He was so matter-of-fact. He wanted her. He knew she wouldn't go, so he just took what he wanted.

"Jake! But I have talked to him all this week about you . . . and I have said things to him about you that . . . I mean, have you any ears left? Well, he'll have to go. I couldn't trust him anymore. I'm afraid you've cost my assistant his job."

"I don't think so," he said simply, calling her bluff, or her threat, or whatever it was.

Rachel lapsed into silence on the phone. There was something deeply surreal about this. Here she was, talking to Charles on the telephone, and there he was, not six feet away, driving her to Kennedy half against her will. There was an arrogance about him that was staggering. She felt totally without power, shorn of the stuff that was her lifeblood, and some of her said, Good, and the rest of her said, Who the hell do you think you are?

She wanted to punish him. She wanted to reward him. Was there any way she could do both at the same time? Not on the telephone.

"Charles, do you think I might *see* you?"

"Yes," he said. The car slowed and pulled over to the curb.

The passenger's door opened. He leaned in toward her. A charcoal-gray suit, a cream-colored silk shirt, and a Turnbull and Asser tie. His face showed an expression of calm certainty. There was no hint of weakness or doubt. She searched for it in vain as she did a lightning inventory of her feelings, those formerly alien things that were now what she cared about. She was glad to see him, ridiculously so. She smiled, and hated herself for it.

"Well, what a macho thing you've just done," she said. The words lied about her emotions. She just *had* to be unkind to him. It was the least she could do after the week of torture . . .

He didn't answer her. He put out his hand and threaded it into hers, and he looked into her eyes. She tried not to respond, but it became apparent to her that her hand no longer belonged to her. It belonged to him, because it squeezed his right back, and as if on cue, tears sprang to her eyes.

"Oh Charles," she said.

And he leaned in toward her as the cruel and unusual punishment she had just suffered became nothing more than the hors d'oeuvres to the kiss. What were the peaks without the valleys, she found time to think as she melted toward him. How could you know without them just how good things were?

Well, now she knew.

Thirty-nine

At the airport, there was a chartered Gulfstream 3. A man from immigration checked their passports, Rachel's retrieved from the trunk with her luggage, side by side with his.

"I can't believe Jake was in on this. I don't even know where we're going."

Rachel laughed in disbelief at the dream, but Charles's hand was in hers and it tied together all the loose ends. A vision of her diary flashed briefly before her eyes like a horror movie. But presumably, Jake, the love conspirator, had sorted it all out somehow or other. She walked slowly toward the stairs of the plane.

"We're flying direct to Nice. It's a short drive from there to Antibes, where we pick up the boat."

"How were you so sure?" she said in wonder.

"Some things have to be," he said.

There were so many questions she had to ask him. When had he decided? The morning after the night before? Or had there been two or three days of agonizing indecision as he fought with personal demons and ghosts of the past? Had he waited to see how he felt, an observer of his own emotions, to check whether or not this was the "real thing"? Or had he known right from the start, as she had known? The steps of his airplane were not the place where those questions would be answered.

"Good afternoon, Mr. Ford. Good afternoon, Miss Richardson," said the air hostess.

Inside, the plane was small but elegant. Was there a bed? Rachel tried to suppress the thought. It was around seven hours to Europe in a big plane. Presumably longer in a jet this size. They'd get into Nice around one in the morning, she calculated, around six A.M. the next day, local time. There were armchairs rather than seats, and the decor was eighteenth-century American, with chintzes and Persian carpets. It looked like a small town-house in Georgetown.

He flopped down into one of the chairs, looking up at her.

"How near did I come to failure?" he said with a gentle smile.

"Near enough," she said, smiling back, and herself settling down opposite him.

"A glass of champagne to celebrate?" he said.

"I suppose so," she said. "This is actually quite amazing. You know you are ruining my career."

"Denting it," he said. "It was ready to be dented, I think."

"Thanks for letting me choose to bend my own fender." There was no malice in her remark. She was almost out of malice.

"Sometimes I think choice is an illusion."

"And therefore freedom," said Rachel.

"But we have to pretend we're free. Even when we aren't. Especially when we aren't."

"Or there'd be no point in getting out of bed in the morning."

"Not necessarily. The Calvinists believed that everything was predetermined and that either you had been chosen for salvation or you hadn't been. They tried like mad to be ostentatiously 'good,' even though it didn't make any difference, because God had already made up his mind. But they wanted desperately for other people to think that they were among the ones who had been chosen."

The champagne arrived on a silver salver. It came with smoked salmon rolled in brown bread, and caviar scooped onto endive leaves. It was Dom Pérignon, vintage '92.

"To us," said Charles.

"And to the south of France, a sunny place for shady people."

They laughed in the conspiracy of lovers. Charles Ford was deeply unpredictable. That, now, she knew. But his unpredictability was not rash or foolish. It was preplanned, like some brilliant military campaign. He decided, and then he acted, and nothing was allowed to stand in his way. He hadn't sent flowers or called. He had hired a plane and made ready a yacht and launched a conspiracy that had included her friend, employee, and confidant, and all because he wanted her. Why? There were so many questions, and so gloriously long for them to be answered.

"I should make some calls," said Rachel.

"On one condition."

"Oh, Charles Ford, you and your conditions and deals. You sound just like me."

"Perhaps that's what happens to opposites. They come together."

"I don't think I want you to be like me. Anyway, what's the deal?"

"You make the calls after takeoff."

She laughed. "You're quite cunning, aren't you? You cover the angles ahead of time." It was wonderful, this. Getting to know him. Getting to know all about him. The song was right.

"You agree?" A bottom-line man, despite the romanticism. Apparently the two could go together.

"Yes," she said.

"Good. I imagine there are loose ends."

"Your grandmother's British understatement lives on."

He smiled. "One Christmas, my father leaned forward at lunch and his hair caught fire on one of the candles. My grandmother said, 'Darling, your hair's on fire,' and went right on eating her lunch. My father said, 'So it is,' and put it out with his napkin. I always remembered thinking that it was a little odd. Drama was frowned upon. I suppose understatement is an expression of horror at the whole idea of emotional incontinence."

Rachel picked up a piece of smoked salmon. She sipped the

wine and looked at him, her heart full of warmth for his cold childhood.

"Were you happy as a child?"

"I think so. Very, really. But happiness wasn't a word we used, and therefore not a concept we conceived of much. Everyone was always there. I think that's about all you can ask for as a child, don't you?"

"You *are* an American, aren't you?" said Rachel in wonder.

"Yes," he said. "More than most, probably, with the Indian blood."

"You're proudest of that, when for most people it might be the bit they gloss over." She was acutely aware that he was not most people.

"Yes, I am. I love the silence, and scents, and I love the dark."

"I remember," she said quickly, and the lust crackled inside her like flames under old twigs.

He heard her and smiled a lazy smile that said he, too, remembered. She knew he didn't really enjoy conversation, but bits of him were blossoming everywhere, like cactus flowers in the dry desert. He seemed not to mind it, actually to like it. Was that what he saw in her? The person who could tease him out of himself with her gentle probing? Was he longing all the while, all his life perhaps, to escape the shell of protection that his family had grown around him?

"Tell me about the boat you've chartered."

"It's my boat," he said.

"Oh, I didn't know you had a boat."

"It didn't come up, did it?"

She laughed. How many millions more things were there to bubble to the surface over the next few glorious days . . . weeks?

"It's a sailboat," she said. "No, don't tell me. A wooden boat. Not vast. Not a gin palace, but very comfortable, and with a captain who has worked for you for, oh, fifteen years. And it is white with a . . . with a black sail, and you steer it yourself and you know how to find your way by the stars."

"Not bad, not bad. I never thought of myself as being transparent. But then I don't surround myself with people who have X-ray vision. Actually, twelve years for the captain, John, and yes, a sailboat, seventy feet, not vast. Black with a white sail."

"Called?"

"The *Myth*."

"The *Myth*. I like it. Why?"

"Because life has no rules, and you go where you like when you like, and you follow the wind behind your sails. The rest is myth, the conventional wisdom of the importance of this, the vitalness of that. My boat reminds me that I am free, and so does the desert. Nowadays there is a retreat from responsibility, a fear of freedom, a cult of the victim. In the land of the free we prefer to believe that we are in psychological chains, predetermined by our past, our childhood, our genes, our environment. But freedom is merely a question of choosing to believe in it. On my boat I'm free. On my horse I'm free. I feel free now. Do you?"

"Not quite yet. Still lots of thoughts about next week and what I'm missing, and will it matter and how much? But they're fading with every sip of champagne, and each time you open your mouth and say something bright that shows more of you. And I'm getting freer, thinking of your boat. Is there a crew apart from John?"

She tore the conversation away from them. It made her feel just a tiny bit too free. Free to do what I want any old time. She could sense the looseness beginning. Already they were lovers. They would be again. Soon. How soon? Very soon. But she wanted to wait. To anticipate. To savor every moment.

"Well, there's Tracy, who gets the drinks and cleans up, and lives with John, and there's Mariel, the cook. And then there's another deckhand who changes all the time. I haven't met him yet, but he's called Tom. That's it."

The door to the cockpit opened.

"We are cleared for takeoff, sir. Any time you want. Just say the word. We have a five-minute window time."

"Let's go," said Charles. The hostess began stowing things away. He reached down and found the seat belt. Rachel did the same. Private planes were not new to her. Matt's was several times the size of this one, all high-tech, futuristic design with little charm but much "attack." This was like flying in a study. There were Georgian wall brackets, leather books in bookshelves, what looked like Sheraton furniture. It was incredibly stylish.

"Do you always charter this plane?" she said, as the engines roared and it thrust forward on the runway.

"Yes, when I can," he said.

Which led to the whole business of Rose. Suddenly, Rachel could feel her in the cabin. It wasn't a threatening presence. There was no enemy there, nor even a rival, but it was a hurdle that would have to be jumped. She had the strange sensation that someone was telling her . . . , "Be brave, you have my blessing, make him happy." The plane soared into the sky, toward the heavens where Rose was, and the closeness of her spirit was absolutely inescapable.

The hostess emerged from the cockpit.

"The captain says it is all right to unfasten the seat belts now."

"What's back there?" said Rachel.

"The bathrooms, the bedroom," he said.

"Can I take a look?"

"Of course."

She stood up. She felt her heart thumping. Was this it? Was this the time when the seal would be set on the destiny the bones had predicted? Was this the time for the assault on memory to begin? He stood up too.

They walked toward the back.

"Bathroom," he said, opening the door on the left.

"Bedroom," he said, opening the door on the right.

Rachel walked inside. The bedroom was small but perfectly formed. She turned toward him. "It's nice," she said. But her throat snagged on the word "nice," and she swallowed hard.

He stood close to her, sensing the moment too, but not frightened by it, not trembling as she was. She knew that, because very slowly and tenderly, he took her in his arms, bent down toward her, and kissed her.

Forty

Rachel opened her eyes and woke up properly. She knew the
bed was half empty. And she knew, too, that all the perfect night
it had been full. He had slipped from the bed as the fingers of
dawn poked round the corners of the drapes through the port-
holes, and the old yacht squeaked easily against its lines. She
had dozed on, knowing that she was not supposed to wake yet,
and she had heard the preparations for casting off. The engines
had purred into life, and there had been footsteps and muffled
orders, and the smell of strong French coffee. She had felt the
movement as the yacht slid from its berth, and then more as it
negotiated the waters of the narrow port before setting out to
sea. She had thought of him in the cockpit, the vast wooden
wheel beneath his hands, and she had remembered him, too,
and the passion they had shared, which made her happier by
far than she had ever been. She had thought also of escape and
freedom and of the future they would share.

She sat up. The sun was already high, but it was still only
nine o'clock French time. She had had precious little sleep, but
she felt wonderful. She got out of bed. On the back of the
bathroom door was a robe of terry cloth, thick and luxuriant.
She pulled it on and looked at herself in the mirror, deliciously
wrecked by the short night of love.

She splashed some water on her face and smiled at herself.

Had she been a cat she would have been purring, her body
arched in a stretch of self-satisfaction, as she strutted back

across the stateroom. It wasn't a big cabin, but it was magical. Everywhere she looked there was old teak, polished to a shiny patina over the years. Books lined one wall, a detachable teak bar holding them in place for the days, unlike today, when the boat pitched in storms at sea.

Rachel sat down on the bed and hugged herself with joy. What had she done to deserve this? Simply allowed destiny to have its way with her? She didn't think so. Luck favored the prepared mind. She had *earned* this. The good Lord had awarded her this prize as the cherry on the top of all the other things she had fought so hard to get. Now, she was going to enjoy it. She got up and walked into the saloon.

"Good morning, Ms. Richardson. Did you sleep well?" John, the captain of the boat, was in the navigation section. He jumped up as she entered.

"Fits and starts. This boat is so perfect it seems a waste to sleep on it."

"She is a fine boat," he corrected her. "And good in a sea. Lots of class, really. Don't make 'em like this anymore. There's some breakfast up on the main deck. Mr. Ford's at the wheel, and it's clear skies and warming up. Should be a scorcher."

"Where are we going?"

"Mr. Ford wanted to run to the islands off St. Tropez. We should make them by lunchtime, and then anchor in their lee for the night."

"I think I'll get up there and find that bread I smell."

"Fresh from the market in Antibes this morning. Fruit's good, too. Figs, Muscat grapes, nectarines, *fraises du bois*. Just say the word and Mariel will cook you up the whole English bit."

"Mmmm," said Rachel. She walked up the companionway, her bare feet in delicious contact with the cool, shining wood. On deck, bright brasswork gleamed against black ropes, the polished wood of the deck offset by the brighter shining varnish of the gunnels. The two masts of the schooner rig rose high above the boat.

"Good morning, Rachel."

He was at the helm, and he turned as he spoke. He wore navy-blue shorts made of a parachute material, and a simple cotton T-shirt with no writing on it. He smiled his welcome.

He put out an arm to her, his other still on the wheel, and drew her in to him. "You finally got some sleep," he said. "I didn't want to wake you."

"This is paradise," she said. It was. The old town of Antibes rose up the hillside behind the boat. The big yachts were clustered around the seawall, the sails of the tall sailing-ships rose behind them. In front of them was the gently rolling Mediterranean, green and blue, fresh and sparkling in the early morning sun. She looked up to the cloudless sky and breathed in the salt air, the aroma of the coffee, and the warmth of him. "I could live like this forever."

"You *think* you could."

"Just let me dream on. Tell me lies. Make up stories. Anything . . . But now, I am faint with hunger," said Rachel.

Mariel, hovering over the breakfast table, poured a cup of coffee into one of the outsize cups the French love, and handed it to her. Unwillingly, she let go of Charles's hand and loaded a slice of baguette with butter and honey.

"Are we really going to Italy, too? Can we just go there anytime we like?"

"Oh, yes, we can. We can go anywhere. I think we ought to swim the caves in Porto Veneri and dive down to the underwater statue of Christ. That's magnificent. And then Portofino for some really good shopping and eating. Then we can go to Sardinia, if you like. All that is for when we tire of the south of France."

"We might never do that. I came about fifteen years ago. I loved it . . . and I loved last night," she whispered, threading her hand into his once again. "On a plane, on a boat. Where next?"

Her voice was husky with longing.

"In the sea," he said. It wasn't a joke. His voice cracked with sudden desire.

She snuggled in, burrowing against him.

"Behind the wheel of a sailboat?" she tried.

He laughed. "It's good, isn't it?" he said.

"It's very, very good. Does it just go on and on like this?"

"Yes," he said, quite certain. "It does."

Until the betrayal, thought Rachel. Not mine. Therefore his. She battled to keep the thought inside where it belonged. Tessa? Surely not. Then who? Nobody on this ship. Not now. Live for the moment. But she cared too much. It was too good not to worry about losing it.

"Remember the bones and betrayal? It won't be me."

"Nor I."

"Does that mean that one of us will one day be a liar?"

"Rachel, look at the ocean, the flying fishes, the sun on those buildings in the distance. It shone on them in medieval times. On that church. These waves surged beneath Roman galleys, and they were the parvenus of the Mediterranean. What of Carthage, the Greeks, the Gauls, the Phoenicians? This boat was a boat when the bits of you were scattered throughout the universe, not yet come together as beautiful Rachel Richardson. Is there time to worry about what can't be changed, what might happen in the future, when joy is here now?"

"But I just want it not to stop. That's all." She knew he was right, but so was she, and she knew there was nothing that could be said or done to make things different. That was the trouble with prophecies and the telling of fortunes. They gnawed away at you until you forced them to happen through your very own fear and insecurity. She felt destiny's dark cloud scud across her sun, and she shivered against him in her sudden cold.

"Jake helped you set all this up?"

"Yes. I had to know that there was a chance for me."

"But you didn't tell Tessa? She didn't know what was going on?"

"No."

"I thought Tessa liked you, you know. After that book thing. I thought you rather liked her."

"I do."

"But not like that."

He was quiet. Then he said, "She's a beautiful person."

It wasn't quite what Rachel had wanted to hear.

"Yes, she is. You know, when I first met her, she was the expert on romantic love. I didn't really know what she was talking about, going on and on about her husband and the magic and things. I heard the talk, but I'd never walked the walk."

She looked up at him. Tessa is in love with her husband's memory, had been the point she was making.

"And you're a beautiful person," he said. "But you're *my* beautiful person."

"Like Rose." She held her breath. She knew she shouldn't be doing this. It was as wrong as it was inescapable. But the demons had to see sunlight. They couldn't forever lurk in the shadows, ready to pounce.

"Are you ready for Rose?" he said simply. "Are we?"

"I don't know," she said. "I think that's for you to decide."

He looked straight ahead at the sea.

He wasn't a talker at the best of times. About Rose he didn't know what to say.

"What do you say about the past, about what's gone? That you miss it? Yes, I miss her. But I didn't miss her last night with you in my arms. I missed her this morning as I cast off in Antibes. I saw her on the deck, because she would help me do that. Sometimes I miss her a little, and sometimes a lot, and it comes and goes like the waves on the sea, big, small, choppy, smooth. The truth is, she is gone and you are here, and so very different from her, that's the extraordinary thing. She was quiet and mystical, and she was content to be. She was in harmony with herself. She had found peace. She was whole. You, you are being and becoming, always moving, striving, battling, dreaming. She was an old soul and you are a desperately young soul and . . . and . . . I don't know what else to say except that I am falling in love with you and I can't stop."

The last bit, that very last bit, was what she wanted.

"Don't stop. Don't ever stop," she said.

"Have you ever been in love?" he said suddenly, almost fiercely. And then, "With another man?"

"No, never," she said quickly. "Not before."

"Not with Matt Harding? He seemed to think that he had stock options in you, or futures contracts or something."

"Are you jealous?" She laughed delightedly. Was he vulnerable after all, standing so tall and powerful at the wheel of his wonderful ship?

"I don't know. Maybe." He shot a sidelong glance at her, a funny, rueful smile on his face that she hadn't seen before. He wasn't going to beg for information. He wouldn't ask again.

"He wanted to marry me. Merge with me, I used to say. He made perfect sense for the old me, Rachel upwardly mobile Richardson. He pursued me like a takeover target with all the élan he saved for his acquisitions. It was tempting, but I was never engaged. I mean emotionally. I never loved him. Fond, yes. He's interesting, even fascinating, but I gave him up, told him no because of you."

"But you didn't know me."

"I'd met you, though. That, for some reason, was enough."

"I felt that about you."

"You *did?* You kept it pretty quiet."

"I had my memories, and . . . I wasn't certain that it was all right to feel things like that again . . . Guilt, I suppose. Then there was our . . . well . . . our falling out . . . ."

"But now we're here," said Rachel, letting him off the hook.

"Yes, here we are," he said.

"And I'm going to sit down at that table and watch you do whatever it is you do, and I'm going to shut the hell up until we've eaten an incredible lunch and moored the boat off the islands and gotten into the sea. Because you did mention the sea a little bit earlier, didn't you, Charles Ford, and the sea sounds *very* good to me."

Forty-one

"There simply isn't room," said Rachel.

He laughed at her. "Watch me."

The cardinal rule of berthing a boat is to take as much time in the world, especially when the harbor is St. Tropez, where the yachts are layered against each other like sardines. To the untrained eye, the *Myth*'s slip was maybe as wide as the boat itself, maybe not. Either way, the boats on either side had cause for alarm. Indeed, the deckhands on both were lolling around pretending not to be interested in their fellow yachtsman's maneuvers, but were at hand to fend him off, nonetheless.

John was perched in the bow of the yacht, controlling the anchor. Charles pushed the gear that controlled the port engine forward and thrust the starboard engine into reverse. Slowly and majestically, the sleek boat turned on itself until its stern was pointing at the harbor wall. Charles eased it out farther into the harbor.

"Anchor," he shouted. John pulled the pin from the chain and the anchor slid into the murky water.

Charles began to reverse the boat gently toward its berth. A brisk breeze blew from the hills. The boat slipped sideways. To Rachel, the boat next door, a 100-foot Broward, was clearly threatened. She saw two crew members leaning against its guardrail tense for action.

"Don't panic," said Charles with a smile. "This has been done before."

A touch of acceleration on the port engine's reverse thrust, a slipping of the starboard screw into neutral, then a shot of forward momentum to starboard halted the sideways drift as John, forward, allowed the anchor chain to tighten for stabilization.

Rachel breathed again. In a few seconds they were snugly into the berth and Tracy and Mariel were crossing the stern lines on the dock while Tom tightened the anchor chain on the capstan to prevent the boat from drifting back into the stone wall. Charles cut the engines. Silence descended. Rachel fought back the desire to clap. John could presumably have done this in his sleep. Charles had not done it for several months. That she knew. Or thought she knew. He could do such odd things. Docking a boat in St. Tropez harbor. Telling the future from an Indian baby's bones. Making love to her in the sea. She shuddered at the extraordinary memory.

"Over to you, John," he shouted forward.

"Right, captain."

There were yellow cables to be hooked to the shore electricity supply, and hosepipes to shore water; the boat to be washed down; telephone lines to be connected, and cable TV plugged in for the crew. But for the master and mistress of the *Myth* there was only more magic to come.

They walked hand in hand along the harbor amidst the throng of tourists. They looked back at the *Myth,* now crawling with activity as the white-T-shirted, navy-blue-panted crew went to work.

"She's the most beautiful boat here," said Rachel, squeezing his hand.

"But always someone has one a little bigger, quicker, faster, tighter in the turns."

"That's the sort of thing I usually say. I'm infecting you with my ambition."

"I want your infections. Have you ever felt that? Wanting the cold of one you love, to be closer to them?"

"No," said Rachel. "Never." Some of her felt pleased by his remark, the jealous part didn't like it. Everyone but her was an old hand at all this. Tessa would have known all about it, and so would Carol. From her postcard, it sounded as if Carol had made a brave new start as an artist in Santa Fe, and already there was a new man in her life. Good for her!

"Freud thought love was neurosis," said Charles suddenly.

"And lovers suitable cases for treatment."

"Oh, yes, and everyone else. In love you project what you want to see on the blank screen of your loved one. It's not real to a Freudian. It's a sort of sickness."

"But you feel bad when you're sick. Who wants to be cured of an illness that makes you ecstatic?" said Rachel.

"When maniacs are manic, they feel pretty good."

"Yes," said Rachel. "I remember my mother's manic phases. She wouldn't sleep or eat. Spent all the money we didn't have. Talked rubbish from dusk till dawn, and different rubbish from one second to the next. I used to far prefer the depressions. Of course, she didn't."

"Was there more of it in your family?" he asked.

She heard the question. Manic-depressive illness was a hereditary condition. If they had children, then those children would carry some sort of genetic predisposition to manic-depression in their genes.

She let go of his hand.

"A great-uncle. Why?"

"Oh, I don't know. Just wondered."

She turned and looked at him carefully.

"Just small talk?" she said. The sarcasm showed.

"Just talk," he said. The "I'm not small" hung in the scented evening air.

Rachel felt it coming. They were going to have some sort of argument.

"You know manic-depression is an inherited disease?" she said, pinning him down.

"Yes."

Silence descended. Disagreements could defuse themselves, be defused, escalate, or be escalated.

"So if we had children, then those children would be at risk. That was what you meant by your question, wasn't it?"

"I'm not a politician on your show, Rachel."

"You're the lover in my life."

"Perhaps the mirror in your neurosis."

She had walked right into it. On purpose. Why? Why did she want to fight with him? Because he steered his goddamn boat so well, and she didn't know the sharp end from the blunt end of it? Did she want to cross swords with him to show him her bladework, to spill a little of the psychic blood of Mr. Excellence, Mr. Aristocrat, Mr. Europe, with his effortless skills and disdain of competition and struggle?

"You're saying I'm neurotic?"

She stopped and turned to face him. This was no longer a walking conversation.

"I'm speaking plain English, Rachel. You seem to be having difficulty following me. Am I speaking too fast for you?"

"Don't *patronize* me."

"Don't try to bully me. I'm not an employee."

"Now you're suggesting I'm rude to my employees."

"You're so good at it. You must have practiced on somebody."

"I'm n-*not* good at it," spluttered Rachel.

"There you are," he said, a smile beginning to crease the corners of his face. "We've discovered a weakness in the woman. Self-admitted. Not good at bullying."

His smile broadened. The sun was peeping round the storm clouds.

"I'll practice and get better and better at it. That's what I do with my weaknesses."

She, too, began to smile. She felt the ambivalence. She hadn't won, but she hadn't lost. It had been a draw. She hadn't seen the color of his blue blood. Nor he the bright, burning red of hers.

"Well, practice on the crew, won't you? You have my permission. They're English. They rather appreciate the lash of a curled tongue."

Now she laughed outright. He had gone up in her estimation. She hadn't seen even the edge of his temper, but she sensed it existed. And in the meantime, he would take no nonsense from her. Even when he was in the wrong. Because he *had* been asking her about familial diseases.

"I have diabetes in my family," he said suddenly, admitting it. As he did so, Rachel was aware that, actually, he had never denied it in the first place.

"Does that mean we should line up doctors as godparents?" Rachel reached for his hand again. He made it available, but he hadn't reached for hers. Their relationship had sustained a surface crack.

He only laughed, not answering her, and now Rachel regretted picking the fight.

They walked on. She felt the coldness. It wasn't a disaster, but the temperature had dipped. He was wary now, watching his words lest he set her off again. Was this how it began, the seeds of the death of love already being sown at its birth? Maybe there were no rules, only lovers, all deliciously different, every box of magic unique in content.

"Would you like to sit at that café for a while?" he said suddenly. "We could drink some absinthe and go blind and pretend we're old pessimists who've seen it all before, and not optimistic Americans into finding ourselves and making dreams come true."

The fun was back, banishing the melancholy. Once again it was a conspiracy, us against them. They stood united, recovered from their stumble. He ordered pastis and some almonds, and they settled down to watch and be watched by the evening paseo.

"Mr. Ford, sir."

It was Tom, the deckhand.

"John sent me to find you, sir. There's a call for you from a Mrs. Andersen. Says it's very urgent and she needs to talk to you right away."

Charles looked at his watch. It was around lunchtime in New York. Damn! What could Tessa want that was so important?

"I wonder what she wants," said Rachel.

"Only one way to find out," said Charles. He stood up. "Will you wait for me here?"

"Yes, of course. Hurry back."

He was gone, and Rachel was alone but not idle. She was thinking. Tessa. What *did* Tessa want? *Really* want. Money? Security? Success? Yes, Rachel's antennae told her that Tessa was drawn to that alien goal. She had certainly started the game late, but that in itself didn't lessen the force of what Rachel knew only too well could become the most potent addiction. Did Tessa want Charles? Yes, a part of her did, despite the grand gesture in "giving" him to Rachel in the name of friendship and feminine solidarity . . . an animal as strange and rare as Bigfoot. Here she was, on the telephone for Charles, not her, with something that couldn't wait. Hell and damnation. They could have been making love and been disturbed. Had Tessa's subconscious hoped for that? "I'm still here. Don't forget me." She took a gulp of her pastis.

He was gone a long time. She sat there looking at her watch. Ten minutes, almost fifteen. How long did an urgent message take? She shouldn't be waiting. She never waited. Stop it, Rachel. It's called a holiday. She was with her lover, and it felt far more exciting than fantasy. Fifteen minutes. What *was* this? The betrayal by telephone? She would go back and stand beside him while he discussed his vital business with her friend . . . hell, with *his* friend. She would pay for the drink. Damn! She hadn't brought any money, and the waiter, Gallic, with eyes like tank turrets, wouldn't let her travel five paces without paying. She was nailed to the spot. He could talk for hours, muttering sweet nothings across the Atlantic, while the holiday lover cooled her heels at the café. Again, she tried to get a handle on this. Love was like being on drugs, she imagined . . . an upper, a downer, a sideways pill, a pop of antihistamine, a shot of bourbon, something to make you sleep, a little something else to wake up.

Crack, smack, and pop, and pretty soon you didn't know whether you were bottom up or top down, and the feelings rushed hither and thither like marbles on ice. Was that the romance trip . . . . ecstasy and jealousy, passion and paranoia, in a cocktail that tasted too good and then turned you into the jumbled junkie of Dylan's jingle-jangle morning?

She felt a funny feeling at the back of her neck. It was as if something was focused on it, neither hot nor cold, just a presence, an imprint of eyes. She turned around and there he was. He was sitting at a table three back from her and behind. He was staring at her. Now he smiled and she saw what he was doing. He was drawing her. A sketch pad was on his knee. He didn't stop as she opened her mouth in surprise, irritation, and relief.

"What are you doing?"

"Drawing."

"Damn, Charles, I didn't know where you were."

"I was here."

He continued to draw.

"Well, I'm cross," said Rachel. She said it more to record the fact than for any other reason. Actually, she had ceased to be cross seconds after she had seen him. She just didn't want the emotion to have been wasted, although it already seemed like ancient history. He was drawing her, so now, of course, she was self-conscious. She fiddled with her hair and tried to strike poses.

"I'm blushing," she said.

All around, the French were totally disinterested, absorbed, as always, in themselves. But Rachel felt she was the object of all eyes. Usually, she was.

He stopped then. The moment had gone. Rachel was not a sitter.

He stood up and moved to her table.

"How long have you been there?" How long were you on the phone to Tessa? was what she meant.

"Ten minutes." He threw the drawing down onto the table. Like an alibi?

She picked it up. It was very good. Every line counted, and

he had captured her anxiety, her churning thoughts. Her expression told the inside story . . . a person in fish-out-of-water mode, the energy, the ambivalence, the power-on-a-leash element that was the vitality of her. She looked pretty, too, but that paled beside the other revelations.

"You should have been a psychiatrist," she said.

"No patience for patients."

He drummed on the table with his fingers, as if to emphasize his point.

"It's a wonderful drawing," she said. "It's beautiful, but more than that, it's revealing. It says everything in a few lines."

"Maybe I should have been a writer." He laughed.

"Maybe you should have been a waiter. I'd love another drink."

They laughed together, almost back to square one.

"What did Tessa want?" Not quite.

"She's had an offer on the apartment. A pretty good one. She wanted to know whether to accept or not."

Rachel went quiet.

He said nothing. A thought was occurring to him. She could see it happening, as he had read her mind for the drawing. If they were going to share their lives, then decisions about the sale of apartments would become, at some point, joint decisions. Had that point been reached? he was asking himself.

"Are you going to sell it?"

"I was going to."

"Why?"

He paused. "Too many memories" as an answer could play either way. He was wary of her now, after the spat, not frightened, not cowed, but aware that she could flare up and that for Rachel words had consequences, and that some attempt had to be made to predict them. He seemed not to like the idea of that, because he said . . .

"Too many memories. I thought maybe something more uptown . . ."

"Our memories, too," she said. "The bones. Before. Afterward. Those aren't memories I want to lose."

"Nor I," he said gently. "So I told Tessa no."

"You did?" said Rachel, brightening. She loved that apartment. She could live in it, damn the driving and the inconvenience. She didn't even mind the memories of Rose. Rose, she felt in some mysterious way, had become her spiritual ally and not her rival.

"Yes. Tessa was not best-pleased, as the English sometimes say."

"Well, realtors always want to sell, cop the commission, and then move on to the next."

"It was within five percent of the asking price," he said. It was a defense of Tessa and a reasonable one.

"Poor Tessa," said Rachel, forcing herself to see the point. "And she really needs the money."

"Apparently not so poor Tessa. She's getting a lot of interest on that house in the Hamptons."

"She *is?*" said Rachel. "That would be some commission."

"And she's picked up another several millions' worth of listings. The Sinclair friends are coming in like lemmings, apparently."

"Good Lord, that's incredible," said Rachel. "I always thought of Tessa as a sort of gilded victim."

"Yes," he said with a laugh, "the English rather like one thinking that about them. Then, when the going gets tough, they revert to type . . . Vikings, Celts, Saxons, Normans, Angles. The veneer of British civilization is thin, but well maintained. Actually, they're all pirates, plunderers, and buccaneers at heart. Look at a soccer crowd loosened up with a little vino for veritas."

Two more pastis arrived. Tessa was over. Once again the future was the place.

"So tell me what's next, Charles Ford?"

"Back to the boat," he said. There was a catch in his voice. Desire sparkled in his eyes. Rachel felt the surge of feeling inside her. She stood up and smiled at him.

Forty-two

Thirty feet beneath the surface of the sea, they held hands with Christ.

The previous night, they had made love . . . so gently and tenderly that Rachel had almost wanted to die in the moment that would not be bettered until the next time. In the morning they had awoken to find themselves swinging at anchor in a bay at the foot of steep cliffs. They had breakfasted, and Charles had made a mystery of what was to follow, as only he could.

The crew had lowered the Zodiac into the water, and it bobbed on the wrinkled sea by the yacht's edge. They had put on swimsuits and loaded the tender with a bag of skin-diving gear, and set off to an area of the bay near the cliffs, where a buoy marked their destination.

"What is it, Charles? What are we going to do?"

"We're going to meet our Maker," he had answered with a laugh.

"Not before tonight, we're not. Or before this afternoon," she had answered, totally in love with him.

"You did say you were happy with skin diving, didn't you?" he said.

"Yes, and there are no sharks in the Mediterranean."

They had put on fins and masks, and he had orchestrated the deep breathing that would prepare the lungs for the oxygen lack. "Hold my hand and we go straight down for thirty feet. You know all about equalization."

Rachel had nodded, her heart suddenly thumping. She trusted him completely, and it was that realization as much as anything that speeded her heart.

Together, they had dived from the Zodiac and swum straight down into the clear water. Rachel had seen it at once—a vast statue beneath the water, its huge hands outstretched, a crown of thorns on its head. It was a statue of Christ submerged in the blue sea, lit from above by sunlight and from the side by the reflections from sparkling fish that swirled around its stone robes and sandaled feet. Rachel had turned to Charles in wonder, and he had nodded, signaling her deeper until they were there, touching the wounded hand that reached up to them in supplication. Three hands in one. Joined by Christ for fleeting seconds before the rush back to the air and the surface.

Now they broke the surface, lungs screaming, and gulped air. "Oh, Charles, that is so beautiful. I can't believe it. It's so huge. It's like a miracle."

"I knew you'd like it."

"It was like . . . it was like a marriage," she said.

"It was, wasn't it," he said. They were quiet as they watched each other, treading water. "Would you like to get married again?"

"And again and again," she said, and she took a mighty breath, flipped herself up, and headed down once more, this time the leader.

Later, tired, they lay still in the Zodiac, warmed by the sun, their hands intertwined. She had never felt closer to him, to anyone. It had been like some form of sacrament, and he had sensed it, and planned it, and intended that it should be.

"There's more," he said.

"What?"

"The caves."

Rachel felt completely indulged. It was a magical mystery tour of adventure, the sort you never experienced as an adult, only as a child, as a *normal* child. There was a glorious feeling of letting go. It was like falling from a great height, eyes closed, secure in the knowledge that you would be caught. It was about trust and certainty. For many women this was familiar territory. For Rachel, it was not.

"Take me to your caves," she said.

He started the engine and in seconds the Zodiac was skimming across the surface of the bay toward the rocky cliffs. Within thirty feet of them, he cut the engine and threw the anchor over. The base of the cliff was honeycombed with caves, a strange rock formation that canopied the sea and put down legs here and there in a geological Swiss cheese carved over centuries by the waves. There were alleys and passageways, corridors and black holes, and the gurgling blue sea washed through them all, crashing against them as spray, bubbling into the nooks and crannies, ebbing and flowing through the natural maze it had created.

"Follow me," he said, and she did so gladly, slipping into the sea beside him and swimming close as he headed for a columned entrance in the cliff.

She didn't ask him if he knew what he was doing, where he was going. There was no need. Ahead of her, he disappeared, kicking down below the surface, and she did so too, swimming strongly after him in what was now a six-foot underwater corridor of rock. She twisted around and looked up. They were in a tunnel. There was an air space above when the waves flowed out, but it disappeared in a cloud of bubbles when the sea came in. He turned around and held his thumb up in the diver's question "Are you all right?" She held her own thumb up. "Yes."

In front of her, he was going up, and she did too. They broke the surface in a grotto half open to the blue sky, half rocky ceiling. The water was calm in there, and warmer. Sand stretched into a cave at the grotto's edge. There was no way whatsoever of entering the place except by swimming underwater. It was splendidly lonely, a place of staggering beauty that could only be experienced if you knew its secret. It was a place for lovers.

She pulled off her mask.

"Oh, Charles, this is so beautiful."

"Isn't it? Not many people know about it. I've never seen anybody else here."

He had come with Rose. Rachel could feel him feel the memories.

It was quiet. Somehow the roar of the sea against the cliffs, all around their oasis of tranquillity, didn't count as sound. There was a faint echo as they spoke.

"Can you stand?" She reached down with her feet. A sandy bottom sloped gently to the cave.

She moved toward him, bathed in sunlight, and he reached out to hold her. His arms were around her and she felt the womblike protection of him.

"Make love to me," she whispered.

She held him tight, plastering herself along the length of his hard body. She could feel him against her, growing, becoming, despite the water's chill. She ground her hips into his and eased her thigh between his legs, the better to feel him, the more to excite him.

"Here?"

She nodded, her lips parted in lust for him. They knew each other's bodies. They had shared each other slowly, and they had devoured each other hungrily. Now, the intensity of their intimacy demanded newness, like this, in unexpected places, at unknowable moments. She wanted to anoint the places they went with the seal of their lovemaking.

She reached down through the circle of his arms and found the hardness. She slipped her hands inside his trunks, and she reached for him, watching his eyes widen, his chest rise and fall with desire as she touched him. The sea swirled around them. It lapped at the lovers. It murmured in the caves. Sunlight bathed them, hot on their faces, the rays leaping from the deep blue water. Above them flew gulls that called to each other, oblivious of the fierceness of the human need below.

She slipped his trunks down, watching him all the time, loving the longing in his eyes. He sighed deeply and closed his eyes in ecstasy as she guided him toward her. She eased back the thong of her bikini and touched him against her. He reached down behind her with both hands and pulled her toward him, and she felt the sublime feeling as he entered her, slipping into her body as effortlessly as, on that long-ago night, he had slid into her mind.

She breathed out a long breath of contentment. It felt so right, and so good. It was the sweet harmony of body and mind. She was held by both him and the sea. It bore her up, seemingly weightless in his arms. And he held her to him, deep within her body as she, too, was in his heart. She wrapped her legs tight around his waist and she threw back her head, to the blue sky and to the God that had made this joy possible. He moved quietly inside her, caressing her with his gentleness. It was slow and easy, the peaceful feeling of love. She rose and fell about him as the sea ebbed and flowed around them both.

"Yes. Yes. Yes," she murmured in time to the rhythm of his lovemaking. She felt so light. Every sensation danced deliciously in her mind. She captured every movement he made in the velvet prison she had made for him, encircling him with both her body and her soul. She sensed it before she felt it. And then she felt his legs go loose, and he swayed to the side as he unleashed his passion inside her, and she held on tight to his shuddering body, milking him of the moment, drawing the love from him to bathe her own, as she bathed his.

But it was not over. He carried her across the sandy floor of the grotto to the warm darkness of the cave.

Forty-three

Carol woke, and she knew somehow today was going to be different. For months she had been deep in a deliciously un-thinking orgy of work, stopping only to eat and sleep. She had barely allowed herself to think. There had been a rhythm to her life that allowed her to concentrate totally on painting. She got up and she did it. There was no pain, no struggle to create, just an almost mechanical loss of herself in the process. It was what she had needed. But today, her eyes still closed, she knew it was going to be different.

She opened her eyes and the desert sunrise greeted her through the small window of her room. Usually, she would get up instantly, instant coffee, instant shower, going through the process on autopilot.

Today, she decided to scrap the Taster's and break open the Colombian Supremo blend that had sat for an age unopened in the cupboard. She watched it dripping through the percolator, and before the glass was full she poured herself a cup and sipped it, feeling the caffeine rush that speeded her thoughts. She walked from the kitchenette into her studio and surveyed the work-in-progress, but she couldn't concentrate on it.

She looked around the studio that she wouldn't be able to bear leaving. She had never loved a place like it, not even the perfect home of the perfect years when she had lived with Jack. It was where she had become Carol, as she had vowed to do all those months ago at the Hacienda Inn. She thought about

Rachel and Tessa. She had kept in touch with them by postcard. Her life had been so busy, she had hardly had time for anything else. Now, she felt she had made it. She had found self-respect. How proud of her both Rachel and Tessa would be.

Then she thought of Charles Ford. He had returned, briefly, from Europe and then made a precipitous second disappearance to his boat in the Mediterranean. That had brought him more sharply into focus in Carol's mind. He had always seemed like a man with clipped emotional wings, unable to fly. Not now. If he had found another woman, what might that mean to Carol? A wife! Her heart reared against the thought, and her mind raced to the secret weapon that existed in both her subconscious and her closet for a moment such as this.

She stood up in the cool studio and walked across to the storage bay. The painting was against the wall, covered by an old rug. She removed it and her own face stared back at her from the petals of the rose. She hadn't looked at it in a month, and as always its beauty, and its originality, took her breath away. She had never given him the painting. She had never properly said thank you for all he had done for her. She had never really told him of the incredible admiration she had for him. The painting could put all those things right, and Carol felt that the moment had come. He must see it soon. Before commitments were made. He had to have a chance to think about her . . . as a woman. She didn't know if she wanted him, but she knew that she wanted him to have a chance to want her. Was that a woman's trick, to try to sabotage something wonderful even without knowing for certain her own desires? The old Carol would have cared about those things. But the new Carol was the equal of her femininity, and her conscience was clear.

She had a packing case in the storage area of the studio that fitted her painting perfectly. She lowered the canvas into it, securing it with bubbled plastic.

Next, she sat down at her desk and wrote a note. She didn't

have her own writing paper, but she had borrowed some from Charles's ranch. It was this that she used now.

"Dearest Charles," she wrote.

"This is for you, with all my love and all my gratitude. You saved me from death, and more important, from my life. I owe you everything, always. Carol."

She put the note in an envelope, wrote "Charles" on it, and stuck it to the back of the canvas with tape. Then she closed the packing case, hammering in the nails carefully, and sealed it with heavy-duty tape until it was totally secure. She wrote the Manhattan address of Charles's studio in three separate places in indelible black marker. She wrote her return address. There was only one thing left to do. She took another envelope and another piece of paper, on which she wrote "To Charles, in endless admiration."

She taped this second note securely to the outside of the packing case, wrote "Charles Ford" on the outside, and stood back to survey what she had done. It was a bomb of sorts. She knew that. It was her statement. It was her gift to him of a chance with her. A last chance, perhaps, before it was too late.

Forty-four

Portofino had been best of all. The old fishing village clustered at the bottom of the hill was enchanting. The ocher buildings with their balconies looked as if at any minute they would reveal baritones bursting with song while the tourists below clapped and the locals cheered. Open-air restaurants surrounded the boats, and the backstreets were full of stores selling leather items, sweaters, and the chic, practical fashions for which Italy is famous. It was a terra-cotta world of peeling paint and bright colors set against the backcloth of olive-green Italy, and everywhere there was pasta and shellfish, and tomatoes, wine, and the love of life that, in this oldest of countries, was still the specialty.

Rachel couldn't bear for it to end, but she knew she had to get back. More than that, she had to go on. On this boat ride of pleasure they were outside reality. Their world was on hold. There were no decisions except where to eat, when to swim, how long to make love, and Rachel wanted decisions. His decisions. Her decisions. They hovered on the brink of marriage, but they would not confront the fact of it until they were home. For now, it was enough to make magic.

She hurried from the changing room of the boutique in a pink cashmere sweater of spectacular softness and style. "I can't believe this stuff. I want it all. Where has it been all my life?" she said.

He looked up at her, smiling. "I know how you feel." He wasn't talking about clothes. She laughed with him.

"I'm going to buy it," she said. "Are you going to buy me?"

"Would you consider a lease option?" he said.

"No. Cash in full, up front. Closing today. I should tell you that somebody else is seriously interested. But if you move fast . . ."

"As is?" he said.

"No. Everything guaranteed in working order, except possibly the mind, which has taken leave of its senses."

"Nonsense. The mind is the most attractive part of the property."

"Charles! You're talking to a woman, remember."

"How could I ever forget? Men don't wear sweaters like that."

"Do we have to go back today?" she said, changing the subject, but only just.

"I thought you had to go back. I have brush, will travel. With my model and inspiration. Ms. Television, however, has schedules and an audience she mustn't disappoint."

Rachel sighed her ambivalence. She wanted to be home with him, to visit his ranch, to be with him in Manhattan, to do cities and the desert after having so beautifully done the sea. Hell, she wanted to marry him and get pregnant, and in her heart, *that* was what she was flying back to. At once, the doubt pricked at her. He hadn't said the four words, "Will you marry me?" There had been talk of togetherness, of endless togetherness, of "them" and what their children would look like. He had mellowed in her arms. Now his smiles and his laughter flowed free, whereas before they had been rationed, forced from him by her cunning and charm.

The flight to Rome was a few hours from now. By tomorrow morning they would be in Manhattan. It would be a Saturday. They would spend the weekend in his loft, holed up where the bones had clattered onto the polished wood of the floor. On Monday it would start again, only different because now, of course, she was deeply in love and everything else was a side-show to the main event in her heart.

"I'll take this. And the bottle-green one. The canary-yellow and the navy, too. And those shoes, and the cream ones, and I'll take him. The man in the corner. The mahogany-brown one that fits like a glove."

"I've never been a sweater before," said Charles, laughing.

"Liar!" said Rachel.

Forty-five

They said their goodbyes at the airport, and Rachel could
hardly bear to let him go. They had gotten the call on the yacht
before they had left. The farm manager at Charles's ranch had
telephoned to say that they had a major problem. The cows were
going down with pneumonia and dying like flies. It was necessary for Charles to fly straight from Kennedy to Santa Fe. Rachel had asked one favor. Could she stay Saturday and Sunday
nights at Charles's downtown apartment? She wanted to remain
close to him, and that would be a nice way to do it, cocooned
in the comfort of the place where it had all begun. Charles had
willingly agreed, and the parting was bittersweet. It had been
agony to leave him, but the sadness of saying goodbye was
alleviated by the thought of his place, private, secret, that she
would be mistress of for the weekend. The getting-to-know-him
would not stop. It would continue in his closets, in his furniture,
in the books in his bookshelves, as she wandered the loft alone
yet still with him.

So now, her baggage around her ankles and the superintendent hovering at her elbow, she slipped the key into the lock as
if into Charles's heart. The door swung open and the super fer-
ried her bags inside.

"If there's anything you want, miss, just phone down and
ask. Pick up the intercom and I answer. Would you like me to
show you around?"

"No," said Rachel. "I've been here before." She thanked him, eager for him to be gone so the memories could begin. The door closed behind him, and the apartment opened in front of her. She sighed. It was the end of the beginning. She was looking forward to the solitude. The office would be messengering a large package that would help her prepare for next week. She would read it between the Chinese takeouts and the Domino's pizza . . . and thé guilty little voyages of discovery that she had already promised herself. She wanted to see his toothbrush and his shaving apparatus, all the things that would have been closest to him. Then there would be time for his clothes, and, oh, wicked Rachel, the desk with its fascinating drawers. She thought, No, I mustn't, and the thought was canceled immediately by Oh, yes, I will.

There was still so much mystery about him. Freud had said that the neurosis that was love could be relieved in therapy. Was that all she was, a suitable case for treatment, as she projected her wishes and libidinal urges onto poor Charles? Was the man she saw simply a mirror to what she wanted, the absent, inadequate father, the foil for her narcissism, as fake and as phony as smoke in the shape of a man? Hell, she didn't care. She just wanted to get on with the business of discovery, and she was starting now.

The intercom rang loudly, startling her. She went to it and pressed the button marked Answer. It was the super.

"I have a UPS delivery for Mr. Ford," he said. "Looks like a big painting. Can I have it sent up? Will you sign for it?"

"Yes, of course." Rachel was intrigued. A painting, a big painting for Charles. She waited, interested. When it arrived, it was indeed big. She signed for it and had the two men lean it against a wall. It would be quite a job to open, requiring hammers, screwdrivers, and God knew what else. The door shut behind the deliverymen. Rachel looked at the packing case. It was addressed to Charles in a big, florid hand. It was the writing of a woman. There was no doubt about it. Yet the return address was Santa Fe. A woman in Santa Fe had sent a painting to Charles in New York. A secretary, possibly. But he had never mentioned such a person. Then again, he didn't mention people. Mmmmmm. It could be a Charles Ford painting, but sent by whom, and why? Then again, hadn't he been blocked until recently? Maybe this was an old Charles Ford canvas. The mystery deepened as the woman whose living was made by asking questions circled the packing case.

There was an envelope taped to the case. "Charles Ford," it said. It did not say "private and personal." It wouldn't have mattered if it had. The toothbrush was now way down the list. This was where discovery began. She detached the envelope from the painting, being careful not to tear it. It was definitely a woman's writing. What was her excuse for opening it? Curiosity. "I opened it because I thought it might be urgent, and that in the general rush you might have forgotten something important." That would do. Sort of. She ripped it open. The words screamed up at her.

"To Charles, in endless admiration."

Still no name. But now an admirer. An endless admirer. An admirer who would be around endlessly? Around Charles Ford, admiring him, a woman admiring the man that Rachel was going to marry? How sweet! A crush! An employee? The note was written on Charles's own letterhead. The faithful servant, the distant master admired from a distance. Oh, bull*shit!* Where was something big and sharp that could open up this mother and get to the truth? She looked down at the polished floor. Betrayal. Was this where it all began?

She stalked into the kitchen and pulled a butcher's knife from a drawer. It bent on the nails, but it did the job. She redoubled her efforts. It was well packed, the bitch. But she could see the edge of the canvas now, and the little plastic balls that prevented it from being damaged. She tried to peer down into the box, but she couldn't see. There was no shortcut. She would have to take out the whole bloody thing. She worked fast, sweating as she did so in the air-conditioned cool. Oh, no! This was terrible. The weekend was off to a tragic start. "In endless admiration"! This couldn't be happening. Not so *soon.* Finally, the top of the

packing case was free. She pulled on the canvas and it slid out
onto the floor, the wrong way up, of course. On the back was
another envelope from the endless admirer. Once again it was
stuck tight. This one had "Charles" on the outside. She ripped
it off, but first she wanted to see what the painting was.

She turned the canvas over. It was a rose, a great big one,
beautifully painted, so well done that Rachel could all but smell
it. And there, nestled in the center of its petals, peering out in
endless admiration, was the painter, or the sitter, or whatever. It
was Carol McCabe. Rachel had not set eyes on her since the
Hacienda Inn. She drew in her breath sharply. Her world stopped
as her mind raced. What the hell was Carol doing peering out
from the petals of a rose in what was no doubt Charles Ford's
studio? Carol had disappeared in the desert. She wanted to paint.
She had wanted to live for herself. Somewhere near Santa Fe,
presumably. In endless admiration. Charles Ford! Oh, no! It
couldn't be. But you couldn't lie with paint. Whose paint? Whose
canvas? The answer was in the bottom right hand corner. The
answer was Carol McCabe. Carol's postcard flashed into Rachel's photographic memory. Carol had met a man in Santa Fe,
a stormy, unpredictable, tortured artist who had become her artistic mentor. It couldn't be. But, already, Rachel knew that it
was.

Rachel turned the envelope in her hand. It would be inside.
She knew it would be revealed in there. But it was already revealed in the expression on the face of the artist. Worship. Admiration. Hell, let's face it—love. She had sent the picture to him
in New York, knowing he would find it on his return from the
Mediterranean. But there had been a mistake. Rachel had found
it first. Charles had gone straight home to deal with the cattle . . .
or to deal with Carol McCabe. It had been Carol all along. Not
Tessa. Rachel had chosen the wrong friend to play the rival. Carol
McCabe. Ms. Suburbia no longer. The attorney had moved out.
The artist moved in. Oh, God! Rachel ripped open the letter, and
there was the rest of it, in blue and white.

"This is for you, with all my love and all my gratitude. You saved me from death, and more important, from my life. I owe you everything, always. Carol."

Rachel zoned in on the important parts. Love. Saved me from death. The death of life without you, presumably. How gloriously over-the-top. Always. Endless. Throughout eternity. Infinity. Love. Life. Death. Betrayal. Rachel looked at the telephone. She looked down at the painting. God, it was good. It was spooky how very good it was. The cows were dying, were they? Hell, the cows hadn't started dying yet.

Rage rushed into the vacuum left by shock. Here it was. Carol McCabe and Charles Ford were lovers. Carol knew all about Rachel, and she was a rival. She had painted the picture as a last-ditch stand to sabotage Rachel on Charles's return. Sometime today the mess would be revealed. Carol would mention to Charles that she had sent a painting to the apartment. Or would she? Maybe she wanted it to be a surprise. And had Charles told Carol about Rachel? Possibly not. It was the cell principle. Great for secrecy. Nobody knew anything about anyone else. Tears rushed to Rachel's eyes. It had all been a lie . . . a great, big, gigantic lie . . . and she had fallen for the oldest trick in the book. She had believed a man because she wanted to, and for no other good reason. Welcome to romance, Rachel Richardson. Welcome to the land of the fool.

Forty-six

Charles's ranch had not been hard to find. Mostly, south of Santa Fe, you drove in it. In the back of the limousine, Rachel was ice cold. The air-conditioning was only partly responsible. She had worked through anger on the plane. She had worked through very nearly everything, but still she was operating on emotion rather than reason. Did killers feel like this? There was a sense of nothing mattering anymore. All action was random, meaningless, shorn of consequences. Nothing could ever be as bad as the present pain, and so what came next was irrelevant. Except that she was here, on Saturday morning in 120 degrees of heat, in the desert loved by the man she had loved.

"The entrance to the ranch should be a few miles up the road to the left," said the driver.

She took a deep breath. What would happen now? Would there be a confrontation? What would she have to say to Charles, to Carol? What would they find to say to her? This was pointless. Everything had to be taken one second at a time. She wasn't here for recrimination. She was here for confirmation. She wanted the facts, now more than ever before in her life. Once again, she was the old Rachel, clear-eyed, unstoppable in her search for truth.

The entrance to the vast ranch was unpretentious. There was simply a gate, which was open, with a wooden structure erected around it as a frame. A small sign in handwriting above it said "Las Olivas." Away behind it stretched the driveway, lined by trees farther than the eye could see. Charles had not lied about one thing—the size of his estate. They entered and drove, and continued for what seemed like ten minutes. Then, out of the heat haze, Rachel saw the ranch house nestled in trees, a green oasis in the desert. It came clearly into focus, the outbuildings, the red-tiled roofs, the stable block off to the right, another set of buildings flanking it on the left. Where were they? Making love in the hot afternoon? Painting, turning each other on with the care and consideration of their brush strokes? Where was the betrayal taking place? Here? There? Everywhere? Still, Rachel had no plan. She was trespassing. She was an intruder. She had no rights apart from those of ex-lover and fool. She smiled bitterly. When would Carol get hers? In a week, a month, a year? Less? Because men like that were men like that. They were the wolves beneath the disguise, who ate romantic Red Riding Hoods like Rachel for breakfast, lunch, and dinner.

"Shall I take you up to the front entrance?" said the driver.

"No, he's not really expecting me. It's a surprise." She looked around. They were passing beneath an arch that served as a gateway to the compound. Off to the left was a garden with fountains, grassy walkways, and flower beds. At the end of it was what looked like a pool pavilion. Rachel's instinct said, "There."

"Can you pull up over there on the left?"

She walked into an English garden, but there were no roses here, she noticed, no source for Carol's artistic inspiration. The rose was Rose. Carol was emerging from it. The symbolism was inescapable. "I can replace her," she had been trying to say. She heard the sound of splashing, a muffled shout. Up ahead would be a pool. Two people would be swimming in it. They would be playing, joking, chasing each other. Rachel's stomach lurched in a wave of nausea. She knew how Charles Ford played in water. She remembered the things he had done in the sea.

Another arbor was the entrance to the pool and its pavilion. Already she could see the blue of its surface, the ripples on it

that would be made by her lover and her friend. She took a deep
breath and a step forward. Like an Indian. Like him. She wanted
to see and not be seen. She wanted to find out but not be found
out. When the evidence was there, she would creep away and
they would never know the hurt they had caused her. She would
trace her footsteps back through the English garden, back into
the car, back to the airport and New York, back, back, to the
old Rachel forever and ever. Never again would she open herself
up to this hurt. Never again would she allow herself to sink to
this, a common spy, her life in the hands of others.

She peered around the corner. They were at one end of the
pool. Carol, burned dark as the Coppertone that covered her,
trim, athletic, and looking wildly happy, stood against the pool's
wall. She was radiant. Her hair, wet and long, ran down her
back. Her head was thrown back, and as Rachel watched, Charles Ford moved toward her, taking her head in his hands, tenderly, carefully, as so very many wonderful times he had taken
Rachel's. He moved in close to Carol, so close, and he was
moving in closer still when Rachel tore her eyes away. She could
not deal with the kiss. Somehow, although it had happened in
all but fact, she wanted not to have it in her memory. Look, she
commanded herself, but her eyes closed. Look, fool, idiot, silly
little stupid woman. Look and see how it happens in the big
wide world. The bones had spoken of betrayal. Watch it, see it,
believe it, learn from it. But she couldn't. Something wouldn't
let her. And so she closed her eyes and backed away and, as she
walked through the garden in a daze of horror, and as the tears
streamed down her cheeks, she was already back in Manhattan,
building on the shattered ruins of her life.

Forty-seven

Rachel came into the office at a run, and Steve simply didn't read the smoke signals.

"Well, look who's here," he drawled. "All bronzed, bright-eyed, and bushy-tailed from an impulse holiday. I must say, Rachel, I never expected you to pull a stunt like that. You were always a pro. But you live and learn, I guess, that's life, and all the clichés are true."

He sighed a world-weary sigh and looked up at her slyly. The two weeks had gone without a single hitch, largely because of the accuracy and depth of the research Rachel had organized. Mary O'Hara, her stand-in, had just had to read off the questions and the interviews had come out fine. But Rachel wasn't going to hear that. She was going to get the acid rain. She must have been expecting it.

"I hear," said Rachel, cutting through the discouraging words, "that in my absence Matt Harding has upped his stake in the company."

"Yeah. Should have signed on with him, dear, rather than chasing around the Med with mystery men. Very bad for the blood vessels. Not so hot for the career."

"Steve," she said. "What sort of job are you thinking of after this one?"

His eyebrows arched upward. Oh, she's attacking as the best form of defense, is she? Good for Rachel. He felt like a cat fight. So good for sharpening the cutting edge.

"Threats, Rachel, so early in the morning, and you the one who's just dropped me in the shit, major-league? Is it *my* job we ought to be worrying about? Is it heavy weather in the land of romance novels, dear, or are you just trying to shift guilt?"

"Do you know what I think?" said Rachel. "I think that Matt Harding would be good for another interview. He's making lots of moves. Hot topic. The last appearance was great. He gives good TV. Some people thought the chemistry between us was positive Nielsen."

"Yes, he'd be okay, but it wasn't so long ago. Don't want to get repetitive. And there may be conflict of interest now that he has a bigger position here. You'd have to be extra tough on him to avoid the impression of favoring him. We don't want people to think we're puff pastries."

"Don't disagree with me, Steve," said Rachel.

She sat down at her desk and smiled a hard smile. Watch out, world. She was back. It was cold as ice in her soul.

"I was being businesslike," said Steve. "You asked me a question. I answered it."

"No," snapped Rachel. "I didn't ask you a question. I stated a fact. I said that Matt Harding would be good for another interview. He would be. He will be. No question, Steve."

Steve stood up. "Well, excuse me for breathing," he huffed. "Put Harding on if you like. I don't care either way."

"Are you saying you think it's a bad idea?"

"The mood you're in this morning, it doesn't matter what I say."

He was on the run. Good. Great.

"Good idea," he said at last, as he stalked out of the room without another word.

Rachel reached forward to the intercom. "Jake, can you come in here for a second?"

"Welcome back, Rachel," said Jake. "I hope you had a wonderful time."

There was the tone of the co-conspirator in his voice. He had helped set the whole thing up. He had a vested interest in its success. There had been a card from France that hinted at promotion, happiness, bliss for all and everyone. But his boss had not come pounding into his office with presents and thanks, and her voice sounded distant on the intercom.

She didn't answer Jake's question.

He appeared in the doorway.

"How did it go?" he said with a hopeful smile that diminished as he saw the expression on Rachel's face. "It sounded like fun from the card . . ."

"Jake. This is what I want to say to you. I'm sure when you got into all the little psychodramas that you thought you were doing the right thing. I'm not criticizing your motive, just your judgment. In the future, I want you to remember that my personal life is completely, totally, out of bounds to you and to all employees. You are not my friend. You are my assistant. You do nothing, repeat *nothing,* without telling me. You do not make judgments about what I might like or might not like. You ask. You listen. You carry out instructions. Is that clear? Is that very, very clear? Because if it isn't, you'll have to go."

Jake took a deep breath. He paled in the doorway.

"I just thought, from the p-postcard, I mean . . . ," he stuttered.

"Don't think. Just obey. Right?"

"Right."

"Oh, and if Mr. Charles Ford calls, I am very busy. Okay? In meetings, script conferences, whatever. Tell security downstairs that he is not allowed up to this office. Understood? If you let him through to me, you are fired. Got it?"

"Yes."

"Good. Now get me Matt Harding on the phone. Immediately."

"Yes, Rachel."

It was another Rachel Richardson that spoke on the telephone to Matt Harding. It was not the new Rachel, but it wasn't the old one either. She had changed. Oh, dear God, how she had changed.

"How are you, Rachel? Heard you went away. Spur of the moment thing, was it?"

He was cool but friendly, in deal-investigation mode. He was fishing for information.

"Yes, I had the overwhelming desire to get away. Took a boat in the Mediterranean. It was bliss."

"With friends?" he said, innocent as an asp. He still wanted her. She could feel it.

"No. I just wanted to cool out. Do some thinking. Pamper myself. It was wonderful."

"But not inexpensive. For one," he said.

"Oh, Matt, I leave worrying about money to people like you who have so much of it. I gather you've been spreading it around in my absence. You've taken a pretty substantial stake. Wow! More to come?"

"Who's asking? The journalist or . . . the friend?"

He paused on the word "friend."

"Maybe neither," said Rachel.

"Oh?" he said. "And what sorts of conclusions did you come to out there in the Med, bobbing about by yourself in an expensive boat?"

Probing. Digging. Sniffing around for information.

"Well, for one, I decided to invite you back on the show."

He seemed genuinely surprised.

"In my role as substantial shareholder . . . or what?"

"No, because I want to see you again." She paused for a split second. "Just joking," she added quickly.

"Ha, ha," he said. There was a smile in his voice.

"You know how it is, Matt. You're always hot, but right now you're hotter. You're making moves. The superhighway got a little flat and dull for a bit there, but now it's developing some nice curves, interesting scenery. We talk well together. I think it'll be good. Steve agrees."

"Do I get a list of questions?" he asked.

"The hell you do. You sink or swim like the rest of them."

"You going to ask me about us?" he said.

"On the air?" Rachel was suddenly off balance.

"Wherever."

"I'm not Rivera," she said.

He laughed. "I got you there, didn't I?"

She didn't reply. He had.

"Well, okay, Rachel. I'll do the show. Last time it was fun. You dug up that thing about me cheating at college. That was hardball. If I was the type to give a shit, I wouldn't have forgiven you for that."

"All's fair in love, war, and live TV," said Rachel with a laugh. "I'm a journalist number one. No quarter given." Was all fair in love? Was it fair that Charles had betrayed her? Was she a journalist number one, or was she a woman?

"When do you want to schedule this?"

"How about tomorrow night?"

"Short notice. Can you dig up enough dirt on me in that time?"

"You should see my Matt Harding file. It's bulging."

"Maybe as a big shareholder I'll send over for it and have a read myself."

"You'll need fifty-one percent for that, and you have to step over my dead body to get to the filing cabinet."

"I suspect the first would be easier than the second." She could hear the admiration in his voice. He still wanted her. There was no doubt about it. Had his buying the extra shares been because of her? No. It made good business and strategic sense on its own, but she would have been the icing on the cake.

"So, do we have a deal?"

"Yeah, why not."

"Shall I get my assistant to fix the details with yours?"

"You do that, Rachel Richardson. Do I get to take you to dinner afterward?"

"Yes, you do," she said.

Forty-eight

Charles Ford grabbed the telephone and punched in the number. Where was she? She had disappeared. On Saturday Louis, the super, had gone up to the apartment half a dozen times, but she hadn't been there. Charles wasn't sure what he was, . . . worried, irritated, nervous, or bits of all three. The parting at the airport had been sweet harmony, and by the time he got to the ranch, it had been too late to ring her. At eight-thirty on Saturday morning there had been no reply.

Well, she was a busy woman. That was part of what he loved about her. Maybe the office had intervened. He'd better get used to it. Life with Rachel would be very different from life with Rose. He smiled at himself and his impatience. He was getting set in his ways. He liked to be the center of things. He was used to that. So was Rachel. There would be lots of moments like this, when those two desires clashed. He put the telephone down. Once again, there had been no reply.

It was Sunday morning. He walked to the window and looked out at the desert shimmering in its heat haze. The cattle were a mess, but the vet was doing everything he could, and there was insurance. The ranch manager was on top of it. Charles's return had been mainly a hand-holding operation to show that the boss cared. That part was accomplished. There was nothing preventing his going back to New York. But he had lost Rachel. Until he could locate her, there was no point in going up to Manhattan. He felt a twinge of fear. Had something gone wrong? He couldn't imagine what. Their journey had been the most beautiful and exciting of his life. He had been reborn. He felt the newness, the excitement, once again, as he had felt it in the early days with Rose. There was a heightened sensitivity, smell, taste, touch, the senses on fire with possibility. He could paint again, create once more. There was a world outside full of fun and joy and laughter, and Rachel had conjured up the change in him. And now she was gone. He laughed out loud. Gone? For one day? God! He was behaving like an adolescent. At last he understood how Rachel must have felt during the week that he hadn't called her, before the limousine kidnap.

"Missing the Mediterranean?" said Carol from the doorway of the dining room.

He turned, pleased by the distraction.

Carol had called early that morning and mentioned that she would be taking him up on his open invitation to come out to the ranch to paint. He had asked her to join him for breakfast.

"Frankly, yes. No worries on the boat except the tides and winds. No cattle dying. No responsibility."

"Just special people," said Carol.

"Yes," he said, allowing the light to filter through his defenses. "Just a special person."

Carol walked to the table and smiled very slightly.

"How's your eye?" he said.

"Fine, thanks. If you hadn't fished that thing out, I think it would have stung me. I'm surprised the chlorine in the pool didn't kill the critter. Thanks, Dr. Ford."

"Some breakfast?" he said.

"Yes, but I'm on a roll. I just want to grab some coffee and a piece of toast and get right back to it."

"The mountain?"

"Yes. It won't sit still for me."

"No, it never does."

He sat down at the head of the table. She went to the sideboard and poured herself some coffee, and then hovered by the table as if unwilling to actually sit at it. She looked at him. He looked disturbed. Was romance doing what romance did, shifting about like the mountain and never sitting still?

"Are you okay?"

"Oh, yes. I'm fine. A bit fed up to have to return to all this chaos."

"I guess it's part of ranching. The weather, diseases, catastrophes of one kind or another."

"Yes," he said. But she knew he wasn't thinking about the ranch.

Carol thought of her painting. It would be sitting there in the Manhattan apartment this very minute, unopened, her statement unmade. She wondered if she should say something about it. No. It would dilute the drama of surprise. She was so proud of the picture. It had such power. To move him? He would see it in time. Perhaps best not now, when his emotional waters looked troubled.

She sat down. There was the unavoidable feeling that he wanted to talk. That was so rare.

"I went away with someone," he said.

"Yes, I imagined you had," she said.

He seemed surprised by that.

"Oh."

"Women's intuition," she said with a smile.

"Ah, yes, they have that, don't they."

"And you had a wonderful time?"

"Yes. Actually, I have fallen in love," he said. He pushed out the words suddenly, as if worried that they wouldn't make it past his lips unless he hurried with them.

"Oh, Charles, that's marvelous. I'm so happy for you," said Carol. She audited her emotions. There *was* a part of her that was pleased, but it was also disturbing to hear him *say* that. What did she feel about him? A million things that the painting described best of all, and her letter that went with it. Oh, damn, why was the beastly thing in Manhattan? It was out of play when she needed it.

"Yes, it is a sort of happy feeling, but not without anxiety attached. You see, she's disappeared."

"What do you mean, disappeared?"

"Well, I left her at the airport on Friday evening, and everything was fine. Then on Saturday she just disappeared. And this morning, still gone."

"That's not a very long time, Charles, and she's just gotten back from two weeks with you. Does she work?" Does she have a life? Carol wanted to ask.

Charles laughed apologetically. He wasn't used to conversations like this. They were totally beyond his character.

"Yes, she's in television."

"Well, then. She's just dropped back into a series of mini-disasters at the office, like you have at the ranch. No big deal."

"No, of course not," he said.

Carol tried to move the conversation back to Charles and his lover.

"In television?" she tried, but he had gotten as personal as he was able to get.

"Yes," he muttered distantly. There would be no further amplification.

Carol stood up. "Well, I've got to get back to my mountain."

"Good luck," he said absentmindedly.

"And to you, Charles," she said.

Forty-nine

It was at lunchtime on Sunday when he got the call from Louis in New York.

"Mr. Ford. It's Louis. I thought you ought to know that Ms. Richardson just moved out of your apartment with all her suitcases and with the painting that arrived Friday. I wasn't sure if it was okay for her to take it, but she assured me it was. She seemed a bit strange to me, in her attitude, like."

"She did?" said Charles. He felt the shock. It was strong and unexpected. The early anxiety had hardly prepared him for it. "What did she say?"

"Nothing, really. Just 'I'm going.' She had a limo pick her up with two men, and they handled the painting."

"What painting? I don't know anything about any painting."

"Miss Richardson signed for it late Friday. Arrived UPS. I don't know where it came from."

"Where did she go?"

"Didn't say, sir. Do you want me to go up and check the apartment? She might have left a note."

"Yes, please, Louis. I'll hang on."

No note. He knew that. Something had happened. The question was, what? A mysterious painting, or something in a crate that looked like a painting. Had Rachel had it sent to the apartment? Was it a gift of hers to him that she had decided for some reason not to give him? Had she had second thoughts? Gotten cold feet? There were no answers at all. He called her office the moment Louis confirmed that there had been no message left for him in the apartment.

A secretary carefully instructed by Jake was very firm when Charles gave his name. "Ms. Richardson is in and out today, but she's tied up in meetings. I'll give her your message as soon as I can, but I know she is desperately busy."

"Listen, Rachel and I have just been on holiday together. I'm a close friend."

"I know, sir."

He heard the message loud and clear. This girl had been ordered to stonewall him.

"Please ask her to call me in Santa Fe as soon as possible. It's urgent," he said.

"I will, sir."

Fifty

Rachel sat on the end of her bed, and the anger filled her. God, how it hurt. She couldn't eat. She couldn't sleep. Why did people put themselves through this misery? Above her, hanging on the wall, was Carol's painting. It would be there forever to remind her of what life was really all about. Treachery. Betrayal. Cheating hearts. She had been charmed, and she had fallen into the snake pit. She had been made crazy by the lust for love that was supposedly a woman's birthright in this injured culture, and she had paid for it with pain and fury. But it was not too late. She could go back to the safety of the person she had been. The old Rachel's wounds would heal. The scars, however, would remain always, and she was glad of them and of the painting that had both destroyed her world and saved it. Never again would she be tempted into the quicksands of emotions. Reason would rule her, and by reason alone would she rule. All would be calculation and planning, cold decision-making shorn of feeling, unclouded by passion and lust.

But first there was revenge. Charles Ford would not escape from this unscathed. She had tried to figure out what his game had been, and she thought she had some sort of answer. He was a man who loved all women. He did not know about faithfulness. Ford had made love to Rachel on a grand, great scale, and at the same time he had been keeping Carol as a reserve in New Mexico. Men did things like that all the time, didn't they? He had loved her in his warped way, that she knew. He was in love with love, and that was why he would be wounded mortally by what she was about to do to him.

She looked up at the painting to give her strength for what she would do. Carol's face, so exquisite, so disarming, stared down at her. Here was innocence in a thin layer over calculation. Her expression made her seem so vulnerable, so sweet and dependent as her face emerged from the velvet petals of the rose. Carol McCabe. Oh, Carol! How far and fast you moved from your own little domestic tragedy. Rachel remembered the horror of Jack's betrayal when Carol had told of it at the Inn. But betrayals bred betrayals. You learned from them. You learned how to perform them. And right now, Rachel was planning a betrayal of her own.

She looked at the telephone. Would he answer? No. José would. There was no chance of coming voice to voice with him. She caught her breath at the thought, and at once a wave of tenderness broke over her. The love again. The remains of it, still in her psyche or her heart or wherever those things lived. She took a deep breath and thought back to the Hacienda Inn, where it had all begun. She had wanted romance and she had found it. She had turned down Matt Harding and his power and his millions just for the possibility of it. She had compromised her career for it. She had dreamed of babies and alien things such as families and togetherness forever with a man who could conjure up the magic, a world free of doubts and fears in which loneliness was forever banished and the good friend and lover was always by your side. She had undermined her own strength, learned during a lifetime in the hardest school—experience— and now she had been repaid for her foolishness. In this life you could never have it all. You had to learn to live with what you could get. You had to become what you were suited to be.

Rachel picked up the telephone and dialed the number.

The butler answered.

"José, this is Rachel Richardson."

"Hello, ma'am. I'll tell Mr. Ford you are calling."

"No!" She barked the command. "I'm in a fearful hurry. Just

give him a message, please. From me. It is very important that he watch my show tomorrow evening. Just that. Nothing else. It will explain everything."

"Watch your show tomorrow, Ms. Richardson?"

"Yes. Just tell him that." She hung up. It would explain everything to the bastard.

Fifty-one

It was going well. Rachel could feel those things. Matt was on a roll, and she had turned the whole interview into an examination of success and how to attain it. These days, salacious revelation was not enough. People wanted information they could use. How to get on. How to survive. How to gain some pleasure from the process of getting and becoming.

"Aristotle Onassis said that the most important element in success was a suntan, Matt. You certainly have one of those. Is it as simple as that?"

"And you have a good tan, too, Rachel, from your holiday in the Mediterranean. No, I think Onassis was not being entirely serious, but he *is* right that you have to look the part and, more important, feel the part. People want your trumpet sound to be certain if they are going to help fight your battles. I think luck is ninety percent of it. Oh, I know that's not the fashionable view. You're supposed to be able to force things to happen, and hard work and focus will deliver. But you can do everything and try everything and still fail. And then again, failure so often replaces success. Here you are, asking me about success today. In ten years time, it may just as well be 'Whatever happened to Matt Harding?' "

"Somehow, I don't think so."

"And then there's the business of defining success. I haven't been a very successful husband. Maybe not the greatest father, though my children are too polite to say so. Right now, I have no one in my life, Rachel, even though I am a very rich man. There's loneliness. Is that success? There are thousands of people out there watching tonight who make me look like a complete failure in very many vital areas. Billionaires, football stars, actors, aren't real heroes. Sometimes we forget that."

"So do you have plans for success in the areas you've just mentioned? Perhaps our viewers know, or should know, that there was a time when you and I discussed marriage, Matt."

"Yes, we did, but you turned me down." He laughed, only just in control of his end of the conversation.

She could see Jake in the shadows over by the right-hand camera. Usually he was in the control room. She was calm. Ice-cold calm.

Rachel watched Matt Harding. He was sleek and slick and he smelled of cedar wood and safety. He was aggressively sane. He might be a womanizer, a chauvinist, a wheeler-dealer, a rotten father and a C- husband, but by God he was there with his brilliance and his billions, sitting across from her in front of the cameras. And out there, somewhere, in Santa Fe to be precise, was Charles Ford. *He* was watching. Curiosity would draw him to the TV. And any minute now, if he had a heart that had cared even a little bit, he would be hurt. That made it okay. That was worth something. It would be some small compensation for the walk on the romance side with the cheat who had betrayal in his bones.

The voice crackled in her earpiece.

"What's the matter, Rachel? You've dried up."

But she hadn't. In the control room they didn't know what was about to hit them. They always wanted ratings. Well, they were going to get ratings. This would be a first. She felt the loathing for Charles bubble up in her throat, the bittersweet taste of revenge. She paused for the briefest of moments, and then she plunged in.

"I've changed my mind, Matt," said Rachel.

There was an awesome silence.

"What?" he said. She could see the flush rising on his cheeks.

"About marrying you," she said.

He rocked back in his chair in shock.

"Rachel!" said the voice in her ear.

But Rachel was tuned in to the desert. He would be listening there.

Matt Harding laughed. It was one hell of a joke for live TV. He had never thought of Rachel as a prankster. Now she had really thrown him. Good for her. He had expected some sort of surprise. Nothing like this.

"Now I know why everyone watches your show, Rachel."

"Okay," said Rachel. "Let me put it this way. Will you marry me, Matt Harding?"

She didn't smile.

"I think I may just have become a ratings spike," he said. His hand rushed to his neck and he tugged at his collar. Then he said, "Are you serious?"

"Yes," she said, and she smiled slowly, because she was. In her mind's eye she could see this segment rolling and rolling for weeks. The day the tip-top journalist asked the billionaire to marry her on live TV. She would be killing birds all over the place with her single shot. Matt Harding. Steve. The Nielsens. Carol McCabe. Charles Ford. There was no romance, but there was tons and tons of business and upward mobility, and from now on that was who she was and that was what she wanted.

She never doubted his answer. Matt was like her. For him, this was as good as it got. The audience of millions. His network. All stars together, making up their own rules, and screw the roses and the bended knees and the silly engagement rings of the rest of the world. A good deal should not only be done, it should be seen to be done. Then it would beget lots of tiny deals that would grow tall and strong and be a credit to the man who had fathered them. Oh yes, nice one for Rachel Richardson, he would be thinking, one of the very few women on earth whom he deemed worthy of him.

"This is not a very private moment," he said.

"We're not very private people."

"Let me get this straight. You are asking me on live TV to marry you, and you are totally serious."

He leaned in toward her and spoke slowly, milking the drama from the situation. She applauded that. It was not a moment to throw away.

"Yes. I am. I am asking you to marry me."

They would be in close-up now. There was a stunned silence in her ear microphone. In the control room they would be transfixed. Out there in America, time would have stopped, too. Hands would be frozen with beer cans inches from mouths. People would be hovering by the set, staying that second or two longer to catch the answer, conversations dead in midsentence, deeds left undone.

"Yes, all right, yes. Of course I'll marry you, Rachel."

Watch it, Charles Ford. Watch it, you bastard. Don't miss one single second of this. This is what the bones meant. This is the real betrayal. Eat your heart out, Charles. Because I am off and running again in the race I should never have left.

Fifty-two

"I'll be gone for a bit," he said.

The old servant knew what he meant. His master would walk away onto the mesa with a blanket and a water bottle, some matches and a knife, and it was not José's job to ask why, where, or when. So he simply nodded. It was high summer and the desert was never safe. But then, life ended in death, and the ancient servant had learned the indifference that made the people who lived here different.

"Be careful, sir."

Charles nodded, but it was carelessness he sought. He had stood in the study where the television lived to tell its tales of silliness to the world, and he had received there the blow that had shattered once again his half-mended heart. It had been premeditated murder of love. She had called to set it up. What hatred was there in her heart, how had it hidden itself, and how had it acquired such artistry in wickedness? But there was no answer to the questions. On the mesa there would be survival to concentrate on, and the mind could only do one thing at a time.

"Are my things in place?"

"Where they always are, sir."

He walked to the gun room and opened the cupboard. The old Indian blanket lay on the bottom shelf, as old as himself, faded and torn but still thick and warm. On top of it lay the knife, shining brightly and whetted to razor-sharpness by José every week for years. The bottle was battered, and he picked it up and filled it from the tap, emptying it once before filling it again and stoppering it. He could live for three days on that bottle in 120 degrees of heat, but he would have found water by that stage, supplemented by the cactus he would suck and the streams he would find where no streams should be. He felt the surge of excitement flowing in and through the sorrow. His plan was working as he knew it would. On the shelf above was his father's blanket, his knife, his canteen. They stood together as father and son had stood together in the bitter cold and the burning heat, bonded at the soul. Timelessness broke over Charles, bringing back perspective. Was his father looking down now upon him, loving him but unable to speak that love now as then? "I am with you, my son, now as you hurt. And Rose is here with me, watching over you. We will be close to you in the desert, as we always were."

Charles felt the tears build in his eyes. He tried not to think about what had happened. He had to find the dispassion of the desert. That was what he had learned to do. That had made him different. Striving, being, becoming, was Rachel's world. It made traitors of humans, and for what base goals . . . success, materialism, fame, and power.

"Are you going somewhere?" said Carol.

"Yes," he said, turning to see her in the doorway.

"What's happened, Charles?"

"I'm not quite sure," he said. He shook his head and laughed bitterly. What had happened? Why had it happened? How could he be so wrong about a person?

"I'll be gone for a few days. It's better out there," he said. He looked stricken, not safe to be alone in the emptiness. Carol wanted to touch him. She wanted to bathe his heart in aloe.

"Don't go," she said suddenly. She put out her hand and touched his arm. He did not withdraw it. "I'm your friend, Charles," she said, as if to prove it to herself.

"I have to do it my way. I have to find my own way back to sanity," he said gently.

So she let him go, and he went through the house and into the driveway, and she watched him walk away until he was out of sight.

"You will be back, Charles Ford," she said to herself.

Fifty-three

Carol sat at breakfast in her studio. It had been a few weeks now since Charles had left. Even in the wild desert there was news. A maid at the ranch had heard from an uncle over the hill that he had seen Charles wandering by the Big River, that he was heading for the high ground away from the blistering heat of the flats.

Carol picked up a copy of the *New Mexican* from the pile of old newspapers that sat by the table. She was thinking of Charles as she half-concentrated on it. She had let him go and his absence hurt. She realized that now.

"Talk-show host in sensational 'live' proposal. Rachel Richardson asks billionaire to marry her in prime time. Matt Harding says 'yes.' "

"What?" said Carol.

She read through the article quickly. "Ohmigod, Rachel. Boy, did you turn your back on romance," she said aloud to herself.

The article had been short on background, long on the drama of the live TV proposal. This was thought to be a first for famous people on TV, although it was always happening on the tabloid talk shows when the faceless masses did anything for their Warhol minutes. There was a brief discussion about whether or not it had been a Roseanne-type quest for ratings. Probably not, was the article's verdict. Rachel and Harding had no comment, but it had been rumored that they were engaged some months previously but had broken it off. Oh, well, no date for the wedding yet, but yes, it *was* for real. Harding had just upped his share in the company that Rachel worked for. Rachel Richardson was clearly one ambitious woman, was the journalist's implication.

Carol put down the paper and sipped her coffee pensively. She remembered Rachel in the dining room of the Hacienda Inn. Her cheeks had flushed as she talked of the romance she had promised herself. The words of the Cat Stevens song drifted into her mind: "You will still be here tomorrow, but your dreams may not."

Quite suddenly, Carol had an overwhelming desire to talk to Rachel. And what had become of Tessa and Camille? Had they managed to stay afloat in the big city? She stood up and walked over to the telephone.

It hadn't taken her long to get through to the Rachel Richardson show and to Rachel's secretary.

Carol explained that she was a personal friend of Rachel's and very much wanted to congratulate her on her engagement.

"I think she's in a meeting, but I'll just check," said the secretary in standard reply to unknown entities on the telephone.

Carol hung on. She was excited. She knew that Rachel might regard her as some sort of conscience and be abrupt and defensive at first. But Carol would rush in to say that she was sure Rachel had made the wise decision, and they would pick up where they had left off. Carol was sure of that. Carol was wrong.

It was the secretary back on the telephone.

"Uh, I just spoke to Rachel and she gave me a message for you, uh . . . uh . . . she said that she didn't want to speak to you now, or ever, and she was amazed that you had the nerve to call her. That's what she said. I'm just the messenger."

"Oh," said Carol. She sat down. Plonk. "She said that?"

"Yes, she did," said the secretary.

"Oh," said Carol again. And then, "Oh." Her face reddening, she put the telephone down.

"The nerve to call her"? What did that mean? Surely the secretary had gotten it wrong. But there was no way to find out. Wow! Carol was not used to being talked to like that, talked about like that. She was nice, sweet Carol McCabe. Okay, she had learned how to be a bitch around Jack, but that was Jack, that was different. Women liked her. They really liked her. She was likable. Very. To a fault. She couldn't remember feeling so confused about anything, apart from Jack and Page Lee.

In the confusion she searched for answers, but she couldn't come up with one. Maybe Tessa would know what was going on. She got the Sotheby's number from directory assistance, dialed it, and asked to be put through to Tessa Andersen.

"Hi. This is Tessa Andersen. I'm sorry I can't take your call personally, but I'm out showing property. Please leave your message after you hear the tone."

"Hi, Tessa. This is Carol McCabe. I've been out of the loop, but I just called Rachel Richardson and got blown away. Are *you* speaking to me? I hope so. I'd love to hear from you. Call me back."

Fifty-four

"Well, what do you think?"

"Sort of . . . big . . . grand . . . over-the-top."

"Yes, but that's right, really, isn't it?"

"Yes, I suppose it is," said Rachel. She walked over to the hold-your-breath view. God's view. La Guardia. Both rivers. Central Park just a postage stamp below. "Low-flying aircraft might be a problem though. I didn't know Carrara had so much goddamned marble."

Tessa laughed. The penthouse apartment at the Metropolitan Tower on West 57th Street was the ultimate architecturally exciting New York space. Its sleek black angles and gray stone invited the high-flying clouds in as visitors as they drifted by. "I mean, you've got your pool down below, and the restaurant is perfect: the food's a dream and they deliver. So you can pretend to have whipped something together for Matt in the five minutes since you got in. He won't notice for months, and then he won't mind."

"I think that he would be appalled at having a meal cooked by a wife. *Such* a waste of valuable achievement time. I think if we take this place, we get the apartment below for the staff and the gym and things."

"Well, it's all for sale. The market's still soft. You can come in quite low on this one."

"It's great to see you doing so well, Tess," said Rachel. It was easy to see why Tessa was selling so much real estate. She made buying fun. Her enthusiasm was contagious.

"Thanks, Rachel. It is a relief. I never thought I'd get to enjoy this." She paused and then headed for the bottom line again. "What will Matt think of it?" she said.

"Oh, whatever. He'll look at the deal, want to know the average cost per square foot of comparable space. If he thinks he can sell it for as much as he pays for it, he won't worry. He'll just move on if it doesn't work."

"Home sweet home," said Tessa.

Rachel was silent for a second. Her mind drifted to the Mediterranean. She pulled it back again. She could afford no regrets.

"Matt's a realist," she said.

"I'm longing to meet him," said Tessa.

They went through the kitchen fast. "Oh, what a lovely kitchen," said Rachel, her eyes set straight ahead, looking neither to right nor to left at the gleaming bits and pieces she would never use. "And I imagine that's the lovely laundry room."

"It was very stunning, that TV thing," said Tessa. "I saw the action replays. Actually, it was quite romantic."

"Yeah, and the following evening I scored my best market share ever. Even better than the President."

"Don't pretend with me, Rachel. I know you're not that tough."

"Thanks for reminding me. I sure got done-over in the romance thing."

They had reached yet another room with a view. The bedroom.

"I still can't believe that Charles would behave like that. Or that Carol would. I mean, all that time, her being involved with him and us not knowing. It's such bad form."

"I suppose the bed would go here," said Rachel without much enthusiasm. She had changed the subject, but it would be returned to. Both women recognized the conversational diversion.

"You know what I'd do. I'd stick it right against the window. You'd wake up in the sky. It would be magic."

For a second, Rachel imagined that magic. It was all to do with the view. Not Matt. Yes, she could imagine the bed against the vast picture window, and rain driving against it, snowflakes the size of quarters drifting against the glass, high in the clouds above the Manhattan that she and Matt would conquer together. She would be warm and snug in bed in the early morning, and he would be beside her, immaculate in silk pajamas from Sulka . . . until they decided he would be better off sleeping in the big dressing room next door because, well, he snored, and she had to get up earlier than he, or he earlier than she, and it made sense, and after all . . .

"Why didn't Charles tell you about Carol, Tess? I can see why he didn't tell me."

"I've thought so much about it, and I honestly think that he didn't think it was anybody's business. It was his relationship, if it was a relationship . . ."

"It *was* a relationship. Believe me, I *saw* it."

"Well, yes, if you saw it. God, how awful that must have been, Rachel. I'm so sorry. I know how much it must have hurt."

"And you saw the painting. I mean, that's a kind of proof in itself."

"I suppose so," said Tessa. She took a deep breath. Rachel was marrying Matt Harding on the rebound. That was the bottom line. It was not a good business, except that it would be good business if she could sell them this apartment. The commission would go straight into Camille's education fund. She tried to reconcile the two emotions in her mind. But they would not reconcile. So she left them both where they were in their separate piles. She was getting rather good at this business of surviving.

"You know, Tessa, I don't love Matt. But I admire him, I respect him, and I for sure don't hate him. I loved Charles, but I don't respect him, I don't admire him, and I'm trying to learn to loathe him. So far, it's going reasonably well."

"I keep trying to understand it," said Tessa. It was true. Charles had always been an intriguing mystery, but she had never imagined for one second that he would have turned out to be a bastard.

"I guess he was like Carol's silly husband after all," said Rachel. "Ruled by his ego and his dick. Everything else was a smoke screen, mirrors, bullshit. I mean, those bones and the betrayal. That wasn't hard to predict. He was at it when he threw the damn things on the floor."

"Why, oh, why can't I help feeling that this whole thing is just some giant misunderstanding?" said Tessa.

"Because he was so good at acting. That's how I feel. The performance was just perfect. But facts don't lie. If I hadn't gone down to the ranch and seen it with my own eyes, I wouldn't have believed it."

"Could you possibly . . . *possibly* . . . have made a mistake?"

"There is *no* way. None. Zip. I am not a fool."

Tessa sighed. "But it may be for the best. I mean, that night at the Hacienda Inn. You'd as good as decided to marry Matt then. So, a few months later, what's changed? You make a dynastic marriage, and you get to live in this fabulous apartment when you're not jetting round the other homes. And screw Charles Ford. Write him down as experience."

"The name men give to their mistakes," said Rachel.

It wasn't as easy as that. There were the memories. The black cloak flying in the air. The magic of the moonlight on a silver sea, the touch of Christ beneath the waves at Porto Veneri, the touch of cashmere on her skin in Portofino. She took a deep breath. Her life had never been easy. Not for ease should one's prayer be, but for the courage to face difficulty.

"Why didn't he call?" said Tessa. "Why didn't he try to make some excuse? He didn't know about your seeing him and Carol together at the ranch. He maybe didn't even know about the painting she sent up to his apartment."

"Perhaps it was a merciful release for him. I mean, he'd had me every which way for two weeks. Perhaps that's par for his course. Or maybe he knew he was cheating and suspected that I'd found out and couldn't face the truths I'd be telling him about his character and his morals, and his mother!"

Tessa laughed. "Oh, Rachel, I'm sorry. It's not funny. But I would like to have heard you putting him straight on a few things."

Rachel smiled ruefully. "Maybe one day I will. Except that he'll get his somehow, somewhere. They don't do well in life, people like that. They're not happy. You can't be bad and happy, can you? Doesn't God guarantee that, at the very least?"

"I think He does . . . long term . . . ," said Tessa, not quite sure about it. "You know," . . . she paused . . . "I've never even allowed myself to think this, not really, but I'm going to tell you. I rather think that Pete might have been a bit of a loser. Not bad, not really bad, but just, well, you know, flaky, irresponsible."

Tessa took a deep breath. The revelation, to herself, to Rachel, was immense.

"Heavens, Tess. You adored him."

"Yes, I did. Yes, I do. But you know, when you got all excited about the idea of me and Charles being a possible . . . relationship, well, I suppose there was just a tiny bit of truth in it. I was comparing him to Pete all the time, and he kept coming out ahead. Then I got this job, and things went so well and I began to see what life was like when you lived it for yourself and took the credit for it. You've always known that. I'd never experienced it. I was always 'beautiful Tessa,' destined to do nothing except decorate places and just be, and I wasn't much more than that with Pete. And now here I am, making money doing something that is exciting and challenging from dawn till dusk, and Camille's happy and back at Brearley, and we have this nice new apartment—on our own. Pete blew all our savings. He blew our life. Quite frankly, Rachel, what's to adore?"

"Thank God you didn't realize that earlier and jump onboard the Charles Ford lifeboat. A leaky vessel, that one, with the benefit of hindsight."

"Perhaps it's better without men," said Tessa with a laugh.

They paused. There was a moment rich with feminine solidarity.

"Do you know something, Tess? I love you. I really do. I think you are wonderful."

"Oh, Rachel," said Tessa, surprised and flattered. "You are sweet."

"No, I mean it. You had a chance with Charles and you didn't take it, because of me. You put me first over what could have been a great future. You did it out of friendship and loyalty, and all sorts of things that women have in abundance until some man comes along. Then all the bets are off. But not you, Tess. You said 'go ahead,' but you had seen him first. I had absolutely no right to him when I blew my top with you. That counts for one hell of a lot. And it's great to see you working so well, and enjoying it."

Tessa laughed. "Showing you this beautiful apartment and gassing on about everything and everyone is hardly hard work," she said.

"Believe me," said Rachel, "anything you get paid for is work."

"Do you want some champagne?" said Tessa suddenly.

"You keep champagne in an empty apartment?"

"Yes, I do, actually. I offer it to the clients that look serious, and they sit there sipping Dom and imagining themselves living here."

"God, that's a good idea."

"I keep some Perrier for the Californians. They like to pop their pills in the loo and then come out and be holier than thou about the alcohol."

"Well, champagne gives me gas, but if it's booze, it'll give me a buzz, and I feel like a buzz."

"You look like a buzz."

The two friends giggled as they found the bottle in the Sub-Zero and wrestled it open in the immaculate kitchen. There were flute glasses in the freezer, but no nibbles. "Interferes with the flow of alcohol to the brain, where I want it," said Tessa.

Then, each with glass in hand, they walked to the vast picture window with its view of the only world that mattered . . . of Manhattan's dramatic skyline. Because there were no chairs, they sat down on the cold marble, side by side, backs propped against the wall.

"Isn't this great?" said Tessa. "You know, when I first met you, Rachel, I thought you were a bit of a Martian. I liked you, very much, but you were sort of an alien. You didn't just do things, you were a vast success . . . and in America, the real thing. Now, in my small way, I'm beginning to see the world through your eyes. In the office they look at me in a different way. With some it's admiration and respect, with others it's envy and malice, but it's different. They know I'm doing well, and it changes them. And every day I'm more assertive and people listen, when in the beginning they just used to talk all over me. I don't have to tiptoe anymore. I asked for a bigger office, and they gave it to me—with a decorating allowance. It was amazing what that felt like. The power. The pride. And yet nothing had changed. I was still me. I'd just sold a few houses, a few great apartments, and suddenly I wasn't invisible anymore. The men stopped patronizing me, and I started to come in earlier even though it wouldn't have mattered if I'd been late. That's the stupid paradox, isn't it? You start to achieve, and you thought the only reason you wanted it was so that you could relax, and then you find yourself working harder than ever."

"Boy, are you learning," said Rachel. "Here's to the relaxation that never comes." Then, suddenly, she said, "To Charles Ford"—raising her glass in another toast—"who showed me the cruel Roman side of romance, and turned me into a soul survivor."

"To Pete Andersen. Dear, lovely Pete, who left and let me find myself," said Tessa. "You know, back at the Hacienda Inn, I wanted security and you wanted your Cary Grant affair-to-remember. The real thing that came out of it was what we agreed to do, to help each other. You helped me get my job. I helped you get Charles. You helped me after my accident. Our friendship was the most important result."

"To our friendship," said Rachel, and they drank again.

"A friendship that proves women can network and stick together and not end up waging secret wars against each other."

"And then there's Carol," said Tessa.

"Ah, Carol," said Rachel. "The exception that proves the rule."

"I never did understand that expression," said Tessa.

"It's just that you never question that all swans are white until you see a black swan. When you see a black swan, you realize that whiteness is a pretty strong characteristic of swans. It's the exception that draws your attention to the rule."

"Oh," said Tessa dreamily. The wine was beginning to take hold. "Shall we have another glass?"

"Oh, yes, I think we should," said Rachel, "very definitely." She could feel the pain and the anger beginning to fade.

When Tessa returned with the two full glasses, Rachel said, "You know, careers *do* love you back, in a sense. They are always there. Occupational therapy. Self-respect. Material things to make your life easier. Men love you back, but they can't be trusted to be there, and if they're not there, they can't love you back. There's always a Carol lurking somewhere."

Tessa was quiet. "Why is it that I just can't help feeling that Carol didn't know about Charles and you?"

"You mean Charles is that secretive?"

"Well, he is that. I mean, he's enormously private, isn't he?"

"No wonder he likes to keep his life in separate compartments."

Rachel shook her head as if to clear it of the memories.

"Oh, Tess, I never want to think about him, ever again. I never want to hear his bloody name. And you know what I'm going to do right now? I'm going to buy this fabulous apartment."

Fifty-five

Jack McCabe drove the car down the familiar, leafy streets until he reached the garage of his house. He reached up for the door opener, and soon he was inside. He did not turn the engine off. He just sat there, empty and alone. He got out of the car and moved like a sleepwalker into the house. The drapes were drawn and the fetid smell of old cooking and dust permeated the rooms. He climbed the stairs to the bedroom, and his heart hung in his chest, beating but lifeless. He paused by their bed, and he imagined Carol lying there, and he remembered how the house had smelled when she had breathed her life into it, fresh and flowery, clean and astringent. The crumpled bed stared back at him, an affront to her memory. It was the bed he and Page Lee had made love in, and it was the place where, in illicit joy, the music had begun to die. Carol's picture was by the bed. It was his favorite one of her, lying in the hay field with the straw hat, as pretty as summer and as comforting. He picked it up and stood there, still, and held it to his chest. The tears came now, and with the melancholy some energy returned.

He walked into the bathroom. In the medicine cabinet he found the paracetamol, a great big bottle. And way back there was a jar of Valium that a friend had unloaded on Carol in a misery-loves-company gesture. He took those out, and the tricyclic antidepressants that the doctor had given him a few weeks before for the weight loss and sleeplessness. Even now, the thought of food revolted him. He had lost thirty pounds, and his diet was strong coffee and strong whiskey. He poured a big carafe of water and stood in front of the mirror as he swallowed the pills. What were his chances of actually dying? Good. Very good, he reasoned. Carol would be sorry for this. It was all her fault. He walked downstairs to the garage.

The car's engine was still running, and he climbed into the front seat and opened the windows. Carbon monoxide did not smell, but somehow the whole garage reeked of fumes. They made him feel queasy, but he sat there and waited. How long would it take? He felt wide awake. In fact, his heart was pumping. He looked around him. Carol's picture was on the passenger's seat and the Bible was in his lap. He had planned to read the Bible in these last minutes, and to look at the picture of his wife. But already he felt the first gentle fingers of drowsiness, and he feared the long sleep even as he welcomed it.

Fifty-six

"Shit, Mom, thank God you're here."

Whitney jumped up from the chair as Carol rushed into the sitting area of the Emergency Room reception. A pile of surfer magazines cascaded off his lap. He looked worried, like he had looked the day the police came to the house about the missing bicycle. She had seen the expression on his face only a couple of times in his entire life. She hugged him tight, loving the great big, woolly feel of him, and she asked her questions into his neck, which smelled slightly of his sweet sweat.

"How is he, darling? What do the doctors say? Is he going to be all right? Where's Devon?"

"Devon's in Manhattan with that Karen friend of hers. I don't have her number. The doctor said there's no way of knowing yet. Do we know what he took? He took some pills as well as doing the garage thing with the engine."

He stood back from her, a bit pale, a bit fazed, but hanging in there with the detachment that his generation had cultivated as a protection against the energy of their baby-boomer parents.

"Oh, Whitney, darling, why did he do it? I mean, your dad, it's so unlike him."

"He hasn't been like Dad since you left." The accusation was matter-of-fact and without malice. That made it harder to take. Carol tried to get a grip on her feelings. She had to take control here. Had to do the sensible thing. Had to be Jack. The old Jack.

She hurried over to a nurse and introduced herself.

"Hello, Mrs. McCabe. He's still unconscious. We don't know for sure what he's taken. Some antidepressants, we think, but he's almost certainly taken some other things as well, sleeping tablets, maybe, or benzodiazepines. Did he have any access to Valium, Librium, or Xanax? Cold medications?"

Carol thought hard. She could still picture the inside of the medicine cabinet. Had it changed since her day?

"There was Valium, and, yes, Tylenol P.M., I think. And some Contac. There was a whole bottle of Valium."

"Valium's not really the problem. It would be good if he took just them. You can eat hundreds of them and be okay. We're worried about the carbon monoxide and the antidepressants. Can we find out which doctor he has been seeing? I gather you're divorced."

"Not quite," said Carol. The pain speared into her. She had done this. To Jack. To the man who had been her love, her life. She had committed the sin of jealousy. She had not had a big enough heart to forgive him when he had begged for forgiveness. She had thought only of herself and her foolish pride, not of her children, of her husband, of her for-better-for-worse-till-death-us-do-part promises. Well, here was death, so near. The death that would part them and give her, paradoxically, the freedom that she had been seeking. Jack had been unfaithful. So had many men. But she had broken her most solemn promise, a promise made before everyone she loved on the happiest day of her life. She had not taken Jack for worse, only for better. She had deserted him in sickness. He had gone alone to a doctor and the doctor had treated him for the depression that her leaving had caused.

"I can ring the family doctor. It's Dr. Josephson. You probably know him."

"Certainly I do. I'll give him a call. One more thing. Do you think he's taken any aspirin or anything like that?"

"There was a big bottle of paracetamol in the cupboard."

"Oh, dear. That's a bad one. It can cause liver damage. If he's taken those, then just getting him conscious might not be enough. We've done gastric lavage and aspirated stomach contents. The lab is running tests right now. We'll know what we're dealing with soon. I'm afraid it's just wait and see. Thank goodness the neighbor heard the car running in the garage."

"Can I see him?" said Carol.

"Yes, I'll take you in."

"Do you want to come, Whitney?"

"No, Mom, I'll wait here."

He didn't want to face it. His father had been Jack the jock, Jack the strong. He didn't want to see him ill. He didn't want to see him dying. It was too threatening.

"Shall I keep calling Devon?"

"Yes, darling. Do that. Thank you," said Carol. She squeezed her son's hand. He hadn't the emotional apparatus to handle this, but she knew the feelings were in there somewhere, all bottled up for later. Hers were.

He lay there, white and still and helpless. Numb with shock, she sat by his bedside and tried to make sense of the unthinkable. All her life Jack had been her hero, first a real one, then a fallen one. But he had never been helpless and hopeless. He and suicide were an unthinkable combination. He and death were. As the emotions rolled through her, she realized that he was, in the most basic way, still the center of her life. The painting, the desert, the finding of herself, were all done with Jack in mind. She had been punishing him, hating him even, but always he had been there. That she knew now. Silent tears fell down her cheeks as she realized it. Now he had to live. After that, there would have to be a rethinking of both their lives. She tried to concentrate, but her thoughts were jumbled. They tumbled about in her mind with no sequence but with powerful meaning. How unlike Jack, but how like him to get his own way. Here she was, back beside him. On his terms. If he survived, she would have to nurse him, be kind to him, in effect to forgive him. *If* he survived.

The doctor tapped her shoulder. He introduced himself briefly, saying much the same things as the nurse had said, but

Carol found it difficult to follow his words. She knew she was in shock, so she simply nodded, and answered in monosyllables.

"I am afraid we're going to have to ask you to leave for a bit while we put in a C.V.P. line," he said.

"Let me know if anything . . . happens . . . ," said Carol.

Outside, Whitney was thumbing through magazines. He looked up as she came out. "How is he?"

"He's not very good." Carol burst into tears. Two or three people looked up and then looked away, embarrassed.

"Don't cry, Mom," said Whitney, and he held her in a loose embrace, with tears in his own eyes. "Dad will be okay."

She hung on to him tight. God, she loved this awkward, wonderful boy whom she had had with Jack on the second happiest day of her life. What did anything else matter? How ridiculous it all was. How pathetic to care about Page Lee and silly, stupid infidelity when there was Whitney and Devon and the wonderful life they shared. She felt so small and so petty, a shamelessly self-centered thing who had been cruel, and this was the result of her cruelty.

"It's my fault," she wailed.

"No, it's not, Mom. It's not anybody's fault," he said. There was an alien certainty in his voice, usually so diffident. "It's just life, and sometimes life sucks."

"They're putting in something called a C.V.P. line," she said to fight off the silence that separated her sobs.

"Oh," said Whitney. "Is he, like, conscious?"

"No, darling. It's not good. It's not very good at all."

"But he's in the hospital."

"Yes, that's good."

"Devon's gone shopping, but she'll be back later. I left a sort of ambiguous message for her to call."

"Did you drive over from college?"

"Yeah."

"Whitney." She sat up and wiped her eyes. The tears seemed to have stopped.

"Yes, Mom."

"If Dad gets through this, I'm coming back to live at home," she said. She hadn't thought about it. The words just came out.

"You are?" he said. He smiled. For him it was quite a show of emotion.

"Yes," she said. "Yes. I'm coming back. I love Dad. I've always loved Dad. And he isn't much good without me. I didn't know that. I do now."

"He for sure isn't." There were tears in Whitney's eyes again. "He's been drinking, Mom. I told you about it, but it's been worse than I said, and the house is a mess, and the garden. He stopped working out, and I don't think he's been eating properly."

"I know, darling, I know. But he'll get well and we'll get things straightened out, and it'll be back to normal. I promise you."

"He will be all right, won't he?"

In answer, the doctor hurried through the swinging doors. "Mrs. McCabe!" he said.

Fifty-seven

Charles sat down against the wall of a white building beneath the pale wood of cedar beams. He reached behind him and found the water bottle and brought it to his lips, wetting them but not drinking. Everything was slow. Each sip of water was a decision of moderation, a gaining in survival. There could be no weakness. But still there was the ache inside, the memories from the world of plenty where man and woman could reach for faucets and count on food and shelter and had, therefore, to find diversions to add salt to the tastelessness of life. Was that all Rachel had been? The ultimate diversion to replace the agony of losing Rose? No! His love had been real. She had been the other half to his puzzle. Rachel was being and becoming, wanting and longing. She was ambition and drive and determination. She needed. She succeeded. She achieved. But he was more of the Indian—not one of them, but like them, and admiring of them.

He looked with a jaundiced eye on the impermanence of achievement and material things. So they had fitted together, his melancholy a foil for her enthusiasm, his spirituality a brake on her here-and-now longings. For a short time he had dared to dream again. He had found the improbable woman, and he had been lost in the wild excitement of the moment. And then, and then . . . the parts of her that had drawn him in had pulled her away. Matt Harding made such perfect sense for the caricature of Rachel, but he had never seen her as a caricature. That had been the blow. That he could fall so completely into water so shallow. So much for the wisdom it was his pride to pretend he possessed. What did he know, Charles Ford, about anything but the dusty road and blood-red sunsets, and the bright brilliance of the sun rising over the desert, bleaching his soul with heat? Perhaps that was enough. It was why he was here. And it was why he would stay here until the thoughts of the world he had left no longer crushed his soul.

Fifty-eight

Tessa marched into the office. All around, respect, even fear, shone from the eyes of her fellow workers. Now there was even more reason for it. The Met Tower penthouse was knocked down to Rachel Richardson and Matt Harding. It seemed there was nothing that Tessa couldn't sell. She sat down at her desk and called her secretary on the intercom. God, what a day! And it had been fun, too. She had been drinking champagne with a person she loved, and making hundreds of thousands of dollars while she sipped it. Was there a better way to go? Where had this been all her life?

"There was a Carol McCabe, who left a number in New Mexico. Lord Bruntisfield called, and the man about the burglar alarm in your apartment."

"Carol McCabe?" said Tessa.

"Yes. She left a rather odd message. Said to call if you are still talking to her."

"Give me her number," said Tessa.

Tessa dialed it. It was Carol's answering machine, and Carol was weeping on it. "I've had to go to Connecticut. Jack's in the hospital. Call me at . . ." She gave a number. That was it.

Tessa took a deep breath. Jack in hospital. Carol in tears. It sounded serious. Her mind raced back to the dining room all those months ago. Carol had been so brave, so all alone. Tessa put down the phone, picked it up again, and called the number she had jotted down.

"Mom's not here. She's gone to the hospital. Who is this?"

"I'm a friend, Tessa Andersen. And you are . . ."

"I'm Devon, her daughter."

"I remember Carol talking about you. Is everything all right? I gather she rushed in from New Mexico."

Devon's voice broke. "Not really. My dad's really sick."

"Oh, how awful. Is Carol okay? Is there anything I can do?"

"They think he's going to die," Devon sobbed.

Tessa took a deep breath. She looked at her watch. She knew what she had to do. She was going to Connecticut.

Fifty-nine

Rachel stood in front of the long mirror and the moment that was supposed to be magic simply wasn't. Her wedding dress stared back at her. On one level there was nothing wrong with it. It was beautiful, stylish, even trendy, and yet it retained a classic elegance. Maria Galana, the designer, had done her job to perfection . . . sheer silk panels, a veil with a lace-encircled visor to frame the face of the bride, and a train of crushed silk that would flow along the aisle like a wake of bubbling champagne.

"It's magnificent," said Maria, bending down to straighten a fold of material but keeping her eye on the dress in the mirror.

"Yes," said Rachel without enthusiasm. "It is," she added for emphasis.

"Don't you think so? Oh, I'm so pleased," said Maria for both of them.

It wasn't the dress that disturbed Rachel, it was her lack of the appropriate emotion to go with it. Just once, in the little thing called marriage, she had wanted to break the mold. She had wanted to tremble at the altar. She had wanted to say the words and mean them. She had wanted to flow toward her man and melt into his lips with a kiss that would be a symbol far more strong and enduring than a mere ring of gold. And she had tried . . . God, how hard . . . and she had come so close . . . God, how close . . . but she had lost. She had been betrayed more callously and more unexpectedly than she had believed possible. And it hurt like hell, and it would continue to do so always.

"It's a little tight in the waist," she said.

"Oh, do you think so?" said Maria. "I think you want it to hug there. It won't be forever. I think the look is wonderful. A waspish waist."

"To be able to breathe would be nice," said Rachel, spreading a little of her angst.

"Of course. I'll let it out a bit. Will you be going up or down between now and next week?"

"I haven't the faintest idea," said Rachel. She presumed the designer was talking about her weight. Maria Galana didn't look like an amateur shrink. But a question about the emotional roller coaster ride would have been more appropriate. Basically, this marriage was an act of revenge. She was striking out at Charles, and she didn't even know if he would feel the blow. Had he been totally without feelings for her? Had it all been the disgusting game of a cunning and ruthless Don Juan? No! The answer screamed back at her. He *had* cared for her. There had been moments about which it would be impossible to believe otherwise, shuddering body memories, and memories of a tender closeness. No, Charles had loved her in his fashion. But he had been incapable of genuine love. He had wanted more. Different lovers. The thrill of novelty and the chase. That was immature, common to many in the species but never, she had believed, to a man like him.

She sighed. A man like him. How little one knew about people, perhaps especially those one loved. Were they camouflaged by the smoke screen of emotion puffed onto them by their lovers? Could they move behind it freely, practicing their egotistical games, free for deception, safe from detection? Apparently. She tried to picture him as villain of the piece. But it didn't work. She felt the shift somewhere in her stomach. Oh, Charles! Why? Why couldn't you have been the man I believed you to be?

The telephone rang.

"Can you get it, Maria?"

Maria picked up the receiver.

"Rachel Richardson's house," she said. She turned to Rachel. "It's somebody called Tessa Andersen. She's calling from Connecticut and she says it's urgent that she speak to you."

Epilogue

Mendelssohn's Violin Concerto in E Minor floated out into the scented desert night. All around the pool the sodium lights stared upward, lighting the branches of the trees and illuminating insects as they meandered through the aroma of jasmine on their endless journey to nowhere. There was the chink of glass as a servant laid out the flutes for the champagne they drank each night before dinner, and Charles was alone on the verandah, waiting for his guests. He looked out to the distant mountain illuminated by the light of the full moon. Who would be first down? Each night it was someone different, and Charles liked the adventure of that as he stood sipping the delicate pink wine.

"A painting waiting to happen, if only the mountain would stay still," said Carol from behind him. He turned around, smiling gently at her.

"Almost too pretty to paint," said Charles. "Like you."

She did look wonderful. It was strange how personality could revitalize beauty, how lack of it could drain physical appearance. She wore a plain white dress and a single string of pearls. Her skin was baked a golden brown. Charles had watched her change before his eyes, and he knew that he had been the catalyst for the new Carol. He remembered her, half frozen in the lonely desert. He could feel her body soft and hard against his as they rode through the night to the ranch. And he could see her now, fast asleep in Rose's bed, her head poking out above the sheets. When the car had been retrieved from the desert and he had seen her drawings, he had known immediately that Carol had talent. Harry Wardlow had been representing her for this past year, and although her reputation was small, it was growing. But if he had some responsibility for her artistic rebirth, she had been the beginning of his. Without Carol, he might still be lost in the memories of Rose, condemned to a twilight world of half-manhood, where the past was the present and the future, too. She had helped him to relearn what he had forgotten, to be able to paint and to love again. They had helped each other, and in her gratitude she had made the painting for him, the painting that had turned his life—their life—upside down.

"I painted myself once. Remember?"

"How could I ever forget?" said Charles with a laugh.

She walked toward him and threaded her hand into his. He took it, squeezing it and feeling the love hurry out of him, through his fingers to her.

They laughed at the memories.

"Some champagne?" said Charles.

The servant hovered at her elbow with the silver salver. Charles took a glass of wine and handed it to her.

"Thank you, sir."

She looked up into his eyes as she took it.

"There's no way I can ever thank you, Charles. You know that, don't you? For what you have done for me."

"Being here is thanks," he said. "Every painting you paint is thanks. Just watching you, the new you, the real you, that's more than enough. And anyway, my debt to you is as great. You know that. Remember what I was."

"You were sad."

"I was a mess. And I was in danger of turning it into a profession. This music—I can actually enjoy it now."

A man strode onto the verandah, immaculate in his tuxedo. It was Jack, but somehow changed. He walked over quickly to kiss his wife. She turned her face up to him, and he bent down tenderly. He knew the truth now, that without her he was a tinkling glass and a rattling cymbal, empty, meaningless. Without Carol he had fallen apart as comprehensively as it was possible to do, and in his so-close brush with death he had learned the realities about himself, his wife, and their relationship. What looked weak had been strong, what strong, weak. It had taken near-tragedy to prove it.

"How's your serve coming along, Jack?" said Charles. "I saw you practicing this morning before you were so rudely interrupted."

It was the kind of easy remark he had never been able to make, but he could now, in these surroundings, among the people he had come to love.

"Yes, I'm afraid Matt's tennis court-helicopter landing rights take precedence over an attorney's service practice. Still, Matt's promised me a game tomorrow."

"Make sure you lose," said Carol.

"He'll probably thrash me anyway," said the new Jack.

Carol took his hand. "Why do I seriously doubt that?" she said. Their magic was back. Oh, the tricks were not so new now, and she knew how most of them were performed, but still it was there, and it had held them together through the bad times, as it was supposed to. Jack might be masterful at tennis, witty giving a speech at the office dinner, silver-tongued before the judge in court, but now she knew the effort that went into maintaining the appearance. She knew all about the little boy inside the man, who would screw up big-time if left on his own. It was better in a way, more real, free of silly fantasy. And his deep-down weakness allowed her deep-down strength to come to the surface. There was a balance now, a respect between equals, and Carol felt the strange freedom and reveled in it. His life had hung by a thread, and she had felt the commitment strong within her as she had made the decision to return to him. She had tipped the balance in his headlong retreat from life. She had willed him to live, first through the drama of coma, and then through the long months of drug jaundice that had followed the overdose. Carol had pulled everything back from the brink . . . Jack, his job, his relationship with the managing partner, the garden, the house. Page Lee had been a casualty. She had resigned when Jack had gone back to work.

But the white tornado that had been Carol's return to her old life had brought dramatic differences. There was an old adobe studio in the desert now, outside Santa Fe, and Carol was free to go to it at any time, without comment or criticism. Her art was a fact, not a diversion. It was what she did, it was who she was. Jokes about it were not tolerated. It lived full center-stage in her life. No longer was she Carol McCabe, the successful attorney's wife. She was a painter now.

"You got a lot of sun, darling," said Jack, who'd gotten even more himself.

"Yes. I just lay by the pool all day, sleeping and listening to the children argue. Thank God, your children, Charles. I had to give them a lecture this morning on sharing. I hope you don't mind."

"You are their godmother. It's your responsibility to give them lectures." Charles laughed.

"Actually, Camille had the situation pretty much under control. She's an awesome policewoman."

"She's going to be president one day," boomed Matt Harding. He stood a few feet away, pausing for a second before joining them to maximize the drama of his arrival. They knew him too well to be irritated. Over the years, they had gotten through the surface to the real Matt. The externals were just part of the tricks of his trade to impress strangers, and couldn't be turned off when not needed. He looked far larger than life, in great good health, his silver hair making him an instant candidate for senior statesman in anybody's movie.

"Where's your wife, Matt? Why are you keeping her from us?" said Charles.

"Do you believe on the telephone? Has been all day, apparently. I thought I was the telephone man. Then I married her and discovered I was an amateur. She thinks I'm lazy. Told me so while we were changing. Never been called that before. Lazy. Matthew Jefferson Harding. Work-shy. Ha!"

He advanced into the room, kissing Carol, squeezing Charles and Jack by the elbow with an older man's "steering" grip. "My word," he boomed, "what a magnificent house this is, Charles. Never expected anything else, really. An artist's eye. An aristocrat's past. Damn it, though, Charles, you've got to talk to Wardlow about your prices. I bought a couple the other day. Brought tears to my eyes. The prices, I mean."

"You should have bought one of Carol's," said Jack proudly.

"I'm thinking about it," said Matt. He turned to Carol. "You know I love your work, don't you? I've been seriously tempted."

"I'm always telling him to buy your paintings," said Rachel as she walked up to them.

They turned toward her. "I spent all day reading this book about the origins of the artistic personality. Total psychobabble, but brilliantly done. So tonight, Carol and Charles get psychoanalyzed in public. If I make any mistakes, Charles, it's because *your* children spent the entire afternoon fighting in the pool until Camille straightened them out, with a little help from Carol."

Matt hurried over to her, bending to kiss her tenderly. "I shall feel totally left out if you spend all your time on Carol and Charles," he complained. "What about art collectors? Didn't your book say anything about them?"

"Straight anal retentives. Very dull," laughed Rachel. She squeezed his hand to show she was joking.

Charles watched her. God, she was so confident, and so brilliant, absolutely bubbling with life. There would be many engines at dinner this evening, but Rachel would drive the conversation. He smiled his pleasure. But now everyone was arriving at once—Tessa, radiant in a strapless Chanel evening gown that enhanced her elegance . . . Camille, almost as regal in a severe black dress and sweet, buckled shoes of black velvet; the young adults, Devon and Whitney and their friends, laid-back and trendy, sauntering loosely, terrified to look as if they cared. Only young Charles and Victoria weren't there, already tucked up in their bedroom with bears and dolls and Nanny droning her way through a long story.

The servants poured the champagne and the conversation partitioned itself off.

"Sorry to be late, darling," said Tessa, threading her arm through Charles's.

"You're allowed to be late," he said, smiling tenderly.

She looked so beautiful, more than ever. Marriage had brought it out in her. Unto them that hath it shall be given.

"What a glorious day it's been," she said.

Rachel joined them. "But, darling, you've spent the entire day on the telephone by the pool, and Matt says you've just done another couple of hours in the bedroom."

"That's right," laughed Tessa. "Total business. All the problems solved. Adversaries overcome, career advanced, money made. How could a day be more glorious?"

"Oh, Tessa," said Rachel, hugging her. "You are amazing. You are *exactly* like I used to be. Exactly and precisely. And look at you now: the hottest realtor in Manhattan. Wheeling and dealing as if to the New York-manner born. What would your poor parents think?"

"They'd be horrified, but they'd guzzle the first-growth claret and live in the Boeing. We'd never get them out of it, and all the time they'd be complaining how vulgar it all was. Typically British. Take with one hand, cut down with the other."

Charles laughed. It was true. Everything was true, and God, how everything had changed.

"You were made for Matt. You know that, don't you, Tess? All the time you were a businesswoman waiting to happen, and then I introduced you to Mr. Right," said Rachel.

"I was off and running before I met Matt," said Tessa. "He was just the icing on the cake."

"Icing on the cake? God, Tess, what is this? First you call me lazy, and now I'm merely icing on the cake. This isn't my night," boomed Matt.

He walked over to her, grabbing his wife around the waist and squeezing her in delight. "Why do I love her? What have I done to deserve this? It's all Rachel's fault. Rachel, if you hadn't forgiven Charles for being in love with Carol, we'd have been married and I'd have been safe from all these insults."

There was an uproar of good-natured denial.

"I was never in love with Carol." Charles tried to sound righteously indignant.

"Why not?" laughed Carol.

"Right, why not?" said Rachel with a broad smile, enjoying her husband's discomfiture. She felt the thrill of ownership. It had all come right after the nightmare of the betrayal that had never been but that had seemed so frighteningly real. Now she could look back on it and laugh, even enjoy it. Then, it had seemed like a cunning hell, and it was only a few short years ago. To this day, she remembered the strange confrontation when a distraught Carol and an excited Tessa had burst into her apartment straight from the hospital in Connecticut.

Carol and Tessa had tried to explain the giant misunderstanding. At first, Rachel had not believed them. "Don't lie to me, Carol. Don't lie to yourself. I saw you together in the swimming pool. I saw you kiss him. I saw him kiss you. I was there, damn it. I saw it with my own eyes. I flew all the way down to the ranch to see for myself, and I saw, Carol, I *saw*," she had said.

Carol had paused, in shock, her head thrown back in disbelief. Rachel could see Carol's face now and the expression on it. Incredulity. At being caught in the lie? No. Not that kind of incredulity. Surprise, genuine surprise. A puzzle. Something that simply couldn't be. Then a smile had suffused her face.

"That time he took the bug out of my eye," she had said. *"That* time? I remember that time. It flew into my eye. It was a hideous great thing. If it had stung me, I'd have been blinded for life. And Charles fished it out. You were watching? Right then? I can hardly believe the coincidence."

And then Rachel had believed. Because, of course, that had been the second she had *closed* her eyes and looked away. And with the joy of relief had come the sense of horror at the enormity of the misunderstanding. It was too late. She was engaged to Matt Harding. She had asked him to marry her on live TV. Damn it to hell, she had tried on the wedding dress that very afternoon. Where was Charles?

"Where is Charles?" she had said at last.

"He's apparently disappeared into the desert. He's been gone for ages. It's what he does when terrible things happen," Carol had said.

"I must find him," Rachel had replied. "Whatever it takes, I must find him."

And she had.

Jack cut through Rachel's memory, continuing the conversation.

"I used to think you were lovers," said Jack with a laugh. "Couldn't imagine anyone spending time with Carol and not being crazy about her."

"Well, I was crazy about her," said Charles. "It's just that I was in love with Rachel . . . ever since I first saw her."

"Well said," said Matt. "Quick thinking."

Tessa looked up at Matt with admiration. After Pete, she had never expected to experience magic again. She had been wrong. She had heard so much about Matt from Rachel, but she had been totally unprepared for the reality of him. Then, on the day she and Rachel had drunk champagne in the penthouse at the Metropolitan Tower and Tessa had sold Rachel and Matt that fabulous apartment, Tessa had gone to his office to get him to sign the papers at Rachel's request. It had happened instantly. He had taken one look at her, and she one long look at him, and the magic had flared.

"Is that the contract?" he had said. "Are you Tessa? Rachel says you're a pretty damn good realtor."

"Yes, it is, and Rachel is right," she had replied.

Tessa could remember her feelings now, the sudden dryness in her mouth, the electricity up and down her neck, the flush of warmth on her cheeks. The power of the man. The raw energy of him. The effortless competence that would overcome all obstacles even before they had become obstacles. Matt Harding would never leave her and Camille penniless on the streets of New York City at the mercy of the world. All around him were the trappings of the high-powered businessman—discreet secretaries, museum art, the photographs of presidents like postage stamps on the side tables. And in front of her was Matt, vibrating with an animal magnetism that Rachel had not mentioned, nor presumably had ever experienced. He had looked at the contract, then back at her.

"I suppose I should read it," he had said, waving it in the air like the irrelevance it had become.

"I suppose you should," she had said, entering immediately the conspiracy of hearts, quite unable to do otherwise. Rachel and this man were getting married. The thought had pounded into her brain. And Rachel had as good as told Tessa that she didn't love him.

She had seen the doubt and confusion in his eyes, and she had known completely that she was its cause.

Somehow she had gotten out of that room, but it was not the same person leaving as the one who had entered. For the second time in her life, Tessa had fallen in love.

She had walked back to her office in a daze. It was wonderful to feel she could love again, be loved again. It was terrible to know that the object of her affection would marry her best friend. Then, sitting at the desk, only half there, she had got the message that Carol had called. The wild roller coaster ride had begun, and within hours of her meeting with Matt Harding, Tessa had uncovered the truth about Charles and Carol and the terrible series of misunderstandings that had led to the breakup of Rachel and Charles's relationship.

She looked down. A beautifully manicured hand had threaded itself into hers.

"Hello, darling. My, you look so beautiful and grown up tonight."

"Thank you, Mummy," said Camille. "You know, when we

get back Matt says I can come and work in his office as a summer job. Is that all right? I'd love it if I could. He said he'd pay me, won't you, Matt?"

"If that's what you want, darling, of course you can," said Tessa. "But you have to stick at it, even when you don't feel like going. And you have to take orders and do what you are told. You can't boss people around."

"Yeah, just like her mom and her stepfather," said Matt with a laugh. He tousled her hair. He adored her. He was already grooming her for business success, and Camille loved every second of it.

Rachel watched them. She sighed. Their lives had worked out so well. It was a question of balance, of hearing the secret harmonies that made the magic melody. Before, she had cared only about career. Now she was a wife, a lover, a friend, a mother. She had given up her nightly TV show, but she still had important work. She had not made the mistake of forsaking everything to concentrate on her husband and children, and Charles was not the kind of man to expect her to. Each year, her contract with Matt's company called for six prime-time specials, in-depth interviews with the people that mattered. They lived in Manhattan for the school year, and in Santa Fe for the holidays. Her life was balanced now on her scales of happiness. She took Charles's arm.

"Come with me," she whispered. She led him away to a corner of the verandah, away from the animated knot of their friends. The fragrance of night-flowering jasmine was strong in the air. Behind, there was laughter and joy, sparkling like the pink champagne in the frosted bottles.

She turned to him. "Sometimes I can't believe how we saved this," said Rachel, "and sometimes I can't believe how we so nearly let it go."

He moved close to her, his eyes suddenly hooded with desire for her. He was thinking back through the years. She had come to the desert to find him and it had not been easy to do. For days he had heard of the famous white woman on his trail.

There had been questions asked in the pueblo, a helicopter seen searching at dawn, the rumor that a powerful woman from the city sought Cnawen, the man who knew everything, who was now living like an Indian on the burning plains of the Southwest. He had known who it was and guessed at her purpose, but his pride had not let her find him, his pride and the indifference he was cultivating hour by hour, day by day, on the edge of survival where love was a luxury that few could afford. But she had found him, as his heart had known she would. Rachel achieved her objectives. It had been part of what he had loved about her.

Dusty and thirsty by the well of the ghost town, he had stood in the shimmering sun, dazed by the heat, thinking only of the cool water he must find. He had filled his canteen in the silence and began to think about food, and he had seen her silhouette against the late afternoon sky.

"Charles?" she had had to ask, so different did he look, but she had known it was him as he had known it was her.

There had been the words, the explanations, the bones of the "betrayal" laid bare, the sources of the actions that had flowed from it . . . but it had been unnecessary. Rachel was there, and he was there, and time had already expunged the pain. He had moved toward her, as he did now, dirty and threadbare as now he was sleek and scented, and he had held her for an age as the words fluttered like leaves on the dry breeze of the desert, hardly heard, hardly mattering. She had drunk water from his bottle, and he had wiped her mouth with his fingers, and the tears of love and sorrow from her eyes, and she had simply whispered, "Marry me."

"Yes," he had whispered back.

Now they held each other's hand as the shafts of moonlight bathed the far-off mountain.

"You know," said Rachel, "I think I've solved Freud's mystery of what it is a woman wants."

"You have?" he said, smiling and squeezing her hand. He turned his head to one side, waiting for her revelation.

"Yes. What a woman wants is to *know* what she wants. It's taken me half a lifetime to find out."

"And what do you want, Rachel?"

But he knew the answer, and he leaned forward to kiss her in the still of the desert night.